Claxfelwestane

A
KENTISH
INSURRECTION

Paul Anthony Greenstreet

Matador
Unit E2 Airfield Business Park,
Harrison Road, Market Harborough,
Leicestershire. LE16 7UL
Tel: 0116 2792299
Email: books@troubador.co.uk
Web: www.troubador.co.uk/matador
Twitter: @matadorbooks

ISBN 978 1803130 729

British Library Cataloguing in Publication Data.
A catalogue record for this book is available from the British Library.

Printed and bound in Great Britain by 4edge Limited
Typeset in 11pt Adobe Jenson Pro by Troubador Publishing Ltd, Leicester, UK

Matador is an imprint of Troubador Publishing Ltd

To my wife Veronica,
in memory of our wonderful days of research.

INTRODUCTION

Have you ever wondered how your ancestors performed during turbulent times in history? Well, maybe not – but it is interesting conjecture, isn't it? On my retirement, soon after the new millennium, my wife and I researched my Kentish family history. This was a fascinating journey involving many churches in Kent and the cathedral at Canterbury. We traced a direct line of male descent back to the English Civil Wars, and my dynasty back to 1250 AD. A coat of arms and crest was borne by Sir Lawrence Greenstreete, 1451, son of John, Prior of Rochester Cathedral. In 1642, the coat of arms was altered by Peter Greenstreet, Lord of the Manor of Ospringe, who resided at Paynter's Farm. Lord Peter was in league with Oliver Cromwell. He espoused the Commonwealth cause until he died, aged just twenty-nine. Life was short in those troubled times. If festering wounds didn't claim you, then pestilence might. My ascertained line of descent dates to my eighth great-grandfather, John Greenstreet (Jack in my novel), who came to Wingham during the time of the civil wars. His son, also John (my seventh great-grandfather), lies buried in the churchyard of St Mary's, Wingham, the grave marked by a granite headstone, inscribed with legible font. John's last will resides in the archives of Canterbury Cathedral. He was a rich yeoman farmer. Due to lack of inscribed records, or records destroyed during the civil wars, we were unable to link my eighth great-grandfather to a specific lineage, or place of origin in Kent. There is little doubt that my ancient family derived from Claxfield, at the end of the village called Greenstreet, in Lynsted, which lay within the Teynham Manor and Hundred, Kent. A late medieval house, once known as 'Claxfeldestane', is still well preserved in Teynham. Here dwelt Johannes Greenstreet, manor reeve, who died in 1494, leaving a well-defined last will and eleven children. Some might say that was enough for a football team! It was certainly enough to create a dynasty and for lines of family pedigree to spread all over Kent. Claxfeldestane was sold by James Greenstreet after the civil wars.

My yarn is fictitious yet surrounded by true evidence and historical fact. It chronicles the life of Jack Greenstreet, a young Royalist at the time of the English Civil Wars. Jack's uncle, Reeve Johis Greenstreet, and Jack's cousin, James, reside at Claxfeldestane. Both men strongly support King Charles I. Throughout Kent there is a strong consensus of Royalist support. Cavalier Jack feuds with his father, William of Maidstone, and his uncle, Lord Peter Greenstreet of Ospringe. Jack's next of kin are in league with Cromwell and espouse the Commonwealth cause. Family division within the dynasty instigates heated argument, breeding hatred, which inevitably turns bloody. The battle for right and wrong intensifies, as Royalists and Parliamentarians clash. Fathers feud with sons, and brothers become hostile and full of hate for each other. The puritanical Parliamentarians seek to attain just laws for the good of the people, without the divine right and interference of the King. Their resolve sets a path of terrifying savagery and destruction – a 'scorched earth policy', which the people of Kent are caught up in. The civil wars will alter the course of British history forever. Royalist Cavalier Jack Greenstreet takes part in various battles and skirmishes, but as the war turns in favour of Parliament, he is pestered by a local Roundhead vendetta and goes to ground. With a bounty on his head, Jack seeks peace and love in an alien place. A place where family, church and farming to attain a good harvest, are the only matters of any real significance to the God-fearing inhabitants who make up the village communities of Wingham and Staple. Events paramount to Jack's survival are avoiding Cromwell's marauding Roundhead troops and steering clear of the advancing 'Great Plague', a terrifying pandemic of the 'Black Death'.

In writing this novel, I racked my brain box in deliberation, but honestly could not conclude which direction of support I might have taken, had I lived in those wretched times of bloody civil wars. Would I have been a Royalist or Parliamentarian sympathiser? There were convincing arguments on both sides of the coin. Of one thing I am certain: the common working man (the peasant or pauper of the lower class) would have fared little better whatever side he was made to support and fight for. Thankfully, I was not born in that era. But I was born at the outset of World War II, a war which brought communities and classes of society much closer together, rather than tore them asunder. The civil wars of the seventeenth century resulted in a devastating loss of life and crippled British resources. Numerous men were shot, spiked, hacked to death, or mortally wounded in the civil wars. There followed a devastating viral plague and the Great Fire of London. With such extremes of death and drained resources, neither Royalist Cavalier nor puritanical Roundhead could possibly claim to be truly victorious. Catholic Charles II was invited to return from France to reign. Small wonder the British capitulated when the Protestant Dutch monarchy was invited into England to rule over them. The eventual accession of Protestants William and Mary led to a 'Glorious Revolution'. It also led to future constitutional monarchies whose powers were limited through Parliament.

Research revealed my Kentish ancestry was split by the events of that seventeenth-century period of civil war. So many families were. My storyline favours the Kent Royalists. Therefore, I agree to have possibly misaligned my ancestor Lord Peter Greenstreet of Ospringe and Paynter's Farm, an avid supporter of Oliver Cromwell and documented to have espoused the Commonwealth cause. But somebody has got to be the bad guy in a novel, for God's sake!

I confess to voting recently, as a Brexiteer, to leave the European Union. That is another storyline! Nevertheless, many families were split over the referendum to 'Remain or Leave', just as they were split all those years ago, in the days of the civil wars, when they had to choose between King or Parliament. What is more, a very uncivilised war has developed in Westminster today, concerning the people's democratic vote to leave the European Union. 'Brexit' underlines the incompetence of modern-day politicians in facilitating true democracy. It poses the question, *Is Parliament any more democratic than it was three and a half centuries ago?* Playing 'Devil's advocate', purely for the sake of argument, had the King not lost his head, and had Parliament been defeated by Charles I during the civil wars, and had Parliament been dismantled by the King, one wonders whether the monarchy today, without the aid of an effective Parliament, might ever have allowed Britain to become embroiled within a European Union in the first place! What is more, had Charles I been swiftly victorious, England would not have been left destitute by years of war and unable to pay its demoralised navy. Then, instead of lying idle and apathetic, the British navy might have repelled the Dutch and altered the course of history. Again, religion would have played a huge part. It always did in those dark days. My reasoning, of course, is a cartload of useless conjecture!

Cavaliers, Remainers, Roundheads, Brexiteers – I digress. Enough of this supposition. Let's get on with my story, which, whilst fictional, is at least based upon true factual evidence.

Paul Greenstreet

PROLOGUE

1642–1643

Following his failure to arrest Parliament's leader, John Pym, and four other members, King Charles I raised his standard at Nottingham, marking the start of the civil wars. But the Battle of Edgehill was inconclusive. Subsequent battles ebbed and flowed, with Royalist victories at Adwalton Moor and Roundway Down, and then an indecisive battle at Newbury.

The village of Greenstreet, in north Kent, split Teynham Manor and Hundred in two. The village straddled old Watling Street, a Roman-built road that linked the City of Canterbury to London. To the north of Greenstreet lay the parish of Teynham, bounded by Tong, Teynham marshes and Conyer Creek, a creek which engaged the briny waters of the Swale estuary adjacent to the sea wall. To the south of Greenstreet lay the parishes of Lynsted and Doddington.

The manor's dominant church was dedicated to St Peter and St Paul, situated off Ludgate Lane in Lynsted. Several smaller churches in the manor included All Saints Iwade, St Mary's in Teynham, and Doddington church to the south of Claxfield and Lynsted.

Claxfeldestane, a large, jettied, half-timbered, Wealden Hall house, built by wealthy yeomen in the 1300s, lay within thirty acres of land, beside woodland called Cripson Wood. The house reclined in splendour at Claxfield, on the western edge of Lynsted, near the London Road. The house and its farmlands were in the possession of the family Greenstreete de Claxfield and had been so since its construction. The old house was mentioned in a subsidy roll of 1327. The family derived from the Norman conquerors of 1066. A John de Greenstreet was known to be Prior of Rochester Cathedral in 1314 and he had brothers in Teynham. Johannes de Greenstreete of Claxfeldestane was manor reeve in 1469, a King's man, responsible for the inventories and accounts of the manor and hundred. The village of Greenstreet was named after the family. At the western side of the property, a long cinder track path led directly to Lynsted church. Over time, the family attained contiguous properties in Selling, Eastling, Ospringe and Faversham, to Canterbury and beyond, across the garden of Kent. Family descendants were mostly yeoman farmers, often responsible for fruit orchards. Since Tudor times, the lands surrounding Teynham were renowned for producing cherry, plum, pear and apple orchards. Henry VIII appointed his own gardener, Richard Harrys, to grow cherries there.

At the outbreak of civil war, Claxfeldestane was owned by Reeve Johis Greenstreet, manorial steward acting on behalf of Lord Teynham, Christopher Roper, the 4th baron, who resided at 'Lodge Lynsted' manor house. Johis' eldest son, James, was a stout lad in his early twenties. All three men were ardent Royalists, in support of the King, as were most of the Kentish population, even though residing next to the Parliamentarian stronghold of London.

The civil wars were bitter. The causes set father against son, brother against brother, and split families wide apart. In 1642, the Greenstreet dynasty was headed up by Peter Greenstreet of Ospringe, Lord of the Manor at Paynter's Farm. The family became split between the Royalist and Commonwealth justifications. Peter espoused the Commonwealth cause and was in close liaison with Cromwell and the officers of Parliament. Peter had the family coat of arms altered from a martlet to an imposing double-headed eagle. The arms were a barruly of eight, argent and azure, on a canton of the second, an eagle displaying two necks. Lord Peter of Ospringe was a dangerous enemy. His manor was an established Roundhead stronghold in north Kent.

The first civil war was turning increasingly in favour of the King. 1643 had, to date, been a year of Royalist successes. The Royalists had taken Adwalton Moor, near Bradford, in June, under the command of the Earl of Newcastle, and Roundway Down, Devizes in Wiltshire, led by lords Hopton and Wilmot. Banbury and Oxford were captured without conflict, and despite a slight hiccup at Reading, the royal campaign was mostly going well from county to county. Then the King's nephew, Prince Rupert of the Rhine, stormed Bristol, losing 1,000 men and exhausting his supplies. But with the City of Bristol captured, the Royalist cause was at a high. King Charles travelled to Bristol to take personal command of his forces and to regroup. He called a council of war, to discuss his next move. The plan was to take Gloucester, via Painswick. Gloucester turned out to be a further hiccup in Royalist advancement, after Edward Massie, a non-partisan mercenary, reneged on a promise to surrender the city and then turned in favour of Parliament. It was incumbent on Charles to lay siege to the city. On 5 September, with heavy persistent rain falling, the Parliamentarian army, reinforced with London Trained Bands led by the Earl of Essex, reached the outskirts of Gloucester and camped on Prestbury Hill. The Parliamentarian presence forced the Royalists to abandon their siege. Wet and exhausted, neither army was in a state to seek battle. Both sides lacked supplies. Essex could not afford to be pinned down, and Charles was losing men through night raids from Gloucester. Essex began a retreat to London, with the Royalists in hot pursuit. At Newbury, the Parliamentarians gathered in strength to 14,000, just 500 men short of the Royalist contingent. A crescent-shaped escarpment, known as Biggs Hill, sat between the opposing forces. At dawn, Essex made a surprise Roundhead attack, leaving Charles on the back foot and low in ammunition. After a heavy battle, with 1,300 Royalists and 1,200 Parliamentarians dead, Essex was able to fulfil his retreat to London. The battle was a stalemate and inconclusive, though strategically it favoured the Parliamentarians, who were able to regroup into a much stronger fighting force and bring the Scottish Covenanters into the war on Parliament's side.

The Royal Standard flew from the top of the grandest marquee. Upon recognition of the Duke of Cumberland, the guards drew aside their crossed halberds and allowed Prince Rupert to enter the magnificent tent. King Charles I sat at a bench table, picking from a bowl of mixed fruit. He bit into a large purple plum. Overly ripe flesh spurted juice over his beard and ruff. The King mopped himself down with a linen serviette and spat out the kernel, before selecting a promising-looking pear and polishing it on his velvet tunic. Charles set aside the pear and wiped the ends of his waxed moustache, then stroked his pointed beard, pondering on matters.

'Well, nephew, we were surprised and outmanoeuvred by Essex and hath allowed him to slip away to London. I doth nay think it bodes well. He should never hath got away. I received news that Long Parliament hath sworn to the formation of a pact with the Presbyterian Scottish Covenanters. Pray, what now, Rupert? Hast thou a good plan of attack up thy sleeve for us?'

The King's impatient nephew and cavalry general flicked aside his dark, flowing locks, then released his red cape, throwing it upon a nearby chair. Rupert spread vellum paper before his uncle. The King of England was not impressed with Rupert's proposals, waving them aside.

'I hath sent the lieutenant to make a truce with the Irish rebels and free up our army in Ireland to return to fight for us here. But 'tis the paucity of ammunition, gunpowder and supplies which is of most concern. How went the Kentish insurgence, nephew? Is there news from Yalding?'

The First Civil War

1642 - 1646

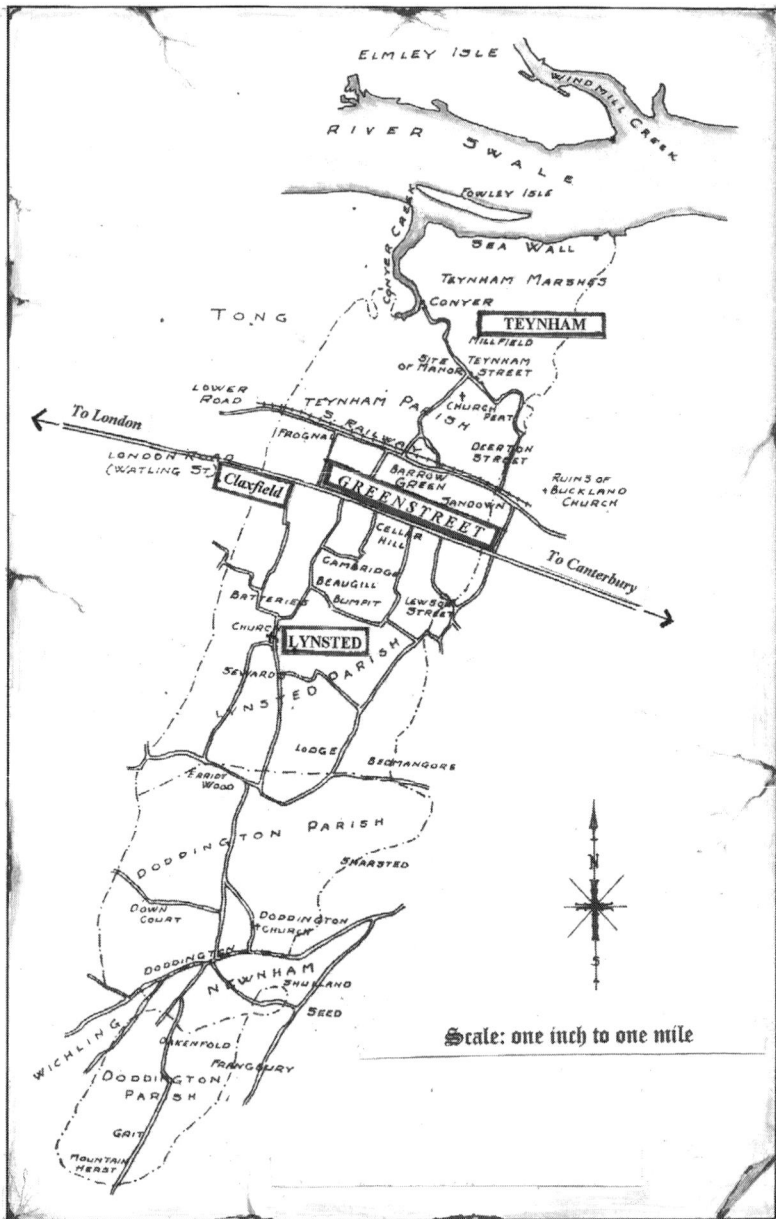

Map of the Manor & Hundred of Teynham, Kent,
incorporating 'Claxfield', Greenstreet & Lynsted.

1

INSURRECTION, KENT, 1643

Jack's leg throbbed unmercifully. Despite the crudely tied tourniquet, blood pumped from the deep slash in the top of his red velvet breeches. A warm, sticky seepage ran down one leg into his leather boot. High in the thigh, the Cavalier's wound was ugly, requiring immediate cauterisation before it turned septic. Jack Greenstreet knew that if the wound turned bad his days on earth were numbered. He urged his horse, 'Acorn', at full gallop, directing the chestnut stallion across the countryside, destined for north Kent. He hoped to find Widow Goody in her cottage at Frognal. The widow's powers of healing were renowned throughout the villages of north Kent. Jack was confident Goody supported the King. The wound was the result of battle at Yalding, caused by a bill, a pole with sharp billhook attachment – a farmer's implement.

The bill had been aimed at Jack by a parliamentary pikeman, as the Cavalier slashed right and left from Acorn with his razor-edged cup-hilted rapier. Fortunately for Jack, his horse had reared and kicked out as the bill was swung, setting the assailant back somewhat and interrupting the arc and velocity of his swing. Had it not been so, Jack's leg might have hung by a thread or been entirely cut away. The Battle of Yalding was hard fought. The Parliamentarians had outnumbered the King's men, who had retreated to Tonbridge with the Londoners in hot pursuit. The Kent men had hidden in the woods and hedges outside of town and fired muskets, whereupon the parliamentary forces dismounted and shot into the woods, discharging small cannon, to little effect. Eventually the parliamentary forces built up their horse and foot, discharging huge volleys of musket balls and pelting the Kent men, who gave ground and were driven into the town of Tonbridge. Two hundred prisoners were taken by the Roundheads. The Kent men fled, pursued by horse cavalry for six miles along the banks of the River Medway. Parliament lost six men and Kent fourteen, plus the many wounded they carried away to die.

Jack had fought on with a small number of Cavaliers, darting in and out amongst the Parliamentarians in skirmishes near Hilden Bridge, whilst the Royalists gathered in regular formation in front of the town and fired some cannon, again to little effect. It was in one such skirmish that Jack received his leg wound. The Roundheads, under Colonel Browne, with the backing of Lord Peter Greenstreet, who sat astride a white charger to survey the battle alongside a few other Kentish gentlemen, resorted, in the main, to saturated musket fire. It was a fierce fight, the Royalists eventually breaking under the strain and fleeing into Tonbridge. Jack had made his way back to Yalding to support the surviving Royalists, numbering approximately 600 men. Miles Levesey, the Roundhead commander, had too much ordnance for the Kent men. Outgunned, 300 of the Royalists fled and the rest surrendered to Commander Levesey.

Ordered to save himself as best he could, Jack set off as darkness fell, resting uncomfortably in a small field, beside a hedgerow along the way. He tightened the tourniquet around his leaking wound and awaited daylight. Jack had struggled to dismount from Acorn's back, to drink from a clear brook. Weak from his wound, he found great difficulty in remounting his faithful stallion. The horse, purchased by Jack's father, William of Maidstone, at Teynham horse-trading fayre, had been proudly given to Jack on his eighteenth birthday. Jack loved his father with all his heart. His mind was in a whirl as he crossed the Kent countryside. In God's name, what kind of issue had torn their close relationship apart? How had it come to this?

A flowing cape, draped over Jack's attire, kept out the morning drizzle. It hung over his English-lace shoulder collar and covered the rump of Acorn, the horse he loved so well. The cape kept his flintlock pistol, powder and the hilt of his sword dry. Weakened through loss of blood, his boot, full of the thick red liquid, squelched in the stirrup. He started to experience dizziness. He could feel the open slash pumping, pumping! The wound burnt fiercely into his groin. Jack spurred Acorn onward through field and orchard, jumping fences and ditches, attempting to concentrate on memory and direction. Acorn was snorting and breathing heavily. Steamy perspiration rose from every orifice of the heavy chestnut stallion's body. A church spire came into vision. Jack was confident he recognised Lynsted church, the church of St Peter and St Paul. He headed in that direction. On reaching the Tudor houses of Ludgate Lane, he reined the horse in and proceeded at walking pace past the parish church and up the winding cinder track path to Claxfield. His vision became blurred. Through the haze he could just make out the silhouette of men working in a field. Figures came towards him and took hold of Acorn's bridle. Johannes and James Greenstreet guided the horse to the house called Claxfeldestane. His kin supported Jack and took him to a spare room on the ground floor. They laid him down on his back, upon an old chaise longue. Jack raised a hand in salute but could not define the men who helped him. Old Johannes, known as Johis, spoke to his son:

'Go ye across the road to Frognal, James. Tell Widow Goody to come as quick as she is able. Thy cousin Jack lieth in terrible trouble. Tell her 'tis a deep wound, cut down to the bone. She is to bring everything she needs to cleanse, apply herbal ointment and to stitch the slash up. I will get some linen and make the boy more comfortable and fix a better tourniquet while ye make haste. Go quickly now, Jamie, Jack hast lost a lot of blood. Look ye sharp now.'

James set off at a trot. Old Johis gazed down at his young nephew with much concern. Jack Greenstreet was a fresh-faced, handsome young man, recently turned twenty, who turned the head of many young women in his manor. His father, William of Maidstone, was a rich gent, owning lands in Faversham, Ospringe and neighbouring villages surrounding

Maidstone. William's riches, until the civil war rift split them apart, were destined to pass to Jack, as eldest son, but would now probably pass to his younger brothers. Shoulder-length dark locks of raven-black hair hung in ringlets below a wide-brimmed leather hat, which he wore tilted to one side, decorated by a single red plume. A leather strap hung from one shoulder to his waist, to which was affixed a scabbard holding his sword. Beneath the strap was a leather jacket, dyed yellow, fixed loosely with cross-lacings and bound together with a blue silk sash. An additional belt at his waist held a brace of flintlock pistols and a short dagger. A large white collar was turned down over Jack's jacket, denoting an undergarment of some considerable quality. The red velvet breeches were covered with leather strap-overs, but the sharp billhook had sliced through leather and cloth to leave the gaping and leaking wound Jack now suffered.

Old Johannes busied himself, carefully removing his nephew's blood-filled boot, hat and flintlocks. He unbuckled the rapier and broad belt, then opened the red velvet breeches. Jack looked vulnerable. No longer was he the brave fighting Cavalier of yesterday. Johis found linen, then cleaned and packed the wound and renewed the tourniquet. He cut away the blood-soaked codpiece, slit through the breeches with a sharp knife and slipped them down from the pumping wound, pulling away fabric from under the buttocks. Johis covered the pubic area, to conceal his nephew's dignity, then called to his wife, Maria, to boil some water on the hearth.

James returned in haste, gripping Widow Goody by the arm and clasping a large wicker basket containing the widow's herbal healing remedies and surgical instruments. In close pursuit was Widow Goody's daughter, Mary, a pretty teenaged girl with flowing golden hair. James was a borsholder, a petty constable for the Claxfield area of the manor. At first, Martha Goody thought she had been arrested, but she came willingly enough when James told her she was urgently required at Claxfeldestane. Widow Goody addressed the reeve in a trembling voice.

'I hath always valued thy kindnesses to me, sir, and like thy good self I am a Royalist, devoted to God and the King. But I am sorely afeard by certain members of thy family, Reeve. Ye hath kith and kin who are Roundheads and witch-hunters, sir. The Lord Mayor of Faversham, Robert Greenstreet, is known to hath recently burnt a suspected witch. I be frightened out of mine wits that, should mine name drift abroad, he will hasten after me. I do nay wish to be tried by ducking, sir. I be nay a gossip, Reeve, nay a blessed gossip. I am but a simple healing woman. That is all I profess to be. I doeth mine best to help ailing souls and hope to oblige ye, Master, but please believe I am but a simple healing woman. I claim nay more than that.'

Widow Goody was in a state and trembling. Mary clung tightly to the back of her mother's bustle, whimpering and quietly pleading for mercy. The reeve's wife, Maria, took hold of Martha Goody's hand firmly and spoke quietly in defence of her husband, old Reeve Johannes.

'Thou hast nothing to fear from Reeve Johis-de-Claxfield, Martha. He hast always been a King's man, as is Lord Teynham, the 4th baron of this manor. They know ye art harmless.'

Reeve Johannes Greenstreet cut in, holding his hands aloft, distraught at the widow's distress.

'Calm thyself, woman. I hereby offer my full protection to ye, should the Witchfinder General decide to come this way.

Hopkins is nay likely to show himself hereabouts. He will be aware of the support for the King in this vicinity and he will nay risk getting his throat cut. As for Robert Greenstreet, he is far too cowardly to put his own life at risk, I assure ye. Should ye see any sign of Roundhead or witch-hunting activity in this neck of the woods, or from thy cottage, then cross Greenstreet immediately and call upon me or my son, Master James here. We will afford thee and thy daughter sanctuary, hath nay fear in that direction. Now look ye, Martha, here lieth a brave Cavalier in distress. His wound is deep and festering. I implore ye to work on him forthwith. Thou wilt be rewarded in honest crowns for thine efforts in mending him.'

Full of thanks, Widow Goody set to work cleaning and washing Jack's wound with boiling water. She ground up hypericum (St John's wort), sage and oregano to make a hot poultice, then heated a rod until red hot in the fire to cauterise veins and areas she suspected were turning bad. After threading a bodkin, she stitched and pulled the wound tightly together with silk thread, cleaning all around with saline beer. Finally, she applied herbs mixed with honey over her fastidious work. All the while her daughter Mary handed out the necessary implements and ointments to her mother and held the linen covering which lay near the wound, protecting Jack's dignity. Quietly her mother went about her work. When all was complete Martha bound the thigh lightly with a linen bandage. Johis and James watched in amazement and were astonished at Martha's skills. All the while she rinsed her hands in hot water and used alcohol to cleanse with. The Cavalier had lost much blood. He was very weak and drifted in and out of a stupor, crying out in agony whilst being stitched and cauterised. Mary mopped his brow and washed the contorted face and body of the sweat which poured from his torso.

Slowly Jack regained his senses. He recognised his uncle Johis, his aunt Maria and James. He raised a hand to them and attempted to smile at the pretty girl who soothed his brow and bathed the sweat from his naked body. He tried to sit up but had no strength in his arms. His wound was on fire and throbbed relentlessly. Martha Goody told the reeve that Jack had lost much blood and needed to drink plenty of boiled water from the well, plus apple and pear juice, milk beer, and dandelion and nettle tea. He should eat as soon as he was able. She suggested eggs, liver, pumpkin, beans and peas, mushrooms, spinach and sauerkraut with garlic. Maria made a list of Martha's instructions. Widow Goody agreed her daughter Mary should stay and attend to Jack's needs, until he regained some strength. Old Reeve Johis arranged for a bed to be placed in an adjoining room and Maria had it made up for the girl. Satisfied with her work, the widow bade the reeve and his family farewell and told them she would come across and dress the wound each day until it healed. The reeve thrust a bag of good English money into the widow's hands and ushered her to the door, thanking her profusely for her fastidious work. Martha Goody walked away from the imposing half-timbered house of Claxfeldestane and crossed old Watling Street, back to her humble cottage in Frognal. The money would be useful in attaining more equipment for her healing work and to assist in combating the pestilences which constantly rained down upon the good village people of Teynham Manor and Hundred.

Widow Goody's husband, Walter, had died from the pestilence six years prior to the outbreak of war. Many people died at a young age. It was this fact that activated Martha Goody's resolve to absorb herself in the powers and knowledge of healing. She was aware that women who dabbled in this type of thing were regularly accused of witchcraft. In fact, such women often had more knowledge of medicine than so-called physicians and were certainly cleaner in their application of healing. Physicians and surgeons were untrained, unreliable, unclean and ill-informed. This was borne out by the results of a military hospital set up in London for wounded Parliamentarians, where two-thirds of admissions died, not from their wounds but from disease and sepsis. The jealousy of physicians and surgeons, when they were upstaged by herbalist healers, or old wives, often led to accusations of witchery and pointed fingers.

With the help of Mary Goody, Jack made steady progress towards his recovery. Mary assisted him up and down from the couch to the chamber pot and, as his strength increased, out of the house to the privy. She cleaned and washed him down and attended on her mother when the widow came to dress the wound and apply honey poultices to assist in the healing. After ten days, Martha Goody unpicked her stitching. The wound still looked angry but had knitted together nicely, and Martha and Jack were well satisfied. He was even able to stand and shuffle about for the first time. With Mary Goody's help Jack started to take an interest in happenings.

Reeve Johis and James interrogated Jack over and over about the Battle of Yalding and how he came to receive his wound. James wished he had taken part, saying he was prepared for the next skirmish. Jack clasped his cousin's hand. They agreed to ride together. Johis enquired after his brother, Jack's father, William of Maidstone, and asked why

Jack had left home. Jack blamed it all on his uncle, Lord Peter Greenstreet of Ospringe, who he swore had radicalised his father in favour of Parliament and then blackmailed him. Peter had threatened to make William a recusant, which could lead to forfeiting numerous lands. Jack explained how the rift came about, prior to the Battle of Yalding, when Lord Peter, with his wife, Deborah, in tow, came to call on William late one afternoon. The meeting had started amicably enough.

Deborah had greeted Jack and ruffled his hair, telling him he was her favourite nephew, but, she said, he had silly Royalist views and misled ideas which needed curbing. Then Lord Peter Greenstreet had waded in, informing Jack's father, William, and all attending, that he had at his disposal a whole battalion of Cromwell's well-armed troops encamped on his farmlands, at Paynter's Farm, Ospringe. They were there, he said, to suppress the insurrections in Kent and those people and insurgents who supported King Charles I. Such suppression and correction would include family insurrectionists, added Peter, glaring hard at Jack. Lord Peter had just had a meeting with Oliver Cromwell and was full of Parliamentarian wisdom. He bragged how he would show little mercy to any Kentish insurgents found to be supporting the King. At first Jack held back, for the sake of his father, William of Maidstone. William and Jack had split views, but they had agreed to set their differences aside and conceal their viewpoints, whilst attempting to live as father and son under the same roof. This time, however, his uncle's baiting had riled Jack, who could contain the coiled spring of his anger no longer.

'Ye are all traitors,' Jack shouted. 'When the day of reckoning comes and King Charles hast restored order, ye will all be tried for treason, and then be hanged, drawn and quartered. Thy heads will be thrust upon pike staffs and displayed over Traitors' Gate. Ye will nay be grinning then, not any single one of thee. How canst thou renege on loyalty to the King, when our family lineage in Kent, from Eastling, Ospringe and Selling, derives from the King's reeves of Claxfeldestane, situate in Teynham Manor and Hundred. Reeves have always been King's men and acted on behalf of the monarchy. We came from the Normans and hath been King's men since the landing of William the Bastard in 1066. Uncle Johis Greenstreet and James of Claxfeldestane are nay turncoats, nor Symon of Borden nor Matthew of Eastling. Why should I be involved in thy treacherous plotting? Shalt all my family members be branded by such treasonable acts of betrayal? Nay, count me out. I support nay part of thy treachery. God save the King, long to reign over us, says I. Be damned to ye, ye yellow-livered turncoats.'

Jack's words were spat out with venom, causing Lord Peter to draw his basket-hilted sword. This threatening move triggered instant reaction from Jack. He sprang backwards, his rapier unsheathed in a flash and a hunting dagger readied in his other hand. Deborah screamed hysterically and hid herself within the curtains of the window bay. William quickly stepped between the dualists, his back turned on his son. He faced Peter, his anger plain for all to see.

'I shalt hath nay family slaughter done in my house for any cause,' thundered William. 'Family feuding is one thing, but murder, nay. Ye will hath to run me through first, if ye art intent on hacking one another to pieces. Jack, thou art to leave my house and nay return until this civil war hast been concluded. There dwell other members of our large dynasty nearby who hath Royalist sympathies. I suggest ye seek them out for thy lodgings. Go now and do ye nay return here again. Ye may take thine horse and all thy equipment. Wat Harrys will help ye load up.'

The swords were sheathed, and Jack departed without a further word. Wat Harrys, William of Maidstone's manservant and Jack's mentor, helped saddle up Acorn. Wat and Jack embraced. Wat had been like a brother to Jack, and they both had a tear in one eye. Jack left to find refuge with Symon Greenstreet of Borden, an older cousin and declared Royalist, known to be in collusion with Lord Teynham. The following day Jack rode out with Symon Greenstreet and Leonard Smith to fight the Roundhead scum at Yalding, south of Maidstone. But the Parliamentarians had much better ordnance and well outnumbered the Kentish men.

2

A RAID ON CLAXFELDESTANE

With Martha and Mary Goody's help and expertise, Jack's wound slowly healed. Soon he started to dress himself without Mary's help and got about with increasing ease. Mary brought the cheerful Cavalier baskets of cherries and soft fruits from the orchards, and Jack enjoyed Johis' home-brewed beer, frequently telling his uncle it was the best beer he had ever tasted. It was a wonderful warm summer. For a brief period, the civil war was not foremost in Jack's mind. His only desire was to build strength in wasted muscle and to get himself fit and agile.

Mary Goody was a buxom wench, causing Jack's sap to rise again. Indeed, he was close to full ardour. Jack helped old Johis and James with the farming chores and, together with the other children, fetched and carried supplies for his Aunt Maria to use in the kitchen. But it was not by chance that Jack ventured across the road, called Greenstreet, one warm summer's afternoon. He found Mary swinging on the five-bar gate at Frognal, and it was Mary, chewing on a length of grass, who unlatched the gate and invited Jack in for a walk through the orchard. They walked arm in arm and exchanged kisses along the way. It was Mary who demanded to inspect the strange lump that had risen alongside the scarred wound in Jack's new blue breeches. Twice they made love beneath the cherry trees. Mary squatted astride Jack, so as not to cause strain on his wounded thigh. Afterwards they picked fruit from the trees and fed each other ripe black cherries, hanging them from their ears and shooting the slippery stones between their fingers. They returned to the gate with red lips, red faces and red-stained blousons. Such liaisons became frequent between them, until the day of the raid at Claxfield.

Lord Teynham, Baron Christopher Roper, frequently called on Johannes Greenstreet, his manor steward. The Greenstreet family came across the water in 1066 under the name of Grensted, Grynsted, Grenstrete or similar, soon after the conquest. Johis and his predecessors were all reeves at Claxfeldestane. Reeves were formerly accountable to the King, though now, as manorial steward, Johis supervised the affairs of the manor for Lord Teynham. Johis Greenstreet prepared inventories and accounts on behalf of the manor for the baron. He arranged help for the poor and paupers and listed fines and collections made, setting each item down on parchment subsidy rolls. Lord Teynham was known to be an ardent Royalist. He led a Royalist attempt to hold Rochester in 1642 but was scattered by Colonel Edwin Sandys and his parliamentary troops. At the same time, Dover Castle was seized by Captain Dawkes in a daring night raid using only ten Roundheads. Edwin Sandys and Sir Michael Livesey raised many troops to secure Kent in 1642 and were active in suppressing signs of Royalist activity in the county. From the Parliamentarian point of view, Kent was an important county to police for three reasons. Firstly, it was a source of Royalist troop movement; secondly, it was a means of communication between Dover and the Continent; and thirdly, and perhaps most importantly, it was a source of iron. The weald of Kent was a major source of iron ore, and it had the trees to provide charcoal. The whole area was dotted with furnaces, employing over 200 men. Many of the cannon and cannon balls used in the civil wars came from Kent. All this iron had to be moved around, and to get it to London much was shipped along the River Medway, as far as Yalding. After the skirmish at Rochester, Lord Teynham was watched closely by the Parliamentarians. For that reason, he chose not to keep arms at his manor home in Lodge Lynsted, but to spread them amongst his loyalist men and to utilise Claxfeldestane.

Time was running out for Reeve Johannes Greenstreet, or Master Johis as he was affectionately known. He was in his seventy-second year, a good age, with soft, flowing white hair which hung shoulder length and blew gently in the late summer breeze. Johis leaned on the gate which provided access to the lane leading to Lynsted church. Across the tree-lined track, his field of golden wheat rustled, ready for harvesting. Next day, the villagers would come armed with sickles, to cut and stook the corn into sheaves. Johis, supported by a stout ash stick, glanced across the field towards Cripson Wood, where he played as a boy. He had such good times with his cousin William, now William of Maidstone. What had caused William to turn against the ingrained family loyalties to serve the King? Knowing William, as he did so well, Johis considered William's support for Parliament was probably motivated by a desire to avoid recusancy and to hang on to the numerous lands under his ownership, whatever the cost. Such desire was to pass the lands on to his eldest son, Jack, but the cost of support for Cromwell had backfired when Jack decided to retain dynasty tradition and go with the Royalists. Now, Jack would probably receive nothing out of William's last will and testament. In God's name, what had it all come to? Then there was the other whippersnapper, Peter of Plumford and Paynter's Farm, who derived from his grandfather's brother, William of Ospringe. Peter was only just turned twenty-nine, yet he had presumed to alter the family coat of arms and had the audacity to espouse the Commonwealth cause. Such presumptions had been made without consultation with senior family members. Peter Greenstreet thought, because he was in league with Oliver Cromwell, that he could walk over everybody and everything without question. Johis paused, then turned from his deliberations and watched Jack pull water from the well. At least he had been instrumental in saving Jack from a certain painful death. Jack was much like James, his eldest son. They got on so well together. That pleased Johis immensely. He wondered what might become of Claxfeldestane after the civil war ended. Praise be, that would be in the hands of the Almighty. Johis was confident James would manage the estate lands, messuages and appurtenances well and look after the rest of his family to the letter of his last will and testament. Johis realised the civil war may yet resolve matters differently.

Jack, being young and sharp of ear, heard them coming up the lane. He knew well the sound of clinking, jingling armour, the ring of spurs and hooves advancing at the trot. He dropped the bucket and limped across to Johis, taking the old man by the arm and out of his daydream.

'Come thee into the house quickly, uncle, we hath company coming up thy track at a rate of knots. I believe it might be a platoon of Cromwell's armoured Roundhead troops on horse.'

They crossed the yard and hurried inside the house. Johis called urgently for James to attend to the imminent visitors, whilst he hid Jack away out of sight. James, who had been inscribing Johis' work because of his father's failing eyesight, ran to the open door and stood tall in the door jambs, calling out loudly after his father and giving a countdown of the company's arrival.

'I canst see the lead commander now. He sits upon a white charger, and for sure 'tis our relative, Lord Peter of Ospringe and Faversham. A platoon of ten Roundheads ride behind him, all with helmets and breastplates. They bear sword and musket and appear to be businesslike.'

'I hear you, James. Greet the buggers in a civilised manner. Offer pails of water for the horses and delay Lord bloody Peter for as long as thou canst, before inviting him across the threshold.'

The platoon entered the rear courtyard in a noisy commotion of jangling metal and discord.

Johis ushered his nephew up a narrow winding staircase to an area on the first-floor landing where the chimney flues gathered into one single stack. Adjoining a bulging whitewashed chimney breast was a section of oak-panelled walling, stretching the length of the corridor.

'Hand me my weapons, Uncle Johis. I will teach yon cowardly Roundheads some manners.'

'There is nothing ye canst do against a platoon of men, nephew, not even with James' help. Put the idea out of thy mind. The three of us wouldst stand nay chance whatever, and thy wound, even though well on the mend, might prove a liability against such odds. We need to be fit to fight another day. Today we art nay prepared and caught short. Let us leave it thus.'

Johis fiddled with the side of the cladding. A section of oak panel slid open to reveal a 'priest hole' in the eaves of the roof. It was low in height to the roof timbers, causing restriction in headroom. The room was packed with arms of every description, including Jack's own flintlocks and rapier, which were laid out on a table. An armchair adjoined the table. Johis held the panel open and bade Jack enter, telling him to mind his head on the purlins and joists.

'In ye go, Jack,' whispered Johis, handing his nephew a lit candle. 'Make thyself comfortable. The arms belong mostly to Baron Teynham, who lies under deep suspicion since he led a group of Royalists in an endeavour to hold Rochester in 1642. The baron was scattered by Colonel Edwin Sandys' Roundheads. At the same time, Dover Castle was seized by Captain Dawkes in a daring night raid. Keep quiet, Jack. Do ye nay set the place on fire. Leave the talking to thine uncle Johis. I can handle Peter Greenstreet. I know well how to address that upstart.'

Johis Greenstreet slid the panel back into position until it secured with an audible click. Well disguised, the priest hole showed no sign of entry. James called out loudly to his father.

'Father, Lord Peter of Ospringe hast come calling on ye. Are ye able to attend upon him?'

As he descended the staircase, Johis had a further thought. He could not recall whether Jack's horse Acorn was stabled, or loose in the adjoining field. It might prove their downfall and could be a complete giveaway. The huge form of Peter Greenstreet stood in the hallway, together with Colonel Richard Browne. Peter looked none too well and was prone to much coughing before he came to the point of the visit. This gave Johis a moment to address James.

'Hath thou nay forgotten something, James? Thou hast nay attended to the horses this morning. They need feeding and mucking out. See to it immediately, son, before ye do anything else.'

But James had fed the horses that morning. Johis had been with him. James quickly grasped the hint his father dropped and departed without hesitation to attend to his formidable task.

'Well now, Cousin Peter, what canst I do for thee? What cause hast ye to visit the Greenstreet ancestral home of Claxfeldestane so early this fine morning and with such a force of men?'

Maria joined her husband and clung tightly to Johis. Lord Peter coughed repeatedly, spat into a kerchief and stood wheezing deeply. He glared hard at Johis before he spouted forth a response, the family coat of arms, a double-headed eagle, visible on the tunic beneath his cape.

'I think ye know well enough the reason for my visit, Johis. Where is he? Speak up! Where hast thou hidden Jack Greenstreet, William of Maidstone's eldest son, who fought at Yalding?'

Immaculately dressed, a white lace collar turned over his leather cape, Colonel Richard Browne rattled his basket-hilted sword in its scabbard. Browne's auburn hair flowed over broad shoulders. A trim moustache and goatee beard adorned his face. The colonel peered out from bushy eyebrows and spoke loudly in a commanding voice, directly addressing the reeve.

'I advise ye to aid our enquiry, Reeve, or a search will be made. 'Tis upon the express wishes of the commander, Sir Miles Levesey, we are here. Jack Greenstreet was observed riding a chestnut stallion at the Battle of Yalding last July and then at Tonbridge. He rode amongst our troops, dishing out considerable damage and wounding many soldiers. Sir Miles is determined to bring certain Royalists to justice. Jack Greenstreet has threatened his uncle here and caused much nuisance along the Medway. He will be caught and hanged, make nay mistake, and those found sheltering such criminals will be dealt with harshly. Speak now and fall on mine mercy.'

Browne glanced at Lord Peter Greenstreet, who was coughing wildly into his handkerchief.

'The reeve is of thine own family, my lord. I shall leave it to thee to give the order to search.'

Peter walked to the door and summonsed half the troop inside. He coughed uncontrollably and heaved into the linen again. Johis detected blood in the sputum of his obnoxious relative.

'Search every nook and cranny. Leave nay furniture unturned. Three men, go ye upstairs and look in every corner and cupboard thoroughly. The other two, attend upon me and thy colonel.'

Old Johis winced hatred at his second cousin but spoke with a calm and insistent voice.

'For what reason do ye come here with troops, Lord Peter? Jack never came this way, so why not sling thy hook and look ye elsewhere? A pox on ye, varmint. If only I was young again!'

Peter stepped forward, as if to slap Johis with his gauntlet, then, thinking better of it, he began to cough wildly again. He heaved and spat a pat of bloody phlegm on the floor.

'Thou art a silly old man, Johannes, and ye too, Maria. If ye were younger, old crone, I wouldst invite the men to have their lustful way with ye, but I wouldst nay want to spoil their breakfasts on an old wrinkly like thee, it might make them throw up. Now, where is the insurgent Jack?'

Johis made to grab Lord Peter by the throat, but Maria restrained her husband. The sudden action caused Peter to cough relentlessly. Lord Peter was obviously in a consumptive state.

'Ye ought to look after thine fearful cough, cousin. Cease drinking from wet glasses is mine advice. It seems ye are unlikely to see the month out, let alone find our brave relative Jack.'

Outside, James handed the waiting Roundheads a glass of small beer each, to keep them quiet, then headed for the stables. Acorn was not there. Jack had led the stallion out earlier, to graze in the paddock adjoining the wheat field. James exited a rear stable door and saw Acorn grazing. He headed towards him with a bunch of sugar beet and enticed the stallion to hand, then, taking hold of his bridle, he led him to a shaded crook in the field, shielded from the lane, and lashed him securely to a tree. Satisfied that the horse was well hidden, James retraced his steps, and came out of the stable whistling. He carried a pitchfork of steaming muck, which he pitched onto a heap of manure in the yard, repeating the process several times. James thought he would hang on to the pitchfork; it was a weapon that might be needed sooner than later.

Claxfeldestane was ransacked. No corner was left unturned, yet the well-secreted priest hole lay undetected. The Roundheads confirmed that Jack was not concealed within the house, but the repugnant Lord Peter did not give up easily. He gave further direction to the soldiers:

'Go and search the stables thoroughly. Look ye for a chestnut stallion. It might be in the paddock,' Peter shouted after them, coughing and rattling severely. 'Go ye into the lane, look over the gate and scan the pastureland thoroughly. His horse must be here somewhere.'

But James had made a good job of secreting Acorn. Colonel Browne turned on Reeve Johis.

'We are aware of thy support for the King, Reeve, and that of Baron Teynham. To some extent it is understandable, because thou art bound up in a history of working for past kings of this country. However, if we find arms ye will be punished severely. We are coming down hard on further Kentish uprisings. If we find the insurgent Jack Greenstreet he will hang. Now, outside in the yard with ye all, whilst my men put a torch to this den of Royalist corruption.'

'Nay, hold fast, Colonel, we won't burn Claxfeldestane,' chirped Lord Peter Greenstreet. 'It is my ancestral home. One day I might return from Paynter's Farm to claim it. Burn the entire subsidy rolls and manor accounts in the yard, they will not be required when Oliver Cromwell comes to power. You may stay for the time being, Johis, until Charles is removed. Then I will return and cast ye and thine out. However, should ye show penitence in favour of Parliament, ye shall hath a small cottage somewhere in the backwoods,' he gaspingly wheezed.

Two men at arms returned to report they had found no chestnut stallion in the stables or paddock, only three mares, two of which were old and had seen better days. The subsidy rolls were piled up in the yard and torched. Colonel Browne muttered something to the men, who mounted, up-holding burning torches. Peter Greenstreet of Ospringe was the last to mount, upon his white charger, and without further ado the platoon left the yard and clattered out onto the track. They spread out along the periphery of the wheat field and threw their torches into the ripened wheat. Flames leapt across the crop field, laying it to waste in an instant. The group of Roundheads and their commanders rode off down Greenstreet. Lord Peter gave a leering backward glance at the destruction. A plume of dark grey smoke rose high into the cabolt blue of the sky.

Old Johis knelt beside the track and watched a year's hard work vanish in a flash before his eyes. White hair hung over his face. The hair gently lifted in the heat of the blaze. It would be a hard winter, and bread for the manor was going to be non-existent for many. From one eye a tear rolled down the reeve's cheek. The other eye burnt fiercely with wrath. James' thoughts were of revenge; his knuckles showed white from the tight grip on his pitchfork.

'Go quickly and fetch Acorn from the paddock, James. He will be going mad with the smoke drifting across the fields. Put him in the stables, whilst I release Jack from his confinement.'

*

Colonel Richard Browne's scorched earth policy across Kent sought to bring the Royalist insurgency to heel, or so he thought. But the upper echelons of Kent were mostly in support of the King, and their dependants were true to their lords. As for Lord Peter Greenstreet, his threats to his Royalist cousin, Reeve Johannes Greenstreet de Claxfield, transpired to be hot air. Peter of Paynter's Farm, Ospringe, never returned to Claxfeldestane. He lay bedridden and slowly drowned in his own consumption. Peter expired in 1644, aged just twenty-nine years. When Johis died, he exceeded his second cousin Peter's lifespan by two score and nine years.

*

Johis slid open the panel concealing the priest hole, to find his nephew's hand on a drawn rapier. Prepared for action, primed flintlock pistols lay on the table in front of Jack, together with a mortuary sword and a backsword, selected from the many arms stacked in the room. Two muskets were propped vertically against a wall primed with powder and shot, and a slow match smouldered ready to discharge them. Jack had obviously prepared to go down fighting.

'Pray, dost nay fire, nephew. 'Tis only me, thine uncle Johis, come to release ye from thy place of confinement. Ye need nay be alarmed, the Roundhead rabble hast departed from Claxfield.'

Jack laid his rapier across the table and struggled out of the low room onto the first-floor landing. He stretched, then greeted his uncle, embracing him in a bear hug and dancing up and down.

'All thanks to God Almighty thou art safe, Johis. I struggled to hear what was going on. When the stench of smoke came through the clay tiles, from thy burning wheat field, I planned to blast my way out of this place of refuge with one of the grenado stored in yon boxes.'

'Well, ye might well hath needed to take such action, Jack, because they were threatening to burn the house to the ground. I was in a quandary to know just what to do. In the end, they burnt the subsidy rolls and then the bastards set my wheat field ablaze. Thankfully they never found thy horse. James caught hold of Acorn and hid him in a clandestine corner of the paddock, where dense trees overhang a small bush-lined offset, along the periphery boundary.'

When Jack saw the state of wanton destruction the reeve had suffered, he was incandescent with rage, and swore an oath of revenge. With the reeve's hard-scribed vellum rolls destroyed and several acres of prime wheat burnt, Teynham Manor was in a state of utter confusion.

'I hath burdened ye and James with thy brave protection and fine hospitality for far too long, good Uncle Johis. Thine goodwill towards me almost cost thee this wonderful house called Claxfeldestane. My wound is healed now. I must move on to pastures new. I shall be forever in thy debt, Uncle Johis and kind Aunt Maria, ye both hast risked thy very lives for me. I am near mended and now I must take the fight to the enemy. I have a few scores to settle.'

'Ay, I will come with ye,' said James. 'We will settle the scores together, Jack. I am nay a fighting man, but, like so many, I can soon learn so to be. Lord knows, I need little motivation.'

Old Johannes was clearly perturbed by his son's statement. He addressed James in imploring, yet kindly, tones, speaking fluently and with firm intent for a man of his advanced age.

'The accounts of this manor very much depend on me as reeve, James. It has been thus in the family Greenstreete, here at Claxfeldestane, for several hundred years. We go through troubled times just now. I am old and shaky. Further, mine eyesight is fast failing. Thy job as borsholder wouldst be better served by helping me as steward. I shall pass on soon. The post of steward to this manor will pass on to thee. I hath already discussed the issue with Lord Teynham. The baron agrees thou art the man best suited to take on my work. It is a post which, depending on the outcome of this civil war, may end as a post of transition. I therefore implore ye not to take off with Jack, for what I agree is a noble cause. The people, especially the weak, disabled and poor of our manor, depend on our ability to fund and feed them. The subsidy rolls have been destroyed by scum, and I desperately require thy help to research, compose and re-scribe the invaluable records of our community onto vellum paper.'

Old Johis paused for breath and held up quivering senile hands. He spoke in desperation.

'Since the outbreak of this terrible civil war, the whole Manor of Teynham and Lynsted has been in a state of turmoil and confusion. Now the manor subsidy rolls hath been destroyed, such turmoil and confusion will be a thousand-fold. There is much to scribe and taxes to gather for Baron Roper. Please don't abandon me now, James. It is my hour of need, nay, the hour of need of the whole community, who reside in Teynham Manor. We all need ye now.'

James crossed the room and took his father's gnarled old hands in his own, realising he had a far more urgent calling to attend to at Claxfeldestane. Fighting Roundheads in skirmishes would have to wait. Johis was right; looking after the poor, weak and vulnerable, and the elderly people of the manor, was considerably more important than fighting the Royalist cause.

'Ay, I hear thee, Father, hath ye nay fear in that direction. I shall remain to do my duty. If we get wind of Roundheads coming this way, perhaps we canst be better prepared next time, with men at arms ready to see them off. To that end, I will organise men in the manor, so they canst be armed and available at quick notice. We must nay risk houses or crops being burned, or subsidy rolls being destroyed by the Roundheads again. We need to make a stand.'

James turned to Jack and shrugged his shoulders, aware he had to help with Johis' failing eyes.

'I'm sorry, Jack, maybe I'm not the Cavalier I thought I might be after all. It seems there is clerking work and manorial matters to attend to. Let us go for a parting drink, cousin. We could go this very evening to the White Swan brewhouse. What say thee? Art thou up for it?'

'I say that is the best idea ye have had all day, James. I will gladly accompany ye for a tankard of ale. By the way, James, ye hath nay need to prove anything to me. I am already convinced thou art a man of much integrity. Uncle Johis must be very proud to have ye as his eldest son, as I am to have ye as a cousin and very dear friend. Indeed, I consider ye to be nay just a cousin, but my closest friend, James. We will drink to that at the brewhouse and toast the King.'

Johis smiled in gratitude. He was profoundly proud and grateful of the support offered by both his eldest son, James, and gallant nephew, Jack. All was not lost if the subsidy rolls could be re-scribed whilst fresh in mind and James was able to set items down in legible font for him.

'I am proud of both of ye, Jack. But do nay disappear from mine house quite yet awhile, nephew. Tarry this night. There is to be a Royalist meeting here at Claxfield tomorrow. Lord Teynham is holding his meeting here because he is held suspect by Parliament, and Lodge Lynsted is constantly watched by Roundheads. Thy cousin Symon Greenstreet of Borden is coming, together with Leonard Smith, James, of course, and my younger brother, Matthew of Eastling. Other Royalist sympathisers will attend. Thou might learn a thing or two, before ye mount thy steed Acorn and wend thy merry way from here. Pray, come thee now down to the dining room, boys. Maria has made us a nice ewe, heron and game pie with vegetables. We will enjoy some good beer and savour a glass of Madeira wine or two. Let us banquet and unwind a little. The past few days have done my ageing carcass nay good at all. I must also discuss with the baron the necessity of fair rationing in the manor since the destruction of mine wheat field. 'Twill be hard-telling on the people of this manor when winter comes a-calling.'

3
—
AN AFFRAY AT THE WHITE SWAN BREWHOUSE

The White Swan brewhouse was situated in Greenstreet, between Mr Wilkins' butcher's shop and the saddlers. Like most villages of the time, Greenstreet was full of stench from a mixture of horse and animal dung, urine, straw, human excrement and rotting vegetation. On hot days, the offensive odour was most rancid. The long street hummed with flies and fleas. Rats and mice scurried here and there amongst the corruption in their hundreds of thousands. The street was best approached by well-booted feet, to avoid getting plastered in putridness, and it was preferable to arrive at one's destination on horseback, which was not possible if a person was poor and had no horse or boots. One always had to be on the lookout for horse-drawn carriages, which passed through the street from London to Canterbury, or vice versa. No mercy was shown to unsuspecting pedestrians, who, on wet days, could get showered by a filthy mixture of flying mud and shit. The street was famous for its fayres and for horse and cattle trading. People came from all over the country to visit Greenstreet's famous annual horse-trading fayre, when Irish horse traders brought their horses and various wares for sale.

Greenstreet was known not only for its bad air but for its arguments. A local proverb stated, '*He that will not live long, let him dwell at Muston, Teynham or Tong*.' The borsholders (petty constables) were kept busy, and many court fines were imposed. Arguments raged over the rights and wrongs of the civil war, over ongoing religious differences of the times, and more often over coveted rights between neighbours. Quite often cudgels or drawn knives were used to settle such arguments. In the 1600s there were many fines or court session orders listed in the Teynham Manor rolls, like a complaint against Richard Cornish for 'suffereth drunkenness in service time, which was very odious in the sight of his honest neighbours'. Then a misdemeanour was brought before mine bishop, when failure of the inhabitants to go to church for a sermon, one Sabbath day after Easter, recorded only six people present in church, and the rest were singing and dancing in an alehouse. Apparently, a barrel of beer was supplied by 'a poor woman', and Symons and Hunt, wandering minstrels of Faversham, were amusing the congregation! Robert West was fined 3/4d for 'breaking open the lord's pounds and taking out his cattle'. Joseph Wyllocke of Bumpit was fined 3/4d for 'making an affray at Greenstreet, upon one Will Donnard'. Further, the court declared Joseph Wyllocke an outlaw for three years. Michael Roper, one of the yeoman family of that name, was fined 40/– for 'allowing a mess of dunge to lie in the highway, between Barrow Green and Frognal'. He was later fined another 40/– because he did not take away his dung. Even the lord himself, Christopher Roper, was fined 40/– for 'allowing trees to hang over the way from Bedmangore to Sharsted'. William Bourne was fined for the same crime but regarding the 'shire way leading from Lynsted to Scuttington, to the annoyance of the passengers of the Commonwealth passing that way'. There were constant fines for poaching, for not keeping dykes clean, clearing overhanging branches from the road, and generally for breaking the many Teynham Manor and Hundred laws imposed at that time by the manor courthouse.

The affray at the White Swan brewhouse was not the fault of Jack nor James Greenstreet, who had turned up at the said premises to wet their whistles, yes, but to primarily see Jack on his way to fight for the King. The owners of the brewhouse, Will Dix and John Caslock, kept an orderly house, but Jack and James, though armed, had certainly not gone there to cause trouble.

Yet trouble was brewing, and plenty of it was heading the way of the White Swan brewhouse!

Will Dix, the landlord, greeted Jack and James in a hearty manner. Will Dix knew James Greenstreet well, as local borsholder and eldest son of Johis de Claxfield, the manor reeve.

'I bid thee good evening, boys. I trust ye are both good in spirit? I hath recently perfected a nice little number. A well-brewed, highly hopped beer named "Mucky Duck". Wilt thou try a tankard or two, or is the porter more to thy taste? How about a yard each, for good measure?'

'Tankards will do us fine, Will. Fill them up with yon Mucky Duck, and good health to us all,' shouted James, licking his lips thirstily in anticipation of the brewed delight being drawn.

'Ay, we need good health around here, Master James,' replied Will Dix, setting two full foaming pewter tankards down on a nearby table. 'I am thinking of asking Baron Teynham if I might borrow a cart to get some of the dung cleared away from outside. For the good baron is just as guilty as many others be, by leaving us plastered in thick shit when his cattle are driven past here twice a day for milking. Baron Teynham has been fined several times, but then he canst afford to pay the fines. He takes nay notice of such fines, nor manor court justice, doth he?'

'Thou canst borrow a cart from Claxfield, Will. I will arrange it for thee. Just find some men to shovel up the dung and let me know a time for thy collection, and then I will yoke up a pair of oxen ready to pull the load. Bring the muck back to bottom field and dump it in the corner next to the rotting haystacks, then return the cart to Master Gabriel in the corner cottage.'

'Thank'ee kindly, Master James, I will arrange a time early next week, if that be alright with 'ee.'

'Fine, Will, just fine. Now, fill us up again. That beer tastes good and strong, do it nay, Jack? I prefer this new hopped beer of thine to thy ale. Thou wilt go a long way with this brew, Will.'

As Jack drained his tankard his ears pricked up. He became less interested in beer and more with a familiar commotion outside. Once more the sound of clinking spurs, armour and rattling swords in scabbards had him readying himself. Jack passed a brace of primed flintlock pistols to James; at the same time, he clutched the hilt of his rapier and loosened the dagger in his belt.

They burst into the brewhouse wearing armoured breastplates, with wide white starched collars turned over leather gimlets. Long leather boots clad the legs, the boots wide and loose at the thigh. There were three of them, each man wearing a mortuary sword with half-basket hilt. They were harquebusiers, from a Roundhead cavalry unit, all helmeted with neck guards, their hair cut pudding-basin length, level with the ear lobes. John Caslock, Will Dix's brewing partner, was roughly pushed ahead of them, and their captain called for Will Dix to step forth.

'Set forth three full tankards of porter, Will Dix, and then go and stand against the wall with thy fellow brewer, John Caslock. Caslock tells me that ye brew in the name of King Charles. After we hast tasted the King's brew we will cut the ears off from thine heads for thy insolence. Ye shalt be hopping and cursing the name of the King forever and a day,' he chortled in mirth.

'But ye will nay be supping the King's brew, parliamentary scum, for 'tis thine own ears which might be flapping upon the floor boards, midst the spit and sawdust of this good brewhouse.'

The sharp tip of Jack's rapier pricked the captain's jugular, staining his white-collar deep red.

As Jack sprang into action, James cocked the flintlocks and trained the pistols at arm's length on the two Roundhead privates. He bade them face the wall and carefully disarmed them, removing their mortuary swords, daggers and firearms, a snaphance musket and a long harquebus. Whilst going about his business, James addressed the Roundhead harquebusiers.

'Pray, let us keep our fight on the battlefield, shall we, gents? After all, the brewhouse is a place for countrymen, of whatever persuasion, to enjoy a decent flagon of good ale or, as is the case here this evening, excellent hopped beer brewed by master brewers. Nay talk thou of carved ears, for if ye enjoy a good tankard of ale I declare yon fellows are the best brewers in Kent and, if I may be so bold, in the whole of merry England. Though England does nay appear to be too merry right now! Good brewers need be preserved to serve folk, nay to be carved up.'

Jack took the captain's weapons and withdrew his rapier. Blood seeped and trickled down the captain's neck, mixing with his sweat. He dabbed at it with a lace kerchief drawn from his tunic pocket, glaring vengefully at Jack. As they prepared to exit the brewhouse, Dix thanked the Cavaliers for their custom. His remarks were purposely designed to help cover their tracks.

'Thank'ee for coming all the way from Canterbury, gentlemen. We are glad ye liked our brew. We are hoping to go into business with Mr Dick Marsh of Faversham shortly and open the first commercial brewery in England. Pray, soon we shall all drink and be merry again.'

Jack and James bade their goodbyes and backed out of the brewhouse door, each carrying an armful of weapons. They dismantled and left the snaphance and harquebus muskets, which were too large to handle, then crossed the road to the Lynsted side of Greenstreet in the nick of time. Within minutes the rest of the platoon arrived on horseback. The two cousins broke into a run. The captain and the harquebusiers ran from the brewhouse. He screamed at his mounted troops, pointing in the direction of the disappearing Cavaliers. The Roundheads charged after them, but James knew all the shortcuts and narrow back alleyways of Lynsted.

'Come, Jack, make haste to Ludgate Lane. We can outrun the Parliamentarians through the back alleyways and take refuge and sanctuary under the roof of Lynsted parish church.'

Fleeing for their lives, they made it to Ludgate Lane. Roundheads on horse were coming at them fast from every direction of the street. The two Royalists veered off, dashing diagonally across the church graveyard, shielded by the headstones. Gasping for breath, they reached the thick oak iron-studded door. James lifted the heavy latch to gain entrance into the church vestibule. As they slammed the door shut and turned the large key in its ornate cast iron escutcheon, lead balls buried themselves deeply into thick English oak. Muskets exploded in a formation of heavy fire, finding their range. More lead slammed into the impenetrable door, adding to the iron studwork. Jack pulled himself onto a sill to peep from the leaded windows.

'What canst thou see, Cousin Jack? How many men do they hath mustered against us?'

'I canst see bugger all, James. Pardon me, Lord! Clouds of discharge obliterate the churchyard like a dense fog. A thick grey blanket of gunpowder smoke covers everything, James.'

A further volley of musket shot embedded in the staunch oak door or flattened against stone walls. A ball shattered the glass in the window Jack had peered from moments before. The fabric and sanctuary of the church of St Peter and St Paul meant little to Cromwell's men.

James quickly hatched a plan of escape. He beckoned Jack to follow him through the pews of the nave to a side aisle, where a small gothic-shaped door opened into the vestry chamber.

'Hurry, Jack, our best chance is to go now and escape via the rear churchyard. Follow me! As churchwarden I know this church like the back of mine hand. A door from this vestry has steps leading to a lower chamber where a slim door opens out into a narrow shaft with railings over. Our heads will be at ground level. When satisfied the coast is clear, we canst pull ourselves up over the railings and run between the gravestones to a thicket of nettle and bramble. I suggest we conceal the weapons in the thicket and come back for them later. We canst then scramble over the stone churchyard wall onto the track and cross the field to Cripson Wood. There we canst be concealed until the Parliamentarian scum hath left. We hath nay encountered this mob of Roundheads before. They will nay connect us with Claxfield. When satisfied the harquebusiers are gone, we canst cross the pastureland to Claxfeldestane.'

'Ay, that seems like a sound plan, James, let us implement it in haste. Hand me the brace of flintlocks, I am probably a better marksman than thou. If ye carry the confiscated weapons, I will take them from ye after I climb over the railings to ground level, then pull ye up by hand.'

James unlatched the low narrow door, and they squeezed out into the tiny shaft enclosure. Standing on tiptoe, his eyes level with the footpath and surrounding graveyard area, Jack could see James' thicket. He noticed the tail end of a foot soldier disappearing around one corner of the church. They were obviously under close surveillance. When clear, Jack pulled himself up over the guard railings onto the footpath, laid his flintlocks ready to hand and took hold of the swords and arms passed up by James. He laid the weapons on adjoining grass, then held one arm down for James to clasp, pulling his cousin up to join him. Gathering up the weapons, they dashed for the cover of a massively tall gravestone. Darkness was creeping in as they flitted between the gravestones and entered the thicket. They hid the confiscated weaponry under a briar patch, slipped over the stone church wall and made their way up the track, then crossed the paddock and the stubble of the burnt wheat field to Cripson Wood. Night fell as they entered the eerie wood. Peering down between the trees, candlelight shone out from the leaded lights of Claxfeldestane. The stench of the scorched wheat field wafted up to their noses.

'Let us allow two or three hours to pass, Jack, before we go to the house, just to make sure.'

The two men settled down on a friendly horizontal oak bough, cracked jokes and listened to the owl's hoot and the rustle of nocturnal creatures in the undergrowth. They watched the creepy shadows of the trees move about in the warm night breeze. A bright moon came out to light up the landscape. There was no sign of the captain's platoon of men. All lay quiet.

'I could do with a tankard of Will Dix's beer right now,' said Jack as he turned away to piss.

'Ay, as could I,' agreed James, 'but we shall hath to make it another day, Jack. We dare nay risk going there to tempt fate this night. We hath our meeting tomorrow with the baron.'

'Yea! I shalt be on my way soon afterwards, James.' Jack took his cousin's hand and squeezed it warmly to his breast.

They had shared quite an adventure that day. 'Please convey my love to everybody, James, including Widow Goody, who saved my life, and her investigative daughter Mary who aided mine recovery in so many wonderful ways! I shall be back again to see ye soon, God willing! Thou, Johis and Maria art my family now, James – God bless ye all.'

4

A ROYALIST MEETING

'Since Charles raised his standard at Nottingham in '42 and the inconclusive Battle of Edgehill, we hath this year seen Royalist victories at Adwalton Moor, near Bradford, and Roundway Down, Devizes in Wiltshire, Bristol and the inconclusive battle at Newbury. Unfortunately, here in Kent, we were outgunned and overpowered by sheer numbers at Yalding, as was I in mine endeavours to hold Rochester. The castle at Dover fell to Dawes, and there hast been many skirmishes over the county, some to the good, others bad. 1644 is fast approaching. We must take the fight to Fairfax and hopefully be victorious in Kent in the ensuing year.'

The 4th baron, Christopher Roper, Lord Teynham, was trim of beard and dressed in embroidered cape, over a doublet and silver leggings. His decorated sword hung snugly at his side, as he paused to survey his audience. Johannes, his trustworthy reeve, James and several other members of the Greenstreet dynasty were gathered, together with Leonard Smith, Ralph Clerke, Thomas Pordage, Stephen Grimsell, Edward Platt, Sir William de Laune, and relations Edward and William Roper, together with several of the baron's trustworthy staff. The baron's gaze fell on Jack, who stood trim of doublet and hose, blue breeches and fully armed.

'I am proud to welcome Jack Greenstreet, the reeve's nephew, to this meeting. This man fought bravely at Yalding, against the odds, and received a nasty wound for his efforts. Jack has recovered well. In fact, so well that he and James caused a skirmish of their own last evening, when they took arms from a captain and two harquebusiers at Will Dix's and John Caslock's White Swan brewhouse, in the village. The Roundhead weapons were secreted in the churchyard and hath been recovered to be turned against the enemy. The arms are secured in our secret armoury. 'Tis a clandestine place, known only to a few of us for security reasons. The weapons will be used in future skirmishes and battles. I understand Jack is departing this day to stay with his older relation, Symon Greenstreet of Borden, here, who we all know so well. God bless ye, Symon. They are planning to join the King's men in the spring, early next year, and to journey west to engage the Parliamentarians. We wish them well and Godspeed.'

'Ay, Godspeed to ye, Jack and Symon,' came a throaty response from the meeting. Lord Baron Roper sipped some elderberry wine from a silver goblet then continued his address:

'It is said the King is inviting foreign mercenaries to help the Kingdom in this war. All kinds of help will be gratefully accepted, as Cromwell's men become increasingly difficult to handle. Many Roundheads started as husbandmen, but Fairfax is building quite a formidable army. We must prepare ourselves better and find more positive leadership. This was sadly lacking at Yalding, despite the odds against us. We need to plan our attacks on those Roundheads from London. Their skirmishes and scorched earth policy are becoming far too frequent. Look ye what happened here at Claxfield when they torched the wheat field. Are they trying to starve us into submission? Incidentally, the harvest yield has been good this year. My grain will be measured out across the manor and folk may go hungry, but nobody will starve. I will not allow that to happen. The instigator of the raid on Claxfeldestane, Peter Greenstreet of Ospringe, who carries the Greenstreet family coat of arms and motto, *Dum spiro spero* (Whilst I breathe, I hope), may not be breathing much longer. I am reliably informed that he lies bedridden and drowning in his consumption. Some say Lord Peter has received his just deserts.'

Baron Roper forced a grimacing smile at the elderly reeve and placed a hand on Johis' arm.

'Of course, it is our reeve's cousin we are talking about here, Lord Peter Greenstreet, the Kent man who espouses the Commonwealth cause, in favour of Cromwell. The man who devalues his own family with such wrath and disdain. Then, backed by a platoon of Roundhead cavalry, he threatens rape, torches his own elderly cousin's ready-to-harvest wheat field, then rides away with a belligerent smirk upon his face. What kind of man does that to his own family? Yea, but so many of us are troubled by split families in this wretched civil war. I suppose I should nay be surprised by such catastrophe. But we have right on our side. Only God chooses a king.'

'Ay,' chipped in Johis, 'and in splitting from us, Peter defiled not only our family name but the coat of arms and motto we so value. I shall never forgive him for that, nor the way he turned against our ancient dynasty. Peter's eldest son, John, is just eight years of age. There will be nobody to continue the Ospringe line until John comes of age. Mine cousin, Matthew of Huntingfield and Eastling, tells me Oliver Cromwell himself advised Peter to have John made a ward of court. He will be known as John Greenstreet of Canterbury. For the cost of a hundred pounds and six shillings, John will remain under the auspices of the Protector General, until he comes of age and marries. Leastways that will ensure the Ospringe line remains open. Meanwhile, when Peter eventually dies of the consumption, which will nay be long from the state I saw of him, Paynter's Farm will be left in the name of his wife, Deborah (nee Sharpe) and her father, James Sharpe. But cast nay doubt, Paynter's Farm at Ospringe will remain a base camp for Cromwell's regiments in Kent for as long as this civil war drags on, I am sure of that.'

'I say we gather a large force together, then surround and attack Paynter's,' suggested James.

'I hath considered that, James,' responded the baron. 'The problem is, most of the Kentish insurgents have left the county and travelled west to support the King, as Symon and Jack are about to do. At this moment in time, I doubt whether we could muster anywhere near enough men to attack a force so large as the Roundhead battalion now established at Paynter's. We could possibly mount skirmishes and aggravate the bastards, but that will only bring about more and more reprisals on innocent people across Kent. I dost nay believe that is our aim, is it?'

'Nay, it is not. I do nay wish to bring reprisals upon folk,' agreed James, backing away from his valiant proposal. 'The Roundheads seem to have adopted a scorched earth policy now, in any case. Burn, exterminate, and question right and wrong afterwards, that is the Parliamentarian way of waging war, but at Paynter's, 'tis under the auspices of our family crest.'

'Ay, 'tis so, James,' agreed Jack, 'but the dragon's head and motto "*Dum spiro spero*" is our family crest also. Unlike mine uncle Peter, I intend to carry the crest in a style worthy of respect for the family name. It shall be carried with more glory than Lord Peter Greenstreet, Cromwell's Kentish puppet, has ever demonstrated from his manor at Paynter's Forstal.'

Thus, the meeting went on all morning. The purpose was to bring the Royalists up to date and to air their views. The Dutch clock in the hall struck half after noon before Jack and Symon tucked into a tasty game stew, washed down with small beer. Maria had insisted they ate well before they left to join the King. It was early afternoon before Symon and Jack bade farewell to their uncle Johis, cousin James and aunt Maria, and finally departed from Claxfeldestane.

5

A GENTLEMAN OF THE ROAD

A touch of autumnal chill had set in as Jack and Symon left Claxfield and made their way down the village of Greenstreet to the forge. The stench of the street was not so bad now that the weather had changed to cool the rancidness of the London Road. Will Dix had men clearing and loading a cartload of manure outside the brewery. As the pair rode by, Will waved a hand, acknowledging Jack as his saviour from Roundhead savagery. Will Dix had obviously taken James at his word and borrowed the cart in the early hours, for the roadway was almost cleared of dung. Jack and Symon were planning a long ride to Devon, to join up with the King. The horses needed shoeing and checking over thoroughly from the outset of such a trek. The journey would be arduous enough without a shoe being thrown, or a lame horse to contend with. The clanging sound of hammer on anvil rang out in the air and meant Tong, the blacksmith and farrier, was already hard at work in his forge. Symon and Tong were well acquainted. Symon always brought his horses to be shod at the Greenstreet forge. Tong's name derived from the adjoining village of Tong. The sound of hammer on anvil also made a metallic ringing of 'tong, tong, tong' when he beat out and shaped red-hot iron. As soon as he could lift a hammer, pump a bellows and steady a frisky mare, Tong worked alongside his father at the old forge, becoming equally skilled at the craft. Tong's huge arms and rippling biceps had built over time, his strength akin to the iron he worked with. The blacksmith was not really concerned one way or the other about the course of civil war, just so long as his trade was steady. He would visit the brewhouse at the end of each day to sink several tankards of good ale and quench his insatiable thirst.

Stripped to the waist and covered in sweat, a youth pumped a bellows vigorously to get coals and metal white-hot.

'Good day, Master Symon and young sir. What canst I do fer 'ee on this gloomy afternoon?'

'Good day to ye, Tong. Jack here, and my good self, shalt be glad if ye wouldst level and shoe our horses for a long journey, Farrier. Do thy job well and ye will be paid in honest coin. We need to visit the saddler's and thereafter partake in a tankard or two at the brewhouse. Do ye nay delay the work, Tong. We must depart before the coming evening darkness makes our way to Borden burdensome. The road beyond Sittingbourne canst be tricky once night sets in.'

Without further ado, the farrier set about reshoeing Acorn, lifting each leg expertly, pulling out old nails, cleaning, filing, paring, levelling, burning and nailing on new iron shoes with the expertise of a lifetime. Symon and Jack visited the saddlers, then walked in on John Caslock, at the brewhouse. Caslock was pleased to see them. He drew two pewter tankards of frothy best beer from the tap of a well-coopered oak cask, which lay propped and wedged on chocks.

'Drink deep on me, boys. Ye mercifully saved us from torture by Roundhead scum last evening, Jack. Will and I will be eternally grateful to 'ee. Ay, and to Master James for his good protection. The Roundheads did nay return here, after they set off in hot pursuit of thee. In his loss of dignity, the captain was furious. He screamed unmercifully what he was going to do when he caught ye, and it wasn't just to carve off thine ears but also thy testicles and all thy other embellishments! He was livid ye made off with his weapons. Will Dix and I saw the platoon return from Lynsted. They took off along Watling Street towards the city, believing ye were heading in that direction. Nay doubt they comb the streets of Canterbury as we speak.'

With their horses well shod, Jack and Symon settled with the farrier. Symon was insistent that they prime and charge their weapons before they set off, knowing that Roundhead activity was prevalent along stretches of old Watling Street. Setting off at a brisk trot towards Sittingbourne, they hoped to cover the seven miles to Symon's abode in Borden, before night closed in on them. A nice grassy stretch through Bapchild village allowed their pace to open into a gallop, but as they approached the Chalkwell crossroad and reined in, to turn down the track road to Borden, a figure stepped out of the murky darkness into their path. The man wore a dark tricorn, pulled low over his brows, from which flowed long straggly black hair. A moustache and beard were equally long and matted. A brown leather frock coat with splayed thigh-length black boots completed his attire. In leather-gloved hands he held a brace of flintlock pistols, their polished brass ends directed at the heads of the two horsemen.

'Stand and deliver thine girdle and purses, or I wilt blow thine heads clean off thy shoulders,' the highwayman demanded in a blood-curdling manner, pointing the flintlocks threateningly.

But in Jack and Symon the highwayman had met his match. Jack's primed flintlocks appeared in his hands as if by magic and were well directed at the highway bandit. The guns were held at arm's length, pointing down at the robber in a state of deadlock. At the same time, Symon's right hand dropped to the side of his mare, Bell. He produced a large blunderbuss musket with a wide-flared muzzle. Leaning over the mare's neck in a prostrated position, his hat and chin resting on the butt and one eye squinting over the short barrel, Symon did not mince his words.

'Now then, mine bold highway robber, ye may discharge thy weapons and blow away one head, perhaps, but thine own swede will immediately disappear, together with thine arms, thine legs, heart, guts and genitals, leaving a tasty mess of carrion for the crows and kites to dine upon. So what is it to be? Our girdles and purses will never grace thy pitifully dismembered body.'

'Ay,' continued Jack, 'and if ye miss me with thy shot, I shall dismount from mine stallion Acorn here, turn ye over and stick my rapier up thy backside and out of thine insolent mouth.'

Unperturbed and still leaning over the mare's neck in a comical position, with the blunderbuss musket directed at the centre of the highwayman's body, Symon sang forth his final ultimatum.

'How now, mine bold fellow, thou art a gentleman of the road, I canst see that, and my cousin Jack here is a gentleman Cavalier. Why don't ye both lower thy weapons after the count of three, whilst I preside over proceedings with my faithful terminator? One, two...'

'If I put up my pistols, pray, how canst I be sure you are a gentleman of thy word, sir, and will refrain from firing?' the highwayman cut in, directing his reasonable question at Symon.

'Well, in all truth ye canst nay be sure, rogue,' replied Symon, 'but then again ye started the argument, I recall. It was thine own good self who intended to rob us of our valuable assets, and whilst we respect thy trade, bold fellow, we do nay propose to part with a half-groat. Nay, not even a copper farthing of our good English money. Now, put ye aside thy weapons and go upon thy business elsewhere, my bold fellow, before one of us gets jumpy. In any case, it is very nearly too dark to see each other clearly now. The killing could get quite messy.'

Still pointing his flintlock pistols the 'gentleman of the road' backed away, and with a sudden rustle of bushes he concealed himself and disappeared into the night without a by-your-leave.

'Well, bless me, he did nay even doff his grubby little tricorn. Hath ye come across the character before, Sy?' enquired Jack, making his flintlocks safe and tucking them back in his waistband.

'I think he may well be the much sought-after James Hind, a highwayman who terrorises this part of the London Road. He fits the rogue's description. I'm glad he backed down, Jack, because I meant to tell ye, my blunderbuss musket has been misfiring badly lately. It cannot be entirely relied upon. But yon fellow was not to know that. I must invest in the new English flintlock musket. In truth, this weapon is a bit ancient, ye know. Let us try it out, shall we?'

Symon Greenstreet pointed the weapon in the direction of the vanished outlaw and pulled back the mechanism, then squeezed the trigger. There was a loud retort. A cloud of white smoke enshrouded them both and a ripping noise as the huge lead ball, together with other rammed metal, ploughed through the bushes, laying a swath of vegetation flat for many yards. They reined the horses in, waved away the smoke and peered along the flattened path of destruction.

'Hmm, it fired alright that time, Jack! Ye wouldst hath been quite safe as it happens, cousin, but ye never knoweth. They really are obsolete nowadays, these old Dutch snaphance muskets!'

Jack laughed so loudly at his older cousin's demonstration, he almost fell out of his saddle, causing Acorn to rear up and whinny. He calmed the horse as the explosion echoed all around.

'Look, Sy, even old Acorn is laughing at ye, ye silly sod. 'Tis a good job thy bluffing was good.'

*

Jack stayed with Symon and his wife, Marion, for a while, helping to plough and harrow the fields. They rebuilt a barn together. One year turned to another. They scattered the seed and erected scarecrows to keep off scavengers. They would be some time away serving their King.

The civil war widened. King Charles negotiated a cessation in Ireland, which allowed him to reinforce his armies with English regiments that had been sent to Ireland to quell the rebellion of 1641. Parliament took an even greater step by signing a solemn league and covenant, sealing an alliance with the Scottish Covenanters. Early in 1644, a Covenanter army, led by the Earl of Leven, entered the north of England on behalf of the English Parliament. The Royalist Marquess of Newcastle was forced to divide his army, leaving a detachment under Sir John Belasyse to watch over the Parliamentarians, commanded by Lord Fairfax in Hull. Newcastle led a main body north to confront Leven, culminating in the 'Siege of York'. The King sent Prince Rupert of the Rhine to relieve York, whilst he played for time in Oxford. This split in forces led to eventual Royalist defeat at Marston Moor, west of York.

Early in 1644, Jack and Symon learnt of the death of Lord Peter Greenstreet. Matthew Greenstreet of Huntingfield and Eastling rode over to inform them. He also informed Jack that his father, William Greenstreet of Maidstone, lay ill upon his bed and was nearing his end. William had asked to see Jack several times, according to Matthew. He sought his son's forgiveness for driving Jack away. Despite their differences, Jack still loved his father. He knew that if it had not been for Lord Peter of Ospringe, they would probably not have split apart, and William of Maidstone might never have sent Jack on his way. Prior to that family row, father and son had agreed to respect each other's choice of sides in the civil war. Jack decided to go at once to see his father. He did not want his father to depart the troubled world without reconciliation between them. Matthew told Jack to be very careful and to keep to the back roads, because Colonel Browne had put a substantial bounty on Jack's head, alive or dead.

6

RECONCILIATION, MAY 1644

Without further delay, Jack set off to see his father. He kept to country tracks, steering clear of the main roads, as his uncle Matthew of Eastling had advised, by giving Watling Street a wide berth. Jack chose not to call on his cousin James and uncle Johis at Claxfeldestane, for fear that Roundhead scouts might have the farm under surveillance or be watching out for him. He did not want to risk the lives of those he held dear, particularly now that he had been outlawed by the Parliamentarians and had a fixed bounty reward price on his head. He rode through the villages of Tunstall and Rodmersham, then cut up north of Lynsted to Lewson Street and down into Ospringe, steering clear of Paynter's Forstal and the Roundhead camp at Paynter's Farm, which was situated a little over a mile from 'Woodlarks', Jack's family home.

Smoke curled up from the chimney pots of Woodlarks, in the still chill of the morning air. All except one terracotta pot emitted smoke. The inactive chimney appeared unused. Jackdaws were busy taking sticks down and building a nest in the top of that chimney. Jack decided it was the chimney stack which once served his active bedchamber. The familiar half-timbered house lay in a dell surrounded by 1,050 acres of farmland, woodland, orchards, pastureland and paddocks. Jack's stomach churned over as he made his way between mature oak and beech trees, walking Acorn slowly down the slope towards the old house. Once upon a time this was destined to be his inheritance. Was it the dread of inheriting his father's many lands which made Jack choose the path he had? No, it was not that, Jack consoled himself, it was for the other inheritance. The inheritance of loyalty, of family values and tradition; that was the path he had chosen to follow. His ancient family had served the kings since the time of William the Conqueror. They had always been reeves and king's men. His great-uncle John was Prior of Rochester Cathedral in 1314. Other family members had been priests, churchwardens and pious men, who served the King. Many continued to do so. The family crest and coat of arms had been granted by King Henry IV to Sir Lawrence Greenstreete in 1400 AD, all those years ago. It should never have been tampered with by Lord Peter Greenstreet, when he altered the arms from martlet to double-headed eagle. Jack had chosen the path of Royalist, in favour of King Charles, for those reasons and no other. Jack, the older of William's sons, was named after his grandfather, carpenter John Greenstreet.

Other than the smoking chimneys, the only sign of life was old Wat Harrys busying himself in the yard. Jack guessed his two younger brothers, William and Thomas, were out in the fields. Wat Harrys was his father's trusty manservant. Wat had been with the family since Jack's mother died of an unknown fever when he was ten years of age. William had married again soon after, but his second wife had died from blood poisoning. She cut herself badly with a sickle in the crop field whilst helping to reap the ripened corn at harvest time. Sepsis set in.

Wat Harrys noticed Jack as he neared the courtyard entrance and hopped over to greet him. He held the bridle whilst Jack dismounted, then led Acorn to a feeding trough and secured him. All the while the old man had a smile upon his face. He turned again to Jack, still beaming, and took hold of the Cavalier's hand, gripping it tightly in his own gnarled palm and not letting go. Pumping his pupil's hand up and down, Wat gazed tearfully into Jack's eyes.

"Tis good ter see ye, Master Jack. Thy father will be so very relieved thou hast come to him.'

Wat Harrys tethered and watered Acorn and left the stallion chomping on a trough of oats.

'Thine father, William, has been full of remorse ever since ye left the place, Master Jack. His health hast served him badly for some time now. I fear whatever ails him is terminal and nearing conclusion. He hast become very weak in the past few days. He had a wicked burning fever, but he is now so very cold. We called in a barber surgeon. The best we could find, mind. He knew all about William Harvey's recent discovery concerning blood circulation. The barber bled the old gentleman, but it doth nay appear to hath made any improvement in him. None that I'm aware of anyhow. Thou hast been foremost on his mind for many weeks now, Jack.

Ever since he lay upon his feather bed with the fever, some five days since, he has been asking for 'ee to call on him, much to the annoyance of thy brothers, I'm obliged to say. Best stay well clear of them, Jack, because they hath turned very nasty agin 'ee, very nasty indeed.'

'Right, thank ye kindly, Wat, for all ye hath done. No master could ask for a more faithful and diligent servant than thou hast been to Father, and ye were always such a patient mentor to me.'

Now valet to William, Wat had been like an older brother to Jack when he was growing up. Wat was then gamekeeper. He taught Jack to snare rabbits using polecats, fire a fowling piece and shoot waterfowl. He mentored Jack in the use of hounds to hunt hares, and to stalk and use the long bow to bring down deer and wild boar. He also taught the intricacies of sword play.

'Ay, but it was my privilege, Master Jack, ye was a good pupil. Come, Jack, I will conduct ye to him. The master lies at rest in the best bedchamber. I must make sure all is tidy fer 'ee and inform the master thou hast come to see him, for I fear he doth nay see too well anymore.'

The old gentleman lay upon his feather bed. Raised pillows propped his head, his eyes were closed and he breathed shallowly. The carved four-poster bed stedle was of the best quality, imposing in its grandeur, with trimmed velour canopy. The chamber was adorned with oil paintings. A large rug, curtain and valences, three ornate chests, a table, a trunk and two beautifully carved and inlaid walnut chairs furnished the room. A sword, belt with powder and shot flasks and a bayonet hung on wall brackets. The fire, which had burnt down, barely kept the room warm and badly needed making

56

up. An earthenware jug and bowl stood on the table ready for ablutions. Wat went to it, freshened a flannel and applied it to William's pale face, washing it gently and drying it with linen. The old man stirred and opened his eyes. His eyes darted about, but he saw little in the room. Barely audible, he spoke in a strained whisper.

'I tried to eat the pottage ye prepared for me, Wat, but I canst find little appetite in me, it seems.'

He referred to a cold bowl of pottage on a table beside the bed. Wat removed the bowl and then took Jack's warm hand and guided it to his father's cold and clammy fingers.

'Here is thy eldest son, Jack, come to see ye, Master. He has come at risk because Colonel Browne has put a ransom on his Royalist head. 'Twill be unwise for him to dwell here long.'

William clasped his son's hand in a weak grip, addressing him in a tremulous but relieved voice.

'Ah, Jack! I am so pleased thou hath come. Our estrangement was entirely my fault. I should never hath turned ye out of thine own home. Ye are so like thy mother, who I loved so very much, as I do ye also, Jack. Please forgive a dying man. This bloody civil war has caused so much damage to us all and split so many families asunder. Pray, let it nay destroy us forever.'

Wat set about raking the fire. The valet placed several oak logs upon the hot cinders, which rapidly burst into flame, causing an immediate glow and feeling of warmth in the bedchamber.

'Father, ye taught me to forgive when I was a small boy. There is no need for either of us to seek forgiveness from each other. Ye should know that. I am sure we understand each other on most issues. Ye also taught me to be loyal, to observe and listen to other people's point of view, and only then to be guided by my own conscience. That I have always striven to do, and that is why I chose to take the Royalist path. Thou hast many lands, messuages and appurtenances, Father, and I canst therefore understand why ye chose to side with Parliament. Was it nay to protect thine interests, as thine brother, Lord Peter of Ospringe, protected his?'

William gripped his son's hand with a last reserve of energy and pulled Jack close to him.

'Nay, Jack! Ye hath followed thine own conscience. I respect thee for that. Thou art wrong about me and the lands. 'Tis sincerely the opposite of what ye say. I believe the people of this country are becoming more and more suppressed by the Crown and there is necessity to bring the King to heel. I shall go to my grave believing we must build a more democratic way of life, rather than be suppressed by Royalty. The lands are not important, Jack. They will be of little use to me on my journey. In many ways, they are a millstone around the necks of this family. I respect the reasons upon which thou hath based thy argument, Jack. This bloody civil war will resolve such arguments one way or t'other. Now, on my deathbed, I want ye to know I bare ye nay ill will, only my love for ye and sincere wishes for ye to enjoy a happy future. To that end, I hath made provision for ye, Jack, but nay in my last will and testament. I cannot grant or pass on lands to ye, Jack, because we do not know the outcome of this war, nor whether you will be permanently outlawed. I implore ye to disappear, in that respect, but I know ye wilt nay heed my warning. Wat, here, is one of my feoffees, along with Matthew of Eastling. I hath made provision for Wat also. He is to have the small cottage called "Moddilyon". The lands are to go to William and Thomas, and I hath made provision for thine sisters. At my bequest, Wat has secreted a bag of coin. Coin of good English money, mind. There is some gold unite, silver pounds, half pounds and crowns, amounting in total to a value of 350 pounds. I hath asked Wat to secure it and pass it on to ye, when it is safe to so do. Take it, son, with my blessing and the blessing of thy good mother, God rest her soul. Do ye nay attend my funeral. I doth nay wish ye to endanger thyself further. It will serve little purpose. Go now, for I am tired and must make my peace with God Almighty, my saviour and redeemer. I hath arranged in my will for a choir to sing for my soul. I crave only free pardon for the forgiveness of my many sins. Thank ye for coming to me, Jack, ye will never know the relief I feel from thine visit, nor the pain I endured from our estrangement. Go now, son, I must sleep. Bless ye and make sure you keep to the back ways, when ye return to thine Cousin Symon's abode.'

Jack released his father's hand and kissed his forehead, backing away slowly from a part of his life he would never forget. His father, William of Maidstone, looked at peace now. Wat came over to Jack, took his pupil's arm and guided him away from the chamber and down the stairs to the living room. Jack had filled up and his eyes were misty. Wat raised an issue.

'Despite my promises to thee, Master Jack, I wouldst prefer it if ye could take the money with ye now. When the master has passed on, I shall retire to Moddilyon. My time for departing this world is also nearing. Hath ye a clandestine place to hide such a vast sum of cash, Jack?'

Jack pondered deeply for a moment, his thoughts slow and deliberate before responding.

'Yea, Wat, there is such a place! A place only one other person knows about and has shared with me. He is also the very person I can trust, all the way to the grave. I will contact him and arrange to secrete the money on mine way back to Symon's farm in Borden. Nobody else need be involved. The money will be safe in the place I know of, I am sure of that. One day, when things art calmed down a piece, I shall recover my legacy and possibly purchase property of my own, and maybe find some fair maiden of Kent to become my wife and have children.'

'What ye say is of great relief to me, Master Jack. At my advanced age I may nay be here to guard such a huge sum of money for much longer. Who else can I confide in as to where it lieth? If thy brothers find out about thine legacy and become aware of mine involvement, they will hang me from the nearest oak tree. I hope to hath some quiet moments of contemplation and contentment at the cottage called Moddilyon before I expire and join the master agin.'

'And so ye shall, good Wat. Do ye nay talk of expiry. Thine retirement will be long and pleasant. I shalt take great pleasure in calling on ye in thy new abode. When this wretched civil war is concluded, we shall enjoy a pipe of tobacco together and dwell upon good times.'

Wat sucked on his clay pipe a moment, then raised his eyes and looked at Jack in alarm.

'Doth ye nay chance coming this way agin on my account, Jack. The last thing I need to see, afore I die, is fer 'ee to be a-hanging from a gibbet on the highway for the corbies and kites to peck at thine poor eyes. Now, make haste to the stables and let us get ye loaded up with thy father's legacy to 'ee and get thee on thy way out of here. The money is nay an inheritance, Jack, 'tis merely thy father's good wishes to ye, that is all. Ye should be running this place, Master Jack, nay thy younger brothers. I sorely miss the good times we had together, Jack. They canst never take those days away from us, whatever else they try to do – eh, Master?'

The two men crossed the courtyard and went to the stable block. Wat removed a mare from one of the stalls and asked Jack to hold her still. The manservant scraped away dung and straw, then found an iron ring in the floor at the back of the stall. Wat pulled hard on the ring and a slab came loose. The old man bent low and removed a bulging leather bag. He replaced the slab, rearranged the dung and invited Jack to replace the mare. The heavy bag was secured by leather strapping with a buckle. Jack strapped the bag to the side of Acorn beneath a blanket. When all was secure, Jack mounted Acorn, then leaned over and gripped Wat's hand firmly.

'Mine father's end is near, Wat. Look after him well until he departeth this life and look after thyself, old friend, until I pass this way again. It will be a short while, mind, before I return.'

'Go ye careful, Master Jack,' said Wat, choking up. He smote Acorn sharply across the rump.

Jack walked Acorn across the yard to leave the stable block. As he went under the slim semi–circular brick arch to ride away, a voice commanded him to halt. Jack's younger brother, Thomas, stepped out of the deep shadows of the yard wall, a loaded flintlock cocked and held at arm's length, his arm visibly shaking. Tom's voice trembled as he gave orders to his brother.

'Brother Will and I guessed that was thy tethered horse, Jack. It was a big mistake leaving him for all to see. Will set off for Paynter's Farm about half an hour ago and will be back with parliamentary troops any minute to arrest ye. Best step ye down and wait for them to come.'

Jack fixed his eyes squarely on his youngest brother. Tom, who had only just turned sixteen, was naturally under the influence of Will the younger. Jack spoke quietly to his sibling.

'It doth nay quite work like that, Tom. I am mounting my horse. Ye need to pull yon trigger and aim to kill me, because I am riding out of here right now, come heaven, hell or high water!'

Wat Harrys ran towards the brotherly altercation, waving his hands in the air. Wat shouted in the name of God for the quarrelling to cease. He urged Tom to put down the flintlock.

'For God's sake, Master Thomas, lay aside thy weapon. What do ye think thy father wouldst say, ye acting this way whilst he lieth upon his bed so very frail and near to death? What do ye think he wouldst say to ye, Thomas, eh? Jack has come to pay his last respects and to mend a rift. Your brother is entitled to pay his last respects to a dying man, especially his own father.'

'William told me Jack has nay father, Wat, so keep thy nose out of it. Royalist scum must be held to account. Colonel Browne will see him hang. This man made an idiot of the colonel's captain, in the brewhouse at Teynham. He stripped him of his arms and those of his men. They wilt hath revenge.' Still shaking, Tom supported the elbow of the extended arm with his free hand; the firearm was getting heavy. 'Step down from thy fancy horse, brigand, like I advise,' demanded Thomas, 'otherwise I shalt blast ye to that place in hell you deserve to be.'

Jack spurred Acorn, who reared, then broke into a gallop. Tom fired with little purpose, the ball whistling harmlessly through the air, leaving Tom shrouded in white smoke. Jack reined Acorn to a halt, then turned to call back to his young brother, who stood white and passive.

'Brigand, ye call me. I am no bandit, Tom, just a true Royalist. Thou best get Wat to give thee some lessons in shooting, Tom. I hath a brace of flintlocks and a rapier here. If it were anybody but thee, Tom, they wouldst be on the ground gasping their last breath of life by now.'

Tom stood trembling; the pistol drooped loose and smoking at his side. Wat put an arm around the boy to comfort him and waved Jack on his way. At the same time, Jack's peripheral vision clocked a row of horsemen on the brow of the ridge. They appeared in line as if by magic. There were seventeen of them, all helmeted, their armour glinting in the rays of the sun, which had broken through the clouded sky. The Roundheads charged down the slope towards the house, brother William in the lead. Jack took off at full gallop to the rear of the house, making haste across the lands he knew so well. He crossed a meadow, jumped fences and rode, with his head kept low. He rode through an orchard and around a lake to a stream, conscious of thundering hooves behind and aimless discharges of musketry in his direction. Making good ground he guided Acorn up a babbling brook to a bridge, climbed the slippery steep bank and left the family estate. He crossed Watling Street, then headed northwards into Faversham.

The rumble of hooves had subsided behind Jack. All was quiet. He took no chances, continuing northwards via Luddenham, Flood Mill and Uplees, until he came to the banks of the Swale and followed the track along the sea wall to Conyer Creek. Conyer, known for its mussels and smuggling, was a wild creek which entered the Swale north of Teynham. Often busy at the quayside, with the coming and going of barges and shipping, Conyer was the port of Teynham. Turning southwards away from the quayside, Jack went deep into the marshes. It was late and getting dark. He found a quiet spot between some trees to lie up and spend the night in contemplation. It had been a narrow escape. A damp mist crept in from the creek.

After securing Acorn to a tree, with grass to graze upon, Jack removed the saddle strapping and the leather money bag and made himself as comfortable as he could on a flat rabbit-grazed plateau. The night was damp. Hunger pangs gnawed within. Yet Jack had enough money beneath his head to purchase a small mansion, with servants to make his bed and serve him a banquet. Exhausted, he attempted to sleep on his cape, burying himself beneath the single blanket he carried. Sleep was intermittent and snatched in short periods. Throughout the long night, his flintlocks lay primed, his rapier naked at his side. Twice he thought he heard rustling and tinkling in nearby undergrowth, causing him to sit up abruptly and strain to listen in the cold night air. It was probably wild animals but could easily have been Roundheads probing the surrounding thicket – searching for him. Smuggling was prevalent in the marshes of Conyer Creek. Perhaps he was near to a smuggling gang's tracks. He did not want to get caught out by rogues. Jack dozed. He awoke at first light, aching in every limb. He was as stiff as a board and hungry enough to eat a horse. Acorn, who had grazed on lush vegetation, eyed Jack suspiciously! The stallion had no cause to worry. His master was only checking to make sure he hadn't been torn, in the mad scramble to get away from the Roundhead platoon.

Reconciliation with his father gave Jack an immense feeling of relief. The journey to Ospringe had been worth it. He knew he would have suffered nagging recriminations, had he not made the effort to visit. He was, nevertheless, both shocked and saddened to see his father so weak. Such a state was not how he wished to remember him. William of Maidstone was a fine gentleman, rich in lands and blessed for his humanity to the poor of the communities in which he governed. Looking back, Jack recalled many occasions when his father had helped the poor of the parishes. To some degree Jack understood his father's argument against the suppression of the man in the street and why he supported a more democratic way of life for all citizens. But what about loyalties to King and country? There had always been kings. They could not get rid of the King who was appointed by God, could they? Could they?

In the early morning dew, Jack strapped the money bag to Acorn's side and concealed it with his cape, before setting off for the village. Jack decided to walk the short distance to Greenstreet, leading the horse by the bridle. He had a plan, but he did not want to arrive too early at his destination in case the would-be recipients of his proposal were not yet abroad from their slumbers. He need not have worried. As he approached the property from the rear, behind the main street, in order that he had less chance of being detected, he saw one of his would-be recipients working in the back yard. John Caslock was already abroad, cleaning a coopered oak tun barrel for his next brew-up. He stopped his scrubbing and, with a wide grin on his face, came to greet his champion, the Cavalier who had saved his ears from butchery.

'What kind of dishevelled rascal calls at the rear of my brewhouse so early in the morning? Doth thou hath trouble with thine sleeping, or was it a wench who kept 'ee from thy dozing?'

'Yea, unfortunately 'twas the former, John Caslock. Could ye find me a morsel or two to eat, John? I am that hungry my arse has been grazing on the wayside grass along with Acorn here.'

'Come ye inside, Master Jack. Will Dix is cooking up some eggs to go with the fresh bread he baked early this morning. Ye are welcome to join us and tell us what on this earth has been happening to 'ee, for ye look like thou hast been dragged through a hedge backwards to me.'

'Well, John, 'tis a story I will gladly tell and a story which ye might be able to assist me with!'

Will Dix was overjoyed to see the man who had saved them from Roundhead butchery. On Caslock's instruction, Will dished up double eggs, oatcake and fresh bread for the starving Cavalier. Warmed and refreshed from the nagging hunger pangs in his stomach, Jack related his story to the two brewers, omitting to tell them of the huge legacy his father had bestowed on him. Jack knew well enough such information was best kept contained close to his heart.

'How then might we assist thy good self, Jack?' chorused Will Dix and John Caslock.

'Well, 'tis quite simple really. Knowing full well the bounty on mine head, I dost nay want to call at Claxfeldestane and put mine uncle Johis, aunt Maria or James at risk. The Roundheads will have scouts out, watching over Claxfield. I was wondering if one of ye wouldst call on James and ask him to meet me in Cripson Wood, at our secret place, say, at eleven of the clock? There are matters I wish to discuss with him. I will use the back track around Frognal and enter the wood beyond Greenstreet, from further up old Watling Street, in a surreptitious manner, ye understand. Then nobody will be any the wiser and I shalt trouble ye no further.'

'Worry thee not about troubling us, Master. I will go on the errand at once,' offered Will. ''Tis a simple favour you ask of us, Jack, and we are both indebted to ye for saving our ears from being carved off by Fairfax's ruffian harquebusiers. I will also give thine horse some mash.'

'Well, 'tis a simple favour from a very simple man, in all truth,' replied Jack. 'Perhaps I could wait here in the good company of John and partake of a tankard or two of thine excellent beer?'

''Twill be my pleasure,' said John Caslock, adding, 'Will Dix and myself are shortly to depart from Teynham Manor. We are going to Faversham to start a brewery business with Master Dick Marsh. 'Tis hoped to purchase several alehouses in which to sell our wares. We are also thinking of purchasing the halfway house at the end of Greenstreet, ye know, the old coaching inn, and opening it as a brewhouse for the public. We might name it the "Dover Castle". We think it is a formidable proposition, and a great location for trade, being as it is approximately halfway twixt Rochester and Canterbury, and on the main road to London.'

By the time Will Dix returned to confirm James had agreed to meet at the chosen place, Jack was quite merry. Twice he slipped in a futile attempt to mount his steed. The first time he tried to leap into the saddle, as he often did, only to fall backwards. Then, midst rumblings of hilarity, he attempted to pull himself onto Acorn's back, only to slide down the stallion's other side, whence he collapsed into fits of laughter, aided and abetted by Caslock. Finally, with John's aid, he got his foot into the stirrup and managed to cock a leg over. Jack put it down to his rough night of sleep, but Caslock knew better. John Caslock's brew had a high alcoholic content, well above the norm for most beers, causing a wonderful effect of inebriation on folk.

Jack set off the way he had come. He walked Acorn across the back fields to Frognal, through the dense orchards of cherry blossom and past Widow Goody's cottage to Watling Street. He saw no sign of Widow Goody, who had sewn him up, nor of her pretty buxom daughter, Mary. Mary had attended so tenderly to all his needs, particularly beneath the trees of ripened cherries. He came to the road boundary and peered cautiously right and left, then trotted across the main London Road and down an overgrown track of nettle and bramble leading into Cripson Wood. The trees were sprouting vigorously into life and the bird song was intense. Woodpeckers drummed, and great titmice gave forth a continuous seesawing song, which needed oiling.

His inebriation dissipating, Jack walked Acorn along a track humming with insect activity. Downwards through leaf-sprouting trees, a narrow path led to the woodland boundary. He found the huge oak tree with its low horizontal bough, dismounted and secured the horse. It was the same shady nook in which he and James had lain hidden, after cunningly escaping the Roundheads and fleeing from Lynsted church. Jack peered through the sap-green vegetation across the harrowed field to Claxfeldestane, seeking clear vision through the hedgerow. He saw James set off from the old house to walk up the inclination, towards their secret hiding place. As James neared the wood, Jack cupped his hands together and made several owl calls.

'Was that ye making those owl calls, ye daft beggar?' asked James as the two men embraced.

'Ay 'twas, cousin. I hath been drinking a good fill of wallop at the White Swan. Will and John's beer gets better with each visit. We shall have to go to Faversham to drink their brew before long. They tell me they are setting up brewing in a big way in that Swale-side town.'

'Good luck to them,' said James. 'I think it takes courage to engage in such commercial activity whilst this war wages on so. Their hopped beer is much tastier than the usual ale, I must say.'

'Yea, I hast to agree with ye, James. I am sure the good brewers are onto a winner. Talking of which, I must inform ye of my good fortune and the reason for my clandestine visit this day.'

Jack went over to Acorn, lifted the blanket covering and unstrapped the heavy money bag.

'Look in there, James. 'Tis a legacy – nay, a gift – from Father. There is 310 pounds of good English money therein. There was 350, but I hath taken some out for a rainy day, and here is ten pounds for thine own good use, cousin, because ye are my dearest friend and the only person who is aware of the existence of this money, other than Wat Harrys, mine father's loyal and diligent manservant.' James gave a whistle of disbelief at the amount.

Jack handed James ten pounds and demanded he pocket it and spend it freely, but wisely.

'Nay, do ye nay protest, dear friend. I want ye to know that, should I perish in combat, or fall ill and die, and should ye hear of mine death, or I do nay return to claim this money, then ye are my sole beneficiary, James. But do nay get overly excited about that, dear friend, for I aim to return as soon as I canst roam freely across this good county of Kent. Now, James, thou art the only fellow I can trust with my life, other than Symon, and he wouldst probably cut mine throat for a shilling. Nay, James, I hath made up my mind. Ye are a brother to me and a man of much integrity. Now, go and get a spade so that we can dig a deep hole at the end of this oak tree bough and bury the leather bag and its contents. I do nay wish it to be incumbent on any other person, or to lie in any other person's property, except it be beneath Johis' land, but he need never know it lieth here in Cripson Wood. In any case, this wood and Claxfeldestane will be thine one day, James. Will ye swear to secrecy on the matter, dear cousin of mine?'

James agreed to go along with Jack's wishes. They shook hands, and James departed to get a spade. He returned with the implement, a mattock and a small oak chest he had found in the stables. The men began to dig a pit some three feet in depth. They put the leather bag of money in the old chest and lowered Jack's inheritance into the hole. After backfilling, they tamped down firmly and strewed dead leaves and bracken over the area to make it as it was prior to excavation. Jack breathed a huge sigh of relief, then slapped James hard on the back.

'So 'tis done, James. I shall wend mine merry way without a care in the world now that heavy money bag has been secreted. Ye and I know exactly where 'tis hidden. The end of the low broad oak bough marks the spot. Shalt thou decide to rob me, James, and go off across the wide world, I canst at least vouch mine legacy went to a good friend and a very fine fellow. Once a borsholder and soon to be reeve. Now, I must prepare to ride back to Symon of Borden.'

Jack burst into a fit of laughter at James' face. James looked sorely vexed that his friend could ever consider such mistrust. When James saw the mischievous look spread across Jack's own face, he also chuckled with mirth. They knew each other well enough, no doubt about that.

'Stay exactly where thou art, Jack. Sit upon yon friendly oak bough, whilst I descend the slope and find a bite to eat for us to share, before ye departeth from our clandestine meeting place.'

'Ah, well ye should be aware I didst breakfast at the brewhouse prior to coming here, James.'

'Yea, but that is not going to fuel thy tempestuous innards all day long, I warrant. Just stay seated with some little patience. I shall return within the shake of a nanny goat's tail.'

Jack perched himself on the friendly stout oak bough and watched his friend descend the harrowed field to the old house. A silence came over the wood. A dove called to its mate. Spotted woodpeckers continued to drum on hollow tree trunks. A song thrush rendered repetitive sweet phrases twice over. The calm and tranquillity of the greenwood was golden. The young Cavalier started to nod his head. Suddenly a cock pheasant crowed and whirred its wings, just a stone's throw from where Jack sat. Startled, he sprang from the bough, drew his rapier and adopted an on-guard stance. Recognising the phenomenon that jogged him from his trance, he sat down again, embarrassed with himself for his jumpy reaction. Yesterday had been that kind of day, but he didn't really expect a party of Roundheads to turn up in Cripson Wood. Yet, woods are spooky places when on one's own. There are always eyes peering from behind trees and imaginary shadows moving forward a pace or two, first right and then left; or for no apparent reason an unexplained rustling occurs in the nearby surrounding bushes.

James soon returned with a wicker basket brimming with food and drink. Almost at once, the woodland at Claxfield presented a far friendlier atmosphere to Jack's way of thinking.

'Now then, my chirpy Cavalier, let us indulge in a banquet before ye go on yonder merry way. Let me see now. We hath cold roasted woodcock legs, cooked in herbs, a slice of cold partridge pasty, capon slices, fresh bread and a smidgeon of oatcake and chutney. This tasty meal can all be washed down with this large jug of cider. How doth that grab hold of thy breeches?'

'Mmm, 'tis a fine tasty platter thou present, James. I shalt need to nap a while after devouring such a banquet,' the Cavalier informed his friend, hungrily chomping away on a woodcock leg.

Good justice was done to the food, midst plenty of joviality. They drained the cider, and the greenwood rang with their laughter. James rummaged in the basket and found tobacco and two clay pipes. They smoked several fills before the friends parted company, as amicably as when they met, neither knowing when their paths might cross again, but wishing each other God's blessings. As Jack urged Acorn to walk on through the woods, he called out to James,

'Convey my best regards to Johis and Maria. I'm joining the King's army at Oxford tomorrow.'

7

OXFORD TO LOSTWITHIEL, JUNE 1644

The stallion's iron shoes clattered across the cobbled yard. The farmyard appeared decidedly quiet. Jack found Marion around the corner of the house, with her three youngest children, feeding chickens with wheat grain. A prime cockerel crowed loudly over its domain to liven the stillness of the afternoon. A dog barked, setting geese hissing. The geese chased forward to see the unwelcome intruder off. Somewhat surprised at Jack's arrival, Marion came across the yard with a besom to shoo the cackling geese away. She helped Jack de-harness his horse and they set Acorn loose in an adjoining paddock, leaving the animal to drink its fill. Marion beckoned Jack into the farmhouse and poured him a glass of small beer. He gulped it down. She poured another to help quench the thirst which had come upon him from the dusty ride.

'Oh, Jack, Symon and Leonard Smith left Borden two days ago, to join up with the King's army at Oxford. They said if ye did nay meet them along the way, they wouldst catch up with ye there. Ye art welcome to stay over for the night, in thine usual feather bed. That might be best. Ye will then be fresh to ride early on the morrow. I have plenty of pottage simmering, and a fresh egg, bread, ham and oatcake to break the fast on the morrow. What say thee?'

'Thank ye kindly, Marion, that I will do. Meanwhile, how canst I assist with thy farm work?'

Marion smiled at his kindness. It was never easy when the menfolk took off to fight for the cause. The farm work was hard enough, and then there were six children to manage throughout each day. Washing and drying was a necessity, and there were meals to prepare and contend with. Marion was thankful for Jack's help. He always did his bit to work his way, whenever he came to stay. Nobody could argue or complain about her cousin-in-law in that respect.

'There are cows and goats to bring in and milk. I was due to perform that task half of one hour ago, but time be my worst enemy right now, with Symon gone to fight for the King and all.'

'I wilt call them in and drive the herd up to the milking barn right away, Marion.'

'Thank'ee kindly, Jack. Take Willow with 'ee to help, he knows what to do.'

Marion stuck two fingers in her mouth and blew a long whistle. The long-haired Old English sheepdog bounded up to Marion. The dog had been napping beneath the timber-framed Tudor granary barn, between the mushroom-shaped staddle stones. Two older children with herding sticks joined

Jack and Willow, and together they set off for the meadow to round up the herd of White Park cattle and goats for milking. They scattered the cockerel and hens on their way.

As he wandered down to the pasture, with Rob and Maisy chattering ceaselessly, Jack wondered if he might one day find a girl like Marion – a girl he could grow fond of and marry and settle down with. Perhaps he might have children of his own. Right at this moment in time, it seemed a very unlikely proposition, outlawed as he was by the Roundheads and with a price on his head. Tomorrow he'd be setting off westwards to join King Charles at Oxford. It was far more likely he would be facing cannon shot and musket balls, rather than meet a pretty maid to pay court to. Willow the Old English sheepdog padded alongside Jack as if he had known him all his life. The children chattered, continuously firing questions at their favourite uncle.

Next day, a dawn chorus awoke Jack early from his slumber. He descended the steep staircase from the attic room to the farmhouse kitchen to be greeted by the smell of cooking. Marion was already busying herself with the new morning. The children were attending to their allotted tasks in the yard. Freshly baked bread, oatcake, patted butter, eggs and pork slices were placed before him, and he thanked her profusely as he chomped away at the hearty meal.

The older children, Robert and Maisy, accompanied Jack to the paddock and helped prepare Acorn for the long ride ahead. He left the farm to a rendering of fare-the-wells and exchanged hand-waving until out of sight. Aware that Roundhead troops used the ancient Watling Street from London, Jack kept an alert mind until he had crossed London Bridge. He rode through the city, north of the Thames to

Brent Cross, Harrow and Gerrards Cross, then rested beside the River Colne near Chalfont St Peter. There he chomped on a slice of ham and egg pie, packed by Marion, and swigged from a pitcher of cider. It was late in the afternoon when he arrived at High Wycombe and sought a coaching inn for the night. The Dashwood Arms seemed a quiet enough place to lodge. It had a sign indicating 'travellers welcome'. The Cavalier led Acorn through the slim archway into the cobbled stabling courtyard area. A servant took the horse to be cleaned, fed and stabled for the night. Jack checked his flintlocks.

Jack had done everything possible to avoid Roundhead confrontation on his ride to High Wycombe, saving the fight for the battlefield. He hoped the inn was free of Parliamentarians and that he could enjoy a well-earned drink and eat a meal in tranquillity. He lifted the latch and entered the room to find one person in residence. A feather-hatted man lounged in one corner. The plump, lazy sluggard had both feet propped up on a table. He munched on a huge round pie with one hand, whilst he slurped ale from a pewter tankard held by the other. He constantly belched loudly from a round red face. His moustache was waxed at the ends and his beard, which was full of pastry and pieces of pie, hung over his expansive barrel chest to the top of his rounded potbelly. Dressed in a red woollen topcoat and baggy grey breeches, a leather body belt supported his sword and scabbard, and from a cross bandolier hung a dozen wooden tubes containing gunpowder and a bag of shot. A wheellock pistol lay on the table in front of him. He spoke in a tongue which was clearly north of Watford, dribbling ale from one corner of his mouth as he addressed the Cavalier who had walked in on his hearty meal.

'Well now, my fine fellow, where doth ye hail from? Ye look like a fighting man to me.'

'I am a Kentish man from north of the Medway and proud of it. I am wending mine way to fight for King Charles. Any man suggesting otherwise will feel the sharp tip of my blade.'

The stout man grinned, showing an uneven row of missing and bad teeth. He extended a hand.

'Nay, stay thee, my good fellow, for we art two of a kind, birds of a feather. I am from Melton Mowbray. My name is Walter of Mowbray. Pray, let us drink together this night. Tomorrow we can find the horse cavalry and join a troop of like-thinking men, what say thee, Kent man?'

'Ye speak a funny tongue north of Watford, my friend, but ye have a similar bent to mine own, and drinking is what I am here for.' Jack eyed the sluggard shrewdly and held out a hand. Mowbray clasped it. Jack drew up a chair and called the innkeeper to attend upon them.

'Landlord, bring me and my comrade a flagon of best ale. Ay, and a pie that I can get my teeth into. I am weary from a long ride across London and trust ye hath a comfortable bed for me.'

'My name is Jack Greenstreet. I come from a large dynasty in Kent bearing that name,' boasted Jack. 'We bear a coat of arms. My crest is a jewel-embellished crown about the neck of a scaly dragon dripping blood. It bears the Latin, "*Dum spiro spero* – Whilst I breathe, I hope."'

Walter of Mowbray held up his hands in part surrender, his mind searching for rapid response.

'I cannot boast of grandeur, my friend. My family are simple pie-men. But thou knowest, ye are not the only man with a family motto. Hark ye, I am considering adopting one right now! "Whilst I eat, I drink!" Pray, doth ye think that will be fitting for a man of my fine stature?'

'Yea, Walt, that wouldst suit ye well enough. Thy coat of arms shall be emblazoned with a pie oozing fat and a tankard of frothy ale. Let us indulge in more ale and drink to thy new arms. Doth ye know we hath brewers in Kent who art brewing beer with hops, Walt? I wilt purchase ye a drop one fine day. 'Tis, by far, a better-tasting brew than the piss we drink here. A mere smidgeon will blow thy breeches clean off. If thy breeches be clean, that is. A pitcher will knock thee out for a week, and doth get ye muddled and seeing double, if nay totally arseholed.'

Jack Greenstreet and Walter Mowbray joined the King at Oxford on 27 June 1644, in time to learn that the third parliamentary army, led by William Waller, had arrived at Banbury, north of Oxford. Waller had taken up position on Crouch Hill. The position was strong. The King was not prepared to attack. The following day, the Royalists moved north along the eastern bank of the River Cherwell, towards Daventry, hoping to draw the Parliamentarians onto a battleground of their own choosing. William Waller followed, shadowing the Royalists along the western side of the river. He planned to surround and destroy the Royalist rearguard, whilst it was separated from the remainder of the King's army. Both sides had forces of equal strength: approximately 9,000 men, of which 5,000 were cavalry and 4,000 infantrymen.

On the morning of 29 June, Waller was at Great Bourton, less than one mile from the Royalist rearguard. Both armies continued north, but the path of the river meant they would need to cross at Cropredy. Charles deployed a small force of dragoons to hold the bridge at Cropredy and to secure his flank. The King also sent a significant portion of his cavalry north to secure Hayes Bridge. The effect was the Royalist vanguard and middleguard moved ahead of the rearguard and William Waller seized the opportunity to attack the King's rear.

King Charles received warning that 300 additional horse were approaching from the north to join Waller's army. The King ordered his army to hasten its march, to cut off this detachment, but the Royalists became strung out. Waller sent Lieutenant General John Middleton across Cropredy Bridge, with two regiments of horse and nine companies of foot to isolate the Royalist rearguard, while he himself led 1,000 men, in a pincer movement, across Slat Mill Ford, a mile south of Cropredy. The Royalist dragoons holding Cropredy Bridge were overpowered, and Middleton's force raced towards Hay's Bridge, but they too became strung out and vulnerable. Middleton's cavalry was halted by Royalist musketeers, who had overturned a carriage to block the bridge, whilst the Earl of Cleveland charged the Parliamentarian foot and artillery from the rear, causing the Roundheads to become trapped.

The teenage Earl of Northampton's men, including the contingent of Jack, Walter, Symon and Leonard, charged downhill against Waller's men, forcing them back across the Slat Mill Ford. The King was alerted that his rearguard was engaged and ordered his army to about turn.

Cropredy Bridge itself was held by two Parliamentarian regiments of foot. The Royalists attempted to recapture the bridge, but were repulsed by Waller's remaining artillery. Waller's men continued to fire from their vantage point on Bourton Hill, forcing the Cavaliers to fall back. As night fell, the two armies were left facing each other across the river. Charles sent his dispatch secretary to parley with Waller, with a message of grace and pardon from the King. Waller replied that he had no power to treat, despite the depletion of his troops and loss of guns.

Finally, upon receiving intelligence of additional Parliamentarians nearby, and as the King was low in food and supplies, the Royalists slipped away under cover of darkness, taking the guns captured from Waller with them. The Royalists suffered few casualties, whereas Waller had lost 700 men, including many who deserted immediately after the battle. Waller's army became demoralised and immobilised by desertion and mutiny. His men were no longer willing to serve so far from their homes. Waller's men came mainly from London. Charles could now afford to ignore Waller and march west to Cornwall in pursuit of the Earl of Essex.

One evening, pausing on the long march to Exeter, a group of cavalrymen sat around their blazing campfire, spinning yarns. The fire was built high, and sparks flew into the night sky and lit up their faces. Jack and Symon Greenstreet, Walter Mowbray and Leonard Smith, amongst many men, drank jugs of cider given by local supporters. After toasting the King and locals, and being warm and merry, the men exchanged tales of past experiences. They were interrupted by a group of officers, including the teenage Earl of Northampton, who bade them 'stand for the King'. It was indeed King Charles I himself who confronted them, telling them to sit down again, as they were, and not to stand on ceremony. He clutched his gloves and spoke quietly and kindly.

'Men, I shall nay interrupt thee long. I have come to thank thee, one and all, for thy loyal support and fighting spirit at

Cropredy. I was particularly impressed by the downhill charge at Slat Mill Ford, under the command of my Earl of Northampton here, and all ye good brave men, whosoever accompanied him. I am afraid I hath received bad news of a defeat at Marston Moor, from my nephew Prince Rupert, but I am sure we can rectify that issue. I believe today is the 23rd day of July. How the time flyeth. Tomorrow we hope to cross the River Tamar and relieve Sir Richard Grenville at Horsebridge. Then, God willing, we will proceed onwards to Launceston and further glorification in our rightful cause. God bless ye, every one of ye.'

'And God save our King,' came back an earthy response of appreciation that the King should ordain to mingle with his troops and address them in such a praiseworthy manner.

On the Parliamentarian side, the Earl of Essex secured a hold over the town of Lostwithiel, in Cornwall, and at various points along the Fowey River, mainly to establish a connection with the navy for supply and support. The naval fleet was entirely in the hands of Parliament and commanded by the Earl of Warwick, but at the crucial time, the fleet was held up by strong westerly winds, prohibiting it from sailing. Essex's estimated strength was around 10,000 men. Part of his army was on Beacon Hill to the east and Restormel Castle to the north, with other positions along the banks of the River Fowey. Essex awaited the support of Warwick's navy. It never came. Essex also awaited support from Waller and Middleton, but Waller, somewhat depleted after his defeat at Cropredy Bridge, no longer had a reliable force of men.

King Charles' Oxford army joined forces with the Royalist western army, commanded by Prince Maurice and then Sir Richard Grenville's force, based west of Lostwithiel.

It gave the Royalist army a combined force of 12,000 foot and 7,000 cavalry, a total of 19,000. The force outnumbered the Roundheads by almost two to one. The Royalists planned to lay siege to the town, in the hope of trapping Essex and cutting off his means of escape. Prince Maurice, the King's nephew, joined with the King as he approached Lostwithiel from the north-east, whilst Richard Grenville was enlisted to approach the town from the north-west. In the King's favour, the country folk of Cornwall were actively hostile towards the Parliamentarians. Many joined the King's army. Others supplied fresh food, meat and drink for the Royalists.

The campaign began with a small number of clashes and skirmishes, but the Royalists attacked in earnest on 13 August, occupying several outposts on the east bank of the River Fowey, thereby making it ever more difficult for help to reach the Earl of Essex. A Parliamentarian attempt to send a relieving force, under Lieutenant General Middleton, was defeated at Bridgewater in Somerset. The Cavaliers were on a roll and left Black Tom scratching his head.

On 21 August, the Royalists attacked Essex's positions north of Lostwithiel, capturing the ruins of Restormel Castle. Jack, Symon, Walter and Leonard rode with divisions of Royalist cavalry into the thick of the Roundhead establishments along the River Fowey embankment. The Royalists cut through pikemen, musketeers and short sword, clashing with harquebusiers and dragoons and risking muzzle-loaded, smooth-bore artillery. They captured train and guns, threatening to cut the Parliamentarians off from Fowey itself. When the Earl of Essex realised there was no hope of relief, he ordered his Roundhead cavalry to break out of the encirclement. Under Sir William Balfour, the

Roundheads forced their way through the Cavalier lines on the night of 31 August, and then fled for their lives towards Plymouth, thirty miles to the east.

In pouring rain, battered and bloody, the increasingly demoralised Roundhead infantry were pushed back towards Fowey, abandoning their artillery guns, which became bogged down in the muddy track roads. The pursuing Royalists captured Castle Dore, another Parliamentarian base, and on the first day of September the Earl of Essex left Sir Philip Skippon, his sergeant major general of foot, in command of the Roundhead divisions, whilst he made good his own escape in a fishing boat. On 2 September, Skippon, having been told his infantry had no chance of breaking out, as the cavalry had done, and having been offered generous terms by the King, surrendered 6,000 infantrymen and all his army's guns and train to the monarchy.

The Battle of Lostwithiel was a great victory for the King. It showed Charles at his best. He fought a resourceful battle and shared great personal bravery, enduring the hardships of his soldiers in the field. What is more, he acted with great restraint towards the beaten foe, considering them still to be his subjects and deserving of his consideration in preserving their lives. However, the disarmed Parliamentarians marched eastwards to Portsmouth in extremely inclement weather conditions and were constantly robbed and threatened by local people. It is thought about 1,000 died of exposure and hunger, and 1,000 more deserted, or fell sick from their deteriorating festering and septic wounds. It was a serious defeat for General Fairfax.

Charles wheeled about and marched towards London. Walter Mowbray bade his Kentish chums farewell and headed back to Market Harborough. Jack Greenstreet, together with his cousin Symon and Leonard Smith, rode back to Kent. But a decisive battle was yet to take place in middle England, and General Fairfax (Black Tom) was training a 'New Model Army'.

8

A WITCHHUNT

Following the Royalist successes at Oxford and Lostwithiel, along the banks of the Fowey estuary in West Cornwall, Jack and Symon returned to Borden. The sound of hooves clattering across the cobbled courtyard brought Marion and the children running to greet them. Symon took Marion in his arms, and they kissed and embraced long. The two older children, Robert and Maisy, helped Jack de-harness the horses and turn them loose to run free in the paddock. Marion took Jack's arm and told him the sad, yet expectant, news of his father's passing. She explained that Wat Harrys had ridden over to Borden to ensure Jack received the news, as near to firsthand as Wat could manage. Wat had brought with him a small package for Jack's personal attention, bequeathed by William, to be opened at his son's pleasure. After the two men had eaten and drunk their fill, Jack went to his room to rest and to surreptitiously open the package. A box contained a heavy gold-encrusted locket and chain. Jack pushed a small catch situated on one side of the locket, activating it to flick open. Inside was a painted miniature portrait of his beloved mother and a lock of her hair. A scribbled note in shaky, thinly scrawled handwriting accompanied the locket. Jack recognised the writing as that of his father, William of Maidstone. It simply said, '*This was my most precious possession. It is now thine to treasure, Jack. I pray for thee – farewell my blessed and eldest son, love William*'. Jack felt himself filling up. He kissed the locket then slipped the gold chain over his head to hang against his naked chest inside his blouson. Emotion burst from within him.

For a second winter's season Jack stayed on with Symon, Marion and the children, sharing the farm labour, ploughing, muck-spreading, harrowing and scattering seed. It was not until the end of April that he started to get itchy feet, wondering how the land lay and how the wars were progressing. Symon needed to drive some of his cattle to Faversham market for sale. Jack accompanied his cousin as drover. Jack had grown a full beard, and both men had dressed themselves in simple farm-labouring attire, with linen shirts, long sackcloth frock coats, short baggy breeches, stockings and leather boots. They donned straw hats and were well disguised from the striking Cavalier style of dress they wore when fighting for King Charles. They set out on horse, on a humid but somewhat grey spring day, driving twelve White Parks, an old English breed of cattle. They went along the ancient Watling Street towards Teynham. The men had flintlock pistols tucked in their boots and ammunition in their belts, but there was little likelihood they would be recognised as wanted men by any Roundhead they encountered. They passed Claxfeldestane on the right and made their way down muckridden Greenstreet, driving the White Parks ahead of them until they reached the old forge. Jack called out to Symon, who was rounding up a stubborn steer. The steer had broken away and gone down a back alley.

'It is stiflingly close this day, Sy. I hath been overcome by a terrible craving of thirst. There do be a paddock at the end of the street. What say we drive the cattle onto that green land and rest up a bit at the brewhouse, and there partake of a tankard or two of good English beer?'

'Yea, I agree wholeheartedly with thy craving, Jack. 'Tis indeed time to rest awhile to quench.'

Jack rode on ahead to open the paddock gate. He dismounted and stood holding the gate open while Symon drove the cattle onto the pastureland with his herding stick. They secured the gate and rode back to the White Swan brewhouse to quench the dust from their parched throats.

On leaving the paddock, the grey sky blackened. Swirling dark cloud rolled in and a rumble of thunder met their ears, followed by sheet lightning and further eruptions. Nearing the brewhouse, a fork of lightning shredded its way through an oak tree, shattering a stout branch, which hit the ground with a thud. The men lashed their horses to a hitching rail and entered the brewhouse vestibule. A streak of lightning, followed by deafening thunder, erupted all around the vicinity, followed by large splatters of raindrops. Day became night. The raindrops turned into a force of water which sheeted down with vengeance before transforming to a bombardment of hailstones. A layer of ice encased the rancid corruption of the village street within seconds. Will Dix came out of the shadows of the doorway and fixed his gaze upwards to the blackened sky. He ushered the men inside and slammed the brewhouse door tight shut.

'Come ye in, gentlemen, ye hath arrived in the nick of time. It doth seem the Witchfinder General, Matthew Hopkins, was correct in his assumptions when he descended on the village yesterday. This cloudburst is surely the work of the Devil himself, brought on by those witches he took away. The gossip and her daughter only confessed when he applied the thumbscrews and by his constant pricking of various marks on their naked skin. He is a terrifying man, but we doth need to rid ourselves of the evil witchcraft racking this country, as well as the constant civil war we endure, day in and day out. There be a purge on witchcraft just now.'

Will Dix averted his eyes from the sky and peered hard at his customers through the sudden gloom which now darkened the room. He lit three candles, setting one on a tun barrel and the other on a table in one corner of the establishment. He carried the third in a glass candleholder and held it up to their faces, examining them as if he were the witch finder himself.

'Is it Symon Greenstreet of Borden? Ay, I recognise ye now, and by all that is holy surely it is ye, Master Jack, under thy good disguise. I needed to look deep under thy straw hat and behind thy bearded mask and frock coat, to ascertain ye as the very gentleman who saved my ears from being carved off by the Roundhead harquebusiers. I declare thou needs to wet thy dry whistles. Pull up a chair whilst I attend on ye. John Caslock has gone to Faversham today to meet with Master Marsh, about the plans for the new brewery in that good town of Kent.'

Without further ado Will Dix took two pewter tankards and filled them from a barrel of beer in the outhouse, bringing them into the darkened room and setting them down on the table. The brew was frothy and inviting. The men drank deeply, and Will repeated the task.

'What was that ye were saying about the Witchfinder General, Will? Who in the village did he interrogate, landlord?' enquired Symon, halfway through sinking his second tankard of beer.

'Why, it was former goodwife, now widow, Martha Goody, and her pretty daughter Mary. Matthew Hopkins and his men dragged the women screaming to the forge, then ordered them to strip naked. He pricked blemishes on their skin with a needle dagger, applied the thumbscrews and heated up a red-hot poker in the coals, threatening to use it on them unless they confessed to witchcraft. Martha Goody kept a cat, which she implored Hopkins to believe was purely to keep away rats from her cottage in Frognal. The witchfinder shouted to the gathered crowd that he had saved them from unheard-of evil. In taking the women away, he wouldst drive Satan from their midst. Everybody had to make payment to Hopkins. Matthew Hopkins clapped the two witches in leg irons and bundled them into his caged cart, then drove off to seek out the mayor, Robert Greenstreet of Faversham, of thine own good-named family.'

Jack leapt to his feet, spilling the precious beer in his tankard. He wiped froth from his lips.

'God Almighty help us! The women ye refer to are both as innocent as the leaves upon the trees, Will. Widow Goody and her daughter Mary saved me from certain death by their good practice and knowledge of herbal medicine. I must nay tarry if I am to save them from the certain vile deaths planned by the so-called witchfinder, Matthew Hopkins, and my decayed second cousin, Robert, Lord Mayor of Faversham. Robert Greenstreet also seeks to rid the county of witches. The pretentious Matthew Hopkins is a fake money-grabber. A fly-by-night. He has no direct mandate nor commission from the King or Parliament. Hopkins travels from town to town, village to village, living on a spree and spreading fear of witches and witchcraft amongst the population. The Witchfinder General churns up mass hysteria and then charges hefty fees for identifying witches. He hangs or burns them without a trace of compunction. My Lord Mayor of Faversham is like-minded and drunk with power. They are both murderous bastards. I am reliably informed Hopkins had sixty-eight people put to death in Bury St Edmunds and nineteen people hanged in Chelmsford in a single day. All without proper trial. Ye canst nay tell me they were all witches. More than 300 supposed witches have been hanged or burnt by this Matthew Hopkins and his accomplices since commencement of the civil war. People are made scapegoats by this self-appointed maniac, who is backed by Roundheads. Hopkins is surely Satan himself. Folk say Cromwell has full knowledge of such torture and execution, because his family were involved when Lady Cromwell met her death by so-called witchcraft in 1590. Come, Sy, in the name of God and all humanity, help me free these innocents from the Witchfinder General, and the man that carries our good family name in disgrace: Robert Greenstreet, Lord Mayor of Faversham.'

Will Dix was disturbed by Jack's words and looked in a manner which sought forgiveness.

'Now ye come to say such things, Master Jack, I see well enough the ladies never were gossips. Widow Goody always did much good by her healing methods. I confess there never was anything wicked or harmful in what she, or her daughter, practised. We have all been tricked. God help and forgive us. I did speak to Master James about the event. When informed the Frognal ladies had been taken to be tried by water, he set off in pursuit, to see Robert Greenstreet and plead for their release. The reeve said he had little hope of achieving free pardon for them, although they may not be able to use the ducking stool test, because a recent legal challenge to cease such trial has been upheld. Go with God, good masters. I will arrange for thy cattle to be taken back to the reeve's pastureland at Claxfield. Ye can collect them later and take them on to Sittingbourne for sale, where ye might get a better price for thy cattle.'

Jack and Symon set off for Faversham without further delay. The storm had abated. The skies cleared as they rode at full gallop down the London Road, their buff-coloured frock coats flying, causing folk to pause and stare and to wonder why two farm labourers rode like bats from hell. They reined in and dismounted near Faversham, primed their flintlock pistols and slipped them back down their boots. Jack unlashed a roll of sackcloth from Acorn's side and unpacked his cup-hilted rapier. Symon followed suit, taking out a cutlass and priming a new lightweight, short-barrelled, flintlock musket, which he slipped into a long leather holder in front of his saddle. They concealed the blades beneath their frock coats and trotted into town. Two villagers informed them that the witch trials were to be held next day beside Flood Mill.

'Fludmyll', or Flood Mill, was known to Jack and Symon. The mill was purchased in 1571 by Thomas Greenstreet of

Eastling, soon after the celebrated Ardern murder. The Ardern murder was written into an Elizabethan play by Christopher Marlowe, or possibly William Shakespeare. Nobody knew which author wrote the play for sure. Sir Thomas Ardern made great riches out of the dissolution of the monasteries. Ardern, a former Faversham mayor, owned Fludmyll, a tide mill in Faversham. The mill was sold by Ardern's daughter Margaret, soon after her father was cruelly done to death by her mother, Alice Ardern. Alice and her conspirators all met cruel justice themselves, culminating in agonising deaths. Flood Mill was now in the hands of another Greenstreet family member, Henry Greenstreet of Godmersham.

The mill was approached via Flood Lane. It lay in an area where streams and tidal waters converged. The mill sat in two acres of meadowland, with appurtenances, ponds and riverbanks. A huge crowd had gathered to view the so-called witches, in their carriage cage, as they awaited trial by water. A ducking stool stood tilted and ready for use on the bank of a nearby deep pond. Two huge marquee tents stood erect for the upper echelons of Faversham town, to drink, dine and pleasure themselves in. Scantily clad girls of ill repute flitted between the marquees selling their wares to certain members of high society. A flag flew from the pinnacle of one tent, displaying the Greenstreet coat of arms, a barruly of eight, argent and azure, on a canton of the second, a double-headed eagle. In this marquee sat the Lord Mayor of Faversham, Robert Greenstreet, his magistrates, judiciary and clerks. They entertained the Witchfinder General, Matthew Hopkins, dining on venison and game pie, washed down with local cider and mead. An adjoining tent had been erected for the Witchfinder General as a courtroom, ready to condemn the witches to trial by water. The outcome was pre-ordained. Recently appointed as reeve, due to his father Johis' failing health, James Greenstreet stood before his relative, Robert, and pleaded the case of Martha Goody and her daughter Mary. He told the mayor that Matthew Hopkins was wrong to accuse two innocents of witchcraft, imploring that he, as lord mayor, should intervene and show mercy by releasing the two women into the reeve's care. In any case, James argued, it was a Teynham Manor affair.

'These women doth nay gossip with others, nor do anything to inflict disease on people. They live quietly on their own in Frognal. They doth nay spoil crops or bring about bad weather. They certainly doth nay indulge in the Devil's work, hold mythical powers, nor practise dark arts. Why doth ye persecute them so? I implore ye to release them both immediately into my custody and find some other misfortunates to satisfy thy misdirected desires, cousin,' said Reeve James forcefully, adding, 'Matthew Hopkins is nothing more than an evil misogynist.'

'And yet they hath confessed,' replied the mayor. 'They hath confessed to dabbling and mixing herbal remedies and so-called healing. That is the Devil's work sure enough. Grateful villagers hath readily paid the witch finder heavy costs, to rid their homes of the Devil's influences brought about by these women. They will be tried by water. Then we shall see whether they be innocent and sink, or whether they be guilty and float – when they shall hang.'

The Lord Mayor of Faversham gave a cruel smile and waved his relative away dismissively.

'Ay, and by that old method they die either way at thine pleasure, cousin. But there hast been a recent legal judgement to abandon trial by water. Ye must uphold the law,' demanded James.

'I hath heard of this, but 'tis only rumour. No such instruction has arrived at my high office.'

As James left the tent, an incandescent Lord Mayor of Faversham shouted verbal abuse after him.

'The Goody witches hath been brought to Faversham for trial under my jurisdiction as lord mayor. I wilt nay tolerate thy false protests – 'tis the Devil's work! A pox on ye, James of Claxfield. Go, before I hath ye arrested as an agent of Satan. The Vicar of Lynsted shall hear of thy meddling. Thy interference goes against the Almighty. These witches hath confessed.'

James paused to look back at his depraved, power-drunk cousin. Robert stood waving a dagger in one hand and a leg of mutton in the other. James spat forth words of family hatred.

'I am the churchwarden at St Peter and St Paul's and I canst vouch our minister wilt turn deaf ears upon thy pathetic methods of evil corruption, Lord Mayor, unworthy bearer of our family name. Our minister is a truly holy and pious man of God, unlike the ministers under thy jurisdiction, who, like ye, crave only power, money and greed, at the cost of any poor lost soul. Doth ye know that to threaten a reeve is to threaten the King himself. King Charles is far from defeated in this civil war. Maybe I should send the King an account of thine own vile heresy. Ha! If Matthew Hopkins is the Devil incarnate, ye are surely the very Devil himself.'

James departed, seething in anger. He realised there was little more he could do on his own to defend the good widow and her daughter. He led his horse away, pushing through the gathered crowd and past the caged cart, guarded by Matthew

Hopkins' armed accomplices. He heard the piercing screams of Mary Goody as she shouted her innocence above a crescendo of jeering and taunting people. He could not bring himself to go over and speak to them. What could he possibly say to pacify the women? They were aware of the horrific fate that awaited them. They had already endured torture by Hopkins, the Witchfinder General. Deeply saddened, James made his way up the incline towards Flood Lane, pushing forcefully through the bloodthirsty crowds. As he neared the top of the incline, he noticed two farm labourers on horseback, their frock coats drawn back and swords at their sides. The men were priming their flintlocks. One of the husbandmen paused in his loading and called the reeve over to him.

'Hath nay fear, James, our good family name will prevail this day. We shall remove the stain which lies so heavily upon our integrity, or die in the process, make ye nay mistake about that.'

Despite the disguise, James knew Jack's voice, and Symon's clumsy outline was plain to detect.

'Praise be to the Lord, ye hath come, cousins. My pleadings fell upon deaf ears, as I suspected they wouldst so do. The mayor and Hopkins, the Witchfinder General, know nothing better than extortion, corruption, torture and the evil murder of good innocent citizens.'

Jack stood tall in his stirrups. Raising himself from the saddle, he drew forth his steel rapier.

'Ay, we concur. Go, James, as fast as ye canst, back to Claxfield. Do ye nay tarry. Consult with Johis and find a suitable place for Widow Goody and her daughter to live, until this wanton witch-hunting and scourging hath ceased. We will meet ye at Frognal after our deed is done. Do ye nay wait on the outcome. Go now, James, and prepare for our return to Teynham Manor.'

James wished them Godspeed and spurred his mount on its way, whilst Jack and Symon made their charge down the slope. With swords drawn and flintlocks readied, they scattered the crowds widely and rode hard towards the caged women, shouting the family motto at the top of their voices: '*Dum spiro spero*, clear thee out of our way, ye pack of blood-crazed zealots!'

Terrified for their lives, mother and daughter huddled together in one corner of the cage. Wet through from their own urine and excrement, they sobbed at the dreadful strife life had served them. Their hands throbbed from the pain of the thumbscrews which had been applied to obtain their confessions. Their legs were rubbed raw from the leg irons around their ankles. The periphery of the cage was guarded by three of Matthew Hopkins' accomplices. They wore the iron helmets favoured by Roundhead soldiers and held muskets, with mortuary half-basket swords at their sides. The men paraded around the cage, chewing on succulent legs of meat, drinking small beer and passing comments with the gawping crowd who had come to witness the state of the vile creatures within the cage. The people of Faversham were there to watch the enactment played out to its finale. To many people in those turbulent times, witch trials were a day out – a day of free entertainment. The convicted witches were mere scapegoats from a country reeling from the first civil war. The crowd, who attended that day, were about to get their free entertainment in spades, as they scattered before the ghost riders.

The yeoman farmers were upon Matthew Hopkins' guardsmen before their old-style heavy muskets could be raised. Jack reined in Acorn and pierced the first unsuspecting guard through the chest. The rapier bent as it glanced off a rib to slip through the witch-hunter's accomplice and out of his back. Jack thrust a foot against the falling man's body and pulled his sword free. Symon's cutlass slashed at the second man, below the helmet, almost separating the head from the body. As he fell backwards, the helmet caught in the bars of the cage. Blood spurted from the severed neck like a red fountain. Symon left Jack to deal with the third guard and went for the lock on the cage door. Sheathing his bloodstained cutlass, he placed the barrel of his new short-barrelled English musket against the heavy lock and fired the flintlock at point-blank range. In a cloud of smoke, the heavy lock disintegrated. The hinged door flew open. Symon beckoned the women out. The third guard managed to raise his musket to fire but was slow in drawing a bead. The lead ball from Jack's flintlock pistol zipped through one eye socket and blew blood and grey brain matter from the back of the man's disintegrating head.

The huge crowd had fallen back twelve feet or more each side of the caged cart. Some people had been forced down the bank into the water in the stampede to get out of the way of the crazy horsemen. The crowd marvelled at the charge made by the husbandmen. They gasped in awe as the guards were dispatched and the women plucked from their caged confinement and laid face down on the horses in front of the riders. The witches' iron shackles clinked as the ghost riders rode silently over hard turf. Only hooves thudded as they headed for the London Road.

White with rage, the Witchfinder General and Lord Mayor of Faversham heard the commotion and dashed from their marquee tents in time to see the end of the precision rescue operation. The accused women had been snatched. Possibly by the Devil's accomplices themselves.

'I am unable to order men after them because they all lie dead on the ground,' fumed Hopkins.

The Lord Mayor of Faversham, Robert Greenstreet, voiced a different logic to the situation.

'Ye hath nay necessity for pursuit, Matthew. Indeed, ye might well come off the worse for it. Consider it this way, Matthew. Ye hath already been paid handsomely for taking the witches. Now thou hath nay need to pay thine three accomplices. Ye need simply to pay me my commission, plus a little extra for each man lost. I will arrange to have the corpses carted away and slipped into the Swale. Meanwhile, ye canst find some cheaper men to serve ye.'

The Lord Mayor of Faversham emitted an evil chuckle and stuck his dagger into a juicy mutton chop. He bit into it, causing fatty grease to run into his short-clipped beard and down his neck.

'Doth ye understand, Matthew Hopkins, ye canst nay really lose? There are plenty more fish to catch in the water, to be gutted, filleted, burnt upon the fire, or hung up to smoke as desired.'

'Yea, I understand thee well enough, Lord Mayor, there are plenty more witches in their covens. Unlike fish, they seldom swim, especially when strapped to a ducking stool, or with their fingers lashed to their toes when thrown into the water to sink or swim. The point ye make is sound enough. 'Tis true I doth owe my deceased incompetent men three months of good English money and, as ye say, I need trouble myself nay more about such payment, except to recompense thy good self, of course. 'Tis also true I hath nay desire to cross swords with those bats from hell. Who doth ye think they were? They were more like Cavalier fighting men than husbandmen, that I will wager, Robert. Dost ye have any idea who they might be?'

'Oh! I hath a good idea of who they might be, Matthew. The battle cry, shouted on their charge, was a giveaway. "*Dum spiro spero*" – 'tis our family motto. I am due to meet with Colonel Browne tomorrow, from the Roundhead camp at Paynter's Farm. I will convey my suspicions to him. He hast already fixed a high penalty on the head of one of my family members. There are others in my dynasty to look at more closely, I warrant. I will name a few to the colonel.'

Jack and Symon paused only to lay their sleeping blankets beneath the stomachs of the rescued women, who could not sit astride the horses because of the leg irons which bound their ankles and chafed their fair skins. The smell drifting from rump to nostril was none too savoury either. Both men found short clay pipes and packed them with tobacco, lighting them thoroughly to sweeten the air as they rode back to Teynham. They reined in at the blacksmith's forge to have Tong strike off the leg irons. To Tong Marshall, the stench of the women was no worse than the rancid street he worked in. The farrier apologised for the women's arrest by the Witchfinder General, at his forge, and for the torture they had endured. But with four armed men there was little Tong could do, other than step back and allow them to use his forge. Hopkins was also prompted by the baying of the hysterical crowd who had gathered around the forge repeatedly chanting, 'Burn the witches and their cats, before they bring a plague of rats.'

Martha Goody and her daughter Mary were taken back to their cottage at Frognal, to cleanse themselves and attend to their sores and tortured bodies. Jack drew buckets of water from the well and boiled water for their use. He told the widow and her daughter to be ready to leave in three hours and to pack only essential items to bring with them. Widow Goody and Mary knelt to give thanks to their saviours. Jack had none of it, telling them they were there for him in his hour of need. He praised God that he and Symon were able to repay the debt owed them.

Jack and Symon set off to quench their thirsts. James met them at the junction with Claxfield and the men went to the White Swan for a well-earned drink and to talk over the success of events. The belief in witchcraft and sorcery had reached an apex, and the men agreed it best for Widow Goody and Mary to move away from the village. James had a small croft available called 'Cook's Croft'. It sat on the edge of a wood in nearby Doddington, just through Lynsted. It was smaller than Widow Goody's cottage, but it would serve the purpose of isolation. James promised to look after the widow's needs. Once established in Cook's Croft, the widow could indulge her interests in herbal and plant medicine and healing, without persecution.

Jack thanked his cousin Symon profusely for his brave and fearless assistance in the rescue of Widow Goody and her daughter Mary. He and James agreed to help Symon drive the cattle to Sittingbourne next day, in the hope of achieving a good market price for the beef stock.

'There is nay need for any thanks, Jack. Ye may think of me as a rough diamond, but I too have an allegiance to our good family name. I was pleased to assist ye in snatching the hapless women from the clutches of that corrupt Parliamentarian cousin of ours. Robert Greenstreet wouldst hath nay scruple in burning or hanging his own mother for half of one crown. He wouldst sell the likes of ye and I for a mere silver groat. Neither do I believe in witches or in witchcraft. It is a figment of imagination, instilled to frighten vulnerable town and village folk by money-grabbing robbers such as the Lord Mayor of Faversham and Hopkins, the Witchfinder General. At least highway robbers are gentlemen who prey mostly on the well-to-do and upper echelons of society. My children shall nay learn of witches or bogeymen from Marion or myself, but only things that are sweet in life. Yea, that is how it shalt be, cousins of mine.'

Symon Greenstreet paused and took a long draining drink from his tankard before continuing:

'To that end I hath decided to partake in nay more battles outside of this county, Jack. Marion and the children need me to be at their sides on the farm at Borden. Ye know well enough I support the King and have offered my life to the Royalist cause on several occasions now, but my family needeth my support as well. I am foremost a yeoman farmer. I canst nay keep leaving the family to cope, ye understand, or I may end my days as a destitute husbandman.'

'I understand ye very well, Sy,' said Jack. 'Ye hast given much to the Royalist cause, as hast thy goodwife, Marion, and if I think of ye as a rough diamond, it is a rough diamond with a good heart. Like thee I hath travelled far and wide for the cause, but unlike thy good self I am without ties. The King hast set off to recover the north and I feel obliged to make one last trip to stand by him and rout the newly formed New Model Army. Royalist supporters are mustering near Market Harborough. I shall ride north to join them and defeat Fairfax once and for all.'

'Yea, Jack, and like Cousin Symon, why not call it a day after that?' implored James. 'There are plenty of young recruits waiting for their hearts and guts to be torn out by parliamentary pikemen or their bodies divided by cannon shot. Why doth thee nay leave the fighting and hath thine heartstrings plucked out by some fair maid of Kent, instead of a well-honed sword?'

'Ay, I shall, Jamie. I shalt attend to that very matter upon my return from Northamptonshire. And now let us take the good widow and her daughter to their new abode at Cook's Croft.'

In a drive to break the Royalists, Fairfax and Cromwell were creating the New Model Army under the command of General Sir Thomas Fairfax, with Cromwell as General of Horse. The New Model Army was made up of Parliamentarian armies, raw recruits and former Royalist prisoners of war. It was becoming well trained, well equipped and well organised. Nevertheless, it was yet to be tested in a full head-on battle. At the beginning of 1645, most of King Charles' advisers had urged him to attack the New Model Army, whilst it was still forming. Prince Rupert of the Rhine, the King's chief military adviser, and general of the Royalist army, proposed instead to march north and join with forces in Scotland. This course was adopted, but it left the King's army weakened, by leaving a detachment (including 3,000 cavalry) to hold the West Country and to maintain the siege of Taunton in Somerset.

9

NASEBY, 14 JUNE 1645

A damp grey shroud of early morning mist lay so dense that the opposing armies could see little of each other. The Royalists lined up on an escarpment from Dust Hill to Long Hold Spinney, looking down across Broad Moor and Broadmoor Farm. They commanded a strong position. The Parliamentarian army was stretched out across Naseby Field to Naseby Covert and Paisnell Spinney. They were the New Model Army, commanded by Thomas Fairfax, with Oliver Cromwell as General of Horse, outnumbering their opponents with a force of some 6,400 foot, 7,200 horse and 1,000 dragoons. The Royalist army, commanded by the King and his nephew Prince Rupert, was made up of 4,300 foot and 5,500 horse.

Slowly the mist swirled, then lifted, leaving a floating blanket to drift quail high across the fields situated north of the Northamptonshire village of Naseby. Jack Greenstreet and Walter of Mowbray sat upon their mounts shivering in the cold morning air, their red braids clear for all to see. They awaited the order to charge. Facing them across Broad Moor, the Parliamentarians wore tawny orange identification sashes tied about their waists. Their drums beat slow and rhythmically. In a few hours, the fate of the nation would be sealed, and the battlefield piled high with dead or mortally wounded male bodies, in a lake of sticky red claret.

As Jack gazed across the scarp his eyes met a strange phenomenon. The mounted cavalry appeared to be floating on horses without legs, such was the illusional eerie mist covering the horses' lower bodies. The weird, uncanny nature of the mist caused him to wonder whether he was already dead and gone to heaven. Reality struck when a foot soldier laid down his halberd, adjusted his broad sword, dropped his breeches and squirted liquid shit onto the ground. Several men had dark wet stains in their breeches brought on by fear. Every man knew he had to carve up his fellow countrymen or be carved up himself. No quarter would be given. Men prepared themselves to die. Jack and Walter filled their clay pipes with tobacco and lit them from a foot musketeer's burning match. This might well be their last smoke. They inhaled the smoke deep into adrenaline-racked oesophageal, nervously awaiting the order to engage.

To date, prior to the imminent battle, the outcome of the civil war had hung in the balance. Across Britain battles had raged for almost three years. Until now, neither the Royalists nor the Parliamentarians looked likely to prevail. True, the Royalists had lost areas of land in the north of England. Nevertheless, the King had seriously defeated the

Roundheads in Oxford and southwards in Cornwall. Now, Charles was desirous to recover the north of his Kingdom.

A strange occurrence was Jack's chance meeting again with Walter of Mowbray, the robust pie-man Cavalier who had befriended Jack and fought alongside him in the West Country. When Jack arrived at the extensive field encampment outside of Market Harborough, he was greeted by a Royalist captain of cavalry, who directed him to join one of the bands out of the many thousands of men milling about with their horses. The huge encampment was under the command of Prince Rupert of the Rhineland. Jack walked Acorn over to a large group of some fifty men, who sat in a ring around a campfire. A few of them poked around and stirred within a huge pot of stew hung from an iron tripod. He was greeted with cries of 'Here's a likely looking Cavalier' and 'Where doth thou hail from, brother, with such a fine steed and all?' 'Join the line, friend, there be enough pottage for all, including thee, if ye art nay a spy in our midst?'

A deep familiar voice called out to Jack. It emanated from a heap of crumpled garments on the grass, topped with a battered black hat. A face appeared, displaying a grin of bad teeth.

'Doth thee crave a piece of my pork pie, Kentish man, and a swig from my flagon of good wholesome cider? For "whilst I eat, I drink" and "whilst ye breathe, ye hope", and I am hoping ye are nay feeling too hungry this day, for my pie is from Melton and nay to be squandered!'

The crumpled heap of garment raised itself from the grass and formed the massive rotund figure of Walter of Mowbray. He came to greet Jack, clasping him in a bear hug and blotting out the skyline. Upon his head he wore a tall black floppy hat, with a leather strap under his unshaven chin. One corner of the hat hung down to act as rainwater drain-off. He supported his frame on the barrel of a long musket. A bandolier of wooden gunpowder tubes, known as the twelve apostles, hung from his left shoulder over a red woollen tunic. A broad leather strap over his right shoulder supported a pouch of lead balls and his sword. Baggy three-quarter breeches sagged over soft leather boots and in one hand he clutched a huge pork pie. Grinning broadly, Walter took Jack's arm and led his friend to his place of rest, tethering Acorn to his own horse nearby. Walter split his pie with a blade, measured one half against the other and handed the smaller division to his friend, who gratefully received it and bit into the pie with the hunger of a starving wolf. The crispy pastry and delicacy of the pork filling was a pie made of ecstasy.

'By all that is holy, that was a wonderfully tasty pie, Walt, absolutely magnificent. If only I had a tankard of Will Dix's beer to wash it down with I wouldst think myself to be in heaven.'

'I knowest, Jack. The family of Mowbray live in Melton, up the track a short way. They are pie-makers by trade and fast becoming famous for their crusty pies all over the region. Here, swig some of mine rough scrumpy. The brew will knock thine boots clean off thy smelly feet!'

Walter leant over to pass a stone jar of liquid to Jack, holding his large portion of pie high in the air. As he did so, a hefty bare-chested bruiser, with muscles of iron, crept up to snatch the pie from Walter's hand. Quicker than greased lightning, a wheellock pistol appeared in Mowbray's free hand. The brass barrel was thrust hard up against the would-be thief's nose.

'Wriggle a bogey, my friend, and I will blast thy brains to feed the birds of yonder rookery.'

Walter referred to a nearby cluster of elm trees, whose apex supported a host of tree-top nests alive with cawing jet-black rooks, who flew up and down like bees over a honey pot. The bruiser had obviously boasted to his cronies that he was going to steal Mowbray's pie. His cronies sat nearby, guffawing and grinning at his inability to so do. With the barrel end of the pistol thrust hard up the bruiser's nostrils, Walter ordered him to sit beside him on the grass. Without taking his eyes from the man, Walter proceeded to slowly devour the tasty pie. When he had finished, he wiped the sides of his mouth and smacked and licked his lips several times. Then, sweeping away the crumbs, he removed the wheellock and ushered the bruiser away.

'Come at me again, sir, and I will nay hesitate to blast thine swede to pieces. Thy remains will fill a pie for thy cronies to eat. With comrades like ye, who needs Roundhead scum to fight?'

'Ay,' agreed Jack, who had drawn his rapier almost as quickly as Walter had magically produced his wheellock pistol, 'and as the best swordsman in this cavalry, I will cut off thy sweetbreads and toast them in the campfire. Return to thy cronies and do nay bother us again.'

King Charles rode up and down in front of his regiments on a white charger, urging his men to fight for the rightful cause of God, King and country. The sides of the shallow valley, known as Broadmoor, were flanked by thick parish boundary hedges. Both commanders, the King and Sir Thomas Fairfax, deployed standard formations of infantry in the centre and cavalry on each wing. The Royalists chose to intersperse their horse with musketeers, keeping back a reserve brigade. The Parliamentarians hid some of their infantry behind the crest of a ridge.

At around 9.30 am, Oliver Cromwell ordered Colonel John Okey to take his regiment of dragoons forward, using the hedges as cover. Okey's men dismounted and under cover of the thickets crept up upon Prince Rupert's cavalry on the right flank. Whilst their horses were held ready, they opened fire with a hail of musket shot. On the other side of the thicket, Jack and Walter were mounted ready with the rest of the cavalry, waiting for an order to charge. Suddenly they were blindly peppered by lead ball from the hedges. Prince Rupert took the only course open to him and ordered his cavalry to ride away and attack the Parliamentarian cavalry on the far side of the valley. Both sides charged into each other, firing their pistols at close range and then setting to with their swords. Initially, the Royalists were driven back, but a second line of Royalist horse entered the fray, causing the Parliamentarian horsemen to flee, hotly pursued by triumphant Royalists, including Jack Greenstreet and Walter of Mowbray, who chased them for miles before veering off and going for the Parliamentarian baggage train. The train was discovered some distance behind enemy lines. It was first blood to the Royalists, but strategically not a good move. Most of Rupert's cavalry had been committed to leaving the Broadmoor battlefield, which left the Royalists vulnerable and outnumbered by the enemy.

Meanwhile, back at Broadmoor valley, the Royalists attacked with venom, initially gaining the upper hand. The Parliamentarians had positioned artillery guns between their regiments, but their range was poor. The salvoes went too high. The Roundhead musketeers managed to discharge a single volley and then the Royalists were upon them, wading in with sword and the butt ends of their muskets and driving them back. The Royalist pikemen pushed forward hard. Philip Skippon, the New Model Army's veteran commander, was wounded in the chest by a lead ball which splintered his armour and struck him beneath the upper ribs, yet he stayed on the field to encourage his infantry. Parliament's colours fell and their foot was in terrible disorder at this stage, but their superior numbers prevailed. There was a stand-off between the Parliamentarian right wing of horse, led by Cromwell, and the Royalist northern horse, neither willing to ride to aid their infantry while the other could attack their flank. Eventually the Royalists charged. Cromwell's troops moved to meet them. Royalist Langdale's men were outflanked and outnumbered two to one. They were forced to charge up a slope of bushes to a rabbit warren and were routed by Cromwell. Cromwell had kept one half of his wing uncommitted and now turned his reserves against the left flank and rear of the Royalist centre. At the same time, Okey's dragoons mounted up and charged from the Sulby Hedges against the right wing of the Royalist infantry, as did other Roundhead regiments, which had partly rallied.

The battle was all but over. Trapped Royalist infantry threw down their arms and called for quarter, whilst others attempted a fighting retreat. Rupert's bluecoats stood their ground stoutly and repulsed all attacks, like a wall of brass. Finally, at Long Hold Spinney they were overpowered by Fairfax on all sides. The King himself was prevented from going upon his death by the Earl of Carnwath, who conducted Charles I from the battlefield to retreat north.

Behind the Broadmoor lines, Prince Rupert's cavalry reached Naseby, triumphantly chasing after the Roundhead cavalry. Some of the Cavaliers, including Jack and Walter, veered off, hoping to capture the Parliamentarian baggage train. Despite the baggage train being surrounded by Royalist cavalry, Cromwell's camp guards and pikemen stood their ground, refusing to surrender. Several charges were made by the Royalist Cavaliers. Jack and Walter rode side by side, firing their flintlocks at close range and slashing at men with their swords, taking great care not to run onto the pikemen, who held their pikes and halberds horizontally in rows around the camp. Unexpectedly, English long bows were deployed by the Parliamentarians. Bows were still an effective weapon, the arrows being quicker to nock than a musket took to prime and load. The arrows were released high, to rain down on the Royalists.

Two iron-tipped arrows thumped hard into the pieman's chest. Mowbray slumped forward over his horse. Jack managed to grab hold of Walter's bridle and rode the horses away from the foray. The incursion had failed. Walter of Mowbray was mortally wounded. Jack could see that Walt was in a bad way and found himself filling up. Ignoring the order to regroup and return to the Broadmoor battlefield, he rode away to the east, across farmlands and fields. He needed to get his friend and comrade away from it all. Tears welled up in Jack's eyes as he spurred Acorn away from the arena of battle. Jack was suddenly sick. Sick from slaughtering his own countrymen. Sick with the killing, but mostly sick at the state of his dying companion.

Unable to capture the Parliamentarian baggage train, Prince Rupert rallied his cavalry and returned to the

Broadmoor battlefield at Naseby. By this time, it was too late to save what remained of the Royalist infantry. Rupert, who should never have left the battlefield in the first place, tried to induce his men to make a further charge, into certain annihilation. The cavalry turned and rode off the field of battle. Fairfax's forces pursued the Royalist survivors fleeing north towards Leicester. Fugitives and Royalist baggage guards attempted to rally at Wadborough Hill, but many were slaughtered on the road and at Marston Trussell, when they were unable to escape their pursuers. The Roundheads also hacked to death some 150 women found with the baggage train, claiming they were Irish whores. Many were thought to be wives and lovers. The Royalist army was destroyed, and with it 1,000 soldiers had died and more than 4,000 captured. The King had lost 500 officers and all his artillery, arms and baggage. The end of the first civil war and military victory for Parliament was almost nigh.

Jack reined the horses to a halt in a quiet spinney near Kelmarsh and took his friend down from his steed. Walter was in a bad way. He cried out as the penetrating barbed iron arrowheads bit deep within his insides to ooze blood. He closed his eyes and Jack thought he had gone. The noise of the battlefield rang in Jack's ears, despite the quietness of the spinney. Only the sweet clear song of a blackbird disturbed the stillness of the area. Walter's eyes opened. He forced a wry grin at his comrade. Blood dribbled from his mouth and ran down his chin.

'I concede thy motto is probably the best, Jack. "Whilst I breathe, I hope – *Dum spiro spero*."'

Jack realised his friend could not go on. Walt was quiet for a while, then choked and sighed.

'Breathing is such a wonderful thing in life, do ye nay think so, Jack?' gasped the pie-man.

'Ay, 'tis the better motto to chew upon, old friend,' agreed Jack, choking on his words. 'Ye lie there comfortably for a while, before we go on our way. There is nay need to rush Walt.'

But Jack was speaking to himself. Walter of Mowbray no longer breathed air and would sink his teeth into no more pies on this earth. Walt was no more than the heap of garments and floppy hat Jack had discovered on his arrival at the cavalry camp. Jack knelt beside Walt and offered up a prayer to the Almighty. He asked God to keep his friend safe until his own arrival at the heavenly gates, where he prayed to be reunited with his comrade-in-arms once more.

Jack took stock of the situation. The whole area was crawling with Roundheads, but he could not leave Walt to the kites and crows to pick clean. He broke away the arrow shafts, then found his companion's sleeping blanket, removed the saddle and laid the blanket over his friend's horse. Walter's dead weight was a problem. He had eaten too many pies over the years, making him obese. With the aid of a length of rope Jack always carried, he managed to pull Walt upright against the mare and lever him up against the horse's flank. By lashing the rope around the steed and tightening it as he hauled, he finally got Walter across the mare's back. He secured the rope tightly beneath the mare and bound Walter's feet to his wrists.

Jack kept to the fields and farm tracks until he arrived at a quiet village hamlet called Harrington, some seven miles east of Naseby. He made for the small Norman church he had noticed as he crossed the fields and arrived at a lychgate. The church was designated to St Peter and St Paul. His mind went to his cousin James and Lynsted church, bearing the same name, where they had sought refuge from the troop of harquebusiers, prior to escaping to Cripson Wood. He dismounted from Acorn, silently opened the lychgate, walked the horses through and closed the gate gently behind him. He paused to listen. Only the rustling of leaves from the tall beech trees, plus the cawing of corbies, nesting high in the treetops, broke the stillness of the churchyard's peacefulness. Jack guided the horses to the rear of the church where they could not be seen from the road and stood in the coolness of the tree-lined shade, drinking in the tranquillity. He watched kites skim over the fields. It was a quietness he had not experienced for some considerable time. A voice interrupted his reverie and deep repose.

'I seek nay to break thy encounter with this peaceful place, brother, but see thou art deeply troubled.'

Involuntary reaction caused him to clap one hand on the cup hilt of his rapier sword. He swung himself round ready for action. A middle-aged man with shoulder-length hair stood before him, clad in a black robe with thick rope around the waist, from which hung a wooden cross.

'Hath nay fear, mine brother. I am the Reverend Buckland of this parish, a man of God and here to help people of every persuasion. It seems thy friend has passed on from this wicked earth. How may I help ye, brother? Hast thou been fighting for thy King and country?'

'Yea I hast, Minister, as hast this good man and comrade-in-arms, now deceased and shot through with arrows. Walter is from these parts. I ask that ye arrange for his burial in this tranquil setting, Reverend, and a choir to sing for his soul? Will ye arrange for a mason to carve a headstone in granite to read, "*Here lyeth Walter of Mowbray, a humble pie-man by trade. He died for his King and country at Naseby – 14ᵗʰ day June 1645.* Dum spiro spero. *Remembered by a comrade-in-arms called Jack.*" In return, Vicar, Walter here bequeaths ye a fine mare and tackle, to which I contribute two pounds of English money from my own coffers.'

'Come into the vestry, my brother, so that I may set thy request down in writing and receipt thy payment,' said the priest. 'Thereafter, ride eastwards and south, keeping tight to the fields.'

Their business concluded, the vicar poured glasses of claret wine and they drank to seal the deal. The minister then took the Cavalier to the rectory to find a platter of food. When Jack was ready to depart, the Reverend Buckland gave the Royalist cavalryman bread and mead for his saddle bags, before offering him sound advice:

'Do ye nay tarry, for I am informed by several of mine parishioners that the area is now saturated with Cromwell's men. They art out of control and committing atrocities of the worst kind. I am given to understand the Royalists were routed at Naseby. Thousands have lost their lives. Many Royalist infantrymen were given the option of joining the Parliamentarian forces or being hanged or put to the sword. King Charles has fled northwards on threat of his own life. I urge ye to skirt the villages and give towns a wide berth. Steer clear of the main roads to London, that is my advice. Lay up during the day and be guided by the stars at night whenever possible. Otherwise, keep to the farms, fields and hedgerows, and Godspeed to ye.' Jack shook hands with the Reverend Buckland and asked the minister to call upon the pork-pie-makers of Melton Mowbray, at his convenience, to inform them of Walter's passing. Walt had no direct living relatives, that Jack knew of, to whom to impart the sad news of Walter's death. After kneeling to pay his last respects to his friend and comrade-in-arms, and to receive the minister's blessing, Jack took leave of Harrington church and the quiet tranquillity of the village. He thanked God for looking after Walter and for directing him to the quiet churchyard.

The trek southwards proved long and arduous. Jack fed and sustained himself from the fields and farmlands. On one occasion he stole eggs and a chicken, which he devoured ravenously. The bird was plucked and dressed in an area of remote woodland, then cooked over a campfire lit from his tinderbox. He snared and roasted rabbit, ate berries, and followed the sun and the stars. He skirted the villages, trusting no one and keeping clear of marauding Roundhead platoons. It was several days before he found his way back to London and crossed the Thames border into Kent. Jack was thankful to be back in the county of his origins. He headed for Borden, hoping his kin were served well and could accommodate him for a short while.

Naseby was the most decisive battle of the first civil war. The King had fled to Scotland, in the hope of raising another army. He would never be able to replace the experienced soldiers he lost at Broadmoor. In the following month, General Fairfax's New Model Army routed the last significant Royalist army at Langport in Somerset. The remaining Royalist garrisons mostly fell like ninepins. Jack realised the Royalist cause was lost at Naseby. He considered it was time to call it a day.

10

TIME FOR REFLECTION

Dispirited and exhausted by the miserable defeat of the King at Naseby, Jack returned from Northamptonshire to reside for a while with Symon and Marion on their farm, much to the children's delight. He deeply pined the loss of his comrade Walter, although he knew such loss in wartime was inevitable. Neither Jack nor Symon could get their heads around the rout of the Royalist army at Broadmoor. Both men were aware the King was now all but beaten.

King Charles had lost not only the fight, plus many men, artillery and arms, but also his entire train and baggage, which contained personal letters, providing the Parliamentarians with propaganda opportunities to exploit – like letters from the Queen, Henrietta Maria of France, indicating she had been attempting to obtain reinforcements, on behalf of the

King, from Catholic powers in Europe. When Parliament made this known, the attitude of many of his Protestant subjects towards the King hardened. Such information led to an increased determination to fight the war to a finish. Parliament's *coup de grace* was now a short matter of time away. Yet elements of the civil wars were complex. Such intricacies were set to boil over into a mishmash of unresolved circumstances. Symon and Jack realised the King was defeated. The disheartened men sat for lengthy periods in conversation, smoking on long-stemmed clay pipes.

'We were seriously outnumbered by Black Tom, Sy, and yet we had the upper hand at first and indeed were winning. The Roundhead cavalry fled for their lives with us in hot pursuit. But leaving the battlefield was a terrible mistake. We left the infantry with no backup. I blame Prince Rupert for leaving the infantry so vulnerable against Tom Fairfax's superior numbers.'

'Ye know what this means, Jack. We are now a republic. Either that or General Fairfax, or even Cromwell, will be crowned King. Imagine that. King Oliver I!'

'That wouldst be against everything the man stood for. I canst nay see that happening, Symon.'

'Yea, 'tis true enough, I agree with ye entirely. Let us bide our time and see what occurs. Hopefully things will quieten down a bit for a while – in Kent at least.'

Jack paused in conversation and pondered a while, blowing smoke rings to amuse the children.

'I still have a bounty on my head, Sy. I think there will be plenty of "witch hunts" across the counties by the Roundheads. They appear to have a lust for blood at this moment in time.'

'Pray, stay here for a while with us, Jack. We see few Roundheads in the Borden vicinity, and there lies plenty of concealment about the place. I have warned the children to hold their tongues and not to speak to any strange persons about thy presence hereabouts.'

'That is a kind proposition ye make, cousin Sy, but I dare nay risk taking such chance. I hath already stayed longer than intended. I refuse to put ye and thine at further risk. Thank ye and Marion for thy goodwill. My last desire is to see thy farm burnt to the ground by Roundheads.'

'Goodwill, nonsense, Jack! It is nothing of the sort. Ye always work thy passage and we are grateful for the extra help on our farm. Ye are welcome to come any time, cousin of mine. Do nay leave it too long before ye return to us, elsewise the farmlands will go to rack and ruin.'

11

THE FAVERSHAM WITCH TRIALS, SEPTEMBER 1645

Whilst the civil wars raged, all over the British Isles a fear of witches and their curses compounded into a hysteria beyond belief. The situation was stirred until it boiled, by witch-finders or witch-hunters who were simply looking to line their pockets with rich pickings from the misguided, or to gain power over innocent town and village people, often where there was an axe to grind. Witch-hunting had reached its peak in 1645, and in Faversham, in the county of Kent, the powerful mayor, Robert Greenstreet, seized the opportunity to hold witch trials of his own. The mayor's examinations led to confessions, trials in the local municipal court and the inevitable executions of several so-called witches. And, it seems, Lord Mayor Robert Greenstreet himself had his own axe to grind concerning at least one of the accused!

In the September 1645 Faversham trials, four so-called witches were tried before Robert Greenstreet – viz: Elizabeth Harris, Joan Cariden, Joan Williford and Jane Holt. The municipal accounts given for the accused, who blamed each other for their witchcraft, were as follows:

A woman from Faversham, in the county of Kent, was identified as the mother of a son who drowned. Elizabeth Harris claimed, during her examination, that the Devil appeared to her in the form of a mouse, nineteen years before; she called the mouse her imp and told her imp that she had a desire for revenge. The Devil promised she should have it, and she sent him to Goodman Chilman, who had accused Harris of stealing a pig. Chilman pined away and died. Harris said that the Devil demanded she forsake Christ, to lean on Satan himself, so she scratched her breasts with nails and gave the blood to the Devil to write the covenant with. About a fortnight later the Devil sucked from her but caused her no pain. Her imp would suck every three or four nights thereafter. When asked how many witches were in town, she replied that Goodwife Dadson, Joan Cariden (alias Argoll) and Goodwife Cox all had bad tongues. Elizabeth Harris also wanted revenge on Goodman Woodcott's High for the drowning of her son, and so when High was cast away, she thought her imp was responsible. Lastly, Harris claimed that Joan Williford told her a boat would 'not come so cheerfully home', that Goodwife Pantery met many times with Williford and Joan Holt, and that Goodwife Gardener also had an ill tongue. Williford claimed that Harris was her fellow and had cursed John Woodcott's boat. Harris was convicted on charges of witchcraft, but not executed at the time of the court accounts.

Jane Holt, a widow from Faversham, claimed in her confession that a creature like a hedgehog started visiting her twenty years before, to suck from her. If it came at night, the pain of it sucking would awaken her from sleep. It would come once or twice a month, and when she struck it off her breast it felt soft like a cat. When jailed, Holt convinced the other accused witches to confess their guilt, while insisting on her own innocence. Holt claimed that if put in water she would certainly sink, but when she was swum, she was seen to float upon the surface. A gentleman asked how she could have spoken so confidently that she would sink, to which she answered, 'The Devil went with her all the way, and told her she would sink, but when she was in the water, he sat upon a cross-beam and laughed at her.' Joan Cariden claimed that Holt told her there was a meeting at Goodwife Pantery's home, which Goodwife Dadson attended. Goodwife Gardener had been expected but missed the meeting. The Devil also attended this meeting and sat at the end of the table. Harris claimed that Holt often met with the gossips.

Joan Cariden, identified as the widow of William Argoll, claimed that nine months before a 'rugged soft thing' lay on her chest in the night; she thrust it off herself. The incident left her thinking that God had forsaken her, for she could never pray so well since, as she could before the event. Later, the Devil came to see her in the shape of a 'black, rugged dog' and crept mumbling into her bed. It returned the next day and demanded her to deny God and lean to him (Satan) and then he would revenge her of any one she owed ill will to. She agreed and promised him her soul. He then sucked from her and had many times since, but she felt no pain. She also stated that Jane Holt told her there was a meeting at Goodwife Pantery's home, which Goodwife Dadson attended and Goodwife Gardener had been expected for but missed. The Devil also attended the meeting and sat at the upper end of the table. Joan Williford claimed that Cariden was her fellow, while Elizabeth Harris claimed she had a bad tongue.

Joan Williford's confession was similar. She also claimed to have signed a contract with the Devil and in return he promised to be her servant for twenty years, and she gave him some blood. That contract was almost up. The Devil told her she would lack for nothing and he brought her money, sometimes one shilling, sometimes eight pence, never more at once. The Devil appeared to her in the form of a little dog, and she called him by the name of Bunne. She also confessed to desiring revenge on Thomas Letherland and Mary Woodrafe, and that Bunne had carried Thomas Gardler out of a window to fall on his backside. Towards the end of her confession, Williford alleged that Joan Cariden had once cursed the mayor, saying he would not prosper. Then Cariden herself told of how the Devil had come to her in the shape of a black, rugged dog, which crept into her bed to suckle her, in exchange for power over her enemies, including, Williford damningly suggested, the mayor himself. This pact, she asserted, was made in the same year that Robert Greenstreet had first been mayor, in 1635, suggesting that the mayor, Cariden had formerly cursed, was Greenstreet himself. This was confirmed by a petition dated 1635, which showed how Cariden was in fact an active, economically integrated and vocal member of the community who aired grievances on behalf of her family, which was more than the product of geriatric malice. Evidently she took issue with Greenstreet and the town council, for not helping her with disputes over property and debts, threatening to take the matter up with the Lord Warden of the Cinque Ports, and it is doubtless significant that she denounced one neighbour as a puritan rogue. Robert Greenstreet was only mayor twice, once in 1635 and again in 1644/5. Like many such independent political and legal jurisdictions, Faversham had a troubled history in the first half of the seventeenth century, and in the 1630s experienced epidemic disease, rioting, religious conflict and mass emigration to the New World. Greenstreet may well have had an axe to grind with Joan Cariden. According to Joan Williford, the mayor had not prospered since he was cursed. The parish register, for example, showed that in the same summer of the trials, his wife died. Strikingly, he had been mayor for just over a fortnight when Cariden was first examined. By this time, if the account is to be believed, the troublesome Cariden had become classed as a classic witch of the Hopkins era, forming a pact with the Devil, and, by her own confession, even attending a diabolical sabbat with other malevolent women, whom, according to Elizabeth Harris, all had very bad tongues.

On 29 September 1645, in the presence of the mayor, Robert Greenstreet, Joan Williford, Joan Cariden and Jane Holt were hanged on a triple gibbet. It is said that a black, rugged dog sat on its haunches and watched their writhing as slow strangulation set in. When a minister stood to shout fire and brimstone and cleanse the air, the black dog vanished from the scene.

12

END OF THE FIRST CIVIL WAR, 1646–1647

A steady rain beat down over Cripson Wood. Waterlogged leaves dripped one to the other, causing rivulets of liquid to gather and pour down the back of Jack Greenstreet's neck as he bent his head beneath the low branches, whilst urging Acorn along the saturated track. The track was banked to one side and fell away steeply on the other. Despite the rain, it was warm and humid. Steam rose from the stallion's flanks as the horse struggled to maintain sure-footedness, where the track had turned to treacherous slippery mud. On the face of it, the civil war had ended. After burying his friend, Walter of Mowbray, at Harrington, Jack decided in his mind to heed James' sound advice and attempt to settle down. He, like so many loyal Royalist men of Kent, had to accept defeat. All was lost at Naseby. The King had fled from the victorious

Parliamentarians, but Charles no longer had an army of any integrity to call upon.

'Bad news, James,' shouted Jack. James rose from the low oak bough of their meeting place.

'Bad news indeed, cousin, but thou art safe at least, praise be to God. I trust you will give a full account of thy deeds at Naseby later. Meanwhile I need to inform ye thine uncle Johis is no longer active and nay always of sound mind. I fear he is fast fading from this life, Jack. Pray, do nay be offended if he doth nay recognise ye. My father hast lived a long honest life, and hast served Teynham Manor and Hundred well as reeve over many years. I hath now fully relinquished my role of borsholder and taken upon myself the work of manor reeve.'

'Ay, 'tis a post to which ye art well suited, James. Johis hast done well to attain such an age, cousin. Though I am sorely grieved to hear of such tidings, for I hath long held such a huge respect and high regard for mine uncle Johis. How doth thy mother, my aunt Maria, cope?'

'She is, as ye are aware, his second wife, and much younger of age than my birth mother, Rebecca, wouldst hath been had she lived. Mine three sisters and the servants see to her welfare. She wants for nothing, Jack. She remains in good enough spirit, and Baron Roper is constantly in touch, sending all manner of things up from Lodge Lynsted, the manor house. My brothers from Doddington and Eastling also frequently come to help out here at Claxfield.'

The two cousins paused to embrace. James took Jack's hand and clasped it hard.

'I have seen nothing of Colonel Browne's Roundheads since they came to Claxfeldestane, with Lord Peter Greenstreet deceased. 'Tis some time ago now, Jack. Pray, come down to the house where we may feast together and drink wine and brandy, maybe smoke a clay pipe of tobacco or two. We shall find thee a nice room and ye canst stay for as long as ye wish, cousin.'

'I will come with thee, James, and give my respects to Johis and Maria and join with ye in a meal, but I will nay stay and put thee and thine at risk. There is still a high bounty upon my worthless head. The Roundheads are turning to unmerciful reprisals all over the country.'

'Yea, I understand thy reasoning, Jack, but I hath a solution for consideration. Until witch–hunting ceases, Widow Goody and her daughter remain securely housed at Cook's Croft. Why not use their empty cottage across the road in Frognal? Leastways until the witch-hunting is superseded by some other hysterical fantasy and the good widow is able to return there again.'

Widow Goody's tenancy agreement was under the jurisdiction of the reeve. Jack concurred with James' idea. It was a good offer and they agreed terms. James immediately sent two servants to the cottage to clean and provision it and to make up the bedchamber. Jack moved into the cottage and adopted a sedate lifestyle, renovating the cottage and helping James with the cherry orchard and farm work. Acorn deservedly rested his carcass, grazing upon the rich grasses beneath the cherry trees and frolicking in the adjoining paddock. In the severe winter months, Acorn was stabled by James. Jack settled himself beside roaring fires on which he made his pottage, and roasted rabbit and venison, hunted in Cripson Wood. Frequently, he was invited across to Claxfeldestane for his meals. The friends often took off to visit Will Dix and John Caslock's new inn called the Dover

Castle, at the far end of Greenstreet. Jack took up carpentry, joinery and ornate carving work with desire and increasing expertise. The rooms in the cottage became somewhat restrictive to this new lifestyle, but James could see his cousin's talented skills. He sent labour to help Jack build a workshop attached to the cottage. Jack's grandfather John had been a carpenter and joiner, and the trade came naturally to the grandson, who, as a small boy, had spent hours watching and helping his grandfather prepare wood, cut dovetails, mortices and tenons and assemble furniture in his workshop. The minister of Lynsted church gave Jack an order, in return for good payment, to replace the oak nave benches which had worn out over the years. Jack set to with relish, and pews with backrests were crafted. Thereafter, his workload in the local churches and in the vicinity snowballed.

The next three years were quieter, although much was going on behind the scenes. Following the decisive defeat at Naseby, the King fled to Scotland, and in May 1646 King Charles I surrendered to Parliament's Scottish allies at Newark. The only Royalist field army remaining was Goring's, but that was no match for the New Model Army. The last pitched battle of the war was fought and lost by Lord Astley on 21 March 1646. Newark fell on 6 May 1646, and the third siege of Oxford ended on 24 June, with a signed treaty. The keys of the city were formerly handed over to General Fairfax. Various castles surrendered, but the last Royalist post, Harlech Castle, maintained a useless struggle until 13 March 1647. King Charles himself, after leaving Newark, spent the winter in and around Oxford, whence, after an adventurous journey, he came to the camp of the Scottish army at Southwell on 5 May 1646.

Potentially the first civil war left England and Scotland in the hands of any one of four parties, or an alliance of two or more, whichever could prove strong enough to dominate the rest. The Royalists were defeated, and yet Charles, who was for all intents and purposes a prisoner, considered himself key to the last. The King was necessary, or so he thought, to ensure the success of whichever party he could parley and come to terms with. In other words, the first civil war, after dreadful loss of life, simply left the country in one huge unresolved mess.

Thus, King Charles I passed successively into the hands of the Scots' Presbyterian Parliament and the Independents of the New Model Army, led by Fairfax and Cromwell. The King attempted to 'cosy up' with each in turn. The Presbyterians, which included most members of the House of Commons, and the Scots were willing to share power with the King. They had strong feelings on religion but disapproved of puritanical groups such as the Anabaptists, Quakers and Congregationalists. The Independents had a strong following in the New Model Army and the support of Fairfax and Cromwell himself, whose soldiers had a persistent nagging gripe because Parliament made no effort to pay their wages, which were long overdue.

Afraid of General Fairfax's and Cromwell's rising power, the Presbyterian members of the House of Commons voted to disband the New Model Army. This caused fury amongst the unpaid soldiers. In early June 1647, while the New Model Army was assembling to rendezvous, at the behest of the recently formed Army Council, Cornet George Joyce, an officer in Fairfax's cavalry, rode with armed men to Holdenby House and seized Charles I from Long Parliament's custody. Cornet

Joyce brought the King to Thomas Fairfax's headquarters on Triplo Heath, eight miles south of Cambridge. This action induced the Presbyterians, the Scots and the remaining Royalists to prepare for a second war, this time against the independency, embodied in the New Model Army.

The Presbyterian Parliament first attempted to disband the army and then, still unpaid, to send the army on foreign service. The New Model Army was exasperated beyond control, and recalling not just its grievances but also the principles for which it had fought, it became most powerful under Fairfax and Cromwell. The breach between the New Model Army and Parliament hardened. The Scottish Covenanters had made a significant contribution to Parliament's victory in the first English civil war, but all that was about to change as they now turned their support in favour of the King, who no doubt gleefully rubbed his hands at such a turn of circumstance. On Boxing Day 1647, King Charles signed an agreement, known as the 'Engagement', with leading Covenanters. In return for the establishment of Presbyterianism in England, for a period of three years, the Scots agreed to join forces with the Royalists and restore the King to the throne. Finally, in 1648, the Presbyterian party, combined with the Scots and remaining Royalists, believing itself strong enough to declare a second civil war, this time against Fairfax, Cromwell and the independent New Model Army. Once again bloody skirmishes broke out over the country.

For a while, Jack Greenstreet turned a deaf ear to Parliament's continual bickering between themselves and the leaders of the New Model Army, Charles and the Covenanters and all issues pertaining. Jack became absorbed in his carpentry work and was called upon to replace elements of the crown post roof in the thirteenth-century church of St Mary's, Teynham, near Conyer Creek. Several timbers required replacement. They had been eaten out and seriously affected by long horn and deathwatch beetle. There was also timberwork in the transepts to attend to. To this end, Jack was granted a labour force of men to direct and assist him in erecting temporary scaffolding and pulley arrangements high up in the vaults of the nave. The crown posts required propping and supporting whilst the maintenance work to them was carried out. It was a highly skilled exercise to perform, but Jack was equal to it and bestowed with much praise from the diocese. Then came another reason for Jack to become involved in insurrection.

For a second time, the stout men of Kent rose in revolt, in the King's name, and they had good cause for so doing. A precursor to Kent's second civil war occurred on Wednesday 22 December 1647, and it happened in the City of Canterbury, following a proposed life-changing announcement by the town crier! The announcement made by the vermillion-coated crier that day affected every man, woman and child in the land. The proclamation, proposed by Parliament and ordered by the County Committee, was an attempt at suppression of the worst kind. The proclamation was designed to be particularly devastating to children, and indeed to young and old everywhere in the British Isles. It released further rebellion and uprising all over the land, and nowhere more so than in the county of Kent. The order led to a second war.

The Second Civil War

1648–1649

13

A SECOND KENTISH REVOLT

A sharp hoar frost gripped the countryside. Roofs and verges sparkled silverwhite, the pungent filth of the highway encased in a continuous clear layer of compacted ice. Branches of adjacent evergreen trees drooped heavily over the roadway, their boughs laden with frozen twigs and leaves. Acorn found difficulty in maintaining his footing on the slippery surface of Greenstreet as he transported his master away from Teynham Manor, along the old Watling Street. The chestnut stallion maintained a slow trot, destined for the City of Canterbury. Both steed and master expelled a steady stream of condensation from their mouths, their breath reacting to the plunge in temperatures. Steamy gases were also discharged from the rear end of Acorn each time he lost footing on the frozen track, causing Jack to rein back and call out to him.

'Steady, boy, steady! Do nay fart away all thine reserves, Acorn. Thou should realise we doth need to come back along this path again when we return to Frognal from Canterbury city.'

It was two days before Christmas Eve and Jack Greenstreet's prime motivation was to finalise his list of gifts. He had already hand carved toys for Symon's large family of children, making whipping tops, sap whistles, some toy soldiers and a hobby horse. He had also manufactured a sturdy chest of drawers for Symon and Marion, after noting they were short of stowage on his last visit to the farm, although he had some concern as to how he would deliver the heavy oak object in its finished state. Now he wanted to purchase some fine ribbon for Maisy's hair and a bow and arrows for Rob. Robert was already into snaring rabbits and trapping game. He had in mind some nativity dolls for Symon and Marion's youngest children and some fine cognac brandy and tobacco for James, plus presents for Johis and Maria. There was no point in making furniture for Claxfeldestane, because the house was full of fine sturdy oak and walnut pieces in every room. It wanted for nothing in that direction. There were beautifully ornate carved dressers, bench tables and chairs, sideboards and occasional chairs in the dining room, and four-poster bed stedles, commodes, dressing tables and wardrobes in every bedchamber.

There was one other person he wanted to purchase a gift for and that was Wat Harrys. He planned to call upon his father's trusty manservant at Moddilyon in Faversham, on the way back from Canterbury. It would be good to see his old mentor again and talk over past times.

On nearing the city, the glorious structure of the cathedral came into view, dominating the surrounding countryside. The high four-spired tower with its cross finials shone out in the rays of the early morning sun, which now sought to burn through the mist and melt away Jack Frost. The duo passed by many pilgrims, dressed in sackcloth, their heads shaven. They had walked miles across the Downs to kneel at the tomb of St Thomas a Becket, Archbishop of Canterbury. In 1170, Becket was slain in the cathedral by four French knights – murdered following his opposition to Henry II's attempts to control the Church. Jack recalled the story. It was said that, as the body cooled in a pool of blood upon the altar steps, lice left his holiness, moving in a line of formation akin to the sign of the crucifix. This version of events might well be more attributable to one of Geoffrey Chaucer's Canterbury tales, than an actual occurrence. Jack, who had chosen to make his way along the banks of the clear chalk waters of the River Stour, passed through the west gate of the walled city and walked Acorn up the cobbled street, passing the friary and weavers, to the market square near the cathedral gates.

A handbell rang out loudly in the market square, drawing Jack towards a huge crowd of people. He found a nearby tethering rail and threw a round turn and two half itches to secure Acorn, then joined the outside of the gathered throng. The town crier stood on a raised platform with two borsholders in attendance. He was fully dressed for the occasion, clad in a vermillion red coat adorned with gold trimmings, a chain of office around his neck, blue pantaloons and knee-length leather crafted boots. The crier adjusted his black ostrich-feathered tricorn hat, then rang the bell several more times with vigour, refusing to make his proclamation until all the people in the vicinity had gathered around him. The crowd became restless and fired questions.

'Hath ye naught to tell then, ye pox-ridden nag?'

'Doth ye need grog to loosen thy fat tongue?'

Jack turned his head towards a young lady and finely clad gentleman who stood next to him. She addressed the gentleman as Father. To Jack her voice was as soft as velvet. She stood just a foot or so away. The man she addressed as Father called her Elizabeth. Jack could not avoid turning to glance in her direction time and again. She smiled at him, a smile that melted his entire inner being. He doffed his titfer and impishly grinned back. She smiled again, a wonderful smile that lit up her whole face. There was an instant attraction between them and an inner feeling he had never experienced before. He was dazzled by her beauty. She was dressed in fine clothes, with a rich, warm cloak of pale blue. Her rosy face was slightly freckled. A lock of fair hair peeped out beneath her fur-trimmed hat. Her open lips pouted invitingly. Jack felt torn apart. Here was a true maiden of Kent. He realised he was totally infatuated by her. Jack was brought out of his trance by the town crier, who began his announcement.

'Oyez, oyez, oyez!'

The crier handed his handbell to a borsholder and unrolled an official-looking parchment.

'Hear me, all good people of Canterbury, ye visitors and ye people of Kent. The proclamation, given on this 22nd day of December 1647, has been decreed by Long Parliament and cometh likewise from the County Committee of Kent. Know ye that Christmas Day is to be outlawed and treated as any other common working day. Such annual Christmas celebrations will forthwith cease to exist, as from the instant of proclamation, on penalty of prosecution. Oyez!'

The gathered crowd erupted in a roar of disapproval. Fists were shaken and staffs raised. It was considered treasonable to attack a town crier, who was a King's man. But the King was now held in custody. Several pieces of ripe fruit were thrown in the crier's direction as he turned to leave in haste. A rotting squash hit him and dribbled down his neck. A cry went up.

'God save King Charles,' somebody hollered. The whole throng noisily exploded again.

'For God, King Charles and Kent,' went up the chant, and when that was exhausted,

'Do ye nay dare to cease decorating thine cathedral, thy church, nor thy shoppe for Christmas.'

'For God, King Charles and Kent,' shouted out the fine gentleman and his daughter Elizabeth.

'Yea! For God, King Charles, Kent and salvation from this overly Long Parliament,' cried out Jack, causing the crowd to erupt again and Elizabeth to laugh at him and drop some of her Christmas shopping. Jack quickly stooped and picked up the packages, piling them back in the arms of the grateful young lady. Her smile of gratitude was reward enough for any man.

'Thank'ee, young sir, for assisting my daughter Elizabeth, she is often clumsy in her transportation of items,' said her father, offering a hand to Jack, with the addition of an affable chuckle. 'My name is John Cartwright of Wingham and Staple, sir. I am squire yeoman farmer of lands at Twitham, Shatterling, Goodnestone and Ash Levels in that good parish.'

'Jack Greenstreet from Claxfield, Lynsted at thy service, sir. Thou knowest Teynham Manor, situated on both sides of the ancient Roman Watling Street, on the road to London.'

'Ay, I often attend the horse fayre there, or pass through on my way to London. Are ye part of the large Greenstreet family dynasty thereabouts? Doth ye know Reeve Johannis Greenstreet, an amiable fellow who I have met on several occasions relating to grain and oats dealings?'

'Yea indeed, I am his nephew. He is a lovely man mine uncle, but now very aged and not so very sound of mind. My cousin James has assumed the role of reeve under the 4th baron, Christopher Roper. But please allow me, sir, to escort thee and thy daughter from this angry crowd. There is rabble amongst them, and some are baying for blood. The good folk of Canterbury and Kent hath good reason to be so heated, but I fear their anger is turning somewhat ugly. The butter market is nay the place for ye and thy daughter to be right now.'

'Thank ye again, Jack, my pony and trap awaits by the River Stour at the Westgate Towers. We hath finished our Christmas shopping and were looking forward to a merry Christmas, prior to the implementation of the very irritating mandate proclaimed and imposed this day.'

Jack took Elizabeth's packages and loaded them into Acorn's saddle bags, then, leading the horse by the bridle with one hand, he placed the other on the hilt of his rapier and proudly walked beside father and daughter as escort. With Elizabeth at his side, Jack became somewhat tongue-tied. Just talking to the girl aroused a deep passion and yearning within him.

'I really doth nay think we should heed the proclamation made by the town crier,' said Jack, adding, 'I doubt very much whether anybody will abide by such a mandate. I know I won't. This puritanical enforcement is going to cause such a stir across the country and…'

His words were cut off by a further loud commotion behind them, as the borsholders, who had attended upon the town crier, ran for their lives They were being pelted by hard root vegetables from the market stalls, and even the stall-owners themselves had joined in the foray.

'That is exactly what I thought might happen,' said Jack. 'We hath nay heard the last of this, I warrant, nay by a long chalk. Such puritanical enforcement will cause another insurrection.'

They left the butter market behind them and walked down the old high street towards the Westgate Towers, crossing the backwater bridge and passing the Pilgrims' Hospital. Just a few paces past the hospital, two ruffians barged into John Cartwright. One paused to doff his cap and offer apology. Jack let go of Acorn's bridle, spun around and drew his dagger, pricking the back of the other man, who froze in his tracks and quickly raised his hands in surrender. The vagabond who had doffed his cap ran off to mix with the pedestrian crowd.

'Turn ye about slowly my light-fingered rat, or I will run ye through like the scum ye are. Now, reach into thy pockets and return the purse ye stole from the gentleman forthwith, and then, maybe, with the season of goodwill upon us, he might ordain that ye lose only one hand and nay both. For if I were left to choose, I wouldst cut off both thy thieving hands forthwith.'

Reluctantly the vagabond opened his heavy cloak, revealing inside linings packed with loot from the morning pickings. He groped in one side of the garment and produced a leather purse and handed it to Cartwright. The belt loop which held the purse had obviously been severed from the girdle by a knife. The purse had the letters J.C. burnt into the leather in one corner.

'Gadzooks, what kind of witchery is it that my purse is in thy possession, ye shabby, uncouth vagrant. Such theft cannot go unpunished, thou art the very pits of earth,' said John Cartwright.

'Ay!' agreed Jack. 'On thy knees, thief, and give forth thy blade,' he demanded, aiming his own dagger close to the pickpocket's gullet. 'Now, scum, open thy cloak wide and let us see inside.'

The pickpocket, a dirty, unshaven rogue, with long matted black hair, stared pleadingly at Jack and removed his razor-sharp knife from a sheath, handing it hilt first to the Cavalier. Jack moved forward and withdrew the thief's takings from the inside pockets of his cloak, handing them one by one to John Cartwright. Mostly they were unmarked pouches, but one had a crest stamped on it. John Cartwright recognised it immediately and drew back.

"Tis the crest of Sir John Boys of Nonnington. He lives a short ride from me. Once a Royalist, he is now a turncoat who hast been made a commissioner by Long Parliament. I suggest we tip the spoils into one pouch and give it all to charity,' suggested Yeoman Cartwright, without hesitation. 'We do nay wish to return money and valuables to a commissioner.'

Elizabeth carefully counted out the money, then checked the rogue's pickings once again.

'I make it total a few groats over twenty-eight pounds. 'Tis a small fortune. We could giveth the money to the friars of Eastbridge Pilgrims' Hospital. 'Tis the almshouse we passed by a moment ago,' she suggested. 'Its aim is to aid pilgrims, and help the poor and the needy.'

'Thine is a wonderful idea, Elizabeth,' agreed Jack, 'and this cretin can hand it over to the chief friar and plead for his sins to be shriven. Come, my ugly rat, knock upon yon studded, arched oak door and offer thy collection for humanity. Ye may yet save thy hands for another day's pickings, rogue. I will ask the chief friar to hath ye locked in the stocks for Christmas. What a wonderful way to spend Christmas Day. After confession, the Minister General may grant thee absolution as a gesture of seasonal goodwill. Perhaps thou wilt consider becoming a friar and wash the feet of pilgrims, rather than pick their pockets! Though, in truth, it wouldst be too much to hope thy soul will be shriven to that extent. If ye hast a soul to shrive, that is.'

'Thine idea is a good solution, daughter. It wouldst be showing seasonal goodwill to both this thief and to the Pilgrims' Hospital, though, as Jack pointed out, I too hath doubts as to the future of such goodwill as far as this pilfering thief is concerned,' said John Cartwright with a chuckle.

They arrived back at the Pilgrims' Hospital and Jack ordered the thief to knock on the door loudly. A small panel slid open at the top of the heavy studded oak door, revealing an iron-barred peephole at eye level. A shaven head appeared. Upon Jack's request, the friar went to find the Minister General. Upon explanation, the minister unlocked the door, giving thanks to God for the contribution and agreeing to the course of action Jack suggested. The thief was taken into custody by two stout friars, whilst the Franciscan-minister blessed the contributors, sending them on their way with praises to God. The vagabond was left to face Christmas Day in the stocks, to be pelted by rancid fruit, rotten eggs and vegetables, and to atone for his sins.

A few paces took the trio to the city's Westgate and the clear chalk waters of the River Stour, where Cartwright's manservant, Tripp, waited with the pony and trap. Jack wished the walk could last forever with Elizabeth at his side. Elizabeth peered over the bridge railings and cast her eyes into the depths of the stream. She glanced back at Jack, looking at him longingly.

'The water is so crystal and transparent, I canst see right to the bottom. There are some trout swimming against the current deep down,' she exclaimed. 'Oh, I wish we were punting upon the Stour, instead of going home. Shall we find a boat to punt, Father? Jack could take me.'

"Tis much too cold for any kind of malarkey on the water, Lizzy,' said her father. 'Thy mother will be wondering what hast delayed us so long. Look, there are snowflakes coming down. We might well suffer a covering before we arrive back at Twitham. We must bid good day to the brave Cavalier. Collect thy packages, daughter, we must wend our way homewards.'

Jack handed the packages to Tripp. Cartwright turned to bid Jack farewell. His daughter's attraction to the young man, and Jack's attraction to his daughter, hadn't gone unnoticed.

'We are indebted to thee, sir. I witnessed ye are a fighting man, Jack. Doth ye have a trade also?'

'Ay, I recently took to my grandfather's trade of carpentry and joinery and am doing well enough at it. I fought with the King at Oxford, in the west, and at the fateful Battle of Naseby. I shall continue to support Charles until he be restored. Today's dictatorial announcement by the crier hast reaffirmed my Royalist resolve, even though after Naseby and the King's capture all appeared lost. I detect a second strong feeling of unrest here at Canterbury today. Like many, I split with mine family over my Royalist support. Mine father, William of Maidstone, and mine brothers favoured Parliament and espoused the Commonwealth cause. Fortunately, I healed the rift with Father before he passed away. He didst nay leave me entirely penniless, though I hath forfeited rights to his vast estates as the eldest son. The estates are left to my brothers in gavelkind. There is a bounty upon my head. I am sought after by Colonel Browne and his Roundheads. Therefore, it is best we are not seen together for too long, sir. However, I am pleased to hath been of service to ye and thy beautiful daughter Elizabeth this cold day.'

'We are of similar Royalist persuasions, Jack, hath nay fear of that, and ye are welcome to call upon us at any time. My farmlands are extensive. We live at Twitham Farm near Staple, just outside of Wingham,' said John Cartwright, gripping Jack's hand firmly. 'There is always work on my lands for a carpenter and joiner, should ye wish to escape the busy part of Kent ye hail from. Ye could settle for a quieter lifestyle at Twitham in the good parish of Wingham.'

'Yes, please, please do come, Jack, please visit us, my valiant Cavalier,' said Elizabeth, removing her glove and holding out her hand for Jack to kiss. 'Merry Christmas to you, dear Jack.'

Elizabeth and her father climbed aboard the trap. Tripp found a blanket and tucked them up warmly for the short journey back to Twitham. Tripp bade the pony 'walk on', and they parted company. Elizabeth and Jack continued to wave until they were out of sight of Westgate Towers. Jack mounted Acorn and trotted back to the market stalls to finish his shopping. A heavy heart accompanied him, for his feelings went much deeper than simple lust. He vowed to visit the girl he had fallen for and take her punting on the river soon. Elizabeth had an even heavier heart, believing Jack was a passing vision she might never see again. The snow fell in earnest as Jack set off for home. Christmas would be a time of deep reflection for them both.

Jack veered off at Faversham and cautiously headed towards Ospringe, destined for the little cottage known as Moddilyon. He approached surreptitiously, having no desire to run into his brothers, or come across a party of marauding Roundheads. The snowfall had eased. Now, only occasional large flakes drifted down from the dirty mauve coloured sky, although, quite obviously, there was more snow to fall. Already the landscape was dusted with the white stuff. Smoke puffed from the single tall chimney of the quaint thatched cottage. Ever active, old Wat Harrys was in the rear garden hacking at a Yule log to see him through Christmas Day. He was delighted to see his one-time young protégé, and Jack was equally pleased to see his aged mentor in such good health, though he was struggling a bit in wielding the heavy axe.

'Greetings, Master Jack, ye hast arrived in the nick of time. Would 'ee mind chopping through the last six inches of this piece of timber? I confess to being just about all done in by it.'

After warmly embracing his former mentor, Jack took the axe and with several mighty blows severed the thick log into two pieces. He carried the requisite Yule log to the side of the fireplace and set it to one side. The fire smouldered with red-hot embers, upon which bubbled tasty pottage. A wonderful bouquet met Jack's nostrils and churned his inner hunger pangs.

'Thank'ee kindly, Master Jack, thou art just in time for a warming banquet of my special woodcock and snipe stew. Pull up a chair close to the fire now and I will serve ye with a platter of this fine mess and some oatcake to fill thy insides. It looks as if ye be half starved.'

Wat poured some orange-coloured scrumpy into a pewter tankard and handed it to Jack, then proceeded to busy himself with the ladle, stirring up the pottage and dishing up a good portion onto a large platter, ensuring he had plenty of meat for his hungry former protégé to feast upon.

'This be wonderful cooking, Wat. Ye hast given a fine enhancement to thine tasty mess, with thyme and other herbs I taste therein, and dumplings as well. God bless ye, old fellow.'

'Ay, I hath also hung up four plump partridge for mine Christmas meal, Jack. Ye art welcome to stay here with me at the cottage and share such delicacy, if thou art so inclined.'

'Nay, old friend. That is so very kind, but I have promised to go to Symon's farm for Christmas Eve. I hath gifts for the children planned. I hath also promised to go across to dine with old Johis, Maria and James on Christmas Day. James hast arranged for other family members to come. I know thou wouldst be more than welcome to join us also. So why doth ye nay accompany me back to Claxfield? Come with me back to Claxfeldestane for the festivities.'

'That is immensely kind of ye, Jack, but I fear I doth nay travel so well these days in bad weather. I prefer to be tucked up here in the confines of my snug and cosy little cottage home.'

'Yea, I understand that Wat. Perhaps I could call on ye soon after New Year has turned.'

'Yea, Jack, a good idea. I will hang some fine hares and make some lardy cake in anticipation. Make it soon after the heralding of 1648, and we wilt drink to better former times.'

The two men clinked their tankards together. Wat refilled them with scrumpy from a demijohn.

'Now then, Wat. I suppose ye never kept that fine yew long bow ye made for me when I was a stripling? I hath been trying to find something suitable for young Rob, Symon's eldest lad. Rob hast past fourteen years of age, but needs to build muscle. He is into hunting and trapping but hast nay enough strength yet to pull back a full-size long bow. I need a weapon of reduced power for him to draw and bend back with ease, Wat, and a quiver of feather-tipped arrows.'

Wat tapped his nose and raised a gnarled finger, beckoning his former protégé to follow him. At the end of the passageway, they entered a well-lit chamber stuffed from floor to ceiling with weaponry, fishing tackle, snares, traps, nets, axes and knives. A workbench on one side was strewn with old tools, grips, hammers and adzes, and bodkins of yarn. Hanging from a shelf above were a score of manufactured fishing flies for every occasion. On one wall hung muskets and fowling pieces, knives, swords and an array of yew long bows, diminishing in size from one end to the other. Wat threw his hands open wide and grinned at his former pupil.

'There thou art, Jack. Take thy pick. I fail to recall which was thy bow, but from what ye hast told me, I recommend ye take this one. This will probably suit the young stripling, Robert.'

Wat selected a medium– to small-sized weapon, found a leather quiver and a handful of cut-down arrows tipped with goose feathers and handed them to Jack with a grin of pleasure. He went to a box and found a sheathed knife. He withdrew the blade and honed it on a wet stone.

'Here is thy first hunting knife, with sheath. Ye had it from me prior to the master giving ye that handsome blade on your eighteenth birthday, which I see clearly hangs from thy side to this very day. When ye had thy new blade, ye handed this knife back to me for safekeeping.'

'Yea, thank'ee kindly, Wat, 'tis exactly what I sought for young Rob. He will be pleased to receive such a gift. I will tell him how you made the long bow and arrows, and how ye taught me to draw the bow back to my cheek, eye through to my target and kiss the string prior to releasing my shaft. There is much ye taught me I will pass on to young Robert, my nephew.'

'Ay and tell Symon he is welcome to bring the boy over to see me. We canst talk over such experiences any time he pleases, for I am invariably at home nowadays, unless in the woods.'

The two men returned to the fire. The cottage was warm and very cosy. Wat found two long clay pipes and some tobacco and they sat each side of the fire, telling yarns, recalling past times and blowing smoke at each other. Jack told Wat about the town crier's proclamation and of the angry riot that had begun to brew up in the butter market at Canterbury. He then told of how he met Elizabeth and her father, John Cartwright, confessing that he was besotted and bewitched by her and couldn't get her out of his mind at any time of the day.

'Sounds to me that ye might well hath found true love then, Jack. I recall I felt much the same way when I met Moll, all those years ago. 'Tis seven long years since Moll departed this life and I still miss her something terrible. She was a wonderful cook, thou knowest, Master Jack.'

'Ay, I remember well, Wat. Moll used to cuff my ears when I crept into her kitchen to pinch one of her freshly baked muffins. I feel the sting of her well-aimed mitt this very day.'

'Well, ye probably deserved it, Master. Ye were always a careless whippersnapper. The art is never to get thyself caught and if ye do get discovered to always have a means of escape. Ye were always too impulsive and reckless in that respect. What ye needed was to hath a plan.'

Jack left the fire and went outside to Acorn. He fumbled in the saddle bag and found a package.

Returning from the cold and snowy conditions outside, Jack handed Wat a thick wooden pack. Wat opened the seal and took out an onion-shaped bottle and two fine crystal glasses.

'It is a double-distilled *eau de vie* from Charente, in France, called cogniacke, Wat. 'Tis bottled from oak casks in Cognac, the very finest brandy. This little number may well blow thy breeches clean off. Some say this finely distilled brew is the only thing the French are good for. In addition, I bought the crystal glasses because I feared ye might pour the content straight into an ale tankard and gulp it down. This drink is for sipping, nay for swigging, Wat. Settle ye down with it by the fireside after thine dinner. Pour a drop into a crystal glass, but before ye let it pass thy lips, caress and warm it in thy hands, like ye might a good woman.'

'Thank'ee very much, Jack, I will treat it with great care, and thank'ee fer calling on an old man and making him so happy this season. Thy goodwill is indeed much appreciated, Master.'

Jack brushed aside snow from the chestnut stallion's back and saddle, before mounting Acorn.

'Long may the season's greetings bide with thee, Wat. Now, I must make tracks, for 'tis snowing heavily again. I hath a few miles to go and do nay wish to get bogged down. I will call upon ye early New Year. Do ye nay drink the cogniacke all in one go, or ye will burn in hell!'

"Twill be treated with respect, Master Jack, do nay worry, and do nay hesitate to visit Miss Elizabeth now. 'Tis wise to follow up such sensitive issues and get them resolved, ye knows.'

*

After Jack had left Canterbury, the rioting turned nasty. Civil disturbances also broke out in London over the mandate to suppress traditional Christmas celebrations. The Lord Mayor of London personally intervened to calm the situation there, though in Canterbury the mayor was driven out of the city, along with several magistrates and clergymen. The Kent County Committee mobilised the Trained Band, an organised company of militia, to restore order. However, on Christmas Day a large crowd gathered. They demanded a church service and decorated doorways with holly and ivy and crammed holly bushes into shop doorways to keep them closed. All the while they chanted, 'For God, King Charles and Kent.' A soldier was badly assaulted, and the mayor's house attacked. Canterbury city was under the rioters' control for three weeks, until forced to surrender by parliamentary forces late in January.

At Twitham Farm, Elizabeth pined over Jack for the whole of the festive season. She lost her appetite, despite the rich fare the household set before her. She tried hard to join in the festivities, but she could not get the handsome Cavalier she had met at Canterbury out of her mind. Her father was aware of her infatuation for the man who had escorted them from the market square riot and caught the pickpocket red-handed. But John Cartwright had other local suitors in mind for his stepdaughter, an agenda of his own to implement. On the spur of the moment he had invited Jack to call upon them at Twitham, but in hindsight, having ascertained Jack was a fighting man who had sold his soul to the Royalist cause, Cartwright didn't think Jack fitted into his plans. Kent was in uproar again. Who could tell where Jack Greenstreet might be? Cartwright needed a man to marry his stepdaughter and to live on the farm, principally to produce a male heir to his vast estates. Having no son of his own, he desired a grandson, ordained as alias by deed, to adopt the Cartwright name. Who else could he possibly bequeath his lands to? Those rich pasturelands at the Ash Levels, and his lands at Wingham, Shatterling, Twitham, Staple and Goodnestone, together with appurtenances, stocks and crops.

John Cartwright had only one barrier to his cunning plan and that was his stepdaughter, Elizabeth Church. Like her mother, Dyonise, she was exceedingly strong-willed. Cartwright married Dyonise Church in 1635, after Thomas Church, her former husband, died in 1628, leaving Dyonise on her own with nine-year-old juvenile, Elizabeth. Elizabeth was twenty-seven now, and in her stepfather's eyes it was high time she was married off and producing children. The Minister of Staple, Emanuel Witherstone, had asked for her hand several times on past occasions, but Elizabeth had refused him, mostly in favour of Wingham's assistant parish clerk, George Wilde. That all changed when she met and fell in love with Jack at Canterbury. She knew, on that day in Canterbury, she had found true love. No advances from either gentleman, minister or clerk, were going to persuade her into an unhappy marriage of convenience to satisfy the machinations of her stepfather. Both Witherstone and Wilde had made recent advances in Elizabeth's direction, but to no avail. Cartwright carried neither man in favour of the other, so long as his stepdaughter could be persuaded to accept one of their proposals of marriage and produce a male heir. He had been in earnest conversation with both men to that effect. Both the minister and the clerk had separately agreed, that should Elizabeth marry one of them and was delivered of a son, they would be prepared to grant a male infant the Cartwright surname, in the form of an alias. The alias would be determined in a deed of indenture drawn up by Cartwright's lawyers. Such alias was planned to be established in Cartwright's will, in order that his estate would pass on, keeping the Cartwright name intact.

*

Moderate snow had fallen outside of Wat's snug cottage, whilst the two men were wrapped in conversation within the walls of Moddilyon. They had closely hugged the well-made-up log fire. Afterwards, Wat had pumped Jack's hand warmly in Yuletide farewell and seen him on his way until out of sight. In an act of desperation, the old man had turned in haste to pee alongside the boundary hedgerow. Like most men of his advanced age, old Wat was suddenly overcome by the need to relieve himself. He danced on one leg whilst he fumbled with the codpiece of his breeches, searching to find his somewhat diminished member in the cold falling snow. His anxiety ceased as he found the mini-beast and released it to spray the pristine white blanket of virgin snow with steaming urine, leaving a pattern of deep yellow indentation. It took a short while to complete his task of nature. Full of relief and happy contentment at Jack's visit, he shook the dripping genital, drew it back into the warmth of its housing, blew a resonating fart of triumph into the silence of the cold night air, then turned to hurry back into the warmth of the cottage. As he backtracked to the entrance of the cosy cottage, Wat was surprised to find a familiar figure waiting to greet him on the doorstep. He assumed he must have come in from the back way. From the young man's belt hung a large hare and two rabbits. He held a flintlock fowling piece by the brass barrel in one hand and a dish with a full round plum pudding in the other. The pudding bore a spray of holly on the top with round vermillion red berries. Two visitors in one day. Things were looking up for the old codger. Yet, considered old Wat Harrys, it was just as well the visits had not clashed! Wat said nothing of the first visitor. The second visitor handed Wat the plum pudding and passed on his seasonal wishes. In his hurry to get away, the second visitor did not stop to bide time with old Wat as the first visitor had done. Having given the compliments of the season and handed over the Christmas pudding to Wat Harrys, the man drew the collar of his cloak up around his neck. Tucking his firearm firmly under one arm, he departed, running into the driving snow, his footprints rapidly obliterated by the heavy falling stuff, which now lay deep, crisp and even.

14

GOODWILL MIDST THE WINTER'S SNOW

The snow was falling heavily when Jack bade Wat Harrys farewell at the cottage. Well over a foot in thickness covered the ground. Jack was pleased to have found Wat in such good health and spirit. He resolved to return to his friend and mentor to see in the New Year as promised. Jack took the shortest route back to Teynham, which meant passing near to Woodlarks, his one-time family home, near Ospringe. Old Watling Street lay hidden beneath the blanket of snow. Only the occasional tracks of a crossing fox or rabbit could be discerned. Behind him the snow was ploughed up by Acorn's dragging hooves. The stallion's hooves normally made a clatter upon the rough flint and gravel. Now, all was deadened to a ghostly rhythmical pounding by the deepening white layer under hoof. An eerie silence surrounded horse and rider, broken only by the hoot of an owl, or a dull thump, as overloaded trees and shrubs dumped accumulated burdens of snow. At the Four Oaks crossroads, near Faversham Stone Chapel, two Roundheads rode out, blocking the road ahead. Jack reined in.

Both men were helmeted. They wore long leather coats with thigh-length boots. Jack halted Acorn. He recognised one Roundhead as captain of the harquebusiers, who had threatened to cut the brewers' ears off at the brewhouse in Greenstreet. The harquebusier addressed Jack in a threatening voice, his open pull-on leather boots filled with snow at the top of thick thighs.

'Well now, look'ee what the Devil hast brought us. 'Tis thine very same cocky Cavalier who pricked my throat at the Teynham brewhouse, whilst his comrade-in-arms held us at bay with a brace of flintlocks. But his comrade be nay here to cover quaint deeds this day, says I. What say ye, Sam? Doth ye think he is a match for me without the backup of other Royalist scum?'

The private harquebusier raised his musket and levelled the long brass muzzle barrel at Jack.

'Nay, do thee nay fire thy musket yet, Samuel. Let us see what a fine swordsman he is on horseback, without friendly backup to oversee his cocky attitude. But keep ye a full train upon him and should he gain the upper hand, ye hast my full permission to shoot him squarely in the front or back, whichever ye choose so to do, so long as ye doth nay hit thy captain, mind!'

Jack cursed himself for being unready. He usually kept his flintlocks tucked in his belt, primed and accessible. They lay dry but useless in his saddle bag. He never expected to find anybody abroad in the inclement weather conditions which prevailed on the London Road that day. Jack managed to draw his cup-hilted rapier as the captain made his charge. The Roundhead swung his basket-hilted sword with a swish aimed at his enemy's head. Jack avoided being decapitated, throwing himself sideways in his saddle in the nick of time. He felt the wind of the blade and reined Acorn in. The captain nimbly turned his horse, but the mare slipped in the snow as the harquebusier charged for a second slash. Jack held his nerve until the last moment, spurred Acorn away, then turned about and slashed the Roundhead high across his back as he passed. The force of the slash cut through the leather coat, opening a deep red wound across the shoulders. Jack had the advantage and met the Roundhead full-on as he turned. Ducking beneath the captain's swishing sword he sunk the cup-hilted rapier under the armpit of the Roundhead and pushed home. The captain fell from his horse into the deep snow, his heart pierced through. The rapier was forcibly wrenched from the Cavalier's grasp.

With the sword buried deep in his chest, the harquebusier's quivering body oozed blood, which pumped from him, spreading and staining the white snow a deep cherry red. Shocked by the rapid demise of his captain, the private soldier hesitated, then levelled his snaphance firelock carbine and steadied his aim. Jack looked squarely at the Roundhead and realised his time had come. A loud shot rang out. Unbelievably, at such short range the soldier had missed him, or the musket had backfired. He would get no second chance. Jack fumbled frantically for his dagger. He had no need to panic. The harquebusier fell dead before him. A lead ball had pierced the temple and literally blown his brains out. His head and helmet were disintegrated.

Jack looked around him. His glance settled on a cloud of grey smoke swirling around a field gate. Through the smoke he made out the profile of a young man. The youth, for he was not much more than that, peered over the barrel of a long fowling musket. The gun rested on top of the five-barred gate to steady it. Slowly the figure moved his weapon away. The young spectre was veiled by a mixture of discharged gunpowder, smoke and heavy falling snow. As the smoke slowly dispersed, Jack recognised the familiar form of his younger brother, Thomas.

'Is that ye, Tom? Hast my younger brother saved me from certain death from the Roundheads?'

'Come ye nay closer, brother Jack. I am nay such a bad shot now, ye agree? I hast my flintlock pistol trained upon ye, so collect thy weapon from this bloodstained stage and be ye on thy way. Inform no person of this bloody carnage, I urge ye. For I doth nay want brother William to get wind of the disgusting act of betrayal I have perpetrated this day. Go now, brother, and remember, my shot was nay to save ye as thou art today, but 'twas for good times past. Call it seasonal goodwill and memories of our dear father. I so wish ye had nay turned traitor, Jack.'

Thomas was obviously torn apart by the brotherly split over the civil war, a war which had destroyed his family and so many like families also. Jack retrieved his sword, cleaned it in the snow and remounted the stallion. Then, turning, with tears burning in his eyes, he sang out,

'Merry Christmas, Thomas. God bless ye and a Happy New Year to ye, dearest brother!'

He cleared his blurred eyes and looked towards the gate. Whether his younger brother was still within earshot, he knew not, for Thomas was gone. The gate stood empty and abandoned, as if nothing had ever happened. The creeping red stain of finality had frozen into the ground and the two men were already half concealed by a white covering, as the snow fell heavily over their bodies. It was doubtful whether anybody would use the highway for the next few days, by which time the bodies would be dragged away by lynx and wolves, to be devoured, together with fox, crow, kite and every kind of animal that survived on carrion. Jack urged his horse homewards, pulling his cloak tightly about his shivering carcass. His trip to Canterbury had not turned out as planned, he mused. But how the devil did Tom know of his whereabouts?

The answer to that thought was resolved early in the New Year, when Jack returned to visit Wat Harrys. Apparently, Tom was on his way to see Wat, bearing a plum pudding from Goodwoman Oxley, the cook at Woodlarks, and a gift of money for Wat from the boys. Tom always carried his fowling piece with him, in the hope of coming across a nice wild boar. Tom had taken a shortcut across the fields to Four Oaks crossroads. He was about to climb over the gate, when he witnessed the fracas between the harquebusiers and his brother. Despite their feuding, Tom decided instantaneously that family blood was thicker than snow or water.

Now, Jack not only had Elizabeth to ponder over, but his brother Tom also. Yet he knew the chance encounter with his younger brother did not mean reconciliation. He wondered whether he might ever return to Woodlarks, even after resolution of the civil wars. It was doubtful whether brother William would ever welcome him with open arms again, and Jack understood well the reasons why. Not only were the brothers of a different persuasion because of the civil wars, but on the death of their father the running of the entire estates had been thrust upon Will. In the normal way of things, as the eldest, such inheritance would have been bequeathed to Jack. In any event, it was all way beyond Will's expectations. Having chosen to espouse the Commonwealth cause alongside his father and Lord Peter, young William had little choice other than to get to grips with the toil and management of William of Maidstone's vast estates.

Christmas 1647 came and passed by with little further incident. Symon, Marion and the children were thrilled with the gifts they received. To Robert, Uncle Jack was the best uncle in the world. Jack took Rob out with the long bow and taught him how to draw and use it to good advantage. He stayed over Christmas Eve at the farm, and shared good food and drink. On Christmas Day he journeyed back to be with James, old Johis and Maria. Many friends came to Claxfeldestane. Everybody enjoyed good fare and made merry, much as any other Yuletide occasion, despite the puritanical mandate announced by the town crier at Canterbury. On two occasions, in his state of considerable dementia and not a little inebriated, old Johis went outside to see whether Lord Peter and the Roundhead soldiers were burning his wheat field. He was quickly pacified by James, who explained that wheat did not ripen in fields of snow.

Christopher Roper, the 4th Baron of Teynham, called in to exchange seasonal greetings and to drink some hot mulled wine with spices. He particularly wished to raise a glass to Johis and Maria. The baron informed James and Jack that

Royalist uprisings were breaking out all over the country again and were particularly prevalent in Kent. Most of the Royalists were not soldiers, but ordinary citizens, cavaliers, seamen and watermen, who demanded that the King be restored to the throne. Cries of 'For God, King Charles and Kent' were to be heard in meeting places all over Kent. Kent and Essex had the strongest insurgency in the country. The situation was becoming increasingly dangerous for Parliament. The baron was convinced it was only a matter of time before the men of Kent and Kentish men were called to arms again.

Throughout the Yuletide, Jack was haunted by his longing for Elizabeth. He yearned to be with her and to tell her about his feelings for her. How tongue-tied he had been by her beauty and in her presence when they met at Canterbury. He wanted to tell her the way he felt each lonely night and every minute of the day. But his mind was sorely troubled by the bounty on his head and the encounter he had had with the harquebusier Roundheads, on his way back from Wat's cottage. He dared not chance bringing such a burden down upon her and her family. Now that Kent was rising again in favour of the King, the Trained Bands and Roundhead platoons would be out looking for him. He decided to write to Elizabeth and explain his position to her. He would find a way of delivering the letter to her when he visited Wat in the New Year. Perhaps he could persuade old Wat himself to make the short journey to Staple on his behalf, when the weather improved for such a journey to be embarked upon, of course. Jack planned to visit Wat to see in the New Year with him. He would broach the essential matter with his mentor then. After all, it was old Wat who urged him to contact her.

15

WAT GOES ON AN ERRAND

The cruel winter weather relented. Old Wat Harrys, on his equally old mare, Patch, journeyed below Canterbury to Bridge, cut across country to Brambling and entered Wingham, passing the church of St Mary the Virgin. He made a right turn to Staple and found Twitham Farm a couple of miles along the Staple Road. Cartwright's rich pasturelands lay between Twitham and Shatterling. A wide cinder track led to the farmhouse. Elizabeth's mother, Dyonise, was feeding a gaggle of geese. The geese paused in their gabbling to hiss and threaten Wat as he dismounted from the mare. Wat doffed his felt cap and greeted Dyonise with a warm smile.

'Good morrow, Goodwife, how doth ye fare? I seek Miss Elizabeth. I am the purveyor of a letter, which I need to place in that fair lady's hand.' Wat grinned wryly and winked one eye.

Dyonise Cartwright finished scattering corn seed for the fowl, then invited Wat to tether his mare and enter the farmhouse pantry. Wat followed her swaying skirts and bum roll, shifting his eyes to the square of linen stitched about her neck to keep the weather out. He tripped clumsily over the threshold, clutching at her attire. Dyonise pointed to a Windsor-style chair.

'Take a seat, old man, ye look weary from thy long journey. Hath ye travelled far this morn?'

'Ay, I hath journeyed from near Faversham on this errand, which I hath made on behalf of mine former master. 'Tis made of mine own choice, mind ye. Pray, is Miss Elizabeth at home?'

'Pause ye for a moment, old man, take the weight off thy feet. Ye hath journeyed far. Make thyself comfy whilst I find ye some refreshment. Then I will go and seek my daughter out.'

Dyonise went over to a larder cupboard and poured out a tankard of small beer, which she handed to Wat. She removed her large-brim pointed hat and set it aside, then found a platter, cut off a huge wedge of lardy cake and set it on a table beside him. Wat's eyes widened.

'There, refresh thyself, old man. I think Elizabeth is in her chamber, busy with her lace work nay doubt. I shall seek her out and tell her ye await her presence forthwith and bear a letter.'

Wat tucked hungrily into the lardy cake and washed it down with the small beer, while he waited for the women to return. He smacked his lips over the lardy cake, which was fresh-baked and tasty. Wat drew in his breath when he saw Elizabeth. She was indeed a girl of considerable beauty. No wonder Jack had fallen for her. She wore a soft satin dress, short-waisted and with full flowing skirts. Her bodice was of blue velvet, on similar lines to a man's doublet, but the neckline plunged low, showing the delicate cleavage of firm young breasts. Her face was framed by a white ruff, trimmed with the finest lace. She approached Wat and offered a hand. Wat kissed her hand and pumped it hard, his etiquette crude and unknowing.

'I am on an errand, Miss, on behalf of Master Jack Greenstreet. I was one-time manservant to William of Maidstone, Jack's father, now deceased. Jack was my protégé, so to speak, and I his mentor. I am also proud to call him a good friend, and that is why I hath turned messenger this day. I am the bearer of a letter from him, which he asked me to deliver into thy hands. He bade me remain until ye hast read it, in case, perchance, ye hath a response to make in his direction. I wilt sit whilst ye peruse, and perhaps indulge in another smidgeon of lardy cake!'

Dyonise Cartwright smiled at the impudence of the rough character and cut him off another slice of lardy cake, then topped up Wat's beer tankard. He slurped the beer and belched loudly.

"Tis a letter from Jack Greenstreet, Mother, the man I told ye about. The handsome Cavalier I met with Father at the butter market, in Canterbury, and who didst safely escort us. Jack held that ruffian pickpocket at the point of his dagger and retrieved Father's purse, as quick as a weasel runs up a drainpipe! Do ye remember me telling ye about him and how brave he was?'

'Ay, daughter, I recall the story well enough. How couldst I forget? Ye hath told me about him on at least six or maybe seven occasions over the Yuletide. Is he coming to court thee?'

'Wait, Mother, grant me time to read the letter through. I hath yet to break the seal.'

Elizabeth broke the seal, unfolded the parchment paper and proceeded to read the scripted font of Jack's neat handwriting. A trembling came over her whole being as she scanned the letter.

5 January 1648

My Dearest Elizabeth,

I hath need to write because of my deepest feelings for thee. Ye hath been close to my heart ever since we met at the butter market, that eventful and momentous day in Canterbury. I recall that now distant day with nothing but many sighs and a pained longing to see ye. I hath a need to set quill to parchment, for ye hath been constantly on my mind every minute of this passing Yuletide. Ye need to understand the reason I dare nay come to thee. The Parliamentarians hath put a high bounty on my head. I am constantly on my guard against the Independents and Trained Bands of Roundhead soldiers.

I was involved in an unpleasant affray with two harquebusiers on my way back from Canterbury, following our fortuitous meeting. I dare nay risk a visit to Wingham, which might by chance draw the wrath of mine enemies upon thee and thine. Fairfax's Independents have turned very vengeful and bloodthirsty since Naseby. Hence, I am currently unable to pursue my strong desire to be with ye. I hope this second civil war will end swiftly. I canst nay ask ye to wait for my visit, it wouldst be unfair to so do. Ye may meet a kind and honest suitor to fulfil thy dreams. Each day I pray

for my situation to terminate. This will nay happen until these cursed civil wars hath ceased. Love keeps out the cold more than any cloak. I hath nay doubt of mine deepest love for thee. I seek love's sublime reward as I wait impatiently for release from my shackles.
My deepest love forever – Jack

Elizabeth carefully folded the parchment paper. She turned to Wat with tears in her eyes.

'Wilt thou wait a few minutes more and take a note back to Jack for me, dear messenger Wat?'

'Ay, lass, of course I shall, if it so be thy wish. Ye take thy time, I shalt sit here and contemplate this homely kitchen parlour and make conversation with thy mother, Goodwife Dyonise.'

Dyonise Cartwright called after her daughter, who had quietly, but hurriedly, left the parlour.

'Well, Elizabeth Church, hath ye been jilted by thy handsome Cavalier or nay?' she shouted after her, before realising she had been duped by her daughter's hurried disappearance upstairs.

Wat Harrys intervened, tut-tutted and waved a gnarled finger at Goodwife Cartwright.

'Come, come, dear lady! Canst thou nay detect the course of true love, goodmother? Nay, Jack will never jilt thy daughter. These are troubled times we live in. Much patience is called for. Do ye nay see, love pulses through the veins of their bodies, like the River Medway goes to the sea, or I be a Dutchman. They are as one. It was the same with me and my goodwife, Moll. Some folk knows when they be well matched. It is pointless to search further afield.'

'Yea, but Elizabeth is nay getting any younger, old man, and there are other able suitors plying for her hand. The local minister of Staple church is like-minded, and the deputy parish clerk at Wingham hast a keen and constant eye upon her, as hath many other less likely local gentlemen. Goodhusband John hast been in close liaison with both men. They art pillars of the community and of much integrity. Know ye that arrangements might be made any day soon if Lizzy wouldst only cometh to her senses. She hast left matters far too long in her waiting, in the vain hope the right man might cometh her way. Both the gentlemen I refer to hath the means to support such union. Hopefully, God willing, one might produce a male child to inherit and carry forward the management of Squire John Cartwright's vast estate lands.'

'Nay doubt, Mistress. Jack also hast more than a little tucked away for such occasion, I vouch for that. But I sayeth, ye canst nay meddle with the course of true love, nay even a smidgeon.'

Wat rapidly changed the subject, knowing that he was making no impression on goodwife Cartwright.

'Doth ye make that wonderful lardy cake thyself, goodwife Cartwright? I hath nay tasted such delicacy since my Moll passed away. 'Tis some seven years ago now, God bless her departed soul. I miss her terrible, but ye adapt to such circumstance as the years roll on by.'

Dyonise Cartwright reluctantly cut Wat off a further slice and stuck it in the rascal's hands.

'That is thy last slice, Wat Harrys. I dare nay contemplate Yeoman Cartwright's words when he arrives hungry from managing his lands and there is nay a crumb of lardy cake to devour.'

Elizabeth returned to the parlour and handed Wat a sealed note. She kissed him tenderly on the cheek and ushered the old man out of the door. Wat's mare, Patch, waited patiently, grazing on the verge surrounding the duck pond. Wat mounted up and bade goodbye to Elizabeth.

'Thank ye, dear Wat, for bringing Jack's letter to me. Ride ye carefully on thy way back home.'

'Pray, hath nay fear, Miss. I will deliver thine response as soon as I am able. I owe it to Master Jack. That fine gentleman came over to me on New Year's Eve. We saw in 1648 together.'

Having successfully completed his errand at Twitham Farm, Wat rode back to his cottage in Ospringe. He slept well that night, exhausted by the day's events. On his journey back, he witnessed houses ablaze. Flames from one house rose high into the evening sky and Wat saw Roundhead soldiers leaving the premises, whilst several unfortunates stood in dismay outside the house, watching their property burn. The uprising by Kentish people was rife again, and they were being severely suppressed by parliamentary troops. The Roundheads were leaving insurgents without a roof over their heads to survive the cruel severity of the elements. Wat rose early next morning and donned several undergarments, a warm cloak and a felt cap. He breakfasted, then mounted his mare and set off down old Watling Street, bound for Teynham.

At his workshop in Frognal, Jack was preparing oak for a set of winding steps, to replace those worn by ministers over many years of preaching from the pulpit of Lynsted church. Surprised by the hammering on his workshop door so early in the morning, Jack readied his sword and cautiously lifted the latch. He was staggered to find old Wat fatigued from an icy journey.

'Come ye inside immediately, Wat. 'Tis a cold raw morning. Ye should nay be abroad in such cold inclement weather. I told ye to wait until it got milder afore ye rode this way to see me.'

The inside of the carpenter's workshop was warm and cosy enough. An open fire, piled high with offcuts from the joinery work, burnt fiercely in the hearth. Logs brought in from an outside wood stack were also frequently added. Flames leapt brightly up the chimney flue.

'So this be where ye spend thy time, Master.' Wat dropped his breeches and raised his cloak to roast his naked arse at the fireside. Shuffling his feet in the shavings he said, 'I recall thy grandfather John had a workshop the same style. A fine craftsman, was thy grandfather.'

Normally Jack would listen in rapture to every yarn Wat told, but he cut him short this time.

'Hast thou been to see her, Wat? Didst ye go to Twitham Farm, as thou promised ye wouldst?'

'Ay, I hath been to Twitham, and what a fine homestead it turned out to be, with its grand farmhouse and all. And Mistress Dyonise Cartwright knows a thing or two about baking lardy cake. Lord, I had three helpings washed down with ale from the pantry. 'Twas very tasty.'

'Yea, but get ye to the point, Wat. For God's sake, get to the point of thine quest for me.'

Wat fumbled within the deep folds of his cloak and produced the note written by Elizabeth.

'Ah, here thou art, Master, a note of response from the girl ye love, and what a pretty picture she was – nay denying. She kissed mine cheek, ye knows. Right here!' Wat touched the spot.

Jack almost snatched the sealed letter from Wat's hand. He broke the seal with trembling fingers and gazed in awe at the delicate handwriting, sniffing desirously at the vellum paper.

Dearest Jack – my noble Cavalier,

I hath little time to set down my longing and rapturous feelings for thee this wonderful day. Suffice to say that I will wait for ye for as long as it takes. My patience is forbearing, and my endurance is forever, dearest heart.

My love always,
Elizabeth

Wat massaged warmth into the cheeks of his frozen buttocks, which were now roasting like a suckling pig against the roaring fire, thawing him out nicely from his freezing journey. He pulled up his breeches, dropped his cloak, advanced from the fireside and sidled up to the recipient of Elizabeth's letter. Wat tried to look over Jack's left shoulder to sneak a peep.

'Well, Master Jack, what news, what news?' cried Wat impatiently, taking hold of Jack's arm.

Jack secreted the letter from Wat's sight, holding it tight against his chest. Elizabeth's vellum paper note was for him and him only, not for prying eyes, though Wat deserved some response.

'She is going to wait for me, Wat. Elizabeth is prepared to wait. Such sacrifice is more than I could ever expect of her,' he surmised, carefully folding the note and placing it in one corner of the long front pocket of his sackcloth work apron, along with the sawdust, tools and nails he kept therein. Jack grabbed Wat and danced over the workshop floor midst the wood shavings.

'Steady on, Master, ye shalt hath me blow up!' Wat perched himself on the carpentry bench gasping for breath, then added, 'I couldst see the love light in her eyes for ye alright, Jack.'

Jack thanked the old man profusely for the journeys he had made. He sighed deeply, his mood changing from one brimming with much happiness to one of a melancholy nature.

'How long are these damned bloody wars going to go on for, Wat? I am done with fighting. Like Symon, all I really desire is to settle down to a quiet lifestyle now. My carpentry and joinery work wouldst sustain me if Elizabeth and I were to join in holy matrimony. Now, Kent is rising up for a second time, demanding Charles be restored to the throne again, even though Parliament holds the King in close custody. It nay bodes well for the King, Kent or our country as I see it. Baron Roper is calling a further meeting at Claxfeldestane next week, concerning this second Kent revolt, and to give forth news and distribute arms. He is in liaison with the Earl of Norwich, who is raising a large army of Royalists. We hath been through all this before and look ye at the bloodshed it hast brought about. I intend to make it clear that if the King is not restored to the throne this year, I shalt nay be offering mine services again. Too much blood has been spilt already by loyal countrymen, whatever side they support. I hath searched mine mind and nay longer do I condone such losses. God Almighty, we shall soon hath only women in this wretched country of ours There will be nay men left if they are slaughtered at the rate they are.'

'Ay, I see thy point of view well enough, Jack. For mineself, I hath ne'er seen the pros and cons of the wretched civil wars from the outset. Only the terrible human killing, disruption and family sacrifice imposed by mankind. Life is short enough, whichever direction thou taketh. Matters such as these are nay worth dwelling upon for too long. Incidentally, I saw houses torched by Roundhead soldiers on my way back from Twitham. 'Twas a terrible sight and sickening to see those poor souls of Kent made homeless. Pray they canst survive to see out this cold spell which has come upon us. Many families will die from exposure, I predict.'

'Ay Wat, and that is why I shall be escorting ye back to thine cottage, just as soon as we have eaten some food within the cottage parlour. I wouldst nay forgive mineself if ye had trouble with Roundheads or highway bandits on thy way back to Moddilyon. Such a trusty messenger, as ye surely are, needs protecting well. Come into mine abode, dear Wat. I hath some pottage bubbling in the hearth to warm our insides afore we set out upon the road back to Ospringe.'

16

A SECOND KENTISH INSURRECTION
AND THE BATTLE OF MAIDSTONE, 1648

Unrest continued to simmer below the surface in Kent. The early months of the year were calm enough, although hotspots of steamy anger broke the surface all over the county due to brutal Roundhead incursions. A Royalist rebellion came to the boil in early May, following a second attempt at suppression by the Kent County Committee at Canterbury. This time the County Committee attempted to suppress a petition calling for the return of the King and the disbandment of the New Model Army. In fact, extensive rioting had broken out in April in several other places around the country, including London, Norwich and Bury St Edmunds, all demanding the return of King Charles to full power. Royalist uprising was strong in South Wales. There was the 'Engager' threat from

Scotland (a secret treaty between the Scottish and the King, whereby Charles promised to impose Presbyterianism in exchange for an army to help restore him to power). Then the navy revolted. The fleet mutinied and a squadron of warships defected to the King, placing the navy under the command of the Prince of Wales.

In Kent, Royalist forces took command of three previously held Parliamentarian castles, at Walmer, Deal and Sandown. Then Dover Castle was besieged. The Parliamentary Governor of Pembroke Castle, John Poyer, declared for the King. Berwick and Carlisle were seized by Royalists, sending Oliver Cromwell scampering northwards to sort matters out in the most brutish manner. Cromwell's army was in no mood for appeasement in 1648.

In late May, a significant part of the Royalist uprising assembled outside of Maidstone, at Penenden Heath. Over 10,000 men had been raised for the Earl of Norwich, who had previously been proclaimed leader of the Kent Royalists at a rendezvous meeting outside Rochester on 29 May. The force was made up of cavaliers, citizens, seamen and watermen, but even though valiant they were, in truth, no match for Fairfax's trained New Model Army veterans. Fairfax, who had been preparing to march north against the Scottish threat, now had a rebellion near to London, and there was real danger that the Kent insurgents might be joined by Royalists from Essex and Surrey. Parliament ordered General Sir Thomas Fairfax to deal with the Kentish threat immediately. On 27 May, Fairfax mustered his troops on Hounslow Heath. Colonel Barnstead's band secured Southwark to the south of London, while the Trained Bands under Major-General Skippon were mobilised to defend the city. Fairfax advanced to Blackheath, dispersing Royalists at Deptford and Dartford. He left a detachment at Croydon to act as rearguard against threat from Surrey, and then, bypassing the insurgents' stronghold at Rochester, he marched on Maidstone, where the Royalist army had assembled. Jack and Symon Greenstreet joined up under the Earl of Norwich. They were ordered, with others from North Kent, to hold Rochester where a Parliamentarian attack was expected at any time.

On 1 June 1648, Fairfax arrived at Maidstone with a force of 8,000 veteran parliamentary troops, to recapture it from the defending 3,000-strong Royalists, who had barricaded themselves within the town. Norwich remained, with some 7,000 men on Penenden Heath, some way outside of Maidstone. Fairfax split his force in half and took 4,000 veterans to encircle the town and attacked an outpost on Farleigh Bridge. From here he crossed the River Medway to the south-west of Maidstone and by 7pm, had secured the perimeter of the town. He stood before the barricaded town centre and laid plans to storm the town at first light.

That same evening, Fairfax's advanced guard, led by Colonel Hewson, came under attack from a group of Kentish insurgents. Following heavy skirmishes with the defending Kent men, other units were drawn into the fight. Fairfax decided it was now or never. As the night clouds darkened, he made a general assault, running his army straight into the stronghold of Royalist rebels. The less well-trained army of men of Kent and Kentish men were far stronger than Fairfax had convinced himself they would be. The battle was bloody and hard fought on both sides. Street by street the New Model Army attacked, winning each Royalist barricade. The barricades were ferociously defended by the Kent men. Both sides faced not only the ferocity of the fighting but torrential driving rain and thunderstorms. Lightning, followed by loud claps of thunder, exploded all around, intermingled with musket fire and the screaming of the wounded and dying, as hand-to-hand fighting raged. The heavens opened and sheeting rain fell upon Maidstone with a vengeance that night. Powder got damp, and both sides resorted to sword, bayonet, longbow, pike and halberd. In the drenching rain, with torrents of gushing and streaming water, mixed with rivulets of life-sapping blood, the Royalists were slowly beaten back through the town, retreating at first towards Gabriel's Hill and then into the darkness of Week Street. At approximately 11pm, cornered in the confines of St Faith's churchyard, many Royalists fled, leaving a tally of 300 of their men dead or dying. Fairfax was said to be utterly astonished when about 1,000 Royalists emerged from within the confines of the Huguenot chapel of St Faith's to offer surrender. A final tally of belligerent casualties and losses was 800 or more Royalists and eighty Parliamentarians.

After their surrender, Royalist prisoners were initially held captive in All Saints church. They were adjudged to have acquitted themselves well in their bloody defence against a professional Parliamentarian attack, and 1,300 Royalist men were allowed by Fairfax to return to their homes. Lord General Sir Thomas Fairfax – nicknamed 'Black Tom' – was becoming sickened by the slaughter of so many of his countrymen. He was said to be a solitary, honourable soldier and a noble Yorkshireman. Following this parliamentary victory, the Royalist force of around 6,000 men on Burnham Heath dispersed, the bulk retreating northwards with a view of regrouping under the Earl of Norwich and taking London itself. They found the city gates closed and moved on to Colchester in Essex, with Fairfax in hot pursuit. On 13 June, they were besieged, and finally surrendered in late August after deprivation and famine.

The expected attack on Rochester never transpired, much to Jack and Symon's relief, for they had ceased to have much stomach for fighting the cause or further related battles anymore. The civil wars and skirmishes had dragged on for far too long. They left the city walls of Rochester, and the Earl of Norwich to his campaigns, and journeyed back to Borden and Teynham Hundred to resume their quieter lifestyles, on the farm and in the carpentry shop. In any case, the King was held captive, and it was true to say he had been the cause of much needless bloodshed through his own selfish principles and arrogance. Even Jack and Symon wondered whether they should declare for King Charles anymore. Many Royalists now felt abandoned, a sense of dissociation and of being sold down the river, by a King who would not compromise with his enemies in any shape or form. Even in captivity Charles had managed to manipulate a new bout of violence, by enticing the Scottish 'Engager' faction to his cause, which had led to this second civil war and the deaths of thousands of his subjects all over the country. Fortunately for Parliament, the Engager invasion was badly co-ordinated with the English and Welsh uprisings. The New Model Army was able to suppress the insurrections.

Fairfax left Colonel Nathaniel Rich to deal with the remains of the Kentish insurrection, and went on to Essex in pursuit of the Earl of Norwich and to quell revolts elsewhere in the country. Rich arrived at Dover on 5 June and quickly snuffed out a Royalist attempt to take control of Dover

Castle. He took the best part of a month to retake Walmer Castle, before moving to Deal and Sandown castles. When he arrived at Deal, he found the castle supported by Royalist warships. The ships managed to land 800 soldiers and sailors under cover of darkness. This force was set to surprise the besieging Parliamentarians from the rear, but a deserter alerted the besiegers, who turned and defeated the Royalists. Less than a hundred men managed to get back to their ships. Three hundred managed to flee to Sandown Castle, further along the coast at Deal. Further attempts at landing men also failed, and the Prince of Wales, who had taken command of that part of the defecting navy, withdrew to the Netherlands, pursued by the Earl of Warwick.

On 23 August 1648, an arrow was fired into Deal Castle, giving news that Cromwell had been victorious at the Battle of Preston. Deal's garrison surrendered, followed by Sandown on 5 September. This finally ended the Kentish insurrections, and when Colchester surrendered at the end of August it finally brought the second civil war to a conclusion.

On that first day of June 1648, whilst he lay against the walls of Rochester Castle, drenched by the rain, sword at the ready and flintlocks primed awaiting a Roundhead attack, Jack's only thoughts had been for Elizabeth and her safety. He knew there would be military movements in her vicinity, on their way to the castles of Dover, Deal and Walmer. Norwich escaped towards London with 3,000 men, but found the gates barred and Skippon's Roundheads defending. Norwich's men deserted. Jack and Symon returned home from their abortive mission. Jack's first thoughts were to inform Elizabeth of his safety and the defeat of Maidstone, heralding the end of the Kentish insurrection. He decided to chance Roundhead

encounters and ride to Wingham with a letter, and there find
means of delivering it to her.

My Dearest Elizabeth,

3 June 1648

I hath just returned from Rochester. Praise be to God, we were not attacked this time, and our forces were nay needed nor tested by this Kentish uprising. Fairfax decided to bypass us and headed directly to Maidstone, where much bloodshed took place before the Kent men were defeated by the New Model Army. Afterwards, the Earl of Norwich took some troops to engage with the City of London. I know nothing of how he fared this day. I pray you were unaffected by incursions in the area of Wingham. Symon and I hath sworn a pact that we shall nay fight under the King's banner again. We hath given our all over the years and now hath to accept a Republican Commonwealth, governed by Parliament and the Council State. So many men are coming home to die of their festering wounds and dysentery and the pestilence is rife again in this part of Kent. It is a pitiful country we live in. How the time drags without thee. I shall die a thousand deaths till we meet again.

My deepest love forever,
Jack

17

A JOURNEY RELEASES RESERVED PASSIONS. A SAD PASSING OCCURS

From Conyer Creek across the Teynham level and Luddenham marshes and then along the sea wall of the Swale estuary to Seasalter was the route he took. Then south-east across country to Herne Common, through Blean Woods and Rough Common, skirting Canterbury to Wickhambreaux, down to Brambling and past the church of St Mary the Virgin, at Wingham. Jack had purposely chosen Sunday, knowing village people would be flocking to their church services. Running into Roundhead patrols was unlikely on the route he chose to take. Staple and Twitham were a stone's throw from Wingham, and if he did come across a Roundhead platoon he'd dismount and intermingle with the country folk who travelled to and fro to their churches, to offer prayers and sing praises to Almighty God. He had purposely dressed in the attire of an ordinary farm labourer, with a smock-like frock coat. He felt very much the same as any other labourer who went about his godly business on the Sabbath day. The fields were full of green wheat crops. The crops had already grown thigh high, and fat ears were starting to form. The cornfields rippled and trees rustled in the light morning breeze. White cattle grazed upon rich pastures, and corncrake and partridge called out from secret hiding places, whilst swifts and swallows swept across the landscape in search of the insect life which buzzed abundantly all about. Chattering congregations of mostly older men, and women and children, wended their way along farm tracks and crossed fields to pass through the lychgates of their places of worship, to pray and to thank the Holy Lord for all things bright and beautiful.

There was a dearth of younger men. So many had already given their lives in sacrifice, run through by bayonet or sword, or crucified upon the spike of a cruel pike or halberd blade. Thousands of men had been struck down by musket balls, arrows, or shot through by flintlock pistols. Some blown to bits by grenado or by cannon shot. Other men, sickened by civil war and not wishing to participate further, had chosen to leave their country of birth and journey to the New World. There was a gender scare. It seemed England was overrun by women. So outnumbered were men that polygamy was already known to have occurred and was considered by many to be the answer. In consequence, sexually transmitted diseases were rife and spread rapidly, at a time when women were expected to be silent, chaste and confined to the household. There were too many women in ratio to men. This was probably one of the reasons for the increase in witchhunting.

Jack sought only one female. Elizabeth Church was the woman in his life. He felt it a strange phenomenon that the woman he loved was probably within a mile or so of the place he now stopped at to refresh himself and to rest his constant uncomplaining companion, Acorn. The Black Pig brewhouse in Barnsole Lane offered the rest sought and a good tankard of ale to quench the thirst from a dusty ride. He had come through Twitham and along the track which led to Twitham Farm. A little further on he passed the long low Saxon church of St James the Great in Staple and heard the singing which emanated loudly from the service held within its stone walls. The mid-morning service had only just begun, and he planned to return to the church after the service. He was bound to find a suitable person to deliver his letter, as the congregation left the churchyard lychgate. Hopefully he could contact some servant or person connected with the farm at Twitham. He planned to pay handsomely for the letter to be delivered to Elizabeth. Jack sank a second tankard of ale and tucked into mine landlord's tasty meat pie with relish.

Jack left the Black Pig brewhouse and led his horse back along Barnsole Lane to the church. Here he stood amongst tall beech trees, with a good view of the church vestibule opposite. The congregation spewed out of the church into fresh air. Near the lychgate, a familiar figure with pony and trap waited. Tripp, Cartwright's manservant, held the bridle of a well-turned-out piebald, quietly munching in a nosebag of oats. He might give Tripp the letter to hand to Elizabeth. Jack stroked Acorn's muzzle in anticipation. Was she there in that very church? He glanced beyond the stone walls and steps leading up from the lychgate to the elevated entrance. Some country peasants with dowdy well-patched sackcloth attire followed the minister out. Then, dressed in finery, John Cartwright left the church accompanied by a tall buxom woman dressed in a long green skirt with bum roll and pointed wide-brimmed hat. Jack assumed she was Cartwright's wife, Dyonise. Cartwright shook hands with the minister and fell into deep conversation with a fully bearded, rather rotund man, who followed in the wake of Cartwright and his wife. Jack's heart leapt when Elizabeth came out of the gloomy vestibule into the hazy sunlight. He was dazzled by her beauty. She was dressed in an ankle-length shift, naturally dyed in pale yellow, with a blue velvet, long-sleeved bodice and ribbons. A lace-trimmed white linen square covered her neck and shoulders. A matching bonnet concealed her long hair. Her attire was obviously that of a well-heeled squire yeoman's daughter. The vicar, Emanuel Witherstone, held Elizabeth in extended conversation, all the while holding up the rest of the congregation. People pushed forward in a ring around the Reverend Witherstone in their attempt to praise the content of his sermon, to shake hands and bid the vicar farewell until the next Sabbath day. Uninterested by the minister's chat, Elizabeth bade him goodbye and pushed through the throng, eager to walk away. She crossed the short-cut grass between tall gravestones and glanced over the stone wall in Jack's direction. Her eyes fell upon the man she loved standing and holding the reins of his chestnut stallion. Her heart skipped a beat. Jack raised a hand in acknowledgement. He pointed to the sidetrack which ran at right angles to the churchyard, then crossed the lane and walked over, leading Acorn by the bridle. Here he was concealed by a high stone retaining wall.

Elizabeth walked over to converse with him. She gripped a tall gravestone for support and looked down over the grassed bank, greeting his impish smile with her own radiance. She raised a slim hand and gave a delicate wave, delighted that he had come to her. She spoke with a tremble, her voice quivering in excitement:

'Go ye down this lane to a five-bar field gate at the back of the church, Jack, and wait for me there. I will ride back with my parents and Tripp in the pony and trap, and then saddle my own pony and return to ye here. We canst ride across Father's lands to the Ash Levels and sit ourselves down beside the bank of the little River Stour. Grant me at least forty minutes. I shall ask Tripp to saddle my mare, Dot, and tell my parents that I need to exercise Dot and am going riding for a few hours. Be patient, my love, for I shall be as quick as 'tis possible to be.'

With her promise made she turned, clutching her *Book of Common Prayer*, and hurried back to John Cartwright and her mother, Dyonise, to free them from the gossip of her father's neighbouring yeoman farmer. She reminded her parents that their patient manservant, Tripp, had been waiting an excessively long time with the piebald and they should be on their way back to Twitham. Elizabeth's powers of persuasion had an undoubted effect on her parents, for they soon bade goodbye to their neighbour and several local villagers, before mounting the steep steps, assisted by Tripp, to settle themselves in the trap. With a crack or two of his whip Tripp set the pony in motion, and squire, mother and daughter returned to Twitham Farm.

She came on her black mare, Dot, riding side-saddle. It was the custom for women to ride aside, to retain modesty and keep their maidenhood intact. Elizabeth yearned to ride astride. Riding aside in a saddle chair with slipper stirrup restricted the rider to walking and trotting the horse. Galloping was dangerous when aside. Her golden hair hung to the bottom of her straight back, flowing loosely over a snug bodice. She had changed to a knee-length linen skirt. Wedge-heeled buckled leather shoes adorned her feet. The skirt revealed more than a usual amount of calf, which aroused her sweetheart, who had waited so patiently for her return.

Jack helped Elizabeth dismount from her mare. They embraced and kissed hungrily and searchingly, as first-time lovers do. She was aware of and excited by his hard-probing manhood as they squeezed tightly together. She had lived around farm animals of every description, since her birth, and was fully aware of the function of an erect male and how he might perform. Jack tied the mare to his own steed, remounted Acorn, then reached down to pull Elizabeth up into the saddle in front of him. She felt his firmness against her body as they trotted across the meadowlands. Elizabeth directed him downwards to the Ash Levels, a vast flat area of divided, rich pasturelands, which bordered the clear waters of the River Stour and stretched between the villages of Richborough on the east coast and west to Pluck's Gutter.

They found a quiet spot on the bank of the Stour surrounded by reed mace, dismounted and tethered the horses to a willow tree. The crystal waters ran clear over long strands of water weed, where trout and grayling hung in lines hugging the riverbed against the rapid flow of the eddies. Jack spread his blanket over the short grass. They kissed, cuddled and released passionate, pent-up love. Elizabeth was twenty-seven. She had kept her maidenhood intact. Jack was gentle but she yearned to have him within her. She spread her legs willingly and guided the tip of his rampancy to her opening, then, clasping his firm buttocks with both hands she thrust herself upon the sword of her Cavalier and gasped in relief as her hymen gave way. His full length ran into her, exploding in a spasm of pulsating jerks. They clung tightly together in release of the sexual tension which had racked them constantly since the day they first met in Canterbury. Jack eased her breasts from her bodice and sucked upon sweet erect nipples. His semi-rigid member became firm again. He pumped her slowly until they orgasmed together. Her skirt was stained by the loss of virginity. It would need a surreptitious wash when she returned home. Elizabeth felt reborn. She decided there and then she would ride astride her pony, Dot, and gallop in the wind, like any normal human being should do. Folk might draw their own conclusions as to why she no longer rode her pony aside and why she had ordered a new leather saddle to be made. Jack was ready for her again. She kissed him tenderly and told him not to be so greedy. In truth, she felt a burning within, where she had so hungrily speared herself upon his taut erection. Jack was concerned by the wound he had caused. Elizabeth giggled and promised no restriction next time they met, but they needed to be careful not to get her pregnant prior to the announcement of their betrothal.

'The answer to thy concerns is for ye to marry me, Lizzy. Then I canst make thee pregnant many times. The sins of the flesh will present nay bounds when locked in holy matrimony.'

'Pray, let us get married soon, Jack. 'Tis safe for ye to cometh over and stay here at Twitham now the wars are almost concluded. We hath seen only a few Roundhead troops in this area.'

'Best give it a bit more time, Lizzy. But our love is not platonic – we canst nay wait forever.'

'Give me the letter ye brought for me, Jack. I need to retain some sweet memento of thee.'

He fumbled deep in his saddle bag and found it with the wax seal intact. He grinned and said, 'It seems I was mine own messenger this day after all, Lizzy. Open it after I hath bade farewell, my love, for 'tis getting late. I must ride with ye to Twitham. Thy parents will be wondering where thou hast got to. It is well after six o'clock by way of the sun's path. I must make tracks. It will be nigh on dark before I get back to Frognal. I wish my visit could last forever, Lizzy. Before long it shall be so. I wilt see ye again in two weeks from now, mine love, as planned.'

'Ay, my sweet Cavalier. Ye hath given me plenty to remember ye by upon thy visit this day. I shalt closely treasure the introduction thou hast giveth me to secret parts of ye I never dreamt existed, my bold lover! Ye hath made me tingle in places long forgotten. I shall find difficulty sleeping tonight. I shalt pray morning never comes, for I wilt imagine, as I lay in mine feather bed, thy lusty sword be inserted safely in its scabbard and we shalt make love all night long!'

Jack chuckled and kissed her many times on her lips and eyes before responding with a grin, 'Ay lass, and I hath nibbled upon the sweetest rosebuds, and stolen and tasted the most perfect, largest, juiciest plum *veneris* in the whole of the Garden of Kent. I canst nay wait to serve ye again and again, *ad infinitum*, for ever and ever, world without end – Amen!'

Jack paused. His broad grin faded away, whereupon his face took on a more serious look.

'You will see from mine letter that I am nay planning to fight again under the banner of King Charles. Symon and I hath given our all for the Royalist cause, but some of the mercenaries the King appointed prior to and after Naseby hath been of dubious religion and integrity. Even in defeat the King has poured scorn upon Parliament, Fairfax and Cromwell, and hast instigated the Scottish and others to fight for his return to the throne in return for Presbyterianism. Even now, if he strove to be a smidgeon conciliatory, I am sure his return to the throne might still be possible. But the King will nay give an inch. Fairfax and Cromwell's New Model Army hath overthrown the Royalist cause now. I think the King will be imprisoned for the rest of his life.'

'Oh, Jack, I do so wish these civil wars were concluded forever. If only the Roundheads were gone from Kent, we could get on with our normal everyday lives. We could get married and be happy forever after. I shall pray for that moment every day, until it comes true for us.'

He assisted her onto her aside saddle, mounted Acorn, and they trotted back from the levels side by side. They walked their mounts the last short distance, holding outstretched hands. When they reached the track which led to Twitham Farm, Jack leaned over Acorn and kissed her long and hard in farewell. They vowed to meet each other every two weeks at the same rendezvous, come fair weather or foul. Jack turned and called to her over his shoulder,

'Remember me, Lizzy, mine own darling girl, until we meet again in two weeks from now.'

'Pray, how could I ever forget any part of thy wonderful anatomy, Jack?' she shouted after him.

He turned again and again to smile and wave goodbye. She returned his waving, until he had gone from sight. She cherished the stinging sensation left between her thighs, proud of the pleasure he had derived from her ripe plum, as he called it. A burden had been lifted from her.

*

Back at Claxfeldestane, old Johis had passed away. Windows were blacked out in the old house as a mark of deep respect for the well-aged gentleman. At James' request, across the road in Frognal, Jack busied himself manufacturing an oak coffin and lining it with quality spun fleece cloth. Ornate brass lifting rings were being fitted when James called to see the carpenter.

'Well, James, doth thee think this resting box will serve the old gentleman proud?' asked Jack.

'Ye hath made a magnificent job of the coffin, Jack. The figure in the wood stands out well. 'Twill be heavy to lift, being 'tis of good solid English oak and accounting for its brasswork.'

'Ay! Take the weight at one end and try it for thyself, dear cousin. 'Twill take four stout men to bear the combined weight of this wood and mine uncle within, though he be but a feather.'

'Well, cousin, with thine agreement, one of those stout men will be thee, Jack, along with myself, and Laurence and Stephen, my younger brothers. They both pull full-size yew long bows, so there will be plenty of muscle. I think between us we will manage the task well enough.'

'I shall be honoured to be a pall-bearer, James. Thou knowest well how much I admired my uncle Johannes. The coffin is ready for us to carry across to the house now, James. We canst place it across two chairs and lay his body within. When is the church service to be held?'

'I hath arranged for it to be next Wednesday at St Peter and St Paul, Lynsted. We leave Claxfeldestane at a quarter past eleven o'clock and carry him from Claxfield down the side lane, through Palmery's gate to the church. I hath paid ten marc to the church for a priest to sing for his soul and for the souls of all good Christians, and to sing again in the space of a quarter of one year and for the quarters of four years thereafter. His wishes will be honoured.'

Warm rain drizzled down that Wednesday as they set out to carry old Johis to his final resting place. They walked bareheaded along the lane which linked the church to Claxfield. Most of the villagers joined the cortege or turned out to pay last respects to their popular reeve. Johis' wife, Maria, was too poorly to travel. In addition to the coat of arms, a shroud of fine linen, worked in silks, was draped over the coffin. It depicted the family crest, a red dragon's scaly head dripping blood from its mouth and with a jewel-encrusted crown about the neck. The motto 'Dum spiro spero' was plain for all to see. Baron Christopher Roper and his family were already there in the front pews, awaiting the arrival of the former reeve. Johannes Greenstreet had been the baron's right hand over many years. Reeve Johis was in fact the baron's dearest and most faithful friend. Jack and James looked at each other, with more than a twinkle in their eyes, as they passed through the sturdy church door, riddled with Roundhead musket shot. The pallbearers set the heavy coffin down on the trestles provided. Despite the rain it was a hot September day and the men had sweated buckets carrying the heavy oak box.

After the service, Johannes was buried within the confines of Lynsted church. A ledger stone was cemented into the floor of the nave. The wake was held at Claxfeldestane, attended by family and friends. Dressed in his best finery, Baron Roper addressed the gathering:

'We shall mourn the loss of our dear relative and friend. Johannes lived longer than most folk can ever expect to live in their short lifespans. Born in the reign of our sovereign lady Elizabeth I, he hast seen the death of a queen and King James I. Yea, and very nearly a second king, for I hast great fear for the survival of Charles I. Many now call for his head.'

The baron paused in contemplation before continuing the eulogy concerning his lost friend:

'Come to think of it, my own head may nay be too secure upon my shoulders, for I am the constant prey of Commonwealth commissioners who believe I hold arms at Lodge Lynsted. These soldiers never find any arms, though, for the arms are better placed! Nevertheless, the time for bearing sword and musket against our own people is over. I see little purpose to it now they hold the King in custody. Nay wishing to digress further, I want to say how much I shall miss my good friend Johis. The reeve hast been my mainstay ever since I took over as Baron of Teynham Manor. Notwithstanding that, I am happy to say that his son James here hast taken over the task of reeve with equal lustre. He hast re-scribed the manor rolls and keeps manor records with great competence of stewardship. His script and font are exemplary. We remain in good hands until the outcome of the civil war is finally put to bed.'

The baron stood aside. James praised his father and recalled his many kindnesses. That done, he offered thanks to the Lord. Afterwards the funeral party was invited to a wake at Claxfield.

*

The Sunday after the funeral proved to be one of the last hot days of 1648. Jack set off for Staple and met Elizabeth after morning church service, in the same manner as before. They cantered down to the Ash Levels, then raced their steeds along the riverbank. She sat astride her black mare, Dot, and felt the warm breeze in her hair as they galloped to their secluded place beside the clear-flowing River Stour. They embraced, stripped naked and made passionate love under the late September sun. Afterwards they cooled their ardour by plunging into the cold river to splash and bathe, shrieking loudly as they were enveloped by the sudden change in temperature, and sending duck, coot and moorhen scooting for cover in the reed beds. They left the breathtaking water of the river, and dried each other with a large woollen sheet cloth, brought by Elizabeth for the occasion. The hot rays of the sun began to warm and dry their bodies. She leaned over him to fondle warmth back into his retracted scrotum, then massaged the flaccidity of his chilled manhood back to life. The long index finger of her other hand trailed through his thick damp pubic hair and downwards to trace the ugly scar left by the billhook in his upper inner thigh. Involuntarily his phallus enlarged, forcing itself beyond elasticity – inflamed, taut, fully stretched and out of control. He was ready for love again, and she more than ready to receive him within her. They continued to explore the intricacies and intrigue of each other's naked body as they made plans for their future married life together.

Elizabeth informed Jack that her parents had begun to suspect something was going on, when she went to order the leather astride saddle to suit her small firm seat. An argument ensued and her stepfather, John Cartwright, intimated she was demonstrating the act of a loose woman. He insisted she was not being virtuous in protecting herself, by keeping herself intact for the men seeking her affection and hand in marriage. She had told her parents that she was twenty-seven years of age, insisting she was no longer a child under their control, and most certainly not planning to remain *virgo intacta* forever, just to suit their needs. Her stepfather repeatedly told her that the minister was the best catch she was likely to make, and the fracas ended by Cartwright pleading with her to marry Emanuel Witherstone, and to make him and her mother, Dyonise, happy. Elizabeth had stormed out of their presence shouting out loudly:

"Tis too late for thy plans, I hath given myself to Jack Greenstreet and am going to marry him.'

Silence now reigned in the Cartwright house. Nobody was on speaking terms except via Tripp.

18

MARRIAGE PLANS

A few weeks later the weather turned autumnal. It was early November in 1648, and the first fall of leaves had already carpeted the ground, following a hard frost. Stiff westerly winds tore away the remaining rich-coloured leaves, which had clung rigorously to tree and shrub. Dressed in breeches with a long top cape draped from her shoulders, Elizabeth was waiting for him in the field at the back of the church. Jack had also donned a warmer outfit. He dismounted and helped her down from her mare. She shivered in the change of temperature and Jack held her tight. One thing that hadn't cooled was their ardour. They pushed their cloaks apart and kissed passionately before she spoke, gazing upwards into his hazel-grey eyes.

'Mine parents hath become quite conciliatory since we last met, Jack. They want us to go to the farm for luncheon.

Ye may nay take too kindly to such invitation, of that I am aware, but it wouldst please me very much if ye came back with me. I doth believe I now understand my stepfather's reasons for being so cold towards our union. He explained to me that he found ye unsuitable because of thy constant need to fight in so many battles and skirmishes over the Royalist cause. Whilst he too is a Royalist, he knoweth well the death rate be extremely high. Daddy was sorely feared ye might be killed, or mortally wounded, leaving me destitute and unable to fulfil his agenda of having a male child to inherit the Cartwright title. He appeared relieved when I told him ye had resolved to withdraw from fighting the Royalist cause. I hast made my parents aware of our bond. Undoubtedly, they assume our consummation. My stepfather makes nay secret of his desire to secure a grandson to inherit his estate lands when he passes on. He wishes to come to an agreement about giving such a child the alias name of Cartwright.'

'Pray, I am nay too sure about that, Elizabeth. Forsooth, I had hoped to keep my family dynasty going strong in name. After all, I shall nay be marrying Cartwright's true blood daughter.'

'There are two thoughts about that, my love. One thought is there is still a bounty upon thy head and the Greenstreet name is known by the Commonwealth commissioners, albeit such persecution may eventually be pardoned, overlooked, or simply forgotten. I shall live in hope of that thought. Even though baptised with thine name, it may prove best if our son does nay initially bear thy name. Meanwhile, my second thinking is that once both parents hath passed on, the alias name of Cartwright canst be dropped and thine own name restored back to thy son, should thou provide for us a son, that is. I mean, after my parents' deaths we canst renege on any indenture made and revert to thy own good and genuine name – our son's true name of Greenstreet. His baptism will be entered into church records and be proof of his real birth name. That way, our son will own many lands. He will be a rich man in this part of Kent.'

'I always heard tale that women are plotters, Elizabeth Church. Now I am convinced of the truth of it. First, we hath to produce a son. Doth ye ever sleep at night, thou sexy witch?'

'Pray, somebody hast to make plans, and it seems to me that men are nay so good at it.' He slipped a hand down her riding breeches and pinched both cheeks of her naked backside hard.

'Ye art a cruel brute, sir. Beware, I shall hath my own back on ye when ye least expect it.'

They mounted their steeds and rode to Twitham Farm in an air of mutual agreement.

Cartwright's farm was much as Wat had described it to Jack. A long gravel track took them to the main house sited near a large pond, which rippled with duck, moorhen and dabchick. The geese half ran and half flew at them as they dismounted from their steeds. Tripp drove off the birds with a stick and then took charge of the horses. Chickens ran between their legs and several loose goats approached, hoping for something tasty. An assortment of horses and ponies grazed in adjoining paddocks, whilst a magnificently powerful, brown-grey-coloured bull dominated its own strongly fenced pasture. The long farmhouse was built of tuck-pointed red brickwork, with high divided sash windows, each sash containing rhythmical glazed windowpanes. A centralised stone portico with generous steps plainly declared itself as the main entrance. Unlike Wat, who had been ushered into the side kitchen parlour opposite the pond, Elizabeth proudly took Jack's arm and directed him to the front portico. She pulled a brass knob to ring a bell. A butler she addressed as Epps opened the oak door and took their cloaks. Elizabeth dismissed Epps and excitedly directed Jack into a grand reception room.

John and Dyonise Cartwright had obviously been waiting for them. They rose from leather-clad carved armchairs and walked over to greet their daughter with an embrace and a peck on the cheek. A pair of lean, grey, long-haired hounds padded behind, occasionally wagging thin dangling tails. Cartwright called them to heel, referring to them as Merryboy and Younker.

'Mother, this is Jack Greenstreet, who I hath told ye about on countless occasions, haven't I?'

Another short embrace, combined with a peck on the cheek was issued to Jack by Dyonise.

'Father, ye need nay introduction to Jack. He is the very same man we met at Canterbury last Christmas. The Cavalier who chivalrously conducted us safely to our carriage and bravely brought that pickpocket ruffian to book on thy behalf, saving ye much grief from pilferage.'

Cartwright gripped Jack's hand firmly. He forced a half-smile, displaying yellowing teeth.

'Ay, ye did us a great favour on that momentous day, Jack. I remain indebted to ye for that.'

Jack, who at Canterbury only had eyes for the stepdaughter, now looked Cartwright up and down. He was an affable enough fellow: rosy-cheeked, small-nosed, tall, portly with silver hair, dressed in brown breeches over pale blue stockings. He wore a white linen shirt with wide collar attached and loose bellowed sleeves, all edged in lace, over which he sported a cherry-red velvet waistcoat with gold buttons. He was obviously a yeoman of considerable wealth. Cartwright beckoned Jack to the fireplace. A roaring fire took the chill off the room.

'Ye canst see I am a man of considerable wealth, Jack. I doth nay lack the odd crown or two. I am the squire of these parts, and as such command respect within the local parish communities. I understand that ye wish to marry my stepdaughter, Elizabeth. I offer nay objection, now that I hear ye hath vowed to refrain from engaging in further battles and local Royalist skirmishes. I am aware that the commissioners seek thy whereabouts, but, in truth, I hath seen few Roundheads or commissioners in our neck of the woods since the capture of the King. If ye came to settle here, nobody wouldst ascertain ye art a wanted man. I could fit out a nice barn for thy workshop, to enable thee to go about thy business of carpentry and joinery without hindrance. I myself hath plenty of projects for thee, and I know the local churches hath areas requiring attention, yea, and many others. Ye mentioned to Elizabeth thy intention to make some fine furniture for your new home together. Such talent is a feather in thy cap.'

Cartwright paused his rehearsed address to acknowledge the arrival of a silver bowl of hot punch, brought to the room by Epps the butler. Elizabeth bade Epps set it down on a side table and informed him she would serve the refreshment herself. In the event, her mother, Dyonise, ladled helpings of the mulled steaming brew into four thick glasses and handed them around. Jack, still a trifle chilled from his morning ride from Frognal, found the brew to be quite alcoholic, herbal and acceptably warming. Cartwright blew upon the hot punch, took a couple of sips, then put down his glass and continued the address he was intent upon finishing.

'Now then, Jack, if I may be so bold, for ye are soon to be my son-in-law, are ye nay? Elizabeth informs me thou art the beneficiary of considerable means of thy own?'

'Yea, enough to purchase property with appurtenances of mine own, and to keep the wolf from the door for a little while,' agreed the future son-in-law. 'I shalt retain my carpentry business.'

'Quite so, quite so,' replied the future father-in-law. 'But ye hath nay need to spend thy money yet awhile. It is my wish that ye live here in one section of this large farmhouse, and to utilise the servants as ye both so wish. That way ye canst save thy cash for a rainy day or for some future occasion. I shall be happy to finance my daughter's wedding costs. Ye need nay concern thyselves with any of that. It is my duty, as Elizabeth's lawful guardian, to so do.'

Jack made to respond, but Cartwright was a step ahead and held up a hand to act as barrier.

'Ye dost nay need to respond this moment. 'Tis but an option we offer ye both. Dyonise and I do nay wish to impose upon any plans ye make as a couple. Ye may well hath ideas of thy own. Carefully think ye upon the offer. Neither doth we require payment in return, other than any recompense ye may choose to make via income from future work. I wouldst leave that to thy good self. On the other hand, I hath nay sons of my own to inherit and manage my lands. Therefore, I must think ahead in respect of future inheritance matters, for I am rapidly advancing in years, and hath need to make a last will and testament to benefit my successors.'

Jack listened carefully to what his future in-law said. At last John Cartwright was getting to the crux of the matter. It was exactly as Elizabeth had intimated earlier.

'To that end, Jack – and this really concerns ye alone – to that end, I request that thy first-born son, should we all be so blessed, be named Cartwright by lawful indenture, so that he may be named in my will as the sole benefactor of my lands and appurtenances. John Cartwright alias Greenstreet wouldst be appropriate. That should nay prove to be too difficult for thee, for thy own first name is John, albeit thou art known as Jack. The future of thine son, should he bear my name, wouldst therefore be set in stone. He will be born into riches, most people canst only dream about.'

Cartwright had finally concluded his lengthy address. Silence reigned for some while, before Jack responded. The long-case clock, in one corner of the room, clunked loudly, and the quietness was deafening. Jack exchanged glances with his intended and dwelt for a while on what she had told him earlier in the day. Eventually the future son-in-law broke the silence.

'Well, sir, I understand thee well enough. I will discuss the issue carefully with Elizabeth and will go along with her desire, for I hath nay wish to upset her in any way. If her thinking is on similar lines to thine own, I shall nay seek to obstruct her or thee, nor stand in the way of any future son's progress, for 'tis a difficult enough life that we all strive to live in these hard times.'

Jack paused to drink down the remainder of his punch, then made a surprise statement:

'When I look at the miserable state of this country, I often wonder whether we might be entirely irresponsible to introduce children into this cauldron of never-ending civil wars, disease, pestilence and evil influences. I know that statement is somewhat blasphemous and not in accordance with the thinking of the Church, nor the instruction of God. We are, of course, put on earth to ensure the continuity of mankind. Ministers will always argue that point. Yet when ye hath fought battles and witnessed thousands of men hacked, impaled or shot to pieces, and seen blood shed on the scale I hath seen, it drives one's thinking in another direction. My point is, I doubt whether an alias name will hath much effect upon the assumed child's development. The lands he inherits will nay restrain him if he is strong-willed and seeks another line of direction. If he takes after me, he will probably tack on a different course in any case.'

'Ay, I understand thy feelings in that respect, Jack, but I need to take a chance on him,' said Cartwright. "'Tis my life's ambition to pass my estate on to kin with my own family name.'

They were interrupted by the long-case clock, which suddenly burst into life, to render forth chimes before striking the hour. Dyonise, who had been listening intently, also burst into life, directing them out of the reception room and down the long hallway for luncheon. Elizabeth took Jack's arm and they followed her parents into the formal dining room, where Epps the butler took charge of matters, conducting them to their seating and opening a linen napkin to place upon their laps. Herbal game soup was ladled into dishes for starters, followed by prime roasted beef with suet pudding. The meal was nothing unusual to Jack, who had been used to a similar style of living at Woodlands, prior to joining the Kentish insurrections. William of Maidstone's estates were even vaster than John Cartwright's. Jack opened the conversation:

"Tis a wonderful clock thou hast in thy reception room, sir.'

'Yea, 'tis a primitive, invented by my good friend and clockmaker William Clement. It is the first pendulum clock of its kind and keeps wonderful time. He will be marketing them within the next year or two. Elizabeth calls it a grandfather clock. 'Tis, without doubt a fine invention. Perhaps ye might like a long-case clock for a wedding present for thyselves. It could be a wedding present from myself and Dyonise? Think about it. Will Clement tells me he has refinements to make yet, to perfect the mechanism. Such future advancements are a good reason for bringing children into this world, Jack. 'Tis a time of golden opportunity as far as discovery and invention are concerned, of that I hath little doubt.'

Cartwright also made a valid argument. In truth, he could not resist a retaliatory dig at his future son-in-law, although Cartwright himself had not witnessed the bloody battles and huge losses of life Jack had seen on the battlefields and to which Jack had previously referred.

Mostly the chat over the luncheon table, and throughout the rest of the afternoon, was devoted to Elizabeth and revolved around the wedding arrangements, her dress and the magnificent wedding breakfast, to be planned by her mother, Dyonise. They set the date for the wedding as 26 December 1649, just over one year, which gave ample time to make plans and for Jack to move to Twitham Farm to set up his carpentry shop. Jack said he would approach his cousin James to act as best man, and from his side he would invite Symon and family, and Wat.

After lunch Jack set off for Frognal. Elizabeth accompanied him as far as Wingham church.

At Wingham church, they tethered their horses, then followed the stone flag path, with its steep bank on one side, walking beneath the yews to the church entrance. The church dated back to the Normans, with an amalgam of additions. They entered the vestibule and lifted the heavy latch of the thick oak gothic door. Monuments were evident to the Oxenden family in a south transept chapel, and to Sir Thomas Palmer, 1st Baronet, 1625, in the north transept. Elizabeth pointed to a monument to Charles Tripp, who died in 1624. She grinned and resolved to ask Tripp the manservant whether he was related. In the nave they held hands, then walked down the red and black tiled floor of the centre aisle, over ledger stones, to the foremost pew. They knelt in supreme quietness and said a prayer together, then gazed through the chancel to the altar and were filled with holy rapture. Elizabeth turned to him and looked into his eyes.

'It is here, Jack. This is where I want to marry ye, here at St Mary the Virgin, Wingham.'

'And so ye shall, my own true love. Let us find the minister and make the arrangements now.'

They went from the church to the adjoining vicarage and requested a brief meeting with the vicar. When the minister ascertained it was John Cartwright's daughter, he bade them both enter his house. The vicar confirmed he was prepared to marry them at St Mary's on the day of their choosing, even though the family of Squire Yeoman Cartwright usually attended the adjoining church at Staple. Both churches came under the vicar's jurisdiction. Twitham lay between the two churches, in the parish of Wingham. The minister was happy to welcome Jack and Elizabeth to St Mary's, on the understanding that any children born from their union would be baptised at that church. Further, their children would be required to attend the same church for religious instruction. Arrangements made, the two intendeds parted company and rode to their respective abodes full of contentment with life and looking excitedly to the future.

The remaining days of 1648 passed by quickly enough. Jack and Elizabeth met frequently at Twitham Farm and spent much of the festive season together. They rode over to James at Claxfeldestane and visited Symon and his family, who were pleased to acquaint themselves with their cousin's intended wife. Marion fussed over Elizabeth as if she had known her all her life. James, who was equally pleased his cousin and firm friend had at last found a partner, confirmed he would be honoured to be best man at the wedding. Then Jack and Elizabeth made a shopping trip to Canterbury. This time without mishap and without father-in-law.

Following the Christmas festivities, Jack informed Elizabeth he had a surprise for her. On a fine afternoon he had Tripp saddle the horses and bade her ride with him to their secret spot on the Ash Levels. The sun sparkled on the crystal waters of the Stour as Jack unveiled his surprise, which had lain secreted in a reed bed. He pulled out a long punt and dragged it down the bank into the transparent waters of the river. Elizabeth could barely retain her excitement. Jack explained how he had purchased the punt from boat builders in Ash. Under his guidance, they had towed the craft up the river to the reed bed. He helped her get seated, then pushed off with a long pole. He punted her over a mile upriver and back, his hands blistering on the long pole as he worked it in the gravel bed, between the water weed, passing mute swans and an assortment of ducks, whilst listening to her contented peals of laughter. The punt was her favourite Christmas present and the source of many happy river trips for many years to come.

On 13 December, the 'Rump Parliament' broke off any further negotiations with the King. In mid-December, the New Model Army had Charles I moved from Windsor to London.

19

EXECUTION, JANUARY 1649

Supposedly the puritanical members of Parliament were true to their mandate and did not celebrate Christmas. If they did, they appeared to have had no recess, because several meetings were held over the Christmas period. On 1 January 1649, Parliament voted to put the King on trial forthwith. He was accused of being a tyrant, traitor and murderer. He was, according to the Rump Parliament, both a public and implacable enemy to the Commonwealth of England. The House of Lords refused to pass the bill, and Royal Assent was naturally lacking, but the Rump Parliament, as it was known, carried on regardless. The King was to be tried by 135 judges. In fact, only sixty-eight turned up for the trial! There were plenty of members who did not wish to see a King put on trial. Most of those had been identified and were prevented from entering Parliament by Colonel Thomas Pride and his soldiers of foot, backed up by Nathaniel Rich's Regiment of Horse. Pride stood at the top of the staircase with a list, probably drawn up by Oliver Cromwell himself. His troops arrested forty-five members and 146 were turned away – mostly Presbyterians. This undemocratic act became known as 'Pride's purge'. The only people allowed in were those Cromwell thought truly supported the trial. Of this Rump Parliament of forty-six men (who supported Cromwell) only twenty-six voted to try King Charles Stuart. For, even though they supported Cromwell, there was no obvious desire to put a King on trial for his life.

After the first civil war, the Parliamentarians accepted that the King, albeit wrong, had been able to justify his fight. Parliament agreed that Charles might still be entitled to limited powers as King, under a new constitutional agreement. But even whilst in captivity, the King had gone on provoking and had instigated a second civil war, leading to unjustifiable bloodshed. Charles Stuart had entered into a secret 'Engagement' treaty with the Scots, which was considered a particularly unpardonable, prodigious treason by Cromwell, more than any other that had gone before. Cromwell could not pardon the King's attempt to vassalage the English to a foreign nation – viz Scotland. The King was unappeasable. In waging war against Parliament, the King had caused thousands of men to die. Final estimated reports were close to 85,000 men killed in the two civil wars and probably 100,000 men dying from war-related wounds and disease. The population of England was thought to be 5.1 million about that time.

A high court of justice was set up and the elected chief judge, John Bradshaw, read out the indictment: the King was accused of treason against England and of using his powers to pursue his own interest rather than the good of England, and that he hath maliciously levied war against Parliament and the people therein represented. That the wicked designs, wars and evil practices of him, the said Charles Stuart, had been, and were carried on for the advancement and upholding of personal interest of will, power and pretended prerogative to himself and his family against the public interest, common right, justice and peace of the people of the nation. The indictment held him guilty of all the treasons, murders, rapines, burnings, spoils, desolations, damages and mischiefs to the nation, acted and committed during the wars.

The trial began on 20 January 1649 in Westminster Hall and was not without moments of high drama. When Solicitor General John Cook rose to announce the indictment, the King attempted to stop him, firstly by tapping on his shoulder with his cane and then by poking him with it. When ignored, and unable to shut Cook up, the incensed King Charles struck the Solicitor General across the shoulders with a blow so forceful that the ornate silver engraved tip of the cane broke off and rolled down Cook's gown to clatter and ring upon the floor between them. Nobody moved to pick it up. In the hush that followed, Charles stooped down and retrieved it himself. When eventually given the opportunity to speak, Charles refused to engage in a plea, stating, with some arrogance, that no court had jurisdiction over its monarch. In all truth he did not recognise the court, believing that his authority to rule was the divine right of kings, given to him by Almighty God when he was crowned and anointed. He said that the power wielded by those trying him was simply by force of arms. Charles insisted that the trial was illegal and that an impeachment could not lie against a king. In his own words he asked, 'I wouldst know by what power I am called hither. I wouldst know by what authority, I mean lawful authority?' Charles maintained that the House of Commons, on its own, could not try anybody, and refused to enter a plea, one way or the other.

The parliamentary court proceeded as if the King had pleaded guilty (*pro confesso*), which was the standard legal practice in such a case, where the defendant refused to plead. Thirty witnesses were summonsed, although some were later excused. The King was not present to hear the evidence against him, and he was therefore unable to question witnesses. At a public session on Saturday 27 January 1649, the King was declared guilty and sentenced to death. His sentence read: 'That the court being satisfied that he, Charles Stuart, was guilty of the crimes of which he was accused, did judge him tyrant, traitor, murderer and public enemy of the good people of the nation, to be put to death by the severing of the head from the body.' Sixty-seven commissioners rose to their feet in agreement to the sentence, and signatures were collected for his death warrant. The warrant was signed by fifty-nine of the commissioners, including two who had not been present when the sentence was passed. When the judgment of the court was announced, Charles finally started to defend himself, but was told that his chance had gone. The King of England was bundled out of the court by the guarding soldiers, the date for his execution set for 30 January – just three days following the public session in which he was sentenced. The Rump Parliament, led by Cromwell, had had enough and they meant business.

King Charles I was beheaded in front of the banqueting house of the Palace of Whitehall on 30 January 1649. It was a bitterly cold day and Charles had dressed wearing two heavy shirts so that he might not shiver and appear to be afraid. He was both self-righteous and arrogant, but he never lacked bravery. He addressed the crowd that had gathered to see their King die, and declared that he had desired the liberty and freedom of the people as much as any:

> "...but I must tell ye that their liberty and freedom consist in having of government those laws by which their life and their goods may be most of their own. It is nay their having a share in the government sirs; that is nothing pertaining to them. A subject and a sovereign are clear different things. And, therefore, until they do that, I mean that you do put the people in that liberty, as I say, certainly they will never enjoy themselves. Sirs, it was for this that now I come here. If I wouldst hath given way to an arbitrary way, for to hath all laws changed according to the power of the sword, I needed nay to hath come here, and therefore, I tell ye (and pray God it nay be laid to thine charge) that I am the martyr of the people."

Thereafter the King spoke quietly to the masked executioner, telling him that he would say but short prayers with the bishop. When he thrust out his hands, that was the time to strike.

*

The well-honed blade of the axe swept through the air and severed the oak log in half with one hefty blow. The divisions were stood on edge, then quartered, the pieces thrown onto a growing stockpile. Jack was sweating from the brow. He no longer felt the biting cold of the frosty morning atmosphere. A peripheral glance saw James standing by, grim of face.

'Good morrow, good cousin. What bids ye to cross the road to mine abode so early this winter's day? Hath thee come to help me cut fuel? Pray tell me, why dost thou hath such a doleful face, James?'

'I bear grave news, Jack. Ye are nay the only person who hast been wielding a sharp-bladed axe. A London tinker called on me just minutes ago. He issued forth the most terrible news. Our King is dead, executed outside the banqueting suite at the Palace of Whitehall yesterday. The travelling tinker watched the execution. He informed me that His Majesty placed his head on the block. After a short while, he stretched forth his hands. At that signal, the executioner severed his head from his body with one blow. The head, after being held up and showed to the people, was placed in a coffin covered in black velvet, together with his warm torso, and carried into his lodging. An unholy wailing erupted from the watching crowd of people. The groan was apparently heard all over London city. His Majesty's splattered blood was taken up by divers for different ends: by some as a relic of a martyr, by others as a trophy of villainy.'

'Ay, James, 'tis a pretty picture thou painteth. Many of us anticipated his end coming, of course. For myself, I am nay surprised by the event. We true Royalists hath witnessed the King to be his own worst enemy. Truly King Charles was self-righteous, arrogant, vain and unscrupulous in so many ways. He made bad decisions and created the unwanted deaths of too many good Englishmen. In the end, King Charles Stuart alienated not only Parliament but his subjects. Now it hast led to his own death and the abolition of the monarchy. Where are we heading now, James? That is my forlorn question. Exactly where will a puritanical republic lead us to?'

'Yea, 'tis indeed a cheerless proposition ye pose, Jack. It seems Charles' problems revolved firstly around religion and the Catholic question, and then money. His marriage to the Roman Catholic Henrietta Maria did nay please his Protestant subjects and led to suspicions of his motives. Yea, and he totally misgauged the sentiment of his Scottish subjects when he attempted to impose an Anglican form of worship on their mainly Presbyterian population.'

'I doth understand, James, that neither General Thomas Fairfax, nor his wife, Ann, desired to take part in the trial of the King. Fairfax is an honourable Yorkshireman, and although Oliver Cromwell has taken over full control of the republic, Cromwell wouldst do well to remember that it was Black Tom's disciplined fighting force which inflicted final defeat over the Royalist armies. If it was not for Fairfax and his New Model Army, the King might still reign over us, and Cromwell's head be the one upon the block for thy worthy tinker to herald news about.'

The two friends paused to stack the split logs under dry shelter. Jack invited James into the warmth of the cottage, found two glasses and poured out double tots of *eau de vie* cogniacke.

'Here's to us, James, and to a Happy New Year! But watch out for the Roundheads. They art in nay mood for reconciliation just yet. I hear tale of many repercussions, shootings, burnings and executions. Hopefully 'twill end soon. Let us drink to more peaceful times, eh, cousin?'

'Yea, but I see little peace will come out of a declared Commonwealth. It is alien to the people of our nation. Heed me, for I warrant 'twill nay last long,' declared James.

20

AFTERMATH

In May 1649, the Rump Parliament abolished the monarchy and the House of Lords. A Council of State was appointed as an executive body, subordinate to the legislative House of Commons. England was finally declared a 'Republican Commonwealth and Free State'.

However, the execution of Charles I merely served to stimulate Scottish and Irish support for the King's son, Prince Charles. The Royalist garrison at Pontefract Castle refused to surrender. The castle lay mostly in ruins from cannon fire, but took two months, after the beheading of Charles I, to finally capitulate its stronghold. Parliament had the remains of Pontefract Castle demolished. The Parliamentarian cause and suppression was out of hand.

The Roundheads, garrisoned at Paynter's Farm,

Ospringe, under the command of Colonel Richard Browne, finally left Kent to join up with Cromwell's all-powerful New Model Army. The mighty army eliminated any threat that got in its way or challenged its authority. In May 1649, the army crushed a mutiny of 'Levellers' in Oxfordshire. Then in September, Cromwell took troops across the Irish Sea to Drogheda, and later Wexford, to subdue the rebellious Irish. More than 3,000 Irish defenders were slaughtered, but the Irish Royalist alliance was eventually subjugated. With no hope of help from Ireland, like his father before him Prince Charles agreed to impose Presbyterianism in England, in exchange for a Scottish army of support.

Further insurrection in Kent was thought unlikely now the King had been disposed of. Yet Kent was unlikely to turn in favour of the Commonwealth, and Royalist support continued to bubble away beneath the surface. Commissioners and Roundhead soldiers were frequently sent to Kent, to seek out and ensure no further uptake of arms. With the Parliamentarian garrison gone and no longer prevalent in Kent, the search for Jack Greenstreet, and many others with a bounty on their heads, faded away. Such persecutions finally disappeared for good.

Following the sentence of death and his father's sudden execution, the young Prince Charles, terrified and sickened by his father's demise and beheading, came to Kent to stay with known friends. Baron Christopher Roper granted him refuge. Later, he was looked after most lovingly by the baron's niece, Mary Roper, who founded the Benedictine abbey at Ghent. Mary was ill when Charles visited her. She received him privately. Charles expressed his gratitude for the comfort she gave him, as he mourned the death of his father, the late

King. Prince Charles never forgot the kindnesses shown by the Roper family. When Mary was taken ill and dying, some months later, Charles sent his own private physician to attend upon her.

Thus, the eventful year of 1649 drew towards its long and weary conclusion. The country, now a Commonwealth and Free State, was a country without a king, and really a country without a defined leader of any consequence and a country without a cause. Tensions and bickering started to develop in the House of Commons. Such strained parliamentary relationships needed resolving and rectifying swiftly, if matters were not to get out of control yet again.

There was one important event to recall at the end of that wearisome year. An event which was a joyful occasion. The wedding of Jack Greenstreet to Elizabeth Church was due to take place on the 26th day of December 1649 at the church of St Mary the Virgin, Wingham, Kent.

The Third Civil War

1649–1651

21

A MARRIAGE GATHERING BRINGS MORE
GOODWILL

At Claxfeldestane Jack spent a quiet but merry enough
Christmas Day with James, and James' aged mother, Maria.
Morning dawned to herald the day of the wedding. The two
men were up and about their ablutions soon after the cock had
crowed. The cousins had spent much of the previous morning
cleaning and grooming their steeds. Acorn and James' horse,
Swift, were pristine, their coats brushed, coarse manes combed,
brasses polished, and ribbons tied to well-carded glossy
swishing tails. The cousins were fitted out in best finery. They
departed from Claxfield looking decidedly eloquent and dandy,
though a little hungover from the consumption of much wine
the previous evening. Groom and best man looked picturesque.
They were similarly dressed in fawn breeches, matching

stockings, white silk shirts with lace collars, red waistcoats and matching woven woollen over-cloaks. Their brown crafted leather boots were highly polished, and brass buckles glinted in the morning light. Both men wore a single pigtail tied with red ribbon, to contain their flowing long hair. Swords hung at their sides. Dressed in their Sunday best, Symon and Marion arrived in a spruced-up cart pulled by two brown mares. Seated within the cart and jabbering with the excitement of the occasion, the children fired a stream of questions at their uncles, mostly concerning the wedding plans.

It was a nippy morning as the wedding cortege set off along Greenstreet, yet a glimpse of sunlight announced the start of a fine day. The weather was set fair for the time of year. Will Dix and John Caslock had got wind that Jack was getting married that day. The brewers were ready for the party of horse when it came into view. Will Dix raised a hand to halt the cortege as it made its way along the London Road, whilst Caslock came out from the brewhouse with a tray of drinks. He offered a stirrup tankard of best beer for the men, and ginger beer for Marion and the children. The brewers also presented a silver platter of warm spiced mincemeat pies, all of which the cousins and children demolished without dismounting. The beer acted well as 'hair of the dog'. The men called for refills. Jack thanked the brewers for their wishes, and they rode on towards Ospringe, where old Wat Harrys had arranged to join them. Once through the village muck, the train set off at a canter, creating a colourful scene as they passed wood and field – a spectacle that would have done justice to any painting to grace a man's wall.

Two horsemen waited at Wat's cottage, Moddilyon. Jack was surprised and delighted beyond all expectations, for holding the bridle of a horse, alongside old Wat, was his younger brother, Thomas. Both were spruced up and looking in their prime. Jack approached with some caution, seeking to clarify recognition and to ascertain that his youngest brother was not a spectre or simply a figment of his imagination, due to the previous night's overindulgence. He was relieved when Tom's face broke into the cheeky smile Jack recalled so well before the civil wars broke out. Jack was somewhat dumbstruck. Thomas stepped forth to speak:

'Since we last met, brother, I hath dwelt much on why I saved ye from death that cold day in the snow, and why ye chose nay to end my life at Woodlarks stables. I hath racked my brain, such as it is, and arrived at a sound answer. For was nay the motivation simply brotherly love? Ye nay more wanted to end my life than I wished to see thine own terminated at the hands of the Roundheads. Now that the wars art concluded, I hope we can come together again, and, if ye will hath me, my desire is to join thy colourful train and witness the union of thy marriage.'

Jack leapt down from Acorn, grinned at old Wat and embraced his brother in a lengthy bear hug. Pushing him back by the shoulders Jack looked deep into Tom's watering eyes. His own eyes had also misted up, causing difficulty in focusing on the face of his youngest brother.

'Ye always were the literate one, Tom. I could hath nay put it better if I tried for a hundred years. Though I hasten to say, whilst I agree we are declared a Republic, and the King lieth dead this day, I am afraid the life-sapping civil wars are nay yet resolved. Our country is too deeply embroiled in its past monarchies to be governed solely by Parliament for any length of time, I wager. But for ye and me 'tis indeed time to heal wounds. I am resolved nay to fight against my fellow countrymen ever again. I am overwhelmed ye hath come, Tom. Wat informed ye about my forthcoming nuptials nay doubt? We must make haste, for time is running short. I need to be at Wingham before noon, so mount ye all up and let us be on our way. I dare nay keep the good woman waiting on penalty of suffering much in consequence.'

Jack's last words caused everybody to ripple with laughter. He linked his hands together to form a step and lifted Wat onto his mount. The ever-lengthening train set off again for Wingham. Their loose jabbering was equal to the pilgrims' chatter in Chaucer's *Canterbury Tales*. Everybody had a story to tell, but none could be heard above the clatter of hooves and rattling wheels of the cart, and the party were unable to stop and listen with real intent. The main purpose was to get to the church on time. In that resolve they soon broke into a canter.

The bells of St Mary the Virgin, Wingham rang out as Jack's party arrived and hurriedly seated themselves in the pews. On the left-side aisle, family members of Cartwrights and Churches were already gathered. A pipe organ musician played quiet, soothing, background music.

Wingham had, so far, avoided the destruction of its pipe organ. Many Anglican churches had seen their organs and many works of art ripped out. Puritanical Parliament thought organs, music and indulgent works of art interfered with the piety of the Church and devotion to God. To them it detracted from religion, which every citizen should embrace without embellishment, particularly on the Sabbath day. Several changes had been made to the mid-seventeenth-century church. Now, appointed priests had to take all the services and were required to call out banns three Sundays ahead of any marriage. Up until this time, boys were legal for marriage at the age of fourteen and girls when only twelve, though marriage was no longer thought advisable at such young ages. Most marriages were arranged by parents. It was considered foolish to marry for love. These issues were not applicable in Jack and Elizabeth's case. They did marry for love and made their own arrangements. After all, they were several years older than the norm and came from society's upper echelons. One thing in common with many marriages of the time was Elizabeth's pregnancy. John Cartwright was well informed, and secretly excited about her state, particularly if it turned out to be a boy and satisfied his mindful plans. Up until the mid-seventeenth century, weddings were mostly held in early June. It was then that people indulged in an annual wash and clean-up, being of the opinion to remain unwashed was the best way to avoid disease and infection. It was for that reason brides carried garlands of sweet-smelling flowers and after the ceremony wore them upon their heads. The garland was designed to disguise the bride's body smell. Jack had no reason to concern himself about the smell of Elizabeth. She arrived sweet in odour, in a long dual-coloured gown, carrying a garland of red roses and pinks scenting of cloves. The organ struck up as she walked down the middle aisle, escorted by her stepfather. Jack rose and stepped forward to greet her warmly.

After the service, Jack and Elizabeth left Wingham to a further peal of bells and the good wishes of gathered villagers. Tripp took the newly-weds back to Twitham in the trap, decorated with enough flowers to make any puritanical onlooker cringe. James followed on his horse, Swift, with

Acorn in tow, and John Cartwright and Dyonise with the maids in another trap. The guests, including Wat and Thomas, fell in behind the procession. As soon as they arrived back at the farm, Elizabeth instructed a servant to make necessary adjustments and to lay an additional place near the top table, next to old Wat Harrys, for Jack's brother Thomas.

A small sextet of musicians playing the lute, fiddle, crumhorn, hurdy-gurdy, curtal and harpsichord kept proceedings cheery. The music was that of Purcell, plus some baroque music. Whilst the music played, welcome drinks of sparkling wine were handed out to the guests.

The wedding banquet, organised by Dyonise, was spectacular. Game soup was ladled out in bowls for starters, followed by roasted peacock, goose and woodcock cooked in herbs. Beef slices were accompanied by a variety of vegetable dishes of spinach, squashes, honey-roasted root and a-many different fruits. The centre of the table had a stuffed peacock with its tail feathers fanned out, surrounded by black and white grapes, shiny red apples and pears. Every setting had a silver candlestick bearing a lighted candle. Expensive decanters of wine were set at intervals and equally expensive wine glasses were continuously filled with red or white wine. As the wine flowed, everybody drank to the newly-weds, wishing them a fruitful life.

John Cartwright rose to his feet and made a speech complimenting his beautiful stepdaughter. He welcomed Jack into the Cartwright family. He referred to his son-in-law's integrity, and how Jack had saved him from being rooked by the pickpocket in Canterbury. He informed everybody that Jack was setting up a carpentry and joinery business at Twitham and invited all and sundry to utilise his good, honest skills. He also thanked his wife, Dyonise, for the wonderful food table she had designed. Then John Cartwright added:

'Hopefully, this marriage will produce a son and heir to my vast fortunes. A grandson I canst adopt to my lineage in name and in title. I pray it be the will of God the Almighty and Father of us all. So, I invite ye to stand and raise thy glasses and drink deeply to that occurrence.'

James, who had conducted proceedings in his usual methodical way, referred to a well-suited happy couple and wished them a long and bountiful life. He kissed Elizabeth on the cheek and said that Jack had impeccable taste in both perfection and the personality of his new wife. Elizabeth was, he said, a wonderful person. James was proud to call her his most beautiful cousin. He praised Dyonise Cartwright for her expertise in organising such a grand wedding breakfast, the likes of which he had never seen before. To which Wat crudely shouted out, 'Yea, but not half as good as her tasty lardy cake, washed down with well-brewed ale, I wager.'

Wat's interruption caused a round of merriment to ripple amongst the guests and a further swig of wine to be taken. James paused to acknowledge Wat's observation, then went on:

'I canst tell many tales about Jack and brave cousin Symon here too. Suffice to say, Jack is a man of, not just integrity, but also bravery. He hast always followed the courage of his convictions. What is more, he is as honest as the day is long and hast been more than just a cousin to me. He is my best and closest friend. I shall miss having Jack near me at Lynsted. Hopefully, we shall meet frequently, either here in the parish of Wingham or at Claxfeldestane.'

James read out messages of good wishes, borne by hand, and then invited Jack to say his piece. Jack took a hefty slug of wine, gulped it down and rose slowly to his feet to make his address.

"Tis surely the most wonderful day of my life. Many thanks must go to my in-laws, John and Dyonise, for throwing this magnificent reception in their wonderful house. I take note of what ye say, John Cartwright. As requested, I will perform to the best of my ability! To my wife, Lizzy, who I love so very deeply, I canst only say: prepare thyself for frequent servicing.'

Jack's latter remark almost brought the house down, causing Elizabeth to giggle and to blush deep scarlet. There was much banging on the table. Jack raised a hand to usher silence.

'On a serious note, before I become too inebriated by the generous helpings of wine ye keep dishing out, I wish to thank my young brother, Thomas, for attending our wedding. I say this from the bottom of my heart. We, like so many families over the Kingdom, or what was the Kingdom and is now the Commonwealth – leastways for the time being 'tis so. I must be careful what I say, or I might find myself arrested for treason! – We, that is Thomas and I, like so many families who were split over the causes of the civil wars, hath come together again. It bringeth joy to mine heart and much gladness to mine very soul to see Tom here at our nuptials. I live in hope that what hast been continuous civil wars are now ceased forever. I pray this is so for the sake of our nation. God knows we canst ill afford to lose any more men to war in this pitiful country of ours. I pray this for the sake of any children that Elizabeth and I mayest be privileged to raise in this wicked world. I pray that estranged families cometh together again to live in harmony once more. Our lives are short. We hath enough to contend with by famine and disease, without fighting forever amongst ourselves to establish a change in constitution. A constitution which will probably never be for the entire freedom of the common man, whatever way thou lookest at it. There, I hath said enough. I am being kicked under the table by my wife. Thank ye, all thy good people who cometh to our wedding today.'

Jack sat down to silence. He had held the company in rapture. A sudden explosion of cheering and handclapping erupted and unknown folk rose to shake both Thomas and Jack by the hand. Jack's speech was greeted with shouts of: 'Well said, young fellow me lad,' and 'Live ye for the day, says I.' 'To hell with this puritanical Parliament,' said another, whilst a well-inebriated red-faced farmer shouted out loudly, 'Bring ye back the monarchy.' 'Never mind governments, we hast our own constitution in Kent, we need no other form,' shouted one yeoman, and 'Let us live only for our families and friends.' Jack had stirred up a hornets' nest amongst the mostly Royalist-orientated gathering. He went over to Thomas and placed a hand on his brother's shoulder. Wat looked on anxiously, hoping there would be no split between them.

'I'm sorry, Tom, I hath put my foot in it once more. It never was my intention to anger ye.'

'I fear thou always will, Jack, but ye will nay worry me ever again. Thy words were well chosen, and well meant, of that I hath nay doubt. I wish ye and Elizabeth a great life of joy.'

'Come over and sit with Elizabeth and me, Tom. Let us enjoy a large glass of brandy together and talk over those unforgettable earlier years at Woodlarks, when life was so carefree for us.'

'Ay, go sit with thy brother, Thomas,' said Wat. 'Jack's speech was right. Both of ye wouldst do well to remember ye are family. Ye two should nay hath been split apart in the first place.'

So large was the assembly of guests that it spilt through the double wide-open doors of the dining room, with trestle tables set up in the hallway. On James' instruction, the entire assemblage rose and made for the large living hall. The room was enormous, with split-beamed ceilings and a huge inglenook fireplace at one end. The inglenook fire was stacked with logs and the flames leapt high into the soot-blackened corbelling of the chimney place. The sextet had moved their instruments and now struck up on a raised platform to one side of the hall. They played several new waltzes, music which was coming out of Vienna. Under instruction, the newly-weds attempted to dance the three-four beat. They were soon joined by other couples. The wedding party was also entertained by Morris men, who danced to folk music and ballads. Folk songs and catches rang out in boisterous crescendo as wine flowed to numb inhibitions.

In the early hours of the morning, people bade their fare-the-wells and drifted away in carriages, leaving John and Dyonise Cartwright and the houseguests to retire to their beds. Old Wat was escorted to his bedchamber, but Jack, Elizabeth and Tom sat talking for a further hour.

'Doth brother William know ye hath come here to witness our marriage, Tom?' asked Jack.

'Yea, we talked long and hard about ye, Jack. Now that Parliament has stamped its authority over the country, I think he is willing to forgive and forget thy Royalist support. But ye know Will, he will nay make the first move at reconciliation with ye. William hast little backup at Woodlarks, now that Colonel Browne and his Roundhead troops are gone from Paynter's Farm. There are many locals who register their disdain relating to Will's espousal of the Commonwealth cause, and there hath been threats made upon Deborah Greenstreet (nee Sharpe) and her father, James Sharpe, who, since the death of Lord Peter, now run the farm and manor at Paynter's, until Peter's son John cometh of age. John is just twelve years of age now. As ye are aware, Oliver Cromwell made him a ward of court. Cromwell hast sent a few soldiers to protect them at Paynter's, but that is of little help to Will. However, when I told Will I nay longer wished to be thine enemy and intended to go with Wat to witness this marriage, he raised no objection, nor made any positive threat. As I departed, William wished me Godspeed but urged me to return as soon as possible to Woodlarks, to assist in the management of the estate. He is nay so good at management, Jack. Will ye nay come back?'

'I am, of course, disturbed by the news ye impart, Tom. But Kent has suffered much at the hands of the Roundheads for its Royalist insurrections. Many lands hath been laid to waste and properties burnt, and now that things hath quietened down and parliamentary regiments art withdrawn, many Royalists seek revenge on families that espoused the Commonwealth cause. I am resolved to refrain from physically fighting the Royalist cause ever again. Nevertheless, I confess I am disturbed by this puritanical, politically correct government we now endure. I submit it is slowly strangling the ordinary folk of what was once Merrie England, by its impounding and restraining laws. That said, I am indeed sorry that I imposed my inheritance responsibilities on Will and on ye, Tom. As the eldest son it was my destiny to be responsible for our father's estates. I walked away from that situation because of my Royalist beliefs, and left Will to embrace responsibilities he never dreamed were his destination – partly because of his own beliefs, for which I now bear him nay ill will. It is a cross I must bear, Tom. It wouldst be totally unfair now to go to Will, cap in hand, offering my services, when he hast born affairs against all the odds by his, and I might add thine own, very honest endeavours. I shall nay do it, nor will I impose my Royalist beliefs on Will or ye, Tom, it would be unseemly.'

22

INTERREGNUM, 1650–1653

The execution of Charles I not only brought about a Republican Commonwealth in England but instigated negotiations between the deceased King's exiled son (of the same name) and the various Scottish parties united behind Charles Stuart. Charles signed the Treaty of Breda and the Scottish Covenanters proclaimed Charles II King of Scotland, and then King of Great Britain, France and Ireland. General Fairfax, who had been deeply disturbed by the King's execution, refused to lead an army against Scotland, forcing Oliver Cromwell, Fairfax's lieutenant-general, to hastily return from a defeated, mostly subjugated, Royalist Ireland. Oliver Cromwell assumed the role of commander-in-chief of the English army. Cromwell wanted a union between all three nations. A Parliamentary Council of State decided on a pre-emptive invasion of Scotland. In this Anglo-Scottish war, Cromwell duly defeated the Covenanter army at the Battle of Dunbar, then marched north into Fife. Charles Stuart invaded England with the Scots-Royalist army. Oliver Cromwell pursued the would-be king, gathering a huge overwhelming force of men at arms on the way, and defeated Charles at the Battle of Worcester in September 1651, his men outnumbering the Royalists by two to one. Cromwell's 'crowning mercy' finally ended the British civil wars. After eluding capture, by hiding in an oak tree at Catholic recusant Gifford's 'Boscobel House', and afterwards laying up in a priest hole, Charles Stuart, despite being unusually more than six feet tall, managed to flee England in disguise. He was shipped across the Channel from Shoreham, in a coal boat called *Surprise*, landing in Normandy on 16 October 1651, where he remained in exile.

Jack and Elizabeth Greenstreet settled down to married life. In June 1650, Elizabeth gave birth to a daughter, Elizabeth, much to her stepfather, John Cartwright's, bitter disappointment. Jack fitted out his new carpentry and joinery shop and built up a good business of clientele, both within and outside of the Wingham area, including maintenance work and additions to the local churches and meeting halls. In his vast workshop he fitted three benches and spent twenty pounds for tools and fittings, including a variety of planes, hammers, a long saw and small saws, augers and wedges for splitting planks from the log, holdfasts, a mallet and two dozen chisels, files, axes and adzes, an awl and compasses, brace and bits, a square and marking gauges etc. Elizabeth soon fell pregnant again and John Cartwright lived in hope of the birth of a grandson.

In 1651, Yeoman Cartwright purchased a publication in Canterbury, called *Hobbe's Leviathan*, an interesting major political work setting down twelve principal rights of sovereignty. It favoured a monarchy. The basis of the argument was for an absolute sovereign, stating that civil wars could only be avoided by strong undivided government. When Jack read the *Leviathan*, he concluded that there was little hope in realising such argument, as the government was far from strong and undivided. It was a weak, puritanical Rump Parliament that now governed the country. Parliament constantly bickered amongst itself. The third civil war was mainly an Anglo-Scottish war and soon snuffed out by Cromwell's huge army.

Snuffed out it may have been, but now the Dutch Republic became belligerent by launching a naval attack on England on 28 September 1652 at the Battle of the Kentish Knock. The Dutch were beaten off by the English under the command of Robert Blake, in his ship *Resolution*. The Dutch lost two ships and many casualties attempting to destroy the English.

In their vain belief that the Dutch had been totally demoralised, if not defeated, the English sent twenty ships to patrol the Mediterranean and Baltic seas, whilst other large vessels remained docked for repair. The English Council of State had made a big mistake. Back came the Dutch, and the English were caught with their breeches down. Vice-Admiral De Witt, who had suffered a breakdown because of his defeat, was replaced by Maarten Tromp as commander of the Dutch fleet. With seventy-three warships, plus some fireships, Tromp escorted 270 merchantmen through the Strait of Dover to France, then turned in search of the

English. Tromp discovered forty-two capital ships of the English fleet, plus ten smaller vessels, anchored in the Downs, between the Kentish headlands of North Foreland and South Foreland. They were under the command of General at Sea Robert Blake. Next morning, at noon, the two fleets moved south-west, the English hugging the coast and the Dutch marking them, but keeping some distance away, due to the Rip Raps and the Varne Shoal. At the Cape of Dungeness, some seventeen Dutch vessels lay in wait. A fierce battle of cannon and musket shot ensued, and the two countries were locked into the Battle of Dungeness off the Kent coast. Blake lost five ships, with two captured and three sunk. The Dutch lost one ship due to accidental explosion. Although himself wounded, Blake and his remaining ships escaped back through the Dover Strait and into the Thames Estuary. The Dutch had no pilot who dared navigate the dangerous estuary waters in pursuit of the English. Blake got away without any further losses.

Early in December 1652, Jack embarked on a visit to see old Wat Harrys. He had just finished a substantial task of work in the manufacture of timber centrings for some elliptical arches under construction by local stonemasons in Goodnestone church. Now, in truth, he desired a break from the mental intricacies and the labour involved in the work. Jack had methodically calculated the chords and scribed the node points of intersections accurately with compasses, to coincide with the exact span of each archway. After cutting, nailing, bolting and assembling the timber centrings, he helped position them, using pulleys to raise each centring into position precisely below the springing points. He cut props, then braced, wedged and cradled his work, leaving it secure and ready for the masons to build upon. Jack left the masons to their task and promised to return and strike the centrings when the stonework had been completed, locked in position, and the bedding mortar had set hard. The masons raised a keystone and set it upon the first centring before Jack left Goodnestone church to return home to the farm at Staple.

At Twitham Farm, Goodwife Elizabeth and little daughter, Elizabeth, kissed Jack goodbye and saw him on his way, waving until he was out of sight. Jack was in high spirits, freed from the complexities and labour of his recent project, which had taxed his brain to some considerable degree. The morning was cold, yet bright enough for the time of year. He urged Acorn into a gallop across the fields and along the highways towards Faversham. When he came upon the cottage called Moddilyon, it appeared inactive. No smoke puffed from the chimney. Wat's dogs, Snatch and Fowler, who normally set up an unearthly din when visitors called, were nowhere to be seen. Jack dismounted and secured his horse to a leaning palisade fence. Jack walked to the rear of the cottage. The back door was wide open. Rats ran for cover in all directions. Sword drawn and flintlock cocked, he cautiously walked in. The cottage was cold and damp. He opened the door to the parlour, where Wat usually sat next to a well-stoked fire with a cauldron of pottage simmering on the hearth to one side. No fire burnt in the grate. The pottage was stone cold. Jack searched the rooms. The bedchamber was as Wat had left it, the bed linen thrown back. The stench of a full chamber pot overpowered his nostrils.

It made no sense. None of this was akin to the methodical ways of his mentor. The rest of the rooms were shut tight and unused. But then the old man rarely used any rooms other than the parlour, his bedchamber and his work den. With some trepidation, half expecting Wat Harrys to be slumped over his wooden benchtop, Jack approached Wat's den at the end of the passageway. Perhaps he had passed away whilst binding a new fishing fly. The door of the old man's retreat was ajar. Jack pushed the door open wide with the tip of his cup-hilted sword and surveyed the workroom and armoury. The fishing rods and basket were in place, so Wat had not gone down to the lake. He sheathed his sword. There was nobody in the cottage, he was sure of that. But Jack was also sure Wat had not been about the place for some time. There was a gap between a row of muskets. One of them had been taken down. He activated his thinking cap. It was Wat's favourite fowling piece that was missing! Jack looked around for the leather belt the old man wore, which supported his bag of lead shot, his powder horn and hunting knife. Both items were missing. Wat had gone off hunting. But why so long? And why had he left the door open wide? The latter question was probably quite easily answered because Jack had noticed Wat's increasing forgetfulness several times at recent meetings. The dogs were another matter though. They usually stuck to Wat like fish glue. The rats had well and truly taken up residence, so the dogs had not been there for some time. In any case, if Wat had been around, he would have set the polecats on the rats. The polecats!

Jack went into the back yard and peered into the cages. All except one of the polecats had died of starvation. In one cage a savage animal bared its teeth and stood over the bones of its companion, which it had obviously killed and eaten. Jack opened the cage and released the animal. The half-crazed dark brown mammal shot out, scattering the rats, one of which the sleek starved polecat caught in its teeth mid-air, dragging it into the undergrowth to devour.

The path from the rear garden, where Wat grew his vegetables, led across a grass track to thick woodland, made up of a mix of deciduous and coniferous trees. Jack followed the track and walked some half-mile into the wood. The trees let in light now that the autumnal fall had stripped most boughs bare. An ochre-coloured carpet lined the floor of the wood. The fallen crisp, dry leaves kicked up in a light flurry with each step he took. Jack was about to give up when he heard the distinct sound of whining and barking. Heading off the track he made for the direction of the agitated dogs. Snatch and Fowler came bounding up to him from a glade.

Wat Harrys lay dead upon the ground, partially covered by leaves, which had blown over his cold, rigid body. Jack knelt beside him and carefully brushed aside the covering of leaves. Seemingly, at first glances, Wat appeared to have died from natural causes. Jack turned him over, then leapt back in a fit of startled horror. The old man's face had been completely blown away on the right side. The gunstock and remnants of the fowling piece were scattered nearby and over the glade. It was apparent to him that his mentor's musket had backfired and blown to pieces in his face. The blast had taken away the right side of Wat's skull. To Jack, it was obvious Wat had not suffered. He would have known nothing about the incident. His faithful dogs, Snatch and Fowler, had remained with him. Both dogs appeared in remarkably good condition. They had obviously found food to eat in the woods. The faithful gun dogs had refused to leave their master unguarded. Jack's dismay turned to sudden grief. He laid his mentor back on his side, so that only the good part of his face was visible, then sat down beside him and sobbed. Wat had been like an older brother to Jack. Such an ending was not fitting.

Taking the woollen cloak from his shoulders, Jack wrapped old Wat Harrys' body within it. He withdrew his well-honed knife from its sheath and cut two stout saplings and some short cross members. By utilising binding cord and rabbit snares found tied about Wat's waist, he lashed together a rough litter and carefully laid Wat's inert body upon it. Jack firmly secured Wat's lifeless form, utilising leather shoulder belts and strapping. Calling the dogs to heel, he dragged the lifeless body back to the cottage on the rough litter and set it down in the parlour. He fed the dogs cold pottage and left them on guard, then went in quest of the local borsholder. Two husbandmen directed him to the house of Gostwicke Buckton. Jack took the borsholder to the glade in the woods and showed him what he had discovered. He pointed out the pieces of musket strewn about the area of the incident, and bits of shattered wooden musket butt. Then he guided the borsholder back to the cottage and showed him the body of his old mentor. Gostwicke Buckton agreed there was no foul play. Buckton agreed to contact an undertaker to attend to the body forthwith and to report the incident to the authorities. Jack decided to call on his brothers at Woodlarks and get them to make the necessary arrangements for their former manservant's funeral and burial, either at St Peter and St Paul's, Ospringe, or St Mary's church, Selling. He whistled up Snatch and Fowler, tied them on a long rope and set off on Acorn for Woodlarks. The dogs knew Jack and ran contentedly behind their new master.

On nearing his former home, Jack was startled to see a huge plume of black smoke rising high into the early winter's sky. He spurred Acorn at a gallop to the top of the rise which looked down over the house and spacious estate of Woodlarks. The stables were on fire. Orange flames leapt high into the early afternoon sky. Twenty or more vigilantes, carrying flaming torches, were gathered in a ring near a mature beech tree. A rope had been thrown over a stout bough, some fifteen feet from the ground. From one end dangled a chilling noose halter. The man being dragged kicking towards the noose was Jack's estranged brother, William. Two burly men were forcing Will to the gallows tree, whilst Thomas was held in restraint by three other men from the imposed *posse comitatus*. Jack could hear Tom begging loudly for his brother's life. Jack checked a brace of flintlock pistols, which he had primed ready before he set out from Wat's cottage. He released the dogs and urged Acorn into a charge down the slope, shouting at the top of his voice, '*Dum spiro spero*.' The blood-curdling motto, 'Whilst I breathe, I hope', echoed all about. Jack fired a flintlock into the air, the retort reverberating about the estate. He drew his cup-hilted rapier. The hunting dogs, Snatch and Fowler, who were familiar with Jack by now and remembered him from past meetings with Wat, ran snarling at his side. Acorn snorted like a charging bull. To Jack it was like the charge at Naseby all over again. With a flintlock in one hand and his cup-hilted rapier swishing in the other, he made straight for the two men, who were intent on stretching Will's neck from the beech tree. Jack reined in, pointing a flintlock at the head of one man and his sword tip at the other's throat.

'Do ye nay move one inch or ye are dead men all,' shouted Jack. 'Throw down thy weapons and burning torches, or I shall nay hesitate in killing thine leaders who art intent on hanging my brothers. Then I shall ride amongst ye and butcher ye all for the cowards thou art.'

Mounted on horse, Jack had the clear advantage. The half-starved dogs were doing their bit, snapping and worrying the rest of the contingent. In the fray, Tom was released and picked up a flintlock. Mostly the men were armed with simple farming implements. Will drew a bayonet from the belt of one of the self-appointed hangmen and pricked the man's ribs with it.

Remaining mounted, Jack called the dogs to heel. Snatch and Fowler came bounding back. The dogs had done a good job darting in and out and snapping at legs, causing the posse to hop around whilst he dealt with the would-be executioners. The assembly could see Jack was a fighting man. They stood listening quietly as he began to address them:

'Pray, under whose authority doth ye come here in force, to burn, plunder Woodlarks and execute my brothers? Who is thy leader? Come ye forth and speak up clearly now or suffer the consequences of thy cowardly actions.' One of the burly hangmen spoke up with clarity:

'My name is Silas Pordage. I confess I am the leader and spokesman of these brave yeomen and husbandmen of Kent, who hath, every one of them, suffered under the hands of Cromwell's Roundheads. We are nay cowards. We are simple husbandmen and farm labourers. All art true Royalist subjects. We are nay fighting men, like thy good self, who cometh upon us like a bat out of hell, with a stallion breathing fire and demon dogs attempting to tear us to pieces.'

Jack called on his brother Will to direct the bayonet away from Yeoman Pordage's rib cage. Pordage pointed an accusing finger at William of Maidstone. He spat forth words of wrath.

'This man – William Greenstreet – is a supporter of the Commonwealth. He rode with the Roundheads last year, when they entered upon my land, and called me Royalist vermin. They made me watch as my house was set alight and burnt to the ground. They churned up my crops, leaving me and mine family destitute. My wife and seven children hath since attempted to live within a rough shelter, which is nay fit for swine. Three of my dear children died during the months of last winter. They suffered slow deaths due to the consumption. I'll nay mention their good names for it will make me fill up with self-pity and inadequacy. Seven children I had and now only four, and one of them be very poorly. These good men that cometh in support today hath all suffered by the hands of the Roundheads, because they dared to shout out "God save the King". Their crops were destroyed by Colonel Browne's men, when the battalion was encamped at Paynter's Farm. Now the parliamentary troops hath gone to fight elsewhere we come to take our revenge, without fear of direct reprisals from the Roundheads.'

Still seated on the stallion, Jack called for the assembly to gather around him in the form of a semi-circle. He sheathed his sword and slipped the flintlock pistol back in his belt, then pulled himself upright. Standing tall in the stirrups and with Acorn reined in, he made his address:

'Citizens. The men you wish to execute are my estranged brothers. True, they espoused the Commonwealth cause, just as we Royalists supported our late King. I backed our poor dead King. Yea, I fought by his very side at Oxford, Cornwall and Naseby, ay and took up arms in the many insurrections of our county. The civil wars hath dragged on for exceeding ten years. Far too many lives hath been lost on both sides of the argument. The wars still rage over the border with Scotland. But I put it to ye – we art finished with it. The civil wars are over.'

This brought a rousing cheer from the assembled company of husbandmen.

'This is the first time I hath met my brother, William Greenstreet, since my family was split apart by fierce argument in 1642. My brother Will is nay different to ye. He is a yeoman, as some of ye art. Rich by birth, I grant ye, but 'twas the wretched civil war that caused such terrible and regrettable actions in us all. Now the wars are over, it is my firm hope that families and our communities can come together again. Men, we must find forgiveness in our hearts.'

Stirred by the Cavalier's message, the men listened intently. The speech was heartfelt.

'Brothers, men of Kent and Kentish men, I put it to you, too many fine Englishmen, ay and Welshmen, hath perished for a cause. Even now, whatever side ye choose to support, the issue is far from being resolved, despite the execution of our sovereign King Charles I. In my humble opinion all the fighting hast nay resolved the argument. It is not likely to be fully resolved for many years to come. Maybe not in our lifetimes. If we go on putting men to death for the sake of revenge, we shall soon be so short of men that we shalt be entirely ruled by women! Is that what ye strive to achieve? Imagine – there will be nay men to fertilise the women and bring forth future generations, let alone men to fight enemies which threaten to invade our shores. The blessed Dutch will rub their hands together in glee at our weakness.'

Jack threw a leg over Acorn and dismounted with agility. He threw his arms wide open.

'So here today, I offer a hand to my brothers, William of Maidstone and Thomas, in the name of friendship and brotherly love. I say to ye all, in God's name, let us come together again, if not in love, for the sake of all humanity in Kent and for the good of our crippled country.'

There were shouts of agreement from the would-be assassins, which gave way to mumblings.

William walked over to Jack, clasped his brother's hand and looked hard into his eyes. Will had just escaped death and was a broken man. He appeared drawn and worn out by anxiety.

'Come back to us, Jack, come ye back to Woodlarks and help run the manor and estates.'

'Ay,' agreed Tom, 'the past hast to be forgotten for everybody's sake. We must make amends.'

Jack turned to Silas Pordage, who had hung his head, whether in despair or shame no one knew:

'We canst nay hope to mend what hast gone before, Silas. War respects nay man. But the civil war is finished in Kent. We need to rebuild, not seek revenge, which will achieve little. In that respect I make a case for ye and thy family to consider. Ye need nay spend another winter in a shelter coupled to an old pig sty. I hath just lost a dear friend and mentor, who lived in a cottage called Moddilyon on the outskirts of Ospringe, near to thy land in Selling. He, having nay family of his own, bequeathed the cottage to me. On this day I name ye as my tenant for a peppercorn rent of one penny, to be paid annually each Michaelmas at Woodlarks. Further, I shall contribute fifty shillings from my own purse for the poor of the parish, to be paid by my brother, William Greenstreet of Maidstone, at his entire discretion.'

'Yea, that is indeed a fair resolution to a bad business,' agreed Yeoman Pordage, 'and, as it has come from a true Royalist, like mineself, I accept thy terms with good heart on behalf of my wife and family. Goodwife Pordage will be grateful beyond belief at thine offer, Master.'

'Good man,' said Jack, 'but give ye me three weeks' grace to move possessions from the cottage and to leave it welcoming. Thou shalt be installed before Christmas cometh. Let us say mid-December. Thou canst cut a Christmas tree from the adjacent woods for thy children. Call here at Woodlarks for the keys in three weeks. Now, please go, Silas. Take thy supporters away from here, that I may converse with my estranged brothers over a glass of wine.'

'I apologise for what occurred, Silas Pordage, but war respects no man,' said William humbly.

Undecided by the apology, Silas Pordage eyed William of Maidstone somewhat sceptically.

"Tis true we were on opposing sides of savage civil wars,' agreed Pordage, 'but I contend ye Roundheads were excessively severe and brutal in the lessons ye applied to ordinary husbandmen and their families. Thou were out of control with thy scorched earth policy. To leave families homeless, facing the severity of winter without shelter, was a death sentence. Nevertheless, as thy brother hath implied, the killing hast to cease. Somehow or other we need to rebuild our communities. I find closure by thy brother's goodwill. I go now, to leave ye in peace and to convey the good news of the cottage tenancy to my wife. To have habitation, with a watertight roof, is the best news I could hope to take back to Goodwife Pordage this day.'

Yanking the rope from the tree, Silas Pordage took leave of the brothers. The *posse comitatus* picked up their weaponry and implements and dispersed, leaving the three brothers to survey the burnt-out stables and to go inside Woodlarks. At least the house was secure from fire.

Inside the house, still shaking from his ordeal, William found glasses and poured three large brandies. He gulped his drink down and poured himself another from a squat glass decanter.

'Well, Jack, thine entrance was, to say the least, extremely fortuitous.' He chuckled quietly to himself, then muttered, 'They didst nay even bring a friar with them to shrive my rotten soul!'

'Thank God ye arrived when ye did, brother,' said Thomas who had clung on to Jack's arm ever since they entered the house. 'Five minutes later and Will wouldst hath been writhing in his last throes. Then it might hath been my turn to be strung up, to choke, shake and wriggle to mine end. I thought it was the end for Will. Ay, and with the stables burning, they were about to throw their torches into the house. Pray, let us nay dwell on it,' said Tom, shuddering. 'Tell us about old Wat Harrys' death. He appeared so well and able on my visit to him last week.'

Jack told his story. How he discovered Wat in the woodland with half his skull blown away and of the action he took in finding a borsholder and reporting the death to the authorities. He asked Will and Tom to converse with local undertakers and to arrange for the burial of Wat Harrys at the local church. Tom said he would ride over to Staple and advise Jack, just as soon as a date had been fixed by a priest to conduct the service, plus a choir to sing for Wat's soul.

'Wat taught ye well to use a sword and discharge a flintlock, brother,' said Will. 'We art in Wat's debt as much as thine own. We all need to pay our deepest respects to Wat,' he said, with genuine gratitude. 'Jack, I swear thine prompt arrival was a miracle from God.'

'Ay, well, ye might be right, Will. A similar thing happened to me once when the snow lay deep and even.' Jack glanced at Tom and smiled. 'But with thine life intact and only thy stables lost and thy horses safely grazing in yon paddocks, ye got away lightly, Will,' said Jack.

'Therein lies the rub, Jack! said William. 'Things are nay quite as they appear on the surface. I must inform ye I hath nay been too careful in handling the estate, nor our father's money. I spent too much money in helping Lord Peter, and Cromwell, in those early days of the Commonwealth cause. Now Tom and I art without ready monies. 'Tis a worthless story Jack.'

'To what degree, Will? Ye might just as well tell me all, even though 'tis nay business of mine. I had imagined ye were handling things so well, with Tom's invaluable assistance, here at Woodlarks and across all the estates. Best get it off thy chest, I might be able to help ye.'

William poured them all another brandy, then conducted Jack and Tom to the study chamber. He pulled a large, heavy, leather-bound ledger book from the shelves, set it down on a desktop and opened it up for Jack to peruse. The ledger was not well kept, the entries interspersed, the writing thinly scrawled in black and red ink with many blotches. There was more red than black. Jack got the gist of the debits and credits. The ledger encompassed many properties, estates and appurtenances over a vast area, which stretched from Maidstone to Ospringe.

'Clearly there is considerable debt here, Will, but it needs a wizard to make head and tail of this messy bookkeeping of thine. Doth thou never sharpen thy goose-feather quill pen?'

'I know, Jack. I never professed to be a great bookkeeper. My handwriting is poor. There is a depletion of ready cash left to draw upon, that is the crux of the matter for Tom and me.'

'Do nay castigate thyself too much, Will. I wouldst probably hath done little better myself. A lot was heaped upon ye because of our family split over the civil wars. This is a huge estate to run. Father didst nay hath to manage the estates throughout the course of the devastating conflict like ye had to. Ye elected to put cash into the Commonwealth cause, just as many people financed the Royalist cause. My suggestion is ye sell off some of Father's vast estate. Doth thee really want to continue the responsibilities of managing those fine houses in Maidstone and Charing and all the journeying it entails? Sell some of it off, Will. Be done with thy concerns. Find thyselves a good woman each, brothers, and perhaps a little happiness in life. I recommend it above all else. That is my best advice to ye both.'

For the first time since they had met, a grin crept across William's face and Thomas looked relieved at his older brother's perfectly sound advice. William looked at Jack and nodded.

'I knew ye wouldst come up with the answer, Jack,' said Will. 'It was staring me in the face all along, but even though we were estranged I kept wondering what ye might say if ye found out I had frittered the estate away. You really ought to return here and help me manage and share the inheritance, Jack. I am sure we could get along again as we did before the civil unrest.'

'Nay, Will. The inheritance is thine and Thomas's to share. I hath made a life of my own now. Elizabeth and my carpentry work keep me contented. I am as happy as any fellow could wish to be. In fact, I am happy beyond compare.

I hath assets of mine own and will lend thee money to tie ye over, until ye hath sold off enough of the estate to clear thy debts and art able to pay me back. I suggest ye engage the help of Cousin James at Claxfeldestane. He is the very man to set ye straight. He will help ye adjust and set out thine accounts ledger in a legible manner. He is the very man to assist in the contact of a good lawyer, for ye will need to appoint such a fellow and retain him to act on thy behalf. A lawyer will draw up indentures of conveyancing and legally set down the terms of sale. Once the properties are sold ye will hath plenty of asset to reimburse James, myself and the lawyer, and to wipe off all thine debts. What is more, ye will retain enough monies to live a comfortable lifestyle of thine own here at Woodlarks, without too many concerns. What say thee to mine indispensable ideas?'

'Absolutely gold-block, Jack. I canst nay wait to set the wheels in motion,' said William. Thomas agreed, nodding eagerly, though more than a little inebriated from the fine brandy.

'In that case I shall go from here to Claxfield to see James this very evening and make arrangements forthwith. I will soon return, bringing to ye a lump sum of cash to tide thee over.'

Jack paused to drain his glass. It had been quite a day. He needed to set off without delay if he was to make Claxfield before dark. He planned to stay over with James until the morning.

'Ye and Cousin James can decide what properties to sell, Will. The sum ye require to clear all thy debts and the amount of cash ye wish to retain in hand. Now, let us partake of another glass of thine excellent brandy before I wend my way to confront Jamie and excavate some ready English money to tide mine brothers over until land sales and transfers art completed. Ye will need to present thy ledger to James and explain thine entries. I will call on ye in a day or two.'

'Now, art thou glad of an older brother, Will?' enquired Tom of his middle brother with a grin.

'Yea indeed I am, Thomas. What catastrophe threatened. Now, I feel a ton weight hast been lifted from us. Such weight might hath dangled from a tree branch, if Jack had nay come to our rescue. I keep pinching mineself to reassure I am nay waiting outside the Pearly Gates.'

After a quick bite to eat, Jack set off at a canter for Teynham. It was dark before he arrived at Claxfeldestane. He banged loudly upon the door. Jerome the manservant drew back the bolts and stood holding a flickering candle high above his head to get a good look at the late-evening caller. Behind him, brandishing a wide-ended flintlock blunderbuss, stood James.

'Who is it that attempts to break down the door of a quiet household this time of night, Jerome?'

''Tis thine cousin, Jack Greenstreet, Master Reeve. He looks cold and damp from a long ride.'

'The saints preserve us all – 'tis ye, Jack. Come ye inside, cousin. Thou art the last person I expected so late. Being situated just off the London Road, as we are, it is wise to be prepared for vagabonds and vagrants. Since the Roundhead raid when Lord Peter came a-calling – ye recall, when ye were hidden in the priest hole – since that time I always answer the door armed.'

James turned to the bent figure of his manservant, Jerome, and issued clear instruction.

'Jerome, take Master Jack's horse to the stables and rub him down with straw. Water, feed and attend to the stallion's needs, and ask Martha to prepare a tray for our guest. There is some mutton stew with new-baked bread and serve my special brewed beer to wash it down.'

James took his caller's cloak, then ushered his friend through the hallway to the front reception chamber. A roaring oak log fire greeted Jack. The room was illuminated by candles, their wicks trimmed and bright. James poured a glass of Madeira wine and handed it to his cousin.

'Well now, Jack, why hath thou called on me at this unearthly hour of the day?' enquired James. 'What ails the need to ride all the way from Wingham to Claxfield this late in the evening?'

Jack positioned himself with his back to the hearth and felt the warmth penetrate his bones. Slowly he began to thaw out. The Madeira wine motivated the brandy back into action.

'Well, James, my journey here wasn't directly from Wingham. I hath a lot of news to impart, coupled with a request of help from mine brothers to present to ye. Secondly, I need a bedchamber for the night. And thirdly, we need to go digging for buried treasure at first light!'

James drew a deep breath, then expelled a long sigh, throwing his hands up in surrender.

'Ay, well, I might hath guessed things wouldst start to get exciting now ye are around, cousin.'

James, who had, to the best of his ability, redeemed and re-scribed most of the Teynham Manor rolls destroyed by the Roundheads, was up to date with his business as manor reeve. He agreed to help his cousins, William and Thomas, in their time of need, mostly as a favour to Jack. After all, they had supported the Commonwealth. Jack insisted the civil wars were over and bridges needed to be rebuilt, and James could see the wisdom of his friend's thinking.

'Inform your brothers I will journey to see them next Thursday. I canst stay over Friday and Saturday if needs be, Jack. From what ye tell me, only William knows how his ledger works. I shall probably need to set up a sound format and re-scribe the accounts and inventories of each property, its land and its appurtenances, before we are ready to proceed to the stage of sales. When needed, I know of a good lawyer who can apply his profession. It will cost them fees, but my own fees will nay be exorbitant. There will be plenty in the pot to cover the small amount of fees expended. Carefully planned, they will be out of debt for the rest of their lives.'

'I am indebted to ye, James. Now, let us retire. In the morning we shall proceed to Cripson Wood to dig up the treasure mine father bequeathed me. Then I will take thee to the brewers' new venue called the Dover Castle at the end of Greenstreet. I am informed they not only serve good beer there, but the most succulent, tasty steak pies accompanied by vegetables.'

On the way back to Wingham, Jack called in at Woodlarks to hand his brothers, Will and Tom, the ready cash he had promised and to inform them of the impending visit from James. His brothers had not been idle. Wat's funeral had been arranged to take place the following week. Jack told them he would be there with Elizabeth. Meanwhile, they were in the process of clearing and cleaning out the cottage ready for Silas Pordage and his family to move in. Jack bade them farewell. He called in at Wat's cottage, Modillyon, on his way, to collect some personal memories of old Wat for himself.

They included several fishing rods, together with basket and tackle, and two long bows with a quiver of arrows, to suit the needs of Symon's boy, Rob, as he grew into manhood. Jack's thoughts turned to quieter moments of retirement. He decided to go fishing for trout in the River Stour, whilst both wife and daughter played happily on the riverbank nearby, making daisy chains or gathering wild flowers.

And of what price the civil wars? On 20 April 1653, with only four years expired since the execution of the King, Oliver Cromwell, together with armed men, stormed angrily into a sitting of the Rump Parliament and in a fit of rage he dissolved it. Red of face and spitting feathers, he made this damning speech, hurling abuse and scourging the worth of those sitting:

'It is high time for me to put an end to thine sitting in this place, which ye hath dishonoured by thy contempt of all virtue and defiled by thine practice of every vice. Ye art a factious crew, and enemies to all good government. Ye art a pack of mercenary wretches, and wouldst, like Esau, sell thy country for a mess of pottage, and like Judas, betray thy God for a few pieces of money.

Is there a single virtue now remaining amongst ye? Is there one vice ye do nay possess?

Ye hath nay more religion than my horse. Gold is thy God. Which of ye hast nay bartered thy conscience for bribes? Is there a man amongst ye that hast the least care for the good of the Commonwealth?

Ye sordid prostitutes, hath ye nay defiled this sacred place and turned the Lord's temple into a den of thieves by thy immoral principles and wicked practices?

Ye are grown intolerably odious to the whole nation.

Ye were deputed here by the people to get grievances redressed. Art thineselves become the greatest grievance?

Thine country therefore calls upon me to cleanse this Augean stable, by putting a final period to thy iniquitous proceedings in this House; and which by God's help, and the strength he hast given me, I am now come to do.

I command ye therefore, upon the peril of thy lives, to depart immediately out of this place.

Go, get ye out! Make haste ye venal slaves – be gone! So! Take away that shining bauble there and lock up the doors behind thee.

In the name of God – go!'

Cromwell's wrath took two months to dissipate. On 4 July 1653, a Barebones Parliament was set up. But that too only lasted for five months, after it became the subject of ridicule and of low social status. The Barebones Parliament was puritanical in attitude but lacked political experience. On 12 December of the same year, the Barebones Parliament was voted out as being not for the good of the Commonwealth.

On 16 December 1653, Oliver Cromwell became Lord Protector of England, Scotland and Ireland, bringing an end to the first period of a diabolical Republican government, called the Commonwealth of England. None of it was satisfactory. What price the death of a king? What price a Republican Commonwealth? There was considerable growing unrest amongst the people of the country. Even one-time supporters of Cromwell felt deprived and called for a return of the monarchy. Such Parliamentarian incompetence, coupled with the puritanical forces that prevailed, were not the reasons men had turned on their own kin, fought their neighbours, or turned against their fellow countrymen for. The whole country had been bathed in blood, and for what? What price civil wars? Two years after he became Lord Protector, Cromwell died. Rump Parliament was restored. Cromwell's son, Richard, took over as Lord Protector. Richard Cromwell was dismissed in 1659 and Long Parliament returned. In 1660, Charles II was restored to the throne. A solitary word summed it all up: 'interregnum'. The result of the civil wars established the principle of limiting the powers of king and monarchy, by requiring Parliament's consent to govern. Ultimately, though not immediately, it strengthened the power of the people to vote through Parliament. The overall cost to achieve this amounted to in excess of 200,000 deaths over the entire United Kingdom throughout the three civil wars.

23

1654–1659

The next six years were relatively quiet in Kent and in the household at Twitham Farm. That is if you can call the cries of a mother in labour and the wailings of her new-born baby 'relatively quiet'! Early in 1654, the household celebrated the birth of a son to Jack and Elizabeth, albeit it was Elizabeth who did the birthing and swearing. Elizabeth's son had been twice as hard to bring into the world as her daughter ever was. Maybe the infant knew the kind of world it was destined to enter. Whatever, John Greenstreet arrived on the scene. John was the infant boy who the doting stepgrandfather, John Cartwright, had dreamed about. At last Cartwright could finalise plans for the inheritance of his estates in the Cartwright name. Without doubt, infant John was born into an inheritance of bountiful riches – provided his parents went along with the wishes and will of his stepgrandfather. Cartwright's machinations were set in stone. Yet even stone can be shattered and swept away. The baby was named John after his father, Jack, and stepgrandfather, John, because all Jacks are Johns, and all Johns are Jacks. Yet Cartwright's designs were not in the forename but in the surname. An alias of which he frequently reminded Jack and Elizabeth. If the infant John were to eventually inherit Cartwright's estates, he had to adopt the alias Cartwright name or forfeit any entitled claim.

Jack went fishing many times in those halcyon days of the 1650s. He became so interested in the pastime of angling that Elizabeth purchased a publication for him in Canterbury, which had come out in 1653. The book was entitled *The Compleat Angler* by Izaak Walton. She thought it might encourage him to bring home larger net results! There was nothing her man liked better on a fine summer's day than to fish, whilst Elizabeth and the children played in the meadow and on the riverbanks behind him. Woebetide any one of the family if they threw stones or other missiles into the water to frighten the fish, as Father stalked his prey and cast his fly, or baited up to sling his hook. Often, they punted up stream to find new fish swims. Sometimes, on hot days, they abandoned fishing altogether and plunged naked into the clear refreshing waters to splash and bathe until their hearts were contented.

Another publication which became of interest to Jack was written by Kent man John Wallis. Wallis, born in Ashford in 1616, became a clergyman, but principally a mathematician, an academic who wrote *Arithmetica Infinitorum*. Many of the principles helped Jack in setting out his carpentry work and stood him in good stead through the latter days of his working life.

Following the cessation of the civil wars, Cromwell's commissioners raised taxes and increased cases of recusancy against their former enemies. Recusancy was a ploy to extract money by heavy fines. Investigations were instigated by the commissioners to ensure there were no further insurrections brewing up. In 1656, Symon Greenstreet and Leonard Smith were again named and recorded by the Commonwealth. They were thought to be in league with Lord Teynham. Again, Cromwell's commissioners were sent to Lodge Lynsted, the manorial home of Baron Roper, to see if he held arms. No arms were found, but a fine was imposed on the baron. He was named a recusant, and lands were seized. Symon and Leonard were pardoned. No further action ensued in respect of their cases. With the withdrawal of Roundhead troops from Kent, the bounty on Jack's head vanished, proving it was a private vendetta by Richard Browne, the regimental colonel of the battalion at Paynter's, Ospringe.

Cartwright, a squire yeoman of the lower upper classes, escaped being compounded for recusancy, despite his Royalist persuasion. He had always played down and kept his Royalist feelings to himself. In so doing he had not attracted the wrath of Parliament. The squire remained wealthy and, unlike so many of his contemporaries, escaped being called to the House of Commons to have a portion of his lands sequestered for recusancy. Squire Cartwright was appointed to oversee the poor, the infirm and the elderly of the parish of Wingham and Staple. He also had the powers to enforce collection of taxes in that respect. Being a rich yeoman farmer, Cartwright kept his table well supplied with fresh meat, vegetables and grain, unlike the labouring men who worked hard in the fields for him day in and day out. They earnt a paltry wage of ten to fifteen pennies per day. Earnings were even less for poor womenfolk.

The only meat low-class peasant families and paupers devoured was gleaned from rancid throwaway scraps, or by their own surreptitious poaching and trapping skills in the dead of night. At night, pheasant and woodcock might be plucked from their roosts and their necks wrung before one could wink an eye! Erroneous early dawn escapades sometimes ended in catching rabbit, hare or wildfowl to enhance the poor man's pottage. This was achieved by a lookout keeping cave, whilst the poacher went about his clandestine business, praying not to get caught and carefully avoiding the dastardly mantraps cunningly set by the gamekeeping fraternity.

Jack considered himself lower middle class, though he was probably upper middle class by association with his father-in-law. He was accepted into the Guild of Master Craftsmen by his good endeavours and professionalism, and soon recognised as a master carpenter/joiner of repute. His skills found him in much demand, both within the parish boundaries and often considerable distances outside. Jack's work took him to Canterbury, where he was engaged by the diocese, under the auspices of the archbishop, in constructing roofs on a mews addition within the cathedral grounds. He had also found spare time to manufacture the beautiful oak and walnut furniture his wife desired. Moreover, it was to the specific style she had chosen. Jack and Elizabeth's half of the large farmhouse was indeed well appointed. The grandfather clock the Cartwrights had purchased for their daughter and son-in-law's wedding present clonked slowly and rhythmically against a wall in the reception chamber.

Rapid changes had taken place in just a few years. By 1656, the belief in witchcraft and magic had subsided and almost disappeared. Jack had started to shave regularly. His beard was cut off and he kept a trim moustache, much to Elizabeth's delight. Newspapers were delivered to the house, and the whole family began to use another invention: toothbrushes! A stagecoach now ran regularly between Dover, Canterbury and London, although it was expensive and frequently held to ransom by highwaymen. People had started to think of personal comforts.

Elizabeth had her hands full with the infant children and did her best to keep them away from contagious diseases. So many children died in infancy. She wore an everyday shift, which she adjusted in size, inch by inch, month by month, for she was already pregnant again. In the spring of 1657, Elizabeth gave birth to another son. Goodwife Elizabeth agreed with her husband to call the new addition Thomas, after Jack's brother Tom, who had saved him from the Roundhead harquebusiers in the snow. John, the older brother, was three years old when Thomas was born and baptised at St Mary's, Wingham. Right from birth, Thomas was a sickly child, often near to death's door from infectious diseases and feverish unknowns. But Thomas, like his uncle Tom, was a survivor, a fighter who would not be beaten by virulence.

Young John was stronger in constitution than his infant brother, Thomas. He caught infections, just the same, but his immune system warded off illnesses without leaving him weak and lethargic, whereas Thomas took ages to rid himself of such problems. Nevertheless, both children survived the years, thanks to good parentage and some constant good fortune in life. Of course, infectious diseases were not only confined to children. In the seventeenth century, death came often and very mysteriously at times. Tuberculosis, jaundice and liver disease, scurvy, measles, rotten teeth, worms, itch, plague, fear and of course the gallows – take your pick!

In Oliver Cromwell's case he suffered from malaria and from 'stone'. Cromwell was said to have died from malarial fever and a urinary kidney infection. He finally expired on Friday 3 September 1658. The eventual cause of death was probably septicaemia. Posthumously, even after death, 'Old Ironsides', as Cromwell was known, did not escape the hangman. Cromwell was succeeded as Lord Protector by his son Richard. Richard Cromwell had no power base in either Parliament or the army. He was forced to resign in May 1659, thus ending the Protectorate. There was no clear leadership from those that jostled for power. The government was in shambles. George Monck, the English Governor of Scotland, at the head of the New Model Army regiments, marched on London and forced the Rump Parliament to re-admit the Long Parliament. Richard Cromwell fled to France. Under George Monck's watch necessary constitutional adjustments were made, leading to a general election and the eventual reinstatement of the throne. The restoration of Charles II was a popular choice.

No precise records ever existed of the actual death toll over the ten years of civil war across the three kingdoms. It is said a range of between 356,000 and 735,000 or a geometric mean of 511,527 people died as a direct result of the wars. That figure is the accumulative estimated loss of men in combat, coupled with civilian deaths, disease, atrocities and genocide attributable to the civil wars. To which might be added many lingering deaths from wounds.

The ordinary man in the street could be excused for deliberating whether the causes he had been caught up in were ever worth fighting for in the first place. Ten years of non-stop battles and skirmishes between Royalists and Roundheads saw the execution of a dictatorial king who believed he ruled by the divine right of God. But mostly it saw the devastating losses of hundreds of thousands of good honest British people. And then, after the Royalist defeats the country was left with shambolic attempts by Parliament to govern. 'To crown it all,' people pressure prevailed in the end. Charles II was ultimately invited to return to the throne. The return of the monarchy was the overwhelming wish of the people, and consent by Parliament and its short-lived Republican Commonwealth was given!

So, besides the usual religious conflict twixt Roman Catholicism and Protestantism and the puritanical extremists, what had the civil wars been for? Was it not to give the ordinary poor citizen, who found himself living in ever-worsening conditions, support for a better lifestyle to ease his miserable situation? That was the spin given when he was asked to fight and to give his life for the cause. Now that the slaughter had ceased, and his friends and neighbours lay brutally slain and his family split apart, could some kind person, whether it be Parliamentarian or King, tell this confused peasant, this poor pauper, just when his lifestyle would improve? In truth, the last thing on his mind was religion, or who governed his existence. His constant quest was to find enough food to feed his family and to find fuel to keep warm through the winter months. To starve or freeze to death had always been his dilemma. Would it continue so?

24

A LAST WILL AND TESTAMENT.
RESTORATION AND DEVASTATION

Cartwright's last will and testament was drawn up in September 1660, as if Charles II had acceded the throne upon his father's death. The will was rather ceremoniously presented to Jack and Elizabeth Greenstreet. The Cartwrights came to Jack and Elizabeth's quarters and knocked upon the door, bearing the document on a silver platter. John and Dyonise were closely accompanied by Tripp, who carried a silver tray with best-quality glasses and a large bottle of sparkling wine. Tripp set the tray down carefully on a tabletop, waited to be dismissed and then departed with well-rehearsed stealth. John Cartwright picked up the will and stood gracefully in front of his stepdaughter and stepson, his white powdered wig fitting snugly on his head, a blue gold-braided waistcoat hugging a baggy-sleeved white linen shirt, and velvet red breeches with pale blue woollen socks pulled up tightly over shapely calves. Black buckled shoes completed his attire. Cartwright carefully read out his will word by word, pausing only at salient points to add comments of explanation, in order to clarify his itemised bequeaths:

'In the name of God Amen

The 23rd September in the twelfth year of our sovereign Lord Charles the Second, by the grace of God, of England, Scotland, France and Ireland, King, defender of the faith etc. In the year of our Lord God, one thousand, six hundred and sixtie, I John Cartwright of the Parish of Wingham in the county of Kent, Yeoman, being sick of body but of perfect remembrance, thanks bee to Almighty God, therefore I doe ordain and make this my last Will and Testamount in manner and forme following (that is to say): First I bequeath my soule into the hands of Almighty God my maker, knowing through the meritorious death and passion of Jesus Christ my only Saviour and Redeemer to receive free pardon and forgiveness of all my sinnes and ask for my body to be buried in Christian Buriall at the discretion of my Executrix hereafter named. Item 1 – I give and bequeath unto Thomas Greenstreet one peece of marsh land; being called the lower peece in Ashe Levill, containing by estimation six acres, more or less, after he cometh unto age of one and twenty years, if hee soe long liveth. And if in case hee dye before hee cometh of the age of one and twenty years, I give and bequeath the said peece of marsh land unto John

Cartwright, the sonne of John Greenstreet. But if hee refuse to be called John Cartwright, then I give unto John Eden the sonne of Robert Eden. Item – I give unto John Cartwright, alias Greenstreet, one peece of marsh land in Ash Levill, being called the upper peece, containing by estimation six acres, more or less, but if in case the said John Cartwright doe chance or happen to dye before he cometh of age of one and twenty years, then my will is that his brother Thomas shall enjoy the said six acres, and further my will is that neither of them shall sell the said peece of marsh land unto any person or persons whatsoever except they doe sell the said marsh land unto each other. Item – I give unto John Eden, my sister's sonne, my house and lands lyeing at a place called Shatterling with all the appurtenances thereto belonging in the Parish of Staple when as the said John doth come of age of one and twenty years. And soe my will is that the above Thomas Greenstreet and John Cartwright alias Greenstreet shall not enjoy the said several parts of marsh land in Ash Levill, next to Sandwich until they come of their several ages of one and twenty years. Item – my will is that Thomas shall hath access through the peece of marsh land, which I hast willed unto John Cartwright alias Greenstreet, without any molestation of the said John Cartwright, alias Greenstreet, or his assigns. Item – I give unto John Cartwright alias Greenstreet all my lands, lyeing and being in Wingham, Staple and Goodnestone, with all and singular their appurtenances thereto belonging, excepting the land and house lyeing at Shatterling before bequeathed and given. Item – I give unto Elizabeth, my daughter, five pounds the yeare soe long as shee liveth by my executrix and after death of my executrix; my will is that John Cartwright shalt pay the said five pounds the yeare unto the said Elizabeth Greenstreet, his mother, soe long as shee liveth. Item – I give and bequeath unto Nathaniell Burk, sonne of Ann Burk, twenty shillings, to be paid by my executrix when he cometh of age of one and twenty years. Item – I give unto the poor of Staple twenty shillings to be paid within twelve months and one day after my decease. Item – I give unto John Cartwright alias Greenstreet all my stock and crops belonging unto me. Item – my will is further that if the said John Cartwright doe take good course in the world, then he shalt hath all the said lands before bequeathed, together with stocks and crops, when hee cometh of the age of sixteen years. Item – I give unto Mary, the wife of Robert Blackman, the summe of five pounds of good lawful money of England to be paid by mine executrix within one whole yeare after my decease. Item – all the remainder of mine goods and chattels, not before given or bequeathed, I give unto Dennie, my wife, after all my debts and funeral expenses being first paid and satisfied and doe make my whole and sole executrix of this my Last Will and Testament, revoking all other wills and testments, this conveying two sheets of paper.

In witness whereof, I hath hereunto sett mine hand and seale, the day and yeare first above written, 1660 John Cartwright his marke. Sealed and delivered in *the presence of Peter Lilley his marke and Charles Wilde his marke.*

Having thus finished the reading of his comprehensive last will and testament, John Cartwright carefully folded the vellum paper and handed the document to Jack for safekeeping.

'This copy of my last will is for ye and Elizabeth to keep safe, Jack. I think our little agreement well and truly looks out for thy eldest son, John, my dear grandson. My younger grandson, Thomas, also hath nay been overlooked. I am sure, if able to keep fit enough, Tom will help his brother manage the estates for fair remuneration, in addition to the acreage I hath bestowed upon him. John needs to retain the Cartwright alias of course. I leave it to thee, Jack, to make sure that constraint is properly adhered to. Thy part of this farmhouse will stay as thine and Elizabeth's for as long as ye both wish to remain. Dennie is also making a will, leaving the farmhouse and its appurtenances to our dear daughter, Elizabeth, here. Consequently, by my wife's will, ye will both prosper, though ye appear to be doing nicely by thine own business, Jack. Ye are now much sought after in the south-east vicinity. I pray that ye, Jack, and my dear stepdaughter, Elizabeth, will stay here to keep an eye on her mother, my dear wife, Dennie.'

'Pray, Dyonise will be looked after, ye need hath nay fear of that,' said Jack. 'But why art ye desirous of bringing this to our attention now, John? Ye still appear in good health this day.'

'Mine looks do nay pity me, Jack. I hath nay felt so good within myself of late. One needs to be careful about such issues. I am getting to be an elderly man, turned fifty now, and I must be prepared to meet my maker. Now, let us drink and seal this, my last will and testament.'

Cartwright popped open the bottle of sparkling wine and filled four fluted glasses with the bubbling wine from France. He topped the glasses up, then handed the fizzing drinks around.

'Let us drink a toast to the success of young John Cartwright alias Greenstreet as he ceases to be a pupil at Wingham St Mary. He hath beaten the bounds, and now, aged six, embarketh upon furthering his education at the ecclesiastical grammar boarding school at Canterbury.'

Jack, who was not happy with the alias arrangement but had nevertheless agreed, to appease both his wife and the Cartwrights, sipped slowly and somewhat distastefully at the bubbly wine in his glass. He preferred a good tankard of beer to wash down any occasion, good or bad.

'I'm not too sure about the clause in your will which refers to John being given all thy lands, stocks and crops at the age of sixteen, should he take good course in the world. He wouldst be a bit young to take control at that age, John,' said Jack with genuine parental concern.

Cartwright sipped his expensive French wine, savouring its pedigree, before responding.

'Well, I hope to be around for some time yet to instruct him in all aspects of my vast estate and the management thereof, Jack, but, in the event of mine passing before he attains such age, I hath good overseers controlling all of mine lands. In addition, thy good self will be there to help and guide him as ye always do. I am sure he will get himself established. I hath also been given good assurance of help from two adjoining yeoman farmers, who are prepared to look out for him and offer advice when and if required. So ye need hath nay concerns in that respect. He will be a very wealthy young man and command much respect in the community will our John.'

'Yea, but he will hath to earn such respect first,' said the boy's father. 'Respect doth nay just turn up at thy door or grow upon trees. I know that from mine own past experiences.'

'John will be alright, Jack,' said Elizabeth. 'He has the same determination as you and always lends his ear well to conversation without attempting to impress. It is there in his blood from thine own line and mine, the line of the Churches of Nonnington. Think about the fine genetic inheritance he hast from thine own father, William of Maidstone, John's true grandfather. Your father was even more powerful than mine own beloved stepfather, John Cartwright.'

'Thank ye for that reminder, daughter dear,' responded Cartwright. ''Tis true what thy goodwife says though, Jack. He lacks for nothing in that direction, doth he? John has powerful forebears.'

'I suppose that is so,' replied Jack, 'but if he takes after me, he is just as likely to decide that farming and land management is nay for him, despite the fortune he wouldst throw away. What if he reacts that way then, John? What if he lacks any interest in thy vast estate and he decides upon another direction in life? I for one wouldst nay stand in his way in that event.'

''Tis a chance I am prepared to take, Jack, and indeed something I care nay to think about. As for thine own direction, that was an entirely different matter. Ye were caught up in civil wars. Otherwise ye wouldst hath done thy father's bidding. Is that theory nay correct Jack?'

'Yea, I hold up my hands, John. I probably wouldst hath done as ye say, even though mine interest in land management lacked in spirit. Yea, there is little doubt about it. I hath always regretted dumping it all upon the shoulders of my brothers, Will and Tom, and leaving that huge burden for them to deal with. I trust I hath been of help to them lately in easing the situation.'

Young John Greenstreet, now called Cartwright, had been attending the petty church school, at Wingham, St Mary the Virgin, since he was four years of age. Each day he had been up and dressed by eight o'clock, ready to be taken by Tripp in the pony and trap and collected again by the manservant soon after four o'clock in the afternoon. As regular as clockwork, Tripp waited at the lychgate to take the infant child back to Twitham Farm. The basic lessons taught were the Bible, early Latin, etiquette and good manners, though John also learned calligraphy, how to scribe his name and to dabble in illumination. John Cartwright Senior had his lawyer, Jerome Bates, prepare an indenture, drawn up in respect of the alias name. There was, however, considerable friction between the church minister of Wingham St Mary and Cartwright Senior concerning the legitimacy of the indenture, due to the indisputable fact that John had been christened and baptised at Wingham in the name of John Greenstreet. According to the minister, only the name given at baptism could be recognised as lawful. The act of baptism had been performed on the child's behalf by the boy's true parents, and the surname of the child's father had been stated and given in the presence of God. Jack was sure the minister had a valid point, but he declined to challenge the situation whilst John Cartwright Senior lived, because Cartwright Senior's health had deteriorated considerably at that time.

Later, young John attended and semi-boarded at Canterbury Grammar School. Then Tripp was able to relax in his old age, as the trap was only required early Monday mornings, and late on Friday afternoons. Young John's curriculum at the grammar school was Latin, the structure of language, the advancing sciences and of course, most importantly, Bible study.

The more Jack thought about his son's alias name, the more he found himself spitting feathers. He had gone along with the Cartwright alias to appease Elizabeth, as much as her stepfather. Now, in hindsight, Jack had grave doubts he had done the right thing. No doubt he had enhanced his son's future by agreeing to the name change, but he realised he was wrong to do so in such manner and form. Jack felt tricked, and yet he knew it was entirely his own fault for ever allowing the alias name to take effect in the first place. The Minister of Wingham was lawfully correct. John had been baptised in the presence of God. It was heresy to make changes to his surname. He was born of the ancient Greenstreet dynasty and should remain so in name and ancestral descent. Jack was angry with himself for ever allowing such misdemeanour. He firmly resolved to rectify the situation, just as soon as John Cartwright Senior deceased.

Meanwhile Jack was not prepared to sit idly by and see the boy mollycoddled purely as a scholar, without learning to fend for himself outside of the classroom. At weekends Jack took John out into the countryside to trap game, stalk wild animals and to teach him the wonders of nature that old Wat had mentored in Jack when he was of similar age. Young John loved to go off with his father into the countryside. During laborious school lessons, he dreamed about the ensuing weekends. But such was the extent of his daydreaming and longing for the weekend breaks to come, that he was often caught out when asked to repeat what the master had just described. He received several beatings for his lack of attention. But his shoulders were broader than his backside, and Latin was no substitute for bending his long bow and losing a straight arrow or snaring a buck rabbit for the pot. As soon as he was old enough, Jack intended to teach his son how to load, prime and fire a flintlock musket, to parry, cut and thrust with a sword, and how to defend himself using sword and dagger. Young John already knew how to ride a horse, and he was thrilled when presented with a pony of his own to take off on.

Thus, it was ordained that young John Greenstreet, alias John Cartwright Junior, would have his childhood and future life presided over by false identity. However, Jack Greenstreet quietly resolved to have his son's true name restored as soon as he was able to so do, without causing unnecessary suffering and friction within the family of the supposed dying Squire John Cartwright Senior, who so wanted a male heir to inherit his estate lands. Squire John, whilst poor in health and frail in body, was quite sound of mind. He did not die until a further seven years had passed, by which time John was thirteen and the alias issue became overlooked.

Earlier in 1660, a positive restoration was underway. With the re-established Long Parliament's consent and invitation, Charles II was proclaimed King. Charles sailed from his exile in the Netherlands and arrived back in Dover on 25 May 1660. He reached London to a tremulous welcome on his thirtieth birthday – 29 May – and was set to be crowned at Westminster Abbey on 23 April 1661. The new so-called 'Convention Parliament' welcomed the Declaration of Breda, in which Charles promised leniency and tolerance towards his enemies. He promised not to exile past enemies, nor to confiscate their wealth. There would be pardons for most of his opponents, except those regicides who signed the death warrant of his father. Nine regicides were identified and hanged, drawn and quartered. Others were jailed for life, or, for those that were extremely lucky, excluded from public office for life. Oliver Cromwell was posthumously convicted of treason. Cromwell's body was disinterred from its tomb in Westminster Abbey and hanged from the gallows at Tyburn, before being subjected to the indignity of posthumous decapitation. A monarch reigned once again!

One other noteworthy incident occurred. A diary started to be penned on 1 January 1660. An exchequer clerk, aged twenty-six years, set quill to paper and recorded events as witnessed through his own honest eyes. His name was Samuel Pepys. *The Diary of Samuel Pepys* chronicled tumultuous London life for the next nine and a half years, an invaluable diary which was set to accurately record events of the era and mark its place in history. Of the Restoration, Pepys wrote, *'The public was full of hope at the restoration of the monarchy. The people rejoiced when Charles 2nd rode into London on a white charger as King. Bells were rung, flowers strewn on the roads, and the wine flowed. Citizens lined the streets from London to Rochester.'* Pepys' many jottings would be preserved for future posterity with provenance.

Charles II was a Catholic at heart and desired to formalise the toleration of Catholics and non-conformists, but he was forced to back down by a hostile Anglican and Presbyterian Parliament. In the latter days of 1660, Charles' exultation at the Restoration was brought to sudden sadness by the deaths of his younger brother, Henry, and sister Mary. Both died from the devastating disease of smallpox. Charles was formerly crowned King in 1661. In 1662, a *Book of Common Prayer and Holy Sacraments* was published for use of the Church of England.

After ten long years of civil war, it seemed, at last, the country was settling down to a normal and peaceful way of life. But these were hard and very brutal times. If it was not war it was witch-hunting, and if it was not witch-hunting it was the return of the 'Black Death'.

Throughout 1664 people commenced to fall sick. At first the virus affected small pockets around the City of London. It then increased in intensity affecting the outer regions of London. In 1665 tragedy of the worst kind struck. It was bubonic and it showed no mercy to people by way of cruel and lingering suffering. The virus culminated in 100,000 deaths in eighteen months in the city and its suburbs. It became known as 'The Great Plague.'

25

—

PLAGUE, 1665–1666

The good practices of Widow Goody and her daughter Mary had taught Jack a lesson as he lay seriously wounded within the confines of Claxfeldestane in 1643. That lesson was the goodwife's belief in keeping clean. Widow Goody insisted on the need to wash the body down regularly with boiled water. Martha Goody had been strict in her administrations in that respect. The widow had a second sense that 'cleanliness was next to godliness,' and keeping clean assisted in healing wounds. Most physicians refuted the idea, believing that to remain dirty kept disease out. Generally, people rarely washed, although they did rub themselves down with rags dipped in herbs and flowers, attempting to kill off lice, fleas and ticks, and hoping to rid themselves of pestilence and intestinal worms. The hands were seldom washed prior to meals.

Bluntly, the rancid stench of people was overpoweringly foul most times.

Jack washed regularly and insisted that Elizabeth and the children adopt a similar routine. The family often bathed and washed themselves in the River Stour, river dipping even in the winter months. In the main, the consensus of people was to wash once each year, usually in May, prior to the May Day festivities. If a member of Jack's family became ill, as Thomas frequently did, herbs were collected, as Widow Goody had prescribed when she helped Jack beat gangrene. Wintergreen, hypericum, sage and oregano. Jack had also purchased Nicholas Culpeper's book called *The English Physician*. Culpeper described and illustrated many herbs and linked them to the signs of the zodiac. He also took note of a physician by the name of Thomas Cogan, who recommended: '*Wash thy face with clean cold water and especially bathe and plunge the eyes therein, for that nay only cleanseth away the filth, but also comforteth and greatly preserveth the sight.*' In Gervase Markham's popular seventeenth-century work *The English Housewife*, he wrote about making pomanders, which were carried around and sniffed at when confronted by a foul stench, be it of rancid material in nature, or wafted from human excrement. Elizabeth made pomanders for Christmas presents, mixing up: two pennyworth of laudanum, two pennyworth of storax liquid, a pennyworth of calamus aromaticus and much balm, half a quarter of a pound of fine wax containing cloves and mace, three pennyworth of liquid aloes, eight pennyworth of nutmegs and four grains of musk; all beaten together till of perfect substance, then moulded to any fashion and dried.

She also made cake soap to rub over them when bathing in the stream. Christmas was back in fashion with a vengeance, now that King Charles II had been restored to the throne, and the dark-clothed puritanical Oliver Cromwell, who had attempted to stop such celebration, had been posthumously disinterred, hanged and decapitated. The first Christmas carol was written. It was a song for all classes of society entitled, 'While Shepherds Watched Their Flocks'.

A suitable privy was an issue rectified by Jack. He constructed a moveable timber toilet near to the rear door of the house, which could be raised akin to a sedan chair. The shelter had a built-in bench seat with circular aperture sited over a deeply dug pit. After bowel relief, each user sprinkled a scoop of sawdust sweepings saved from Jack's workshop. The sawdust was kept in a large wooden box, regularly filled for the purpose. When the pit was full, the privy was picked up by two men and moved to an adjoining position, sited over another deep-dug pit. A pail of fresh water was drawn from the well each day and tipped into a washing bowl outside the privy. A cake of Elizabeth's scented soap and a drying rag hung inside the privy.

The first inkling Jack and Elizabeth had that everyday life was out of kilter was when young John was hurriedly sent home by coach and four from his boarding school. A letter from the headmaster instructed parents to keep sons at home until further notice. There had been a severe outbreak of an unknown disease at the Canterbury school. Four pupils had been taken sick by an unknown infection. Two of the four pupils had been overwhelmed and had succumbed to the pestilence. They died following terrifying fevers, giant blistering and sneezing and choking fits. One other boy had been given the last rites. The boys sharing John's dormitory had been immediately quarantined. On arrival home, John told his mother that he did not wish to eat. Frightened for his life, Elizabeth boiled water and washed her son from top to toe, then sent him to bed. She burnt his clothes and kept her other children, Thomas and Elizabeth, confined to their chambers. The following day, John came down from his room feeling hungry and looking to break the fast. He was delighted when told school was banned. In fact, John did not return to Canterbury for two years. The plague spread rapidly across London, which soon became 'Hell on Earth'. Towns and villages alongside the roads to the city were the first to be infected, before the pestilence engulfed habitations over the whole of the country. People dropped like dead flies. Late 1664 saw the 'Great Plague' out of control.

Jack decided he could not have the boy sitting about, unoccupied and doing nothing. After much deliberation, he set him to work in the carpentry shop for three days each week. John Cartwright Senior was delighted to have his grandson work as apprentice to his farm managers for the other three working days. Squire Cartwright said it was an opportunity to give his grandson a good grounding for what lay ahead when he turned sixteen. Twitham being a countryside place, some considerable distance from London and Canterbury, gave the family hope. They were relatively isolated and prayed daily to God that they might avoid the plague.

As the plague spread, Jack's carpentry work imploded. He became concerned about his brothers at Ospringe, James of Claxfield, and Symon, Marion and their children. He had not seen them since Christmas. Against Elizabeth's advice, he decided to ride over to ascertain the welfare of his kin. Elizabeth had grave concerns about the wisdom of such a trip and pleaded with her husband not to go on such a venture. To dice with death in areas close to London was madness. She did not want him exposed to the pestilence. But Jack felt obliged to go to those who had helped him out in past times, and indeed saved his life. He explained to his wife his innermost feelings, telling her he would never be able to forgive himself if he abandoned any one of them in an hour of need. Elizabeth had bad feelings about her husband's trip, exacerbated by events which occurred on that 9 October day of his departure in 1665.

After tucking into oatcakes plus two boiled duck eggs, Jack sipped his new love: coffee. He opened the *London Gazette* to read an article by Pepys relating to the plague outbreak and the great man's obsession with death. An etched illustration showed bodies being loaded onto deathcarts, to be taken for burial in a mass grave, the handlers puffing hard on the tobacco in their well-lit clay pipes to help disguise the stench of the deceased. Samuel Pepys reported: '*... talking with a borsholder in the highway, came close by the bearers with a dead corpse of the plague; but Lord! To see what custom is, that I am close almost to think nothing of it.*' The *London Gazette* reported: '*... after plagues in 1603, 1625 and 1636, this Great Plague is the most significant since the Black Death in the 14th Century. It is likely to have arrived upon English shores from the Netherlands, possibly carried by rat fleas. 7,000 deaths a week are listed.*'

After breakfast, having scanned the pages of the newspaper, Jack made ready to depart for his visit to north-west Kent. Before he could finish his ablutions, Tripp burst into the parlour, inclined his head, touched his forelock, and beckoned to Jack with a bony finger, calling loudly,

'Thou best cometh quickly, Master, thine horse Acorn doth nay look right to me. He lieth on one side, breathes difficult and canst barely lift his head. He is making weird guttural sounds.'

Jack leapt up and ran to the stables with Tripp hard on his heels. In truth, Jack knew his old companion and friend was nearing his end. The chestnut stallion was a good age and had seen off twenty-five years of faithful service. He had transported his master over much of England and accompanied him many times in battle. Acorn had taken part in battles at Oxford, Lostwithiel, Naseby and in many Kentish insurrections. In no skirmish had the staunch horse backed away from the discharge of musket and cannon fire or attempted to throw his rider. Jack looked lovingly into the stallion's eye. Acorn snorted and whinnied in recognition of his master and attempted to lift his head. Jack squatted on his haunches and stroked the animal's muzzle and forehead knowingly, speaking quietly to his good friend as he always had. Acorn would never rise to his feet again. His master knew that. If left to his own devices, the stallion would simply die a slow and painful death. With tears in his eyes, Jack addressed Tripp:

'Kindly go and fetch a flintlock pistol, Tripp. Elizabeth will direct ye to it. Load and prime it with great care, and bring it to me ready to discharge, wouldst ye, Tripp? When ye hath done that, leave me and mine horse Acorn to say our farewells. Find four good labourers and rope to drag Acorn onto the hay wain and have a large grave of adequate depth excavated between the copper beech trees, so when I look out from mine bedchamber, I know where he lieth.'

'I shall attend to it without delay, Master Jack. There are a dozen men working on raising the beet crop. I will take four of the best of them to excavate the grave. I shall be as quick as 'tis possible with thy flintlock, Master. 'Twill be ready to discharge, hath nay fear of it.'

Squire Cartwright walked into the stables with John Cartwright Junior and made straight for Jack. He put an arm around his son-in-law's muscular shoulders and said not a word. He knew, as most men knew, the value of a good horse and the numerous events and camaraderie that tied man and beast together in a lifetime. Acorn was spent and best quickly dispatched.

Jack squeezed Cartwright's hand for showing kindness, then with tears running down his cheeks he turned to address his young son, John. He spoke in a low voice, juddering with grief:

'Understand, one day in the future, John, ye will hath to face the very same situation I face now. I am so saddened by this day. Tarry with me whilst I put an end to such misery. Then pacify thy father, for 'tis a burden I find hard to bear on my own. 'Twill be over soon enough, son.'

Tripp returned with the pistol loaded with ball and primed ready to discharge. Jack placed the weapon appropriately, turned his own head to one side, looked at his son John and pulled the trigger. With the flintlock smoking in one drooping hand, he held his son's hand tightly with the other and walked out of the stable to the courtyard. Jack gasped and juddered in grief. The bond between father and son strengthened. Squire Cartwright waited outside of the stable.

'I know ye were planning to go to Teynham Manor today, Jack. Tomorrow will do just as well. Ye will nay get to a horse-trading fayre for some time with this plague raging, I declare.'

Aware of his son-in-law's grief, Cartwright took hold of the man's drooping arm to relieve him of the snaphance pistol. Wisps of gunpowder smoke seeped from the orifices of the flintlock.

'Thank'ee, John. I need a short while to come to terms with my loss. Ye go on with my son, I shall right myself in a moment or two. Acorn is a huge loss to me, 'tis like losing a limb.'

'Quite so, Jack.' Cartwright hesitated, then said, 'There are three horses in the paddock, besides mine, and Elizabeth's pony. Take thy pick of any one of them to tide thee over, or keep one for as long as ye need the service of a nag. Try them all. I care little which one thou chooseth to keep. It will at least serve ye until the horse fayre comes around again, in about a year's time.'

'Ay, thank'ee again, John. I was wondering how to get to see my kin. It is imperative that I do go tomorrow. I know Elizabeth wouldst grant the use of her pony, but I hath nay wish to leave her without a mount. She is against such visits because of the plague, but I owe my kin much, verily my own life. I hath a duty to go to them. Kindly hand back the flintlock. I may need it on the road tomorrow. I like to travel with a brace of pistols, in addition to mine rapier.'

Yeoman Cartwright returned the cooling flintlock and bade his son-in-law farewell. He put his hand upon young John's shoulder and guided him away from his distraught father. Jack overheard his son's whispered conversation with his stepgrandfather as they departed:

'Why didst Father hath to shoot Acorn, Grandfather? Hast the horse broken a fetlock?'

'Well, ye need to understand this, young John…' Their chatter faded as they walked away.

Elizabeth came out of the house to take her husband's arm. She steered him indoors and found some French brandy. Filling a wine glass almost to the brim she thrust it into his hand.

'Here, drink this down, 'twill help dull the blow of thy tragic loss, mine poor dear husband.'

'Yea, Lizzy, to tell the truth I knew Acorn's time had come several days ago. I attempted to make him canter up from Long Acre. He wanted none of it. We walked back at a snail's pace, for I desired nay to force him. I was unable to bring myself to come to terms with his wheezing and rattling, but I had a feeling then I wouldst never sit astride his sturdy flanks again. What service he gave me, eh, Lizzy, what service. He was indeed the truest of all mine friends.'

'Father says ye are to take one of his nags from the paddock, Jack, to tide ye over for a while.'

'Yea, I must away and select one now. I am determined to ride over to Ospringe and Teynham tomorrow to enquire after the welfare of my brothers and my dear cousin James. If the plague is nay so prevalent, I might go further along Watling Street to call upon Symon and family.'

'Go thee careful, Jack, ye do nay possess a certificate of health to travel from the authorities.'

'True, but I read in the *London Gazette* that forgers are making a fortune issuing counterfeit certificates. I am nay too sure about the outlying areas, or how badly the hamlets and villages are affected. Rest assured, Lizzy, I shall refrain from taking risks. I will skirt those areas showing signs of the pestilence and will nay alight to dwell in such places, hath ye nay worries.'

Jack chose a good-looking black mare called Molly. He instructed Tripp, who had just returned after burying Acorn, to clean Molly and ready her for the journey early next morning.

Molly and Jack quickly became acquainted. Mol was easy to mount and ride. The mare never shied away. She was not as frisky as Acorn. The October morning was warm and muggy, and clung on to the remnants of an unusually hot summer. Such extremes of heat had added to the spread of the Great Plague. It was reported that 12,000, from a population of 500,000, had died in London in the last week of September. Though whether all the deaths were due to plague was not fully ascertained. People were dying all the time from mysterious illnesses; tuberculosis, scurvy, measles and 'stopping of the stomach' were all known to be heavy hitters. The King and his entire court had fled to Oxford. Even there it wasn't entirely safe, as the disease had spread rapidly to many outlying areas. The roads leading away from the City of London were crowded by a hoard of frightened people, who fled deep into the countryside.

As Jack neared Faversham, he became aware of numerous red crosses painted on doors. The isolation period was forty days. Once a person had been diagnosed, the whole family were locked together indoors, for the entire period of incubation. The signs were red circular blotches on the skin and large pus-filled sacs found under armpits and in areas of the groin. The final symptoms, prior to death, were sneezing fits. In Ospringe, old Wat Harrys' cottage, Moddilyon, was boarded up. A huge red cross was dribbled across the door. Life had dealt one bad card after another to Yeoman Silas Pordage and his family. First it was the Roundheads, who burnt his house down and decimated his crops, now the deathly plague had struck. The cottage Jack inherited from Wat, and in turn had leased to Silas Pordage for a peppercorn rent, was now a den of pure hell. He imagined the whole family inside, trapped and isolated – waiting for death. Or had they already succumbed? He wondered who brought food and water to them, or indeed if any one of the family remained alive within. For the sake of his own family's safety, Jack could not investigate the plight of the Pordage family. He swallowed hard and spurred Mol on to Woodlarks, praying that his brothers had fared better.

The entrance to Woodlarks was fenced off. The high five-bar gate was nailed shut and a bold notice had been erected, its font broad and threatening – *'Keep out – no admittance – no peddlers – trespassers will be fired upon'*. Jack rode along the fence line until he found a lower section for Molly to jump. Then he turned the mare away at right angles from the fence for some hundred yards, turned again to face the obstacle and spurred her into a full gallop.

'Over ye go, Mol, good girl,' he urged, slapping the side of the mare's neck with one hand.

Jack sailed over the fence and raced down the slope towards his family home. He tethered Mol to a rail adjoining the front entrance porch, climbed the shallow steps and banged loudly on the oak studded door. There was no answer. He waited a while then thumped upon the door again with the bone end of his riding crop. A small landing window, situated over the portico entrance, opened slowly with a creak. A gruff voice bellowed deafeningly downwards.

'What do ye want? Step back and identify thyself and make haste. I canst nay wait all day.'

Jack ran back down the steps and onto the gravel. He looked up at the square leaded window which had been opened just wide enough to present the barrel of a short musket. The wide brass muzzle glinted in the midday sunlight, blinding Jack for a minute. The gun was trained fully upon him. Behind the stock he could just make out the head of a man. Long straight black hair drooped each side of the firearm. The brass muzzle was thrust forward in a threatening manner, and the man's larynx boomed forth again, his tone deep and demanding.

'If ye doth nay want thy head to fly from thine shoulders ye had best state the purpose of the visit, sir. What is it ye want? Declare thyself or I shalt discharge this blunderbuss in thy direction. At this range I shalt nay miss, ye canst rest assured. When I say rest assured, at rest ye will surely be when thy swede leaves thine shoulders to rest upon yon gate post!'

'Well, ye impudent rascal, my name is Jack Greenstreet. I am the older brother of William of Maidstone. I demand ye go and find my brother forthwith, so that we might hath discourse.'

The musket was hurriedly withdrawn from the window. Jack had a good view of him now. The man appeared to be a middle-aged scrawny fellow, with a hooked nose and very bushy eyebrows. The deep-voiced aggressive manner was suddenly dropped as the servant adopted a more servile, subservient whining in his tone, causing Jack's grin to broaden across his face.

'Pray, accept humble apologies, Master. Tonks should hath recognised thy likeness to Master William. Pray, wait there, whilst I go in haste to find Master William. I shall go at great pace.'

A full two minutes passed before there was a scratching inside the door, then the sound of several bolts being drawn back. The door cracked half open and William peered out.

'Ye hast nay brought the pestilence with ye, hast thou, Jack?' enquired his brother fretfully.

'Nay, Will, I cometh clean in health, ye silly bugger. Why hast ye hidden thyself away in such a withdrawn manner, and what pathetic scoundrel doth thee employ to address me so roughly?'

'Ah, that is mine servant Tonks. I instructed him to turn away any unknown or dubious characters from the door. We art surrounded by the plague here, brother. The adjoining farm hast been closed, together with many houses in our vicinity. The Maison Dieu, which serves to look after lepers, was also struck by plague last week. It hast been boarded up and marked with a red cross, like so many buildings. I decided to take nay chances. Mine isolation is voluntary, together with mine servants who live beneath this roof. We plan to stay isolated until the pestilence ceases to spread. We hath plenty of cattle to milk and food to live on. We hath duck, chicken, sheep and goat. In addition, there are, as ye well know, wild deer and boar to be hunted. There are plenty of snipe, heron, woodcock and crane in the grounds and rabbit and hare to shoot. Then there are the crops. We are laid to siege by this Great Plague for its duration. The well and stream issue forth good clean water to make beer and wine for drinking. Therefore, we lack for nothing other than our freedom to roam outside of the estate. Come ye in and dine with me, brother. Tell me why ye cometh here to thy family home?'

"'Tis purely and simply to enquire after thy welfare, Will. Nothing more and nothing less. I became much concerned for all mine kin when this terrible plague struck. And what of Thomas, Will? Where is our younger brother, Tom? Is he nay longer dwelling here with ye?'

'Therein lieth a strange story, Jack. Tom met a young lass in Selling, by the name of Margarett Taylor. He took to courting her. After we sold off the lands, as ye suggested, a suggestion to which we are indebted to ye, we split the vast proceeds. Tom bought a house near to the church of St Mary the Virgin in Selling. He moved into the house about six months ago, with intent to marry Margarett. Then the plague struck here at Ospringe, and he told me he intended to stay away from the area. He took his belongings, and I hath nay heard of him since. We parted on good terms. I pray he is in good health, but Tom might also be besieged by plague.'

'Well, well, well, the little whippersnapper. Getting married, eh! Who wouldst hath thought my little brother Tom is planning to get himself married? 'Twill be ye next, Will. Hath ye plans that way? I shall track Tom down once this plague relents and I canst buy a new horse.'

Will poured glasses of wine from a decanter and offered one to Jack. He enquired about Acorn.

'Well, William?' Jack persisted. 'Woodlarks needs a family of children running about its structure. It wouldst bring the old place back to life again. A rich man such as ye now art ought to attract a suitable young lady to cometh in thy direction. Ye canst nay leave it all to Tom and me to produce the next generation for the continuation of our ancient family dynasty.'

'Speaking of wealth,' said William, avoiding the question posed by his brother, 'Tom and me hath set aside a princely sum for thyself, Jack. 'Tis from the huge amount of money we made from Father's estates. Ye advised us well to sell off some of the properties. I admit to ye now I was getting myself into much trouble in managing Father's vast estates. James helped us out very professionally with the bookkeeping and in selling off the lands. We paid him handsomely for his work. We agreed we owe ye ample reward also. It was, after all, thy good counsel and guidance in the first place, which dragged us from the deep mire I was getting ourselves into.'

'William, I hath already told ye I will nay accept monies from Father's estate. Ye know well enough I left ye all to get on with managing the lands, properties and affairs when I left home to support King Charles. It is thyself and Thomas who should reap the rewards of inheritance. Please share the amount equally betwixt thyself and Tom. In any case, Will, I am quite well off myself. Mine children will reap the benefits of Cartwright's estate lands. The carpentry and joinery work also brings in a pretty penny. Any hand I gave in bailing ye out of a difficult situation was just family advice. Ye did the right thing, by the way. Neither of us were cut out to manage vast estates like Father did. Ye applied thy best ability to continue Father's work in extremely difficult times of raging civil wars. I admire ye immensely for that, Will.'

William pondered a moment, then took keys from his waistcoat pocket and unlocked a bureau in one corner of the room. He came back with a bag of coin and held it out for Jack to take.

'Now that we art friends again, Jack, and I pray it is our best intentions to remain so, I wish to give ye a present, from Tom and myself, from brothers to brother. If, as ye say, the monies are all mine and Tom's now, ye will accept our present in good grace. It is a sum of fifty pounds of good English money. Please spend it at thy leisure. Purchase a good pedigree horse to replace the loyal companion ye hath recently lost. Indeed, buy new steeds for all thy family. Once I wanted thy head on a platter, Jack. Then ye saved mine own neck from hanging.'

Jack nodded knowingly. He embraced his brother for the first time since the day of Jack's departure from Woodlarks, when he had argued and threatened the Royalist case, and crossed swords with his uncle, Lord Peter. Jack's father, William of Maidstone, had ordered him out of the house, and young William, having also espoused the parliamentary cause, had witnessed the entire scene through a crack in the door. But Jack had not abandoned Will when his head was in the noose. Now, their broken bond had been repaired by give and take on both sides.

'Now then, Jack, let us see what fine mess the cook has dreamed up for us. It smells alright to mine nostrils. Nay doubt ye still hath a yearning for some tasty food. I remember thine appetite was always keen, and there is plenty of tender meat to devour and good wine to drink.'

Tonks saddled Mol up, ready to leave Woodlarks. It was with a feeling of contentment and a full stomach that Jack bade his brother William farewell. He left the family home satisfied that at least one brother was safe and locked away from the pandemic, albeit in a most extreme manner. Lighter of heart, yet hoping upon hope Thomas was in good health, Jack journeyed on to Teynham Manor. He would try to find his younger brother, Thomas, on the return journey. He would pass close to Selling, which was a small village just a few miles from Faversham.

Jack approached the tightly packed houses in Greenstreet with caution. The Dover Castle alehouse was boarded up. The street was as rancid as ever – full of shit and corruption. The surface of the roadway rippled with rodent activity, akin to a dirty brown sea of mice and large black rats. The rodents fed on garbage thrown out of windows and doors. Many of the houses had red crosses painted over boarded-up doors, warning of the bubonic plague contained within. The Great Plague had obviously hit Teynham Manor hard. 1665 had been the hottest summer in living memory. It had been ideal conditions for the virus and uncontrolled infestations of pests. A sash window slid open. Jack reined Mol in hard as the contents of a steaming chamber pot were emptied from a first-floor bedchamber. A vile soup of bodily excrement and urine landed with a splat, less than five feet from the mare's feet, causing the writhing mass of grey-black rats to run in every conceivable direction. The stench was unbelievable, making Jack retch several times. Some men puffing hard on clay pipes pulled a heavy cart laden with dead bodies. One of them shouted out loudly, 'Bring out thy dead.' It was a cue for those with death in their houses to bring bodies out to be loaded onto the cart for burial in a mass grave. Piled high with corpses, the moving cart scattered the rodents, which scurried to spread disease everywhere. The village was a cocktail of filth and unbelievable human degradation.

Jack had seen enough of the rancid squalor. He veered off and cut down a back alley towards Lynsted church, pausing to lean over the mare in a corner of Ludgate Lane to heave up the full content of his luncheon. Several houses in the lane had red crosses splurged across the doors. One house, near the old forge, was burnt to the ground. He wondered if the fire had been caused in a deliberate attempt to burn out the plague. He passed the church of St Peter and St Paul and found the back track leading from the church to Claxfield. When he came to the rear of Claxfeldestane, he turned into the entrance he knew so well and dismounted from Mol, pausing to relieve himself in a nearby bush. He gathered himself and crept to the front of the farmhouse. Having ascertained there were no red cross markings on the doors, he returned to the rear door and banged hard. There was movement inside. Bolts were drawn back. The door opened slowly. James appeared, looking gaunt, drawn and white from fatigue.

'Ah, 'tis ye, Jack. Ye look healthy enough, cousin. 'Tis glad I am to see thee, but why hast thou come to this village of hell? Ye should nay be riding in the path of this Great Plague. The disease is prevalent in all the villages near to Watling Street, right up into the city. Come ye inside. The servants hath fled in fear of catching the plague and art headed for the countryside. My mother, Maria, has died and I survive here on my own, abandoned by all at Claxfeldestane.'

'God rest her soul, James. Didst mine aunt fall foul of this pox-ridden disgusting pestilence?'

'Nay, Jack, it was consumption that claimed her. They took her away by cart piled with bodies, just the same. The undertakers canst nay handle so many deaths. I pleaded she be given a decent burial. It hast preyed upon mine soul to see her taken to be buried with the stricken.'

James choked on his words and emitted a sob of grief. He gripped his friend's hand firmly and trembled throughout his body. Overwhelmed by emotion the two men clung tight together.

'I could nay find a priest to sing for my mother's soul, Jack. She deserved so much better than that. Mother was always such an uncomplaining goodwife to Father and a wonderful mother to all her children. I pray for her salvation every night, and for all those poor souls I knew well as reeve, who hath been taken by this deadly plague. So many citizens hath expired in the pandemic. The village hast become the

Devil's haven, Jack. I see nay sign of regression in this vile disease. Unsuspecting wretches drop like dead flies. The poor villagers art but a veil of ghosts. I decided nay to venture forth, other than to feed the animals. I hath survived mainly on oatcake, wine and cider for many weeks now. Lord show some mercy on us all.'

'Ay, James, ye hath had a grim time of it, I canst tell. In all truth, cousin, if ye stay here on thy own ye may well catch this virulent pestilence. Best find a horse and come back with me for a while to Wingham. We art tucked out of the way there at Twitham Farm, and hopefully we will avoid this frenzied predatory monster, which is set to ravage everybody in its path. Ye will be safer by far with Elizabeth and I, and more than welcome to stay until this aggressive Black Death subsides. Pray, come back with me now, James. We will look after thee as ye once looked after me. Some good food inside thy belly will see ye chirp up in nay time at all.'

'What about the cattle and chickens, Jack? I canst nay leave them to starve.'

'We will take the chickens back with us and turn the cattle loose to graze as they find. They will have to fend for themselves. I hath one more call to make before we leave, James. I am anxious to learn of the health and welfare of Symon and his family. I must go to see them.'

'Oh, 'tis more bad news, I am afraid to report, Jack. I rode over to seek their welfare myself but was turned away by a borsholder and his gang of men. A red cross was splashed across the five-bar entrance gate. I was informed by the borsholder that the farm was quarantined and told to stay away for mine own good health, as the whole family were succumbed by plague. As I rode back to Teynham, in a poor state of mind, I noticed groups of people digging vast excavations, which I assumed were grave pits. There were mounds of bodies piled high in the churchyards. It is no ordinary epidemic we suffer, Jack. This disease is feared by all.'

'Poor Symon and Marion and my delightful nephews and nieces, all succumbed, I simply canst nay believe 'tis so. I owe so much to Cousin Symon. He fought so faithfully for King Charles.'

Jack pondered a while, shuddered, grimaced, then clapped a firm hand on James' shoulder.

'Go now, James, pack thyself some items whilst I ready a horse for ye and attend to the chickens and cattle. We canst be back at Wingham crossroads by nightfall if we leave within the hour.'

Jack called out to James' horse in the paddock, took hold of the bridle and led the steed to the stables. He prepared and saddled the mare, then found some lidded wicker baskets and caught hold of a dozen chickens, stuffing them into the containers. After opening the top gate to allow the cattle to roam freely, he secured the outhouses and empty stables. By the time he had lashed the wicker baskets to the horses, James was ready. They secured the old Wealden Hall house, leaving Claxfeldestane abandoned and forlorn for the first time since its erection. Leaving the filth of old Watling Street behind them they struck out across country.

On the 16th day of October 1665, Samuel Pepys wrote the following in his diary:

> *But Lord, how empty the streets are, and melancholy, so many poor sick people in the streets, full of sores, and so many sad stories overheard as I walk, everybody talking of death, and that man sick, and so many in this place,*

and so many in that. And they tell me in Westminster
there is never a physitian, and but one apothecary left,
all being dead, but that there are great hopes of a great
decrease this week. God send it.

There was no time to go looking for Thomas in Selling. Nightfall had descended by the time Jack and James arrived at Wingham crossroads. They veered their horses off at the Staple junction to be met by a further unexpected encumbrance. Villagers had erected a barricade across the road. There were fires burning. As the cousins approached the barricade a row of muskets was levelled at them. In no uncertain terms a spokesman called to them to turn about.

'If ye value thy lives come thee nay nearer. The village of Staple is isolated against the spread of the Great Plague. Unless ye hold a certificate of health ye are nay granted access beyond this barrier. We desire to keep our village clean. Turn ye about, or we will fire upon ye.'

Jack recognised the spokesperson as the village slaughterer and butcher, Jesse Sellen.

'Greetings, Jesse, 'tis Jack Greenstreet the carpenter and joiner, together with mine cousin James, that come upon ye this night. We art desirous of reaching mine home at Twitham Farm.'

'I am sorry, Jack. We art protecting the village against spread of disease and know not where ye hast been, nor what disease ye may hath encountered on thy journey. Our determination is final. We hath to protect our sorely frightened families. Access is prohibited this way. Ye are unwelcome and will be fired upon if ye attempt entry. Other roads are guarded likewise.'

Jesse Sellen crossed the barricaded line and advanced on the riders, all the while holding his musket in a threatening position. He walked to within two yards of Jack and spoke in a whisper:

'Pray, find another route back to Twitham Farm, Jack. Ye canst pick thy way along the River Stour. I dare nay be seen to give way in front of the other men or 'twill defeat our objective.'

Jesse Sellen backed away, his weapon still levelled at the riders. Jack raised a hand in acknowledgement and the two cousins turned to ride back towards Wingham village.

'Come, James, we will go via Wingham High Street. I know a route from Shatterling where a bridge spans the river. We canst ride across the ash levels up to Twitham. We shall be there in an hour if we go carefully in the dark. Hath nay fear, I know the trail well enough.'

The two men arrived at Shatterling and picked their way in the darkness. They crossed a narrow bridge over the Little Stour. Glimpses of moonlight helped their navigation in the closing darkness of late evening. Jack urged the horses up grass tracks, making for the lights of Staple which shone out a mile or two above them. James clung on for dear life, the chooks clucking nervously in the wicker baskets. On reaching the church, Jack knew the way back to Twitham like the palm of his hand. Both Elizabeths, John and Thomas greeted the riders with relief.

People saw the plague as a punishment from God, but as colder weather set in the number of plague victims decreased. Deliberate isolation also helped prevent further spread of disease.

26

THE GREAT FIRE OF LONDON, 1666

In February 1666, it was considered safe enough for the King to return from Oxford to London. The plague had abated enormously and James Greenstreet, who had been no burden at Twitham Farm, contended that if it was safe enough for the King to return to London, it was safe enough for him to return to Claxfield. James set out for Claxfeldestane looking plump and healthy from Elizabeth's good cooking. He was a man on a mission. On his return, in his capacity as reeve and manor steward, James planned to instigate a new regime of cleanliness. It would begin with street cleaning and hand-dug pit latrines wherever possible, such as Jack had organised at Twitham. Handwashing was also to be introduced, wells excavated, and village pumps installed. Whilst in Jack's good care, James had scribed a dozen public health bills, in respect of his plans. The bills addressed 'all good and open people', and he planned to have them signed by the baron and displayed around the villages at strategic points of the manor. He also planned to arrange for an extensive cull on rodents and to appoint a chief rat catcher.

It was thought the Great Plague had come from Amsterdam, via Dutch trading ships carrying bales of cotton to the London docks. The Dutch were in fact as much a plague on the British as the Great Plague itself. Some say the Great Fire of London was started by the Dutch, though there was no evidence to support such a statement. The Netherlands had been at war with the British navy since 1663. As usual, it was the British who provoked the war by striking and capturing Dutch bases in West Africa and New Amsterdam. There had been many battles at sea, and the British had largely prevailed. But the Dutch struck below the belt when the British were spent from the Great Plague, and down and out from the ensuing Great Fire of London, which destroyed their capital city. Events culminated in a Dutch raid up the River Medway.

The fire started a few minutes after midnight on Sunday 2 September 1666. Flames took hold at Thomas Farynor's bakery in Pudding Lane soon after midnight. Initially it was thought to be a minor fire, but the flames were fanned by a strong wind that night, which drove the fire through open roof spaces, causing it to spread rapidly out of control. The Great Fire of London raged over four days, decimating the city and rendering hundreds of thousands of Londoners homeless. Samuel Pepys, with his own house under threat, observed and documented the raging inferno from aboard a boat on the River Thames writing: *'So near the fire as we* could for smoke; and all over the Thames, with one's face in the wind, you were almost burned with a shower of fire-drops.' Pepys saw the devastation from the river. Congested higgledy-piggledy houses, built of wood and thatch, pitch and tar, plus warehouses of oil, wines, brandy, cloth and other inflammatory stocks, fuelled the fire's swift impetuosity. A hot, bone-dry summer rendered buildings tinder-dry to nourish the inferno. The Thames acted as a barrier in places, though the houses on London Bridge were burnt down. Bellowing winds fanned the hungry flames north and west to devour the financial centre of the city, where gold reserves were urgently saved from melting down. The following day the winds changed direction to blow eastwards and engulfed St Paul's Cathedral, gutting it beyond its thick stone walls. As the wind lessened, enforced demolition provided firebreaks, effectively saving more buildings from the leaping flames. Eventually some control was established, but the City of London was left smouldering and unrecognisable with more than 13,000 houses and eighty churches destroyed. Miraculously, and mercifully, loss of life was said to be in single figures.

As London was consumed by hungry orange flames, which pierced through a thick umbrella of black smoke, Pepys, who had advanced from civil servant exchequer clerk to high-ranking naval administrator, penned his diary:

The poor pigeons, I perceived, were loth to leave their houses, but hovered about the windows and balconys till they were, some of them, burned upon their wings and fell-down. Word was carried to the King. So, I was called for and didst tell the King and the Duke of Yorke what I saw, and that unless his Majesty didst command houses to be pulled down nothing could stop the fire. We staid till, it being darkish, we saw the fire as only one *entire arch of flame from this to the other side of the bridge and Bow up the hill for an arch of about a mile long; it made me weep to see it. The churches, houses, and all on fire and flaming at once; and a horrid noise the flames made, and the cracking of houses at their ruins. Sir W. Batten not knowing how to remove his wine, didst dig a pit in the garden, and laid it in there; and I took the opportunity of laying within all the papers of my office that I could nay otherwise dispose of. And in the evening Sir W. Pen and I didst dig another, and put our wine in it, and my Parmazan cheese, as well as my wine and some other things.*

The fire, which had raged for four days, eventually burnt itself out, leaving the city a wasteland of smouldering cinder and debris. Jack scanned the single page of his miserly printed newspaper in disbelief, before reading it out loud to Elizabeth and her stepfather, John Cartwright. Elizabeth tightly clutched her husband's arm. She was reluctant to accept the truth, that the great City of London had been burnt to the ground. The people of London had good cause to lay blame at the door of the Lord Mayor of London, Thomas Bloodworth. In the early hours of the fire, Bloodworth had declined to authorise enforced demolitions to provide barriers, in at least some attempt to check the progress of the fire. Bloodworth was reported to have scoffed, 'Pish – a full-bladdered woman could piss the fire out, if she didn't burn her arse whilst squatting over it!'

'One good thing might well come from this awful decimation,' said Jack. 'Hopefully it will hath burnt out the remnants of the Great Plague. That, at least, we canst be truly thankful for.'

'Ay!' agreed John Cartwright. 'Pray we also grasp the opportunity to adjust to a new, healthier way of living. A purge on terminating rat infestations and cleaning our streets might be a good place to start. There will be plenty of work for thee to get thine teeth into, Jack, when it comes to rebuilding our capital city. Skilled, knowledgeable tradesmen such as thyself will be in great demand, of that I hath nay doubt, Jack. Prepare thyself for a call to the City of London.'

The British population had been totally devastated. It had suffered a terrifying loss of life throughout the prolonged periods of fighting during the civil wars. Families had been torn apart. Women were persecuted and tried for witchcraft, suffering public burning or hanging. Tens of thousands of people had died in horrific circumstances by contracting bubonic pestilence during the years of the Great Plague. And, if that hadn't been enough, the heart of the country had been devastatingly consumed by a great raging fire. An inferno from hell, which burnt London, the capital city, from the face of England. Soon after the fire, another cataclysmic event befell the nation. Once again Pepys, a senior figure in naval administration, was at the heart of the second Anglo-Dutch war, and able to write in his diary with clarity. Inadvertently, Jack also became involved in the Dutch raid on the River Medway! Such involvement was through no pre-knowledge, desire or plan of his own making. Indeed, the trip he planned would never have been made had he known about the Netherlanders' intentions.

27

FINDING TOM AND A VISIT TO BORDEN

It was by chance that Jack found Tom's abode at Selling, near the beautiful village church of St Mary the Virgin, with its squat Norman tower and buttressed stone walls. He had no idea where his brother lived as he trotted past the quaint church. A beadle and a dozen boys were partaking in the old English custom of 'beating the bounds.' Each boy had a willow wand to beat with. At salient points, the beadle would pause to tap the boy's backsides with his cane, in order that they remembered not to venture beyond parish boundaries. The beadle's gruff fortissimo voice built to a crescendo. He could be clearly heard as he spouted forth his patter.

'These bounds stretch between Mr Greenstreet's wash-pots and his cherry grounds,' the beadle shouted out. 'Do nay encroach beyond these bounds, nor dare to scrump the cherries.'

Jack reined in Mol and addressed the rosy-faced beadle, who glanced upwards at the rider through bushy eyebrows and equally bushy sideburns, twitching a rather bushy moustache.

'Pardon me, Beadle, pray, didst I hear you say Mr Greenstreet's wash-pots and cherry gardens?'

The beadle, dressed in a long royal blue, gold-braided gown with white stockings, black patent silver-buckled shoes and an ornate tricorn hat trimmed with yellow braid, tapped his ornate silver staff upon the ground and called the boys to order. He bade them keep still. One could hear a pin drop in the hush that followed. He spoke in his gruff, yet high-pitched voice, his ornate staff of office held upright with one hand, whilst his cane swished to and fro in the other.

'Ay, indeed ye didst, sir. Mr Thomas Greenstreet's house sits within these boundaries. If thou art proposing to visit his abode this day, the porched entrance lies situate just around the corner. Doff thy hats to the gentleman, boys. Remove thy cap this very minute, Milner Junior. Acknowledge the gent afore ye taste my stick across thine arse, boy, and bow low, damn ye.'

The boys all gracefully bowed and doffed their caps, holding their willow wands aloft. Jack raised a hand in acknowledgement and continued to walk Mol around the corner to the entrance of a rather grand-looking rendered house, with rhythmical sash windows, a parapet roof and portico porch supported by Corinthian columns. He hitched Mol just inside the gate and walked up a tree-shaded, diapered brick path. Beneath the portico porch was a cast-iron bell pull. He tugged hard upon it. A bell rang out loudly within. Jack grinned to himself. He was impressed. Thomas had done alright for himself and appeared to live in grand style. The door was opened wide, and a shapely woman stood before him, bearing a very pleasant smile.

'Who calls on us, Margarett?' came his brother's voice within, causing Jack to laugh aloud.

"Tis I, Tom, thy brother Jack. Get off thy lazy backside and see for thyself.' Jack took the young lady's hand and squeezed it. 'Ye must be Margarett, Tom's betrothed.' She gripped his hand.

'Hello, dearest Jack. Well, not quite betrothed for we hath been married two months since.'

Thomas arrived at the door and embraced his brother. Both were immediately full of jabber.

'Ye were nay invited to our wedding, Jack, because we dare nay risk the spread of plague. I was surprised ye went to see Will and journeyed on to Claxfield to seek the welfare of James.'

'I understand thy consideration of risk well, Tom. 'Tis indeed a terrible plague we endure. Nevertheless, I felt obliged to seek the welfare of our kin. I found Cousin James in a bad way. His mother, Maria, recently died of the consumption. The servants fled Claxfeldestane in fear of contracting the plague. James was so distressed that he could nay arrange a decent burial for his own mother. He lived on his own, was run down and nay looked too well. I took him back to Wingham, where he stayed until recently. I am afraid Symon and his family hath fared badly. I am sorely afeared for their lives. James found Symon's farm quarantined against the plague. James rode across to Borden and was grieved to see a red cross painted across the gated entrance. He was turned away by a borsholder and his gang. Mine mission was to track ye down, Tom, and then go on over to ascertain the fate of Symon and family. I also wanted to make sure James is fully recovered. As ye say, the plague hast abated considerably, thanks be to the Almighty. Art ye going to let me in, or do we stay upon thy threshold all day exchanging news? I am desirous to learn how ye both met and got thyselves married so soon?'

'Thomas forgets himself,' chirped Margarett. 'Please come ye into our humble abode, brother-in-law. Allow me to find ye some refreshment and show ye the house and cherry gardens.'

'Ay, come on in, Jack, and I will tell ye all about it. It was thy good advice that motivated William to released money from Father's estate, whereby I became the recipient of a very generous apportionment of ready cash. Now, I hath a smallholding to help keep me solvent.'

Thomas explained how he had met Margarett, whilst on a carefree ride between Ospringe and Selling. She was leaning upon her arched garden gate, on a warm day in early spring, clutching a posy of primroses she had gathered from the nearby woodlands. The sun was upon her, and Tom was struck by her beauty. He bade her good day and then sidled over to chat to her about the plague, advising her to keep within confines and not to journey into the town of Faversham, or go to Ospringe, or along the old Watling Street. She told him she lived frugally alone with her mother. The two of them chatted so naturally together, and struck up such a resonance and rapport, that they arranged to meet at Selling church on Sundays and walked together after the service. Tom learned that a house with smallholding, adjoining the church boundary, was up for sale. Since he now had ready cash, he was favourably positioned to purchase the house. In a nutshell, they agreed they were in love. Thomas asked Margarett to marry him, she agreed, and he purchased the house there and then. After the nuptials they were able to move straight into the house, called 'The Beeches'. Tom had not informed Will until a fortnight before the ceremony was due. William had become reclusive because of the Great Plague, which was no bad thing, but Thomas decided he could do without Will's constant ribbing prior to marriage.

'Margarett and I were married in the local church of St Mary, adjacent to mine boundary. The church ye hath just passed by. I wanted to call upon William to act as best man but decided against venturing to Ospringe where the plague was so rife. Brother Will was safe enough isolated and locked away in Woodlarks. I was surprised to learn from Will that you went to see him and then journeyed on to Claxfield. Teynham is such an unhealthy place, and with the plague so rampant it was a risk to thyself and family, Jack. Hence the reason why I did nay ride over to inform ye of our nuptials. Thank God the epidemic now lieth in remission.'

Jack bided a while with Thomas and his new wife, Margarett, and then bade them farewell and set off for Claxfield. As before, on reaching Teynham he approached the village with caution.

This time, Jack had no need to fear! He could scarce believe his eyes. The village of Greenstreet had been cleansed. Gone was the usual thick-caked filth and foul-smelling contamination. It was nothing short of a miracle. Never had he seen the village street so unsoiled. Yet the street appeared strangely quiet and empty. There were no scurrying rats. No writhing infestations. Greenstreet was a ghost of its former rancid being. The Dover Castle alehouse remained boarded up, as was the White Swan. The sound of distant hammering on an anvil rang out from the far end of the street. Mol's hooves clattered over the cobbled surface, echoing from empty house to empty house. Evidence of faint painted-out red crosses was apparent on many front doors. At the far end of the street the blacksmith's shop doors were wide open and Tong, with sleeves rolled up to his bulging biceps, greeted Jack, a red-hot metal rod clasped between the jaws of a pair of grip-irons. Jack spoke first.

'Greetings, Farrier, I am glad to see ye survived the terrible deathly plague then, Tong?'

'Greetings to 'ee, Master Jack. Yea, but many citizens from this neck of the woods were nay so lucky. I estimate half the people in the village succumbed to plague. They dropped like moths flittering around candlelight. I declare thy cousin, Reeve James, has done wonders since he returned to marshal the street cleaning. Folk needed little prompting, mind, after such gruesome deaths. The baron hath implemented fines for any person seen fouling the highway.'

'That surely is a step in the right direction, Tong. I am calling on the good reeve now. When is the next horse-trading fayre to take place? I need to purchase a good healthy nag or two.'

'"Twill be the first week in August, Master. The Irish gypsies always bring along good healthy stock. 'Tis the best trading fayre in the country, as ye knows. Dost thou needest mine help?'

'I shall pay thee well for thy expert advice, Farrier, if ye wouldst help look the horses over. After I hath purchased the horses, I shalt need ye to shoe them for me. Good day to 'ee, Tong.'

James was back to his sprightly self. Two of his manservants had returned, and James had appointed Widow Martha Goody as his cook and housewoman, giving her back her cottage across the road in Frognal. James, who always kept up with the times, trusted Martha's sound knowledge of healing and health matters. He had appointed her as a consultant as much as cook and housewoman. Martha's daughter, Mary, had married a candlestick maker from Lynsted and now lived in nearby Bumpit. Jack owed his life to Martha and was glad she now had a well-paid job within the reeve's household. Jack praised James for instigating the street cleaning. Jack was aware that matters of sound hygiene had originated from Martha Goody's door. Baron Roper's recusancy had been reinstated by a grateful King Charles II, who paid back the baron in full for his sufferance by Parliament. The King had never forgotten the support the Roper family had given him when he most needed help, following the terrifying execution of his father. Money was now readily available for James to apply to his good stewardship within the confines of the manor. Once again there were signs of improvement in the lives of those citizens who had survived the Great Plague and supported the monarchy.

Happy with his best friend's improvement in lifestyle, Jack bade James farewell and struck out for Borden. James had no further knowledge of Symon or the welfare of Symon's family, but he warned Jack not to expect good news in that direction. On arrival at the farm entrance, the oak gate was closed. It had been scrubbed clean of any former warning signs to keep out.

Nevertheless, a faint stain of red dye remained, where the five-bar gate had been marked with a cross to prohibit access. Jack opened the gate and urged Mol onto the steep and winding track which led downwards to the farmhouse. The grass was high and unkempt each side of the bridle path. Symon normally kept it scythed tight to the ground. He dismounted with trepidation to be met at the door by Marion, who was obviously distressed. Her eyes flooded as she welled up. Tears streamed from sunken sockets to run down her gaunt cheeks. Maisy, growing up fast now, came over to slip a small hand into his. Was it love for her uncle or security she sought? The girl laid her head against his arm and gazed upwards, wide-eyed.

'I saw ye coming down the track from the window, Jack.' Marion spoke quietly between sobs.

'Thanks to Almighty God ye are safe, Marion. When cousin James came to visit ye he was turned away by a borsholder and his gang. We thought ye were all claimed by the plague.'

'We were claimed, but 'twas nay by plague, 'twas the measles, we were racked by the measles. It infected the whole family. We lost our eldest dear boy, Robert. Robert was soon to cometh of his fifteenth birthday. He fought so hard to stay with us. Then we lost tiny Bess. She was only just two years old. We placed them together in the barn, not wanting to see their bodies piled onto a cart with those that had succumbed to the plague.' Marion broke into stifled sobs before she could continue. 'Symon and mineself were badly struck down by the disease. We were weak from exhaustion. Maisy here did much of the work, bless her, she was the strongest of us all. When we had regained some strength, Symon and mineself dug a large grave. We buried Rob and Bess together in an embrace, beneath the spinney where the sun shines longest in the day. We laid Robert's long bow and arrows beside his body, along with his knife, so he could protect his sister. It was the bow ye gave him Jack, which he was never parted from. Since then, thy cousin Symon has been affected to such an extent that he sits in silence out in the barn for most of each day. Sy seldom speaks a word to any of us. I am so concerned for us as a family, for Maisy and my other two little ones, who hath survived the cursed pestilence.'

Marion broke into stifled sobbing again and Maisy clung tightly to Jack's hand. At first Jack was choked for words. He had been through such dramatic times with Symon, whilst fighting for the King in Kentish insurrections. He had also been close to his teenage nephew Robert, who often mirrored images of himself as a boy. Jack bit his lip. He knew he had to go to Symon, but he would need to choose his words carefully. He stammered out words of solace.

'I am so sorry for ye all, so, so sorry, Marion. Too many poor families hast been robbed of their children by terrible diseases. Here, take Maisy in thy embrace. I shall go to Symon, nay as a cousin but as a comrade-in-arms. I shall offer him solace, but also urge him into action.'

Engulfed by sadness, Jack left mother and daughter to console each other and strode across to the barn. He cracked open the high-framed ledged-and-braced door. Symon was sitting in the gloom on a pile of hay, fondling the ears of Willow, the Old English sheepdog. Jack went over to him and placed both hands upon his cousin's shoulders. Peering through his own misty eyes he gazed into Symon's weather-worn and tear-stained face, rubbed raw by grimy hands.

'Ye canst sit here all day long, Sy, but 'twill never get thy babies fed. Do nay leave thy goodwife, Marion, to grieve alone. 'Tis unfair. She craves thine arms around her to help soothe away the nagging pain and miseries of thy sad losses. Best share thy grief together as man and wife.'

Symon took hold of Jack's hands and firmly pushed them away from his sagging shoulders.

'Thank'ee for coming here this day, cousin. I see little purpose in life at this moment in time. I hath let the farm go to rack and ruin since the measles struck us down like a venomous snake.'

'Prithee, Sy, sitting here feeling sorry will nay bring thy children back. All over England hundreds of thousands of children hath died from the Great Plague. Many families have died out completely. At least ye hath a goodwife and three dear children to look out for. 'Tis easy for me to say, I know that. Ye also know Rob was very dear to me. I painfully miss thy dear son Robert, and little Bess, God bless her. Sy, we hath fought side by side and slain men in battle. Ye hast butchered many animals for thy table. None of it compares with the loss of thine own dear children. But remember, the Lord provideth and the Lord taketh away. Thy family is dependent upon thee, Symon. Ye hath Maisy and the two little ones to raise up. 'Tis thy duty, old comrade. And what about thy dear wife, Marion? Doth thee plan to abandon her in her hour of need? None of them will survive without ye at the helm, man. Come, Sy, best get on with life now, eh? Grasp the nettle. Go and pacify thy goodwife, who so deserves ye at her side. I shall attend to the welfare of thine animals. I assume my old quarters are available. I canst stay for a few weeks and help ye get back on track. Come, Sy, we will soon hath thy farm trim and working again. Ye need to bury thyself in hard work on thy lands.'

Symon looked at his cousin, grimaced, then held out a hand. Jack pulled Symon to his feet and held the door open. Head hung low, his old comrade walked to the farmhouse and entered the parlour. Maisy came out to assist her uncle. Together they fed and milked the animals and cleaned out the stalls, collected eggs and found a plump capon for the evening meal. Jack pulled the bird's neck and Maisy plucked it whilst warm. It was getting dark by the time they had finished and walked back hand in hand to the farmhouse. Candles were visible through the parlour window. Symon and Marion stood in silhouette. They were bound together in a deep embrace and Symon was clearly planting a lingering kiss on his wife's forehead. Clearing the lump from his throat, Jack gripped Maisy's hand tightly and directed his niece away.

'I think we should just check mine old nag Mol one more time, Maisy, before we go inside. Tomorrow I will ride back to thine Uncle James and ask him to send a messenger to Elizabeth. We shall inform thine aunt I shall be staying for a week or two here at Borden. Are ye alright carrying that chicken in thy arms, Maisy? We best not put it down or a fox might steal it.'

'Thank ye, thank ye, Uncle Jack,' said Maisy, excited that her uncle was going to stay. 'I will carry the capon all day if necessary. Do ye think Rob and Bess will have capon for dinner up there in heaven, Uncle Jack? Do they roast and eat chickens for dinner in heaven?'

'Oh yes, Maisy. I expect Rob is tucking into a huge tender drumstick right now, as we speak.'

'Mmm, I wish I could see him eating it,' said Maisy remorsefully, adding, as only children do, 'Bess doesn't like drumsticks, but she does eat the parson's nose!' Maisy started to giggle.

'Here, let me carry the capon, Maisy, it is far too heavy for ye to manage on thy own.'

Jack took the plucked bird from her and stuck its claws between his fingers, so that it swung freely as they walked back to the farmhouse. Maisy clasped her uncle's free hand tightly. Candles blazed light from many windows now. Tomorrow they would start work in earnest.

28

A FAMILY DEATH.
A RAID ON THE MEDWAY

With the dawning of 1667 came the passing of Yeoman Squire Cartwright. John Cartwright had seen the New Year in and listened to the distant bells of St Mary's, Wingham. He died a day later aged fifty-eight. Seven years had passed since he had, somewhat ceremoniously, presented his last will and testament to his stepdaughter, Elizabeth, and son-in-law, Jack. A further three years needed to elapse before the main recipient of his will, his stepgrandson John Cartwright (alias Greenstreet), would come of age sixteen and be eligible to receive and control his stepgrandfather's lands, crops and stocks. Cartwright was buried in Staple church. A huge gathering had turned out to say farewell to a most popular squire. John Cartwright remained sound of mind to the end, despite being of poor health, with a slow nagging and deteriorating internal problem. Probate was granted to Cartwright's wife, Dyonise. Jack took overall charge of family affairs, on behalf of his young son John. The management of Cartwright's lands was presided over by his executors, Peter Lilley and Charles Wilde.

Cartwright's death had caused much administrative work for Jack. He was not overly worried. His carpentry projects had dried up, due to the recent bubonic pandemic. Tradesmen did not wish to journey too far, until they were sure there was no further threat of pestilence. However, Jack's professional reputation as a master craftsman, and his ability to calculate and control intricate works, had preceded him by way of his work at Canterbury Cathedral. He had visits from master builders who were looking for sound carpentry project managers to help supervise the rebuilding of the City of London, following the Great Fire. Jack intimated he would be ready to journey to London once he knew rebuilding was ready to begin. He had no desire to become embroiled in the mundane work of making safe and shoring up buildings left in a dangerous state by the Great Fire. The newspapers stated that Charles II was in process of appointing architects and city planners. Rough sketch proposals had been submitted for consideration, including a street plan drawn up by a certain Christopher Wren.

Keeping his options open, Jack also considered turning his skills to boatbuilding. Other members of the Greenstreet dynasty had gone across the River Medway to Sheerness dockyard to embark upon boatbuilding. The docks were located on the Sheerness peninsula, on the Isle of Sheppey, at the mouth of the Medway. In need of a break from the mundane affairs left by Cartwright, Jack thought he might look the boatbuilding fraternity up. In 1665, Samuel Pepys, Clerk of the Acts to the Navy Board, measured a site at Sheerness for a new dockyard. Jack's thinking was, if he took a liking to the work, he might become involved in boatbuilding, or seek work on the new docks, rather than journey to assist in reconstructing the City of London.

On 9 June, with his older son, John, tied up with Cartwright's managers and estate lands, Jack decided to take his younger son, Thomas, with him and make an adventure out of the trip to Sheppey. Thomas had been unwell of recent months and Elizabeth agreed that the fresh sea air might do the boy some good. Jack packed warm blankets and fishing lines and tackle and told Thomas they would find an upturned boat or some other shelter and spend the night fishing under the stars. Father and son set out from the farmhouse soon after breakfast. They stopped at Claxfeldestane for an early lunch with James. James, who had been tied up with affairs of the manor, also wanted a break, and decided to join his cousin and nephew in their adventure.

'A fishing trip on an island, eh! What adventures, eh, Tom? 'Tis a long time since I crossed the river to the Isle of Sheppey. In fact, it is a long time since I partook of any adventure at all. I seem to recall the last adventure I got involved in was with thine father here, Tom. 'Twas several years ago now. We were caught up in an affray with Roundheads at the White Swan brewhouse in Greenstreet. Do ye recall, Jack? We ran for our very lives to Lynsted church and escaped via that small ginnel which led out from the vestry basement.' James paused for breath, then with little hesitation continued, 'Wouldst thou count me in thy pending trip, men? We canst cross by ferry-barge at the narrow point of the Swale from Kemsley, near Sittingbourne, to Elmley Isle. I believe the ferry-barge operates on the hour most days.'

'Yea, 'tis what I planned to do, James. There will be a toll which I hath money to pay for. We shall be more than glad to offer ye a berth. Go pack thee a warm blanket and thy flintlock pistol and side arms. Just in case we meet some highway robbers. I understand that Matthew Greenstreet from Eastling and his two sons hath been boatbuilding on the island for two years now. I wish to peruse their work and the rebuilding work along the dockside. The weather is set fair and warm, but it might turn nippy at night, so make sure thou bringest snug clothing.'

'Tell me about the affray at the White Horse brewhouse, Uncle James, I want to know,' pleaded Thomas, getting more and more excited by the adventure they were about to embark upon.

'Thine uncle will tell ye all about it as we journey on, Thomas. Come, we need to make haste now, son, if we are to arrive at our destination before dusk and get our fishing lines out.'

After coaxing their horses onto the wide ferry-barge and paying the toll, the three men were pulled across the narrow point of the Swale by cable, alighting on the Elmley marsh side of the Isle of Sheppey. They rode across the marshes in high spirits, in awe of the wildlife which appeared around them. Harriers rose from the long grasses, and they were startled by rising heron and crane. Corncrake called to their mates, and booming bitterns gave a base note to a cacophony of bird song and buzzing which erupted all around. They rode north-eastwards, past Queenborough, keeping the Swale on their left side, passing west of Minster, until they arrived north of the island at Sheerness, where the North Sea swept in past Sheppey and the Isle of Grain converged with the Swale. Here lay the mouth of the River Medway. Dismounting at the tip of Blue Town, they found a sheltered spot to make their camp. Several holed rowing boats lay abandoned on their sides. Between them they erected a snug shelter, then found a pile of driftwood and built a fire. From the soft clay rock, they dug some clam and ragworm for bait, and cast out their hand lines. James was the first to hook a fish. It was a nice whiting of two pounds or more. Then Thomas, who had quickly mastered his hand line, hooked into a nice Dover sole. Jack filleted the fish off the bone. They used the guts and discarded remnants for more bait. A good selection of fish was caught through the still warmth of the night. The stars shone out brightly in the black sky. They gazed up in awe and chattered about the wonders of heaven. Thomas, a little overly zealous in his casting, slipped twice, attaining wet feet. He finally landed on his butt end, achieving a thoroughly wet backside. Jack, who had least success with his fishing, cooked them up a tasty treat over the open fire. They devoured the fish hungrily, accompanied by fresh-baked bread, which James had loaded into his saddle bags along with a flagon of cider. It was the early hours of the morning before the men lay down to nap under the rowing boats, contented with a great day out and a good night's fishing. Tom was awoken by creaking timbers and the sound of many distant voices.

Naked, Thomas dashed from his warm blanket, beneath the upturned rowing boat encampment, to the dying embers of the previous evening's fire. Near to the fire, his father had laid out his breeches and stockings to dry over some driftwood, prior to them retiring for the night. Tom struggled to pull the semi-dry breeches up to his waist. He buttoned them and glanced towards the sea. He could scarce believe his eyes, astonished to see close to sixty ships near the shoreline. They appeared to have dropped anchor, and flew a horizontal tricolour of red, white and blue. A blaze of cannon fire echoed around. Cast-iron balls and grapeshot hit the adjoining stone walls of Sheerness Garrison Point Fort with a terrifying thump, less than 300 yards from their encampment. The men shot from their beds and hurriedly dressed. Smoke and the stench of gunpowder drifted on the morning air. The noise was deafening.

'Invasion, invasion!' shouted out Reeve James, hopping about on one leg to force on a boot.

Thomas attempted to pull on his damp stockings, struggling and tugging hard with no success.

"Tis indeed invasion by the Dutch,' shouted back Jack. 'Leave thine stockings, Tom. Pull on thy boots and get to horse immediately. We must leave now before we art blown to pieces.'

Jack and James hastily primed flintlock pistols and buckled on side arms. Jack handed a pistol to Tom and drew a musket from the side of Mol. He loaded, rammed and primed the weapon before turning to look towards the sea. The Dutch sailors had lowered their jolly boats. The first contingent of sailors was already running up from the shoreline armed to the teeth with musket, cutlass, pike and snaphance. The invaders' prime objective was to take the fort, which appeared to be unguarded. The Dutch swarmed like bees from an upturned hive. The three fishermen had been spotted. Musket fire suddenly flew in their direction. Jack and

James were already saddled, but Tom had difficulty mounting his pony, having secured the strapping far too loosely. Jack rode over to Tom, bent low, scooped his son up with one arm and drew him up in front of him. There was no time to go after the boy's pony, which had bolted aimlessly as musket fire and lead rained down around them. More sailors landed along the shoreline. Dutchmen raced towards the trio, pausing to fire their muskets and to brandish steel.

A British frigate, tied up just around the corner from their place of encampment, was alight from stem to stern. As the trio spurred the horses to race away from the Dutch, Jack pointed to another British ship which had burst into flames along the length of its starboard side. The enemy continued to fire their cannon broadsides. It was obvious that the vulnerable British ships, moored along the banks of the Medway, were 'sitting ducks' for the Netherlanders.

'That Garrison Point Fort is supposed to protect against invasion, Jack. I didn't see a shot fired from it in anger, did ye?' James shouted across to Jack above the roar of the Dutch cannon fire.

'Nay, nothing at all, nay even a pop from a misfired musket,' shouted back Jack, spurring his horse southwards at the gallop, with his son Thomas clinging on to the saddle for dear life.

The trio headed back the way they had come, towards Elmley marshes, not sparing the horses for a minute. Whether the Dutchmen thought they were on mainland England could not be ascertained. They appeared to come from every direction over the island. Halfway through the marshes a line of Dutch foot musketeers suddenly appeared, heading in line towards them.

'Veer left, James, towards the end of their line. Keep out of range, we canst outskirt them.'

Keeping out of range of musket fire, the trio rode hard for the end of the Dutch line to skirt the advancing foot division. Jack turned and fired a blind shot from his musket. It was a token gesture. He realised all would be lost if he attempted to fight the invaders. When well past the progressing Dutch line, some two miles from the ferry, Jack called out to James to rein in.

'Take Tom on thy horse, James, and get to the ferry. If the ferrymen are not on the Elmley marsh side, do thy best to signal them to bring the ferry-barge across. Fire thy flintlocks to get attention. I am going to set a little distraction to give yon invaders a taste of their own medicine. Get thee gone quickly now before the Dutch advance further across the marshes.'

Jack dismounted from Mol and hitched her to a friendly elder tree. He wet a finger in his mouth and held it up in the breeze, then pulled some grass up and cast it into the air. He calculated the stiff warm wind was southwesterly. Ideal for what he had in mind. He pulled up some tall dry grasses and bound them together with dead wild clematis, making a long torch. He secured the torch at its base with fishing line. Satisfied with his work, he went to the saddle bag and found his tinderbox. Jack rode some considerable distance to his left before dismounting to strike the tinderbox and ignite the long grasses of the flat marshland. He could see the Dutchmen crossing the marshes in a continuous horizontal line. Jack lit his torch from the leaping flames and rode back the way he had come, pausing at intervals to ignite the dry combustible grasses and gorse. A raging inferno of fire spread rapidly over the marshes. The line of consuming flame and smoke leapt high and raced northwards towards the invaders.

'There, my little Netherlanders, that wilt warm ye up,' Jack shouted at the top of his voice. Though it was for his satisfaction only. The Dutch were far from within earshot.

Disturbed by the fire, clouds of birdlife rose high in the sky, causing Jack to feel genuine grief.

'Pray, accept my humble apologies, ye beautiful wonders of nature. Forgive me for such disturbance to thine habitat, but this is England, and nay invader is welcome upon our shores.'

Jack spurred Mol towards the narrow point of the Swale and prayed the ferrymen were there to take them to the mainland. He arrived to find James and Thomas in a state of argument with three bargees, who refused to believe the Isle of Sheppey was being invaded by the Dutch. Accordingly, the ferry was not due to depart for another forty minutes. The ferrymen had dug in their heels. Jack drew his rapier and directed the sharp-pointed tip at the spokesman's heart. James and Thomas cocked and aimed their flintlock pistols at the other two ferrymen.

'Either ye believe what we say, as good honest Kentish gentlemen, or we shalt leave ye here for the Dutch to make mincemeat of. Alternatively, we could kill ye all now, which wouldst perhaps be kinder. To die quickly might save ye from torture at the hands of the Netherlanders. What dost thou sayest, brothers? For whatever ye decide we shall be departing this isle now.'

'In that case I declare we go across without further delay,' said the chief ferryman wisely.

The bargees hurriedly took the horses on board by their bridles and hitched them to a railing. The adventurers went aboard the barge, their firearms well directed. Within a few minutes the ferryboat was being hauled across the Swale waters by cable to Sittingbourne. As they neared the landing point at Kemsley, Jack's raging grass fire could be clearly seen across the Elmley marshes. Further loud cannon broadsides left the ferrymen in no doubt there was an invasion.

'Bring forth a winch and let us get this barge out of the water,' James commanded, 'then one of thee go and find every man available that bears arms and form a line along the embankment.'

A breathless horseman arrived, bringing news.

'The Dutch hath arrived in force,' he proclaimed. 'They are advancing down the Medway firing broadsides into every British ship berthed along its banks and sending in fireships. It seems they hath overrun Sheppey and landed on Grain with little British retaliation. They are causing huge amounts of damage to our anchored fleet. They say the Dutch attempted to sail up the Thames, but were beaten back by a strong southwesterly and had to moor below Gravesend. Apparently, they hath taken and blown up the fort at Sheerness and are scorching the whole Isle of Sheppey with fire.'

Yea, and not only the Dutch, thought Jack, with a wry grimace of satisfaction.

'Pray, tell me, what defences are the English mustering?' Jack shouted after the horseman.

'Nay too sure. They were laying a huge iron chain across the Medway when I left Gillingham, and the ship *Unity* is posted just below the chain. I suspect the Dutch hath far too many ships to be much concerned about the placement of *Unity*. They hath also brought many fire ships with them to be feared. The British hath a strong battery at Upnor Castle, Chatham and Rochester Castle after that. We should hope and pray that the batteries offer some fierce resistance. There are some coastal batteries and no doubt they are being reinforced, but I fear this invasion by Holland is going to give us all a very bloody nose, before 'tis finished.'

'Will the Dutch overrun the whole country, Father?' asked Tom anxiously.

'If every good Englishman stands together in line along the banks of the rivers, with firearms and pike at the ready, we shall prevail. Sixty foreign ships will cause much damage and weaken our navy, but they will nay advance far across our lands. They wouldst need a mighty army with much infrastructure to back it, before they could conquer our country. Even though we lie mortally wounded from the civil wars, the plague and the Great Fire, we canst still muster a good fight if needs be. That it should come to this, our defences weak and our navy so depleted and lying idle and unmanned in home waters.' Tis a wake-up call to us all, for no invasion has succeeded since William the Conqueror. Now, here we are with a Kentish Isle and the Medway overrun by Dutchmen. Lord, hast we nay suffered enough of recent times?'

Even as Jack spoke, eighty or more men arrived with muskets, pikes and arms to stake out their patch along the banks of the Swale at its narrowing. James, who had been talking with the Reeve of Sittingbourne, brought news that armed men lined the narrow point of the Swale from where they stood, to as far as the loop at Chetney marshes, opposite Queenborough and beyond as far as Upnor Castle. They could repel the Dutch but could do nothing to save English ships.

At the Palace, the King had instructed Admiral George Monck to go to Chatham to take charge of the situation. Monck found the defences woefully inadequate, and summonsed artillery from the city to be positioned at Gravesend. Sir Edward Spragg, in command of the ships at anchor in the Medway, could muster only one ship, the frigate *Unity*, to defend against the Dutch invaders at Garrison Point. The frigate fired one broadside before, when threatened by Dutch fireships, it withdrew further up the Medway. Never had the British navy been so weak.

Huge plumes of smoke rose high into the sky over the Isle of Sheppey, mostly from Sheerness Fort and burning ships fired on by the invaders. Jack, James and Thomas awaited the dawning of 11 June, with bated breath, whence came news that a company of English soldiers had arrived to reinforce Upnor Castle. Blockships had been sunk near to the iron chain, which was guarded by light batteries. Further ships were sacrificed and sunk to block the Musselbank channel in front of the chain, and Upnor Reach, near the castle. These measures did nothing to deter the Dutch, who by nightfall on the 11th had towed away enough blockships to open a channel. On 12 June, the invaders advanced up the Medway and attacked the English defences near the chain. The chain was set too deep in the water and the Dutch simply sailed over it. They devastated five more ships and captured the good ship the *Royal Charles* and her crew. Sensing disaster, Monck ordered sixteen remaining British warships further up the Medway to be sunk, in order to prevent capture. This act made a total of thirty British ships deliberately scuttled.

On 13 June, Symon Greenstreet, who had heard news of the invasion via the grapevine, arrived from Borden armed to the teeth. By chance, Symon found his cousins and nephew on the riverbank of the Swale. They were by now both hungry and very dejected. Tom blurted out the story of their adventures on the Isle of Sheppey, much to his uncle Symon's amazement.

'Ye should hath called on me,' Symon exclaimed, 'I too needed an adventure. Woebetide any Dutchman who attempts to come here to Sittingbourne. What a good thing I packed plenty to eat in my saddle bags. Come ye, cousins, back to my horse and eat something to sustain ye. Thou art also welcome to swig from mine flagon of cider. When the Dutch withdraw, as they surely will, ye must all come back to the farm. We will kill some geese and eat a good fill.'

'Praise be to ye and thy goodwife, Marion, Symon,' said James with much gratitude.

'Ay 'tis true we art famished, Sy. We hath eaten nothing since we caught and cooked fish on the beach at Sheerness Point, prior to the invasion,' Jack informed his old comrade-in-arms.

The four men devoured Symon's food, then sat waiting for news to be passed along the line. Tom and his uncle Symon became as thick as thieves. The lad reminded Symon of his deceased son, Rob. The boom of distant cannon kept everybody wondering. Conjecture was rife amongst those waiting to repel the invaders. Word arrived late in the day. A British officer rode the entire embankment to ascertain the force of men at arms in case of invasion.

The news was that London was in a state of panic. Rumour was spreading that the Dutch were in the process of transporting a French army from Dunkirk for full-scale invasion. Many wealthy citizens had fled the city, taking their valuables with them. Factually, the Dutch had continued to advance into Chatham docks with fireships *Delft*, *Rotterdam*,

Draak, *Wapen van Londen*, *Gouden Appel* and *Princess*. The Dutch had come under fire from Upnor Castle and shore batteries. The Netherlanders suppressed the English fire, but themselves had lost a ship in the attack and suffered casualties. Three of the finest and heaviest vessels in the navy perished by fire, with a cost of seventy-five cannon. They were the *Loyal London*, *Royal James* and *Royal Oak*. The captain of the *Royal Oak* perished in the flames, refusing to abandon his ship.

On 14 June, expecting a stiffening English resistance, Cornelis de Witt decided against further penetration down the Medway. He withdrew his ships, towing *Royal Charles* along as a trophy of war, together with *Unity* and her prize crew. It was a great Dutch victory.

As they withdrew from the Medway, Dutch sailors rowed to any English ship they could reach and set it on fire. One Dutch boat re-entered the docks to make sure nothing was left above the waterline of sunken English vessels. The shore facilities at Chatham dockyard escaped destruction. No Dutch vessel reached those docks. That, at least, was fortunate, as it ensured the Royal Navy would later be able to repair the sunken ships. The Dutch fleet, under the command of Michiel de Ruyter and Admiral van Ghent, attempted to attack other ports on the English coast, but were repelled each time, with no further successes, despite their pestering.

Jack, James and Thomas went back to Symon's farm to be treated to a banquet of good food and drink. The fishing trip had turned out to be quite an adventure. Jack never did get to see his boatbuilding relatives on Sheppey. Their work was probably destroyed by the 800 or so Dutch who invaded the isle. Jack decided boatbuilding was not for him, although there would be plenty of work in building better docks, both at Chatham and Sheppey.

Much discussion took place as to the state of the British fleet and the reasons for it being so unprepared. As in many past cases, the main cause was money. Lack of funds. British sailors lay idle and unpaid. Blame was laid at the door of the Palace and Charles himself. The truth was, after the plague and the Great Fire had decimated London and its financial institutions, Charles II could no longer afford war. Naval cutbacks were the only option, resulting in unpaid soldiers and sailors leaving their posts. Ships were left anchored along the banks of the Medway – a sitting target – whilst Charles himself continued to live the good life.

Warm smiles greeted the adventurers when they eventually returned home. Elizabeth, with young John at her side, had heard nothing about the dastardly Dutch incursion up the Medway.

'I expect ye boys need feeding up after such a long trip. Hath ye both had a good adventure? Ye look quite rosy and healthy, Tom. It hast done ye a power of good to go off with thy father.'

'Oh, yea, Mother, we caught plenty of fish, were woken by cannon fire and chased by hundreds of Dutch invaders across the marshes. They were firing muskets at us and bearing cutlasses.'

'Really,' she chuckled, 'thy vivid imagination, Thomas! What wouldst ye fancy for supper?'

Jack beckoned Thomas to his side and spoke to him in a whisper, a wry grin upon his face:

'She is never going to believe ye, Tom. Wait until tomorrow when I read the *London Gazette* to her. Then all hell will break loose! And guess whose name will be mud then? 'Twill nay be thine, Thomas, 'twill be mine own head on the block for ever getting ye into such a scrape. We could blame it all on to thine Uncle James of course. She will nay be able to get to him!'

Tom went off with John to spin his adventures to his brother. John listened intently to Tom's detailed account, wide-eyed and spellbound. It was true, Tom could always tell a good yarn.

Later, Jack spent time explaining to Elizabeth exactly what had occurred on the Isle of Sheppey. Within days he read excerpts from the *London Gazette* to her. The paper gave a detailed account and referred to the low morale of the English sailors. The mood of the people towards their King was lamentable. In Westminster people cried out for a Parliament! A Parliament! It was reported that the King and Duke of York had been below London Bridge on 13 June, since four o'clock in the morning, to command the sinking of blockships at Barking Creek, and other places, hoping to halt the Dutch ships from penetrating into the River Thames.

Samuel Pepys, who had kept a detailed account of the invasion, wrote in his diary:

News is come to Court of the Dutch breaking the chaine at Chatham, which struck me to the heart. And to White Hall to hear the truth of it; and there going up the back stairs, I didst hear some lacquies speaking of sad newes come to Court, saying that hardly anybody in the Court but do look as if he cried.

Pepys drew the conclusion that this would mean the end of Charles' regime and that a revolution was inevitable. The people were already baying for 'a Parliament':

> *All our hearts do now ake; for the newes is true, that
> the Dutch hath broken the chaine and burned our ships,
> and particularly 'The Royal Charles'. Other particulars I
> know not, but most sad to be sure. And the truth is I doth
> fear so much that the whole kingdom is undone, that I do
> this night resolve to study with mine father and wife what
> to do with the little that I have in money by me.*

Then even worse news is brought:

> *Late at night came Mr Hudson, the Cooper, mine
> neighbour, and tells me that he cometh from Chatham
> this evening at five o'clock, and saw this afternoon 'The
> Royal James, Oake and London', burnt by the enemy
> with their fire ships: that two or three men-of-war came
> up with them, and made no more of Upnor Castle's
> shooting, than of a fly.*

After the Dutch had withdrawn and peace talks began,
Pepys noted in his diary on 19 July 1667:

> *The Dutch fleete are in great squadrons everywhere,
> still about Harwich and were lately at Portsmouth
> and Plymouth and now gone to Dartmouth to destroy
> Streight's fleete, but God knows whether they canst do it
> any hurt, or no, but it was pretty newes come the other
> day so fast, of the Dutch being in so many places, that Sir
> William Batten at table cried, by God, says he, I think
> the devil shits Dutchmen.*

And later Pepys laments:

> *The Kingdom never in so troubled a condition in
> this world as now; nobody pleased with the peace, and
> yet nobody daring to wish for the continuance of the war.*

The Dutch victory in the Medway forced Charles II to
make a peace treaty at Breda on 31 July 1667. Navigation acts

were amended to allow Dutch and German goods to enter Britain in Dutch ships and many colonies taken during the Anglo-Dutch wars were returned, although the Dutch kept Surinam, and Britain kept New Jersey and New Amsterdam (later named New York, after the Duke of York).

Jack Greenstreet decided against working on the Isle of Sheppey as a boatbuilder. He was appointed as carpentry foreman to Samuel Pepys, engaged in revamping the Chatham dockyard, then later appointed as clerk of works on a project at Canterbury Cathedral. His ability in resolving complex methods of construction issues preceded him. In 1675, Jack's valuable knowledge and experience was sought out by the new City of London architect, Christopher Wren. Wren was appointed by the King, after the Great Fire. Wren's work included rebuilding many of the city's churches, plus a new cathedral to replace St Paul's.

THE DUTCH IN THE MEDWAY

If wars were won by feasting,
Or victory by song,
Or safety found in sleeping sound,
How England would be strong!
But honour and dominion
Are not maintained so.
They're only got by sword and shot,
And this the Dutchmen know!
The moneys that should feed us
You spend on your delight,
How can you then have sailor-men
To aid you in your fight?
Our fish and cheese are rotten,

Which makes the scurvy grow—
We cannot serve you if we starve,
And this the Dutchmen know!
Our ships in every harbour
Be neither whole nor sound,
And, when we seek to mend a leak,
No oakum can be found;
Or, if it is, the caulkers,
And carpenters also,
For lack of pay have gone away,
And this the Dutchmen know!
Mere powder, guns, and bullets,
We scarce can get at all;
Their price was spent in merriment
And revel at Whitehall,
While we in tattered doublets
From ship to ship must row,
Beseeching friends for odds and ends—
And this the Dutchmen know!
No King will heed our warnings,
No Court will pay our claims—
Our King and Court for their disport
Do sell the very Thames!
For, now De Ruyter's topsails
Off naked Chatham show,
We dare not meet him with our fleet—
And this the Dutchmen know!

Rudyard Kipling

29

NEW STEEDS. JOHN COMES OF AGE.
WREN CONSULTS JACK

So those dark, turbulent days of the civil wars, misogynous witchcraft and the latter years of the Renaissance ended, only to be superseded by equally hard suffering years of Restoration, plague, fire, lack of monetary resource and the significant Dutch raid up the River Medway. It was true to say the Dutch had their teeth well and truly into the British. Despite the Treaty of Breda, the Netherlanders had tasted victory, and after Medway were not likely to let go. The Dutch knew the British were strapped for cash. They patrolled British waters like persistent parasites, buzzing here, there and everywhere, sailing close to the shores of England and testing every British port in the English Channel, the Strait of Dover and the North Sea.

On a fine, warm August day in 1667, Jack took his wife Elizabeth, daughter Elizabeth and their rapidly growing sons, John and Thomas, to the Teynham horse-trading fayre. Jack had made do with riding old Mol long enough. He considered it was time to purchase younger breeds of horses for himself and for all family members. It was time to spend the money his brothers Will and Tom had passed on to him, as a gift for such an occasion. A plethora of people had gathered along the confines of Greenstreet. A much cleaner street since James had stamped his authority on maintaining its cleansing. The street was lined with sweet-smelling hay, which was already glued by a thick spread of horse droppings. Acrobats and jugglers amused the crowd. In one corner a Punchinello wooden stick puppet show kept a ring of children, and young at heart, enthralled in rapture. The children shouted out loudly in delight. The show had recently come to England from Italy. It featured Punchinello, a red hook-nosed humpback, who beat other puppets about the head with his slapstick, whilst tricking and hanging Jack Ketch the hangman, the Devil and just about all the rest of the cast on a gibbet. The doors of the Dover Castle inn were once again thrown wide open. Local men, with frothy tankards of beer clasped in one hand, leaned against the structure, chatting and surveying the street scene. Strawberry and cherry stalls sold ripe fruit, with maids shouting their wares. A pie-man wheeled his cart up and down the street selling meat pies for a half-penny piece, whilst bakers sold fresh crusty bread and bowls of hot stew from a cauldron, to satisfy hunger pangs.

Jack found an Irish gypsy with a dozen good-looking horses. A grey stallion particularly caught his eye. The Irishman informed him the horses were Arab crossbreds.

Tong, who Jack had paid well to accompany him, inspected the horses closely, lifting each leg and peering expertly at the hooves for any signs of rot, opening their mouths and looking at teeth, then rubbing his huge, gnarled hands over fetlocks and flanks. Tong took Jack to one side to speak.

'These are all fine animals, Master Jack, the best I hath seen in a long while. They art well cross-bred. When shod, they will give ye good service for many years. The grey stallion is a magnificent beast. I recommend ye purchase. Ye will nay go wrong with these horses.'

Each family member selected a horse. Jack and Tong bartered long and hard with the Irishman. In the end a deal was struck and agreed. The men spat in the palm of their right hand and the hands were smacked together hard. Jack paid the Irishman, and Tong led five fine horses to the smithy to be shod. The rest of the day was spent enjoying the fayre and visiting James at Claxfield, to fill in time. Tong the farrier sweated buckets to shoe five horses before the afternoon became too long. They departed for home, well pleased with their new steeds.

'My faithful old companion was named Acorn,' shouted out Jack to Elizabeth as they rode along the way. 'From acorns grow oaks. Therefore, I name my fine new stallion "Oak". If he serves me half as well as Acorn, I shall hath nay complaint to render to any man.'

Elizabeth laughed musically, pondering on a name for her own new steed. They continued to ride merrily homeward through country lanes. After much contemplation she declared, 'This old nag called Dot hast also served me well. She shalt live out the remainder of her life on good pastureland. I name my new steed "Little Stour", after the clear river waters which flow through the Ash Levels, where we first met and made passionate love, dear husband.'

Jack reined in, took her bridle and leaned backwards to kiss her, much to the delightful jeers of their children. One by one the children named their horses. By the time they had spurred themselves homeward to Twitham Farm, new names were established by all. They were met at the stables by Tripp, who frowned deeply, then scratched his head in puzzlement.

'My sainted aunt, Lord help me. Pray, how am I going to look after this menagerie of horse?'

*

So, the years passed by. The Hudson Bay Company was formed in 1670. In that same year, John Cartwright the younger, alias Greenstreet, attained the age of sixteen, and in accordance with the will of his stepgrandfather, he inherited the deceased squire yeoman's extensive lands and appurtenances. His extensive training in land management over the years, coupled with his acceptance by the local farming fraternity, by way of John Cartwright's purposeful introductions, stood young John in good stead and ensured he had no problems in taking over his benefactor's affairs at such an early age in life. John had a good understanding and rapport with older contemporaries who resided in the several local sub-parishes which fell under the auspices of Wingham. He listened intently to the advice of his elders. In turn, the local yeoman farmers formed a liking for the young man, steering him away from trouble and keeping him on a straight path. John handled his land managers well, handing out bonuses for handsome profits. Thomas, forever in poor health and often quite frail, helped his brother John whenever able, but it was as much as he could do to manage the six acres of land at Lower Ash Level, bequeathed to him by his stepgrandfather. Thomas maintained the land as a wild meadow, grazing goats for milking and beehives for honey. John was always there to help his brother out when Tom fell sick from ailments. Goodwife Dyonise, Elizabeth's mother, passed away, after suffering a long spell of congestion followed by pneumonia. In her will, she left her daughter, Elizabeth, the farmhouse at Twitham Farm, plus a house at nearby Shatterling.

Always keen on new inventions, Jack became the proud owner of a telescope. He took it with him wherever he rode, surveying the horizons with alacrity, until he alighted on an object of interest. In 1671, Jack, not knowing exactly his age, surmised he was about forty-six. His knowledge of intricate building construction and calculation had become profound. He attained an appointment, at the behest of the Secretary of the Navy Board, Samuel Pepys, as carpenter foreman at the Chatham dockyard, which was undergoing extensive revamping work at that time. Pepys himself, a few years later, recommended Jack's expertise to the new city architect, Christopher Wren. Wren consulted Jack on aspects of design for St Paul's Cathedral, particularly regarding the intricacies of the timber-framed hemispherical outer dome.

The coffeehouses of London were popular meeting places. People gathered to exchange news and discuss commerce. For the price of one penny, a cup of coffee, tea or chocolate could be purchased, plus admission. It was in one such favoured place, near to the site of St Paul's, where work had yet to be started, that Jack Greenstreet waited for Christopher Wren and Nicholas Hawksmoor's arrival. Wren wished to discuss a parabolic construction proposal and had invited Jack's input. Jack sat absorbed in the *Statesman* newspaper, sipping coffee. A runner came bearing news. People were dumbfounded at the story he told: the story concerned a would-be thief by the name of Thomas Blood, who, disguised as a clergyman, had the tenacity to steal the crown jewels from the Tower of London. Blood was immediately caught, being too inebriated to run with the loot. This statement caused an uproar of laughter in the coffeehouse. The thief was condemned to death, and then mysteriously pardoned by the King! The story of the crown jewels was followed by much political discussion in respect of Parliament's address to the King in respect of popery. Anti-Catholicism was a reoccurring theme throughout seventeenth-century England. Religious subjects rose and fell with political events of the time. The French, and much of Europe, threatened a weakened England, and many feared that Charles II, who had French sympathies, was himself espousing Catholicism. King Charles was warned by Parliament of a brewing popish plot to have him murdered and replaced by his Catholic brother, James. Rumour led to a crisis of anxiety amongst the English people, who favoured the Protestant Dutch more than reverting to Catholicism by a French invasion. Such discussion kept the coffeehouses babbling with discourse right across London.

Christopher Wren arrived with his measuring clerk, William Dickinson, and principal assistant, Nicholas Hawksmoor. Hawksmoor spread drawings and sketches over a table, which immediately drew a ring of inquisitive people, who quickly forgot the religious jabber in a jostling to gain information concerning their new cathedral. The architect ordered them back to their tables, telling them they would discern nothing by their ignorance of such matters and to mind their own business. Wren addressed Jack, pointing a finger at the sketches laid out.

'Now, my fine fellow, I hath spent much time and deliberation concerning the dome and finial, as thou well knoweth. It hast struck me, and Will Dickinson here, that the dome needs an inner weight-relieving structure, so that the load is transmitted to spread across the entire mass pier foundations of the crypt, rather than via the outer walls. I want the outer visible dome of St Paul's to be a structure of light timber-framed construction with lead weathering. Now, this is where ye come in, Jack Greenstreet. Ye art valued for thy design solutions. I seek immediate thoughts in respect of the construction of this particular attempt to satisfy my dome design.'

'Sir, my immediate thoughts convey ye art on the right track in transmitting the load in such a way, and by heeding the poor bearing qualities of the London clay sub-strata which ye build upon. Give me indication of the inner and outer radii and height dimensions of thy dome, and I will take away thy sketches and superimpose mine ideas on paper. I need a little time to apply thought as to my preferred method in achieving thy wonderful design. I need to work out and calculate the segmentations, strutting and support work. Allow me a return of two weeks, Master Wren. If ye set a date, we canst meet here at this coffeehouse, or at thy offices.'

'Best make it mine drawing office in Whitehall, there art too many nosey buggers in this coffeehouse for mine liking, Jack.' Wren gave Jack design parameters and sketches, then set a date and time for the next meeting. He bade farewell and departed with a swirl of his cloak.

30

CLAXFELDESTANE

The old farmhouse called Claxfeldestane looked sadly neglected and unkempt. The limewash between the half-timbering was now decidedly drab, mouldy and flaking. Several tiles had slipped from the steep tiled roofs, allowing damp to penetrate. Surrounding grass and weeds were tall and unscythed. The house now lay idle. It had once been a hive of activity with the villagers to-ing and fro-ing to see the reeve, to pay their fines, dues or taxes, or to simply raise queries. Lady Day, Michaelmas and other quarter days, when rents were due, had once been busy times at the old Wealden Hall house. Rents were now collected directly at the manor house in Lodge Lynsted. The lord of the manor no longer had sole charge of manorial matters, and therefore no longer needed a manorial steward to manage his affairs or to keep the subsidy rolls. The parish council and local manor court, in conjunction with parliamentary commissioners, had assumed responsibility for gathering taxes. After the Great Fire, a coal and hearth tax had been introduced, amongst other taxes, to help pay for rebuilding the City of London. The title of reeve had been retained within Teynham Manor as a mark of respect for the Greenstreet dynasty, who had managed accounts and subsidies, as reeves, since the house was first built. Reeve was a medieval title, meaning a King's steward. The post of manorial reeve was no longer tenable, and though he had always been a King's man, James was redundant. Moreover, he was weak in body and very weary.

Redundancy concerned James not one jot. He had turned fifty-six and was not in good health of late. His eyesight had dimmed, and he had become short of breath. He coughed a great deal and was pained in the limbs. James was aware the old house had become dilapidated. It was far too much for one man to manage, especially when feeling unwell and advancing in years. Claxfeldestane had been in the possession of the Greenstreet family since it was first built 200 years ago, in 1473. James decided he had to sell the place and downsize. He knew his deceased father, old Reeve Johis, would not be best pleased in heaven. But times had changed dramatically since the conclusion of the civil wars and the Great Plague, of Roundheads and Cavaliers, pestilence and restoration. James had no children of his own, living brothers or willing nephews to pass the house on to. Claxfeldestane would pass to outsiders, its history and story locked securely within the tight lips of its walls. Many plots of Royalist insurrection had been hatched within the confines of the old house. The arms that the parliamentary commissioners had frequently sought,

338

in raids on Lodge Lynsted manor house, had been successfully secreted within Claxfeldestane's oak-panelled roof spaces.

Luck was on James' side. In 1674, a wealthy friend, Christopher Clerk, who lived in Frognal, just across the London Road from Claxfeldestane, offered James a good price to purchase the property and its farmlands. He said he would be prepared to retain his offer until James found suitable accommodation to live elsewhere. James rode across country to Wingham parish, to inform his close friend and cousin Jack of his intention to sell the ancient house and move on.

'Yea, but where wilt thou move to, James? Ye art connected to the church at Lynsted as churchwarden. Will ye find a place locally to suit thy needs? Thou art nay too well in body and really need to have folk look after thee. What thoughts dost ye hath in that direction?'

'Yea, 'tis true I am currently nay in perfect health, Jack. Hopefully that will improve with time.'

'Pray ye be right, cousin. I watched ye dismount from thy horse a while ago and, well, ye need to face facts. In mine eyes ye were struggling to climb down from the animal's back. Ye needs find a place of rest, James. A place where an eye be kept upon ye night and day.'

'That is emphatically true, husband. I know the very place he should be,' interrupted Elizabeth. "Tis right here at Twitham Farm.' She took James' arm and directed him to a padded armchair, wherein she bumped up a velvet cushion, lifted his feet onto a footstall and made him cosy.

'Well, there ye are then, James, problem solved,' said Jack. 'Mine thinking is the same as Lizzy's. I was going to approach her on the subject later but 'tis nay necessary because we art of the same sound mind. Look, James, there are vacant rooms since Cartwright and Elizabeth's mother, Dennie, passed away. They art good rooms ye canst call thy very own. They overlook the farmyard pond, with the trees and paddock beyond. Every glance out of the window will keep ye amused. We canst share the servants. The food cook serves up is gold-block, I canst vouch for that. So why not come and join us here at Twitham Farm? The two of us hath always got along well. It seems to be the perfect solution to thy problem. What say ye, Jamie?'

James paused. A smile of relief crept over his face, which had been sadly lacking since his arrival. He struggled up from the chair and came over to them, taking Jack by the hand and pumping it up and down, then kissing Elizabeth twice on the cheek, causing her to blush.

'Thank ye, my true friends. I promise to always keep myself to myself and never impose on thy privacy. Money is nay problem; there is plenty to pay towards my keep and our agreed rental terms. I hath lived a terrible lonesome life since the departure of mine parents and the deaths of my younger brothers. It wouldst be so nice to hath kin to converse with sometimes.'

'Well, there ye are then, Jamie. Stay over for a while and discuss our offer in more detail. View the rooms and envisage how ye might hath them arranged and altered to thy liking. Then depart for Claxfield, find Christopher Clerk, and instigate documents of sale to be drawn up. Ye canst move in here any time ye like,' said Jack. 'When thy furniture starts arriving here, I will journey over to Claxfeldestane to assist ye in clearing up and finalising matters. We canst then come back here together, to thy new home, eh, cousin? There is a pony and trap available when ye struggle to mount thine horse. Tripp is always available to escort ye if needs be.'

Jack paused, excited that his friend would live close by and be around to engage in intellectual discourse from time to time, over a long clay pipe of tobacco. In truth, such discourse had been missed since his father-in-law had passed on. Jack smiled, then added whimsically, 'We shall retain many fond memories of Claxfeldestane and Cripson Wood, eh, Jamie? Do ye recall the day we hid in Cripson Wood, after escaping from the Roundheads, James?'

'I do, old friend, and that time we buried thy inherited treasure in a chest beside our oak tree.'

There was a moment of quiet reflection before James Greenstreet spoke again. This time in a melancholy way and with a sincerity of some deep regret, coupled with tremors in his voice.

'Pray God, I shall miss the old place though, Jack. 'Tis a pity the farm and farmhouse will nay longer be there for our dynasty to inherit as a part of our family incumbency. 'Twill always be the home of our ancient Kentish ancestry. Yea, I shalt sorely miss the ancient house called Claxfeldestane, from whence derived so many of our forebears. 'Tis a sad ending indeed.'

341

31

ONWARD TO THE GLORIOUS
REVOLUTION

St Paul's Cathedral began to emerge from its chrysalis of blue London clay. With numerous foundation piers and the crypt walls in place, the restrained English Baroque style of Wren's architecture started to become evident. Pairs of fluted pilasters with Corinthian capitals and the lower part of the portico and towers, designed to support the second-storey pediment, became visible. Crowds of Londoners gathered daily on Ludgate Hill to gawp at the sheer magnitude of the development as the first lift of Portland stone masonry slowly and painstakingly advanced skywards. The construction costs were covered by a special tax levied on coal. The building would take thirty-three years, from its commencement in 1675, and be finished within the lifespan of architect Sir Christopher Wren, but sadly not in Jack's lifetime!

Architect Wren made many visits to the site of St Paul's, tinkering with and altering his design at various stages of its lift. It was on the recommendation of Pepys and the archbishop that Wren employed Jack as consultant, to assist and offer a variety of solutions to John Langland the master carpenter. Gifted and knowledgeable craftsmen, like Jack, were gathered by Wren, not always for consultation but to ensure master skills were passed on to the London apprentices. Wren and his principal assistants, architects Nicholas Hawksmoor and William Dickinson, were always willing to listen and alter a method of construction, often stating, 'There are always a variety of methods.' Concealed buttressing and flying buttresses were frequently added by Wren, who introduced them at late stages of the development to give extra strength and stability. On one occasion Jack expressed his interest in telescopes to Christopher Wren. Wren duly invited him, as his guest, to the newly commissioned Royal Observatory at Greenwich. It was a time of great discovery. Isaac Newton published his 'theory of light'.

James settled in well at Twitham, but it was not long before his wasting disease forced him to walk aided by sticks. No longer was he able to mount and ride a horse. Tripp, or occasionally Elizabeth, escorted him in the pony and trap, whenever he desired to journey out. James took over young John Cartwright's accounts and inventories. He taught Thomas to scribe, illuminate, and to set down the credits and debits of commercial ledger work in understandable and legible form. This suited Thomas well, because, like his uncle James, he was not of good health and was best suited to indoor work of that nature. Thomas also had a great artistic streak and liked to sketch and paint. Uncle and nephew got along famously together. James' plan was to teach Tom in all aspects of accountancy, so that when he was no longer able to see and manage the work himself, Thomas would be well versed as an accountant in his own right.

Young John Greenstreet (alias Cartwright) prospered well in managing his numerous lands, marketing milk, wool, fruit and grain, amongst other crops. The cumulative reward from his lands resulted in handsome profits. Stepgrandfather John Cartwright would have been proud of him. John often journeyed to Ospringe to see his uncle William at Woodlarks, who had turned his land over to orchards and was also doing very well. At the same time, he always called in to see his uncle Tom and aunt Margarett at Selling. John got on well with his uncle and aunt, but the main attraction was Elizabeth Neame, a charming young lady he had met in the village of Selling, just as his uncle Tom had met Margarett, several years earlier. Uncle Thomas's house was a friendly meeting place for the young couple during their courting.

It was not long before John brought Elizabeth Neame to meet his parents and siblings. Young John's betrothal was met with an air of joyous accord by his family. Once again, talk of marriage coursed throughout the farmhouse at Twitham. At the mention of marriage, the sound of female jabber exploded all around, ramped up by a frenzy of convivial, at times incoherent, babble of undeniable ecstasy. The female fraternity became totally embroiled in wedding rapture and planning.

'Wilt thou hath me for a bridesmaid?' implored John's older sister, Elizabeth, excitedly.

'I hath two infant sisters, Elizabeth, and they shalt be my bridesmaids, but I wouldst deem it a privilege if ye wouldst be mine personal maid of honour,' replied a giggling Elizabeth Neame.

'Oh, that is awfully exciting,' said Elizabeth Greenstreet Junior, drooling over the situation and wondering what wonderful garments would be chosen for her to wear on that great occasion.

'Ay, and mine brother Thomas will be best man,' said John, in a more serious, down-to-earth manner, attracting little response other than a nod of agreement from Elizabeth, his mother.

'Well, well, well, all these ladies called Elizabeth! We shall hath to call ye by numbers,' stated Jack with a broad grin settling over his face. 'But mine own goodwife will always be Elizabeth the first to me,' he added, with a twinkle in his eye, whilst surreptitiously pinching his wife's bottom through her shift, causing Goodwife Elizabeth to blush scarlet and give him a black glare of warning. He knew she would have her own back before the day was through.

'But, Daddy, I thought I was Elizabeth the first,' said his daughter somewhat forlornly.

'Nay, nay, ye art my little princess. Indeed, ye might be a queen if ye hurry up and find a handsome young prince to marry ye!' retorted the father, chuckling hopefully in her direction.

John took his father's arm and half pushed, half ushered, him towards the door.

'Sir, I wish to speak with ye about an urgent issue which hast stuck in my craw now for several long years. I need to get the matter resolved before this marriage malarkey canst take place!'

'Yea, I think I know what is ailing ye, John. Come along to the study, we can indulge in a clay pipe or two and endeavour to find a conclusion to thy irritating little problem.'

In the study the two men filled long-stemmed clay pipes from a jar of tobacco mixture and lit them with a taper from the glowing embers of a fire, filling the room with fine Virginian smoke.

'Well, John, 'tis to do with thy false name, is that nay so? Ye hath always been unhappy by it.'

'Yea, Father, ye hath hit the issue on the head in one. I realise I was born into a rich inheritance, but 'tis nay right this alias business. The alias was thrust upon me as a child but 'tis nay lawful and should be rectified. Elizabeth and I hath chosen to get married at Wingham church, where I spent the early years of schooling. I recall the vicar telling me that the alias bestowed upon me was heresy in his eyes, because I was baptised in the name of Greenstreet.'

'Well, the alias was stipulated in Cartwright's will, John, and if it were disregarded it wouldst hath rendered ye ineligible as beneficiary. I must admit to having grave doubts at the time.'

Jack paused to relight his pipe, offering his son the flaming taper before continuing discourse:

'You see, John, both thy mother and I realised the provision in Cartwright's will and testament might be a golden opportunity for thee, when ye came of age. Who were thy parents to throw away such inheritance, before ye were able to speak up for thyself? I proclaimed to Cartwright at the time that ye, like mineself, might turn to address life in a different direction. Nevertheless, 'twas a chance he took when he made his last will. I hath watched ye grow up, son, and both thy mother and I hath been proud of ye and thy achievements. 'Tis one thing being born into riches, but 'tis another matter, entirely, making such inheritance work and function for ye. Thine benefactor, John Cartwright, prayed ye wouldst do so. Ye hath more than fulfilled John Cartwright's expectations of ye, John. If Cartwright were alive this day, he could say nay one derogatory thing in respect of thy management of his legacy.'

'Then it must be in our blood, Father, because ye left thy inheritance behind, but later took up carpentry and joinery work and studied mathematics and mechanics. Now look at ye, thou art consultant to the greatest architect of our time, Sir Christopher Wren, recently knighted.'

'Yea, but times were different then, John. True, as eldest son I was also born to inherit Father's estates. Thy grandfather William was even richer than John Cartwright. I turned against my father and uncle's espousal of Parliament, in favour of support for the King. Nowadays I often contemplate and analyse whether it was all worth it. The civil wars, I mean. The King was executed by Parliament. Then a new King was restored, but 'tis said Charles II is thought to be turning against the true Protestant faith. The latest gossip is that Charles II has married off his niece Mary to the Dutch Protestant William of Orange, to appease the English population and cover up his family's Catholicism. Once again Parliament and the King are at loggerheads. Think of the cost of it all in human life and misery, John. What are we left with after all that has come to pass, plus the miserable losses due to the Great Plague and the devastation and cost of the Great Fire of London? I tell ye, England is a country torn to pieces. Ay, fragmented, and still nay knowing its destiny. Pray, for the sake of all humanity, we doth nay drift into civil wars again in our lifetimes. I doth nay think that will come upon us again, because we hath so few men left to fight such wars, nor willing to take up arms, I warrant.'

'Where art ye going with all this, Father?' enquired John, anxious to get to the point of his alias.

'I set out to make a point but confess to digression, John! Ye grasped thine inheritance and made the best of thy blessing, John. Nobody can deny that of thee. But for a person to demand another person must accept an alias, otherwise he gets nothing from his last will and testament, is surely tantamount to blackmail. In hindsight, I should hath told Cartwright that, when he came to read his last will to thine mother and me. True enough, the vicar at St Mary's stated that such a will was unjust and unlawful, if not heresy in the face of the Church. Ye canst nay marry and give a lass an alias name. In any case thy name is Greenstreet and ye bear a coat of arms with the motto "*Dum spiro spero*". I propose we get thine Uncle James to draw up documents in his good font to "all open people". In effect, it could state thy business will continue under the name of Cartwright Enterprises, but ye, as director, will in future sign all correspondence and documentation in thy lawful name of John Greenstreet of Twitham and Staple. The documents canst be posted to thy creditors and debtors and in the local parish churches of Staple, Goodnestone, Shatterling and Wingham. How doth that strike ye, my boy?'

'Thy plan strikes me as a sound proposal for adoption and immediate action, Father. Ye hath resolved my dilemma profoundly, as I knew ye wouldst do. Let us go to James and get the task implemented without further delay. I hath a marriage to arrange in mine own honest name.'

'That may be so, John, but I hath thy mother to placate first, in respect of her stepfather's will. Leave it to me. When she learns that an alias name will interfere with thine marriage, and when I inform her that her grandchildren shalt all carry alias names which wilt nay be recognised by the Church, I doubt the issue will be anything other than a summary one.'

Elizabeth was duly placated, James consulted, and friends of the lawyer fraternity informed. James scribed a legally binding proclamation in respect of John's alias. The document was laboriously copied many times by Thomas and delivered to all concerned in John's business affairs. Notices were affixed to church notice boards in surrounding parishes, addressed to 'all open people'. No objections were raised. As far as the Church was concerned, John had been baptised and recorded as John Greenstreet at the church of St Mary's, Wingham. There was never any doubt about his true name in that direction. From thence onwards, John Cartwright was accepted as John Greenstreet of Twitham and Staple in the parish of Wingham.

John married Elizabeth Neame at St Mary's, Wingham in the spring of 1679. Their first child, William, named after William of Maidstone, was the apple of his grandfather Jack's eye, but died from unknown disease in 1684, just two years of age. A second child named Thomas was baptised in 1687. Like his uncle Thomas, the child was sickly and frail, yet he was a survivor. Then came John, named after his father, John, and grandfathers Jack and John. He lived until age eleven and died in 1699. Elizabeth, born 1690, and Joseph, born 1691, were stronger children. A late addition was infant James, named after John's uncle, Reeve James.

James of Claxfeldestane turned very poorly in 1681. He passed away without seeing any of his nephew John's children, or being able to witness the joy or sadness each birth and death brought with it. Jack was heartbroken when his cousin James passed away. They had been such close friends over prolonged years of turmoil. The body was transported back to Lynsted church for burial. The church where James had presided as churchwarden. The service was attended by the elderly Baron of Teynham and many old friends from the manor. A choir sang for James' soul. Symon of Borden attended the funeral with his wife, Marion. Other members of the Greenstreet dynasty, from Eastling, Ospringe and Selling, came to pay their respects. Jack rendered a eulogy, and arranged a grand headstone for the grave, which read:

> Here lieth James Greenstreet of Claxfield,
> Borsholder and Churchwarden of this parish
> in the Hundred and Manor of Teynham,
> Last Reeve of Claxfeldestane.
> Died 1681.

Charles II had many illegitimate children by a variety of mistresses but had none by his wife, Catherine of Braganza. His Catholic brother, James, was therefore next in line to the throne. Knowledge of negotiations with Catholic France, together with efforts to become absolute ruler, brought Charles into conflict with Parliament, which he dissolved in 1681 to rule alone.

King Charles II died on 6 February 1685, converting to Catholicism on his deathbed. The British had tolerated the ageing King's unpopular Catholic religion, believing such heresy would perish in his death. James II, second surviving son of Charles I, acceded to the throne. Like Charles I, he was a devote Catholic and pro-French, so when he produced a son, James Francis Edward, leading nobles appealed to

Protestant William of Orange and his wife, Mary, James' older Protestant daughter, to land an invasion army from the Dutch Republic.

Later in 1685, James II faced rebellion, led by Charles II's illegitimate son, the Duke of Monmouth. The rebellion was crushed at the Battle of Sedgemoor, and savage punishments were imposed by the infamous Judge Jeffreys, at the 'Bloody Assizes'. Monmouth himself was messily beheaded. Once again, religion was causing unrest in the British people, with conflict between Crown and Parliament. James prorogued the agitated Parliament, promoted Catholics to prominent posts in the military, political and academic arena, and issued a declaration of indulgence. Anglicans were having none of it. The dark Middle Ages of the Stuarts had to be snuffed out once and for all if Britain were to retain a leading role in the world. Yet, civil wars had to be avoided at all costs. A non-violent solution was required.

At the turn of 1686, Jack recognised he was ageing quickly. He no longer chose to journey to London, or mount and ride his horse, Oak, for any long distance, or short distance for that matter, other than to make his regular trips to the nearby inn at Staple. The 'Three Tuns' brewhouse at Staple, which he frequented, often accompanied by his sons, John and Thomas, was the extent of his desire to travel. There he enjoyed a tankard or two of beer and engaged in discourse with the locals. Occasionally he and Elizabeth mounted their steeds and trotted or walked them down to the Ash Levels. They held hands on the riverbank and gazed into the clear waters of the Stour, recalling blissful bygone days of life together and wonderfully happy moments spent with their young children. Their eldest child, Elizabeth, had at long last married a local clergyman, the Reverend Insole, from Goodnestone church. With the family depleted, other than Tom, who spent his time scribing, and with James dead, the rambling farmhouse was too large. The house had become a monument to departed souls. Upkeep of the farm was fast becoming a burden. Tripp had retired to a small cottage in Staple. The new manservant, Crumble, was never so diligent nor so obliging as Tripp had been. Son John had purchased property at Nonnington and Waldershare, near Dover. When invited on fine days, and if he felt up to it, Jack accompanied John in the pony and trap to peruse John's newly acquired lands.

Twice in 1687, Jack was visited by Wren's principal carpenter, John Langland, who on one occasion was accompanied by architect Nicholas Hawksmoor. The cathedral was advancing well, but there were several carpentry issues to resolve, and they sought Jack's input. It was mostly to do with the dome. New variations had been drawn up by Hawksmoor in respect of the timber-framed outer dome and lantern, which had been the subject of numerous revisions. Wren was satisfied with the design of the inner drum wall which sloped to carry a hidden brick cone, but the outer lead-clad visual dome tormented Sir Christopher Wren. It was his nemesis.

On the first day of November 1688, John Greenstreet asked his father, Jack, if he felt up to a trip to Waldershare. John had some business to conclude on land and a house to purchase at Popshall. John told his father that he had to sign some documents to conclude his business at Waldershare, then he suggested they travel on to the South Foreland, to scan the sea across the Dover Strait for a while. John suggested the bracing sea air might do his father some good.

32

THE DUTCH INVASION, 1688

Feeling stronger than of late, Jack decided against the pony and trap, informing his son John he would ride his fine stallion, Oak. He ordered Crumble, or Crum as he liked to call him, to prepare the steed. Father and son set off for Waldershare at a brisk trot. A strong breeze blew through their hair. Pope's Hall, or Popshall as John referred to it, lay some six miles south of Staple as the crow flies – country miles, that is! John met a lawyer at Pope's Hall and completed his business relating to the purchase of a handsome piece of land with a house. Six acres of grounds and appurtenances surrounded the property. The deal impressed Jack immensely.

'I suppose ye and thy wife will be leaving Goodnestone to live here at Popshall then, John? Ye will be further away from us then. More's the pity, for we like to see the grandchildren.'

'Nay, Father, my plan is to retain it for thy grandsons John and Thomas. Until they come of age I shalt hath the lands maintained and let the house. The house will fetch a good enough rental, I am sure. There is good profit to be made from the rich soil of these lands. I just need to decide what to grow. My thinking is an apple and pear orchard.'

They rode an equal distance from Waldershare to the coast and made their way high up on the white cliffs of the South Foreland. A vast crowd of people had gathered along the tops of the white cliffs. They appeared to be mesmerised. Standing in a hush of silence, they gazed out to sea. Church-like mutterings were drowned out by the stiff easterly breeze. What were they watching? Father and son urged their horses through the gathering towards the cliff edge. John helped his father down from Oak. They pushed through the throng to gaze over the strait. Jack could scarce believe his eyes. He pulled his telescope from his cloak, causing people to fall back. He extended and raised the invention to one eye and focused the magnification. A huge fleet of ships loomed up, making its way along the English coast. The ships stretched out across the Dover Strait. The mainsail of each ship was filled and bellowing in the stiff easterly. Jack counted twenty ships abreast in line. The fleet was about twenty-five lines deep. A quick reckoning amounted to some 500 warships. The armada filled the English Channel from Dover to Calais. A concerned old man called out to Jack. White-bearded and bent at the waist, he leaned on a birch stick, a clay pipe clenched firmly between ochre teeth.

'What canst ye see in thy glass, old man? Are they British? Shall we raise a cheer of pride?'

Jack snapped the telescope shut and handed it over to his son John. He turned to the elderly inquisitive, clapped a hand upon his shoulder and responded in a voice of deep despair:

'Nay, mine friend, thou canst nay wallow in pleasure, for other than the inshore barges bringing Portland stone for building St Paul's, the ships are Dutch men of war. They fly the horizontal red, white and blue ensigns of Dutchmen. If I am any judge, our shores are about to be invaded by Netherlanders. Every deck is packed with soldiers, and their cannon are run out. I wouldst say the force of men is overwhelming. They are certainly not popping in for dinner, old fellow!'

"Tis truly an armada, Father. It is enormous,' said John, extending and adjusting the telescope. "Tis a huge flotilla. I wonder who on earth has planned and instigated this little surprise?'

Close perusal of the *London Gazette* newspaper, and visitations from Wren's accomplices, kept Jack well versed with London gossip. The Stuart royal family had put much strain on the people of England and upon Parliament by their unremitting Catholic faith, in what was mostly a Protestant, often puritanical, society. He was not at all surprised by the Dutch invasion.

'Well, John, I wouldst nay be amazed if this invasion was by invitation from the English Protestant nobles. Maybe even Parliament itself,' said Jack. 'This hast been boiling up for some time now. Prior to the Dutch raid on the Medway, is my reckoning. We should nay be surprised by it. England has no answer to a fleet of this size. Yea, 'twill be an invasion alright. The first since 1066, when William the Bastard came a-calling. Our family dynasty derived from William the Conqueror, now we hath further bastards to contend with in the form of William of Orange and his Stuart wife, Mary. They at least are Protestant, which may stand us in good stead. When England is at its weakest and lowest ebb, invaders sniff us out like lynx sniff out a carcass. Maybe a good conquering will do us some good, eh, John! We canst but pray that is so. We shall all be wearing clogs before much longer and speak double Dutch.'

Expanding in size by the minute, the crowd stood above the white cliffs, shivering in the chill of the easterly wind. Eyes were glued on the armada, peering out to sea, the crowd stunned to silence as the Dutch sailed within three miles of the shoreline near Dover and Folkestone, before turning to run parallel with the coast, out of the straits and down the English Channel.

Jack and his son John left South Foreland with heavy hearts, praying that the country would not be dragged into another prolonged war. Jack had seen it all before. He was too long in the tooth to get overexcited at his age about a Dutch invasion. After informing John's wife of the invasion and kissing his grandchildren goodbye, Jack left his son at Goodnestone to wend his way back to Twitham, hankering for the comforts of home and his goodwife, Lizzy.

A week later the *London Gazette* stated that the Dutch fleet made landfall at Torbay in Devon. Troops disembarked on 5 November. The date was no accident. It was Bonfire Night for the English, a celebration of Protestant triumph over Catholic conspirators of the Gunpowder Plot of 1605. William had planned it that way. There was no British army or militia to offer resistance, only a handful of puzzled West Country folk. William came ashore under a banner proclaiming *'For liberty and the Protestant religion'*. He made slow progress, his army marching through the rain and thick mud of a November English countryside, to cries of 'God bless ye'. William of Orange was unopposed over the length of the route – some 200 miles to London.

Later, Jack's newspaper stated that London was a city rife with rumour and unrest. It took three days for news of the invasion to percolate from Torbay. The number of ships was exaggerated by a number exceeding 700. An anxious King James, suffering from severe nosebleeds, probably due to the overindulgence in wine and rich food, sent the Queen and baby son to France. Abandoned by his officials, and with the royal administration disintegrated, James stayed until an advanced platoon of the elite Dutch Blue Guards had taken up position in St James's Park. In the dead of night, King James was escorted to confinement in Rochester Castle, Kent. On the 18th day of November 1688, William and Mary of Orange made their formal entry into the City of London. They were welcomed by an enthusiastic crowd who shouted, 'Ye hast come to redeem our Protestant religion, laws, liberties and lives.'

King James avoided death. Dutch jailers looked the other way, and he was smuggled to France.

Quietly and orderly Mary, daughter of the deposed King James II, together with her Dutch husband, William, had invaded England, unopposed, and taken the throne. Unmolested, they began to reign as King William III and Queen Mary II, in a joint monarchy. The British people swallowed their pride and willingly settled for the Protestant change of regime. With the one exception of Ireland, the British people embraced the peace offered by the change of monarchy. After all, the British had much in common with the Dutch, sharing a similar cultural heritage, their bond sealed by a Protestant faith. What is more, it kept the dreaded Catholic French away when Britain was at its weakest. The national drink the Dutch brought with them was gin. It was much frowned upon at the time, being described as 'mother's ruin'. That aside, could it be 'Great Britain' was at last being born again into a 'Glorious Revolution'?

Jack preferred his tankard full of well-hopped beer. When offered to try a small glass of the clear Dutch brew, he spat out his sample of gin onto the sawdust spread over the inn floor.

'Ye Gods, what kind of poison is this our masters hath brought with them?' he cried. 'Do the buggers nay understand the sanctity of a decent full tankard of well-hopped English beer?'

John Greenstreet had turned over many of his crop fields to hop fields. In fact, John had gone into hops in a big way, planting numerous acres of the vigorous climbing herbaceous perennials which clung to high poles, strung together in rows. John was one of the first farmers in Kent to construct brick oast houses for hop drying. The brick houses were twenty feet by fifteen in plan, with hipped, tiled roofs, kilns and a single cowl in the ridges. The dried hops were sold to local brewers, and on a more industrial scale to John Caslock, Will Dix and Richard Marsh of Faversham – the forerunners of what was soon to become the Shepherd Neame Brewery of Faversham, Kent. Jack recalled Caslock and Dix well from the White Swan brewhouse in Teynham. They were very advanced in age themselves now, but still brewing tasty wallop. He wished he could go to see them, but he had ceased to journey any distance unaccompanied.

Lizzy attempted to reckon up how old Jack was, because he retained no documentation of his birth, nor baptism records to refer to. Many documents and church records had been burnt, destroyed, or were lost during the civil wars. After much debate it was concluded he was sixty-nine, close on seventy. It was a good age, but he was beginning to feel pain in his hips and joints, and like James before he died, Jack could no longer mount his steed. Nowadays, he travelled by pony and trap, accompanied by Crum or Lizzy. Elizabeth remained sprightly enough, even though of similar age. She could still throw a leg over the back of her mare, Little Stour, and gallop across country with her greying locks flowing in the breeze.

Retired from the carpentry shop, Jack was no longer capable of manual work, though still available for consultation in respect of any intricate structural problem. He was frequently visited by Wren's assistants, seeking solutions to problems relating to the advancing cathedral. If they could not find Jack at home, they knew his whereabouts would be within the Three Tuns inn, where he was a regular customer. These days it was Master Culpepper's brew he drank. Jack was popular with his local contemporaries with whom he played games of shufflegroat, cribbage, dominoes, dice and cards. There were, however, some very puritanical locals and black-habited clergymen who frowned deeply upon such heretic activity. The parson frequently lectured the deviant locals from the pulpit, working himself into a frenzy of rage about devilry, throwing his hands heavenwards and pleading to God for their salvation.

Yet all was not what it seemed. The rector, the Reverend Emanuel Witherstone, despite his black looks and rasping voice of thunder when shouting sermons of hell and damnation at his congregation from the elevated stone pulpit, or pleading for fire and brimstone to rain down upon certain blaspheming parishioners, was in fact the epitome of hypocrisy himself. He was the very same clergyman who, years ago, had sought Elizabeth's hand in marriage. Reverend Witherstone had never married, preferring to teach the wicked ways of the world to young innocent female parishioners at Bible study classes. The rector had aged into a wizened, silver-haired, lecherous character, with long, accusing fingers and a ghoulish appearance. It was of course the rector's duty to damn the heretics who played at cards and dice at the Three Tuns inn. To damn those who drained tankards of strong beer and wasted away the valuable time God had bestowed upon them. Yet the Reverend Emanuel Witherstone himself was often the surreptitious recipient of a case of fine wine, a cask or two of brandy and a large package of tax-free tea, or baccy for his clay pipes. Quite often, in a surreptitious way, he sent one of his virginal pupils through the passage to the Three Tuns with a jug hidden beneath her white linen. The landlord, Master Culpepper, filled the jug to the brim with strong grog. Nothing was ever said by the locals. They knew what was going on but turned their backs on such issues. It was in the parishioners' best interests to retain silence in the village of Staple, to ignore the sins of others, and to ask no questions of those clergymen, churchwardens and clerks who had turned from holy righteousness to join the village syndicate. A band of owlers.

In the cellar of the Three Tuns brewhouse, a stout oak door opened to reveal a brick-built passageway. The passageway, just six feet three inches in circumference, ran below ground to connect to Staple church. Steps led down from the church vestry to the passageway door. The passage link was for one purpose only: smuggling! Jesse Sellen, the village butcher, the landlord of the Three Tuns, James Culpepper, and candlemaker Ginger Baker were the lead smugglers or owlers. At pre-arranged times, Sellen, Culpepper, Baker and crew put to sea to meet French and Dutch ships at Pegwell Bay, Sandwich, trading with bales of Kent wool. The men rowed the exchanged contraband up the clear waters of the Stour as far as Pluck's Gutter. Donkeys grazed alongside the Ash Levels ready for their role in the enterprise. As night fell, the donkeys were loaded up with barrels of brandy, packages of tobacco, untaxed tea etc. When dark, the smugglers and donkeys set off in single file. With padded feet and hooves and flintlocks primed, Sellen led the way with a single shielded lantern. They trekked their spooky journey along a well-worn track, where every moving shadow or tree was a customs officer! The owlers were guided by the lights of Wingham Barton, Ware and Shatterling to the candlelit church of Staple. Cautiously, the contraband was unloaded between the gravestones, blessed by the rector and stored in the passageway ready for distribution at the inn. Those heretic village locals, such as Jack, his churchwarden son John, together with other villagers, who were regularly cursed to hell and damnation by Emanuel Witherstone from the pulpit on Sundays, were never short of a glass of fine Cognac and a pipe of good Virginian baccy to puff upon. Parishioners kept a straight face when it came to the parson's Sunday scourging of their wicked sins. Then the congregation held their hands up high, and, grimacing in pain along with the rector, implored forgiveness for their miserable sins and exorbitant misdemeanours!

One morning, Jack attempted to mount Oak, for his usual trot to the Three Tuns inn. He suffered a stroke. The horse shied from his master and bolted. Jack was dragged along by the stirrup for some way. His long journey of adventure was drawing to its inevitable finale.

33

ASCENSION, 1691

The Ash Levels lie serene, bathed in the warmth of a midsummer's morning. High above, a heavenly canopy is unbroken in a never-ending parasol of cobalt nuance. Larks rise up from the meadowland, their trilling songs reaching a crescendo as they become mere dots in the deep eternity of the atmosphere. The waters of the Stour sparkle in the brilliance of the sunlight. At a bend in the river, shaded by overhanging weeping willow trees, a patch of drifting mist hovers over the water – a ghost waiting to be exorcised by the sun's rays. Swans dip long necks deep into crystal transparency, their heads emerging gracefully with dripping eelgrass.

The tranquillity is broken by an elderly woman driving a pony and trap down the gentle slope of the embankment. She uses a long whip to touch the pony and to check its direction.

The shaft connections groan and clink on the unlevel surface. She halts on a plateau some twenty yards from the water's edge and applies a lever to lock the wheels. She drops the reins and leans across to tenderly kiss the old man who sits beside her. They gaze into each other's eyes as if they are young lovers courting. The pony begins to graze on lush grasses and rich sap clover. A blanket is draped over the gentleman's legs. He speaks softly to her. His speech is slow and somewhat slurred. It has been affected by a stroke and the process of his ageing.

'Go on down to the stream, Lizzy, whilst I bide here a while and watch ye. Be careful at the water's edge, my love, we doth nay wish thy fine dress to become waterlogged, doth we?'

The lady wears a formal emerald green dress with long waistline. Her bodice is low and stiffened. The sleeves show off expensive lace. A matching lace-trimmed shift is evident. The skirt is made to wear open, displaying elaborately trimmed petticoats. Long grey curls hang upon her shoulders. The man wears attire based on the Dutch fashion. He has a short dark purple velvet jacket. Beneath the blanket, crimson breeches hang loose to the knees. He sports a white, laced cravat. His stockings and silver-buckled shoes are black. Such fashion dictates that they are obviously a couple of considerable means.

She pecks the old man on the cheek, kicks off her shoes, picks up a wicker basket, hitches up her petticoats and walks down to the riverbank. All the while she calls out, to reassure him.

'Watch me, Jack, or steal thyself a little nap. I shalt hear ye if thou hast needs to summon me.'

From the open-topped basket, she begins to throw pieces of stale bread and oatcake onto the surface of the water. As

364

if by magic an assortment of aquatic birds arrive to feast upon the banquet spread before them. Ducks, geese, swan, dabchick, moorhen and coot skate across the surface to gobble and squabble over the scraps, driving each other off by pecking and running across the water with open wings. Elizabeth giggles in amusement, then turns to look back over her shoulder at her man. He has a smile of satisfaction and contentment upon his face. Elizabeth raises a hand of salute. Jack attempts a weak wave of acknowledgment and smiles back at the woman he loves. He wishes he is a dashing young Cavalier again. What he senses as a stirring of desire in his loins rapidly turns to a gripping pain in his chest and down his left arm. The old war wound in the top of his thigh begins to throb madly. She turns to smile and wave at him again. He attempts to raise his right arm to return the gesture.

The arm drops limply to his side. His head rolls backwards. Jack groans. Lizzy senses her man is in deep trouble and drops her basket to hasten up the bank. She calls loudly in her anxiety, fearing the worst. She climbs into the rig and takes Jack into her arms. His eyes roll.

Images flash before Cavalier Jack Greenstreet's eyes. He feels the slash of the billhook as it cuts deep into his upper thigh, then the searing pain of cauterisation and stitching – the raid on Claxfeldestane – flashes of Kentish insurrections and Royalist battles – Naseby and the death of Walter, his comrade-in-arms – James and the Roundhead confrontation at the White Swan brewhouse – Symon and the highwayman – reconciliation with his father – the witch rescue at Faversham – the slaying of the harquebusier, Tom saving his life in the snow – his first meeting with Elizabeth. 'Ah dear Lizzy, where art thou now?' The execution of King Charles –

the Great Plague and Fire of London – the Dutch raid on the Medway – the Dutch – the Dutch…!

A red scaly dragon's head appears. A bejewelled crown is draped about its neck. Blood drips from its mouth. It is the family crest, first borne by Sir Lawrence Greenstreete, a knight of Ospringe, Kent, who died in 1451. Jack attempts to raise his head to shout the motto '*Dum spiro spero*' (Whilst I breathe, I hope). No words come forth. His head falls back. He no longer breathes, nor hopes. Life for Jack Greenstreet has expired. His body lies deceased.

Jack's ghost looks down upon the useless shell of his lifeless carcass. The spirit reflects! It had been a good life's experience. There had been much to engage upon during such a short span of time on Earth. He sees Elizabeth sobbing mercilessly over his motionless, cooling body. He will visit her soul and help pacify her tonight, as she kneels and prays for the salvation of his being before she climbs into the marital feather bed without him. His apparition will bring her love, affection and a close embrace, but there will no longer be bodily warmth to comfort her. His spirit can bring relief to her conscious and semi-conscious mind, but no comfort to her body. Four earthly years will pass before his goodwife can join him. They will continue to meet in spirit. Jack's ghost will haunt the clear, misty Stour waters. He will be there whenever she goes on her lonely journey to their secret meeting place. Their punt will rot in the rushes by the river. But they were soulmates, and soulmates can never be parted.

From out of a swirling mist, an enormous grey phantom dome with lantern appears before him. Jack recognises it as the lead-clad finial of St Paul's Cathedral, designed to cap the Whispering Gallery. The dome is yet to be built! Curved timber ribs are evident. The ribs are constructed in the structural form Jack had calculated and suggested to Wren as appropriate to his design. Clouded blue apparitions loom up, towering over and surrounding the dome's circumference. The spirits are linked arm in arm and at ease with one another. The ghosts of the Stuart kings, Charles I and II, stand between Fairfax and Cromwell. His father, William of Maidstone, old Wat Harrys and the huge form of Lord Peter of Ospringe are intertwined in a state of benevolence. Catholic and Protestant, Cavalier and Roundhead, arm in arm together. There are men he has slain in battle, including the harquebusier captain; all are there to welcome him as a neighbour. Oh, and there is Walter the pie-man of Mowbray. Jack draws nearer. Shrouded by the members of his deceased family, past enemies and comrades, he is filled with empathy. Jack reaches out to embrace the ghostly yet inimitable forms of old Johannes Greenstreet and his closest friend and cousin, James – the last reeves of Claxfeldestane.

EPILOGUE

FROM FICTION TO FACT: 2018, THREE CENTURIES LATER

On a bank, in the graveyard of the needle-spired church of St Mary the Virgin, in Wingham, Kent, to the right of the gothic arched vestibule, a small upright headstone, shaped and capped by two skulls, reads as follows:

> *Here lieth buried the body of*
> *JOHN GREENSTREET*
> *late of this Parish. He departed this life*
> *24 October 1719 – aged 65 years*

The deep-cut Roman font is still clearly legible, despite three centuries of weathering upon the inscription. Only the occasional dab of yellow ochre lichen ages the granite face of the gravestone. Could one of the skulls represent the Cartwright alias bestowed upon John, whilst the other skull expresses his true name? The grave is that of John Greenstreet, my seventh great-grandfather, son of John, my eighth great-grandfather (who for the purposes of my novel I called Jack). John (Jack) came to Wingham from the ancient Kentish family of Greenstreet, soon after the second civil war. He married Elizabeth Church of Staple and Twitham, at Wingham church. John (my seventh great-grandfather), son of John (Jack), was born in 1654. John had a brother, Thomas. John was ordained the alias name of Cartwright in the last will made by his stepgrandfather, John Cartwright. The will was made in the year 1660, the year in which Charles II was restored to the throne. Infant John was in fact just six years old at that time. I know not what transpired between the family and John Cartwright, nor the true reason why the alias name came about. I leave that to my fiction. Cartwright's last will and testament is unaltered in my novel. Teenage John Greenstreet's alias was dropped sometime after the burial of John Cartwright, and his surname reverted again to his baptised name of Greenstreet, the true name he carried to the grave. Young John was in fact just thirteen years of age when his stepgrandfather, John Cartwright, died. Elizabeth Greenstreet (nee Church), John's mother, was the daughter of Thomas Church and Dyonise Church (nee Creak), both of Nonnington. Thomas Church was born in 1586 and died in 1628. Dyonise Church married John Cartwright in 1635.

'Where did all those facts come from?' you ask. 'Surely this author is getting carried away, or needs carrying away,' I hear you exclaim. But no – not so! My information is gold-block. I found the history of my descendants, referred to above, buried in the archives of Canterbury Cathedral, together with the last wills of John Cartwright and John Greenstreet, my seventh great-grandfather, and a comprehensive inventory of goods and chattels made after their deaths. Was the alias name given to hide my eighth great-grandfather's identity, or was it that Cartwright, having no sons of his own, simply wished to leave his vast estate to his adopted grandson, so that the Cartwright name might carry on? We shall never know the answer to that, any more than the true life of my eighth great-grandfather, John (Jack), who may not have had the adventures portrayed in my yarn, but, without doubt, encountered nerve-racking experiences and formidable events along his lifespan, in that very turbulent period.

In the lifetime of my eighth great-grandfather, the Pilgrim Fathers sailed for America, whilst four kings acceded the throne. Civil wars raged, King Charles I was beheaded, and a Commonwealth was declared by Parliament. Witch-hunting was prevalent, and William Harvey discovered the circulation of the blood. There followed the restoration of King Charles II. Then came the devastating Great Plague, and a Great Fire ravaged London. Samuel Pepys wrote it all down in his diaries. The rebuilding of London's churches and St Paul's Cathedral, under the direction of Wren, began. Charles II died and after four years of James II, Great Britain was invaded by the Dutch Protestants William and Mary, who acceded to jointly reign. Such an inventory is enough for any human to digest in a lifetime's journey.

Sir Christopher Wren's English Baroque cathedral, which dominated London right up until the 1960s, stands as a symbol of seventeenth-century architecture and craftsmanship of the highest quality. St Paul's rose from the ashes of the Great Fire of London in 1666, and still causes hearts to proudly flutter, though in height it no longer dominates the city as it once did, which is surely an insult to Wren. Yet stand and marvel at the magnificence of its grandeur and you will see it has a rhythm of proportion, and arguably displays the most splendid dome in the world. A dome which outshines any modern-day attempt to lord and tower over it. Modern-day architecture, including the BT Tower, Shard and Gherkin, has attempted to minimise the cathedral, not flatter it. Such high rise has certainly blotted it from view in places. Bad manners, or an evolution of necessity? Call it what you will, but catch just a glimpse of St Paul's, from train, street or river, and the cathedral is immediately London town itself. Indeed, it is certainly not the rhythmical cathedral which is alien to our capital city! Whilst standing in contemplation, admiring and drinking in the architecture of St Paul's, consider the complications of erecting the building without the aid of today's technological advancements. When another great fire of London, called 'the Blitz', raged over the city in the 1940s, during the Second World War, the cathedral remarkably survived. Surely divine intervention saved the cathedral from German bombs and incendiaries, which rained down upon London to obliterate buildings in close vicinity to Wren's masterpiece. One incendiary bomb narrowly missed the lantern, glanced off the dome of the cathedral and rattled around on the exterior stone gallery. In the nick of time the incendiary was dislodged and thrown clear by alert firefighters. St Paul's was miraculously saved, whilst burning buildings and an inferno of fire from hell raged all around its periphery.

Situated in Teynham, Kent, 'Greenstreet' is part of old Watling Street, the Roman road leading to London, or to Canterbury – depending on the direction one wishes to travel. Greenstreet is that section of the road which divides Teynham and Lynsted. The eastern end has a public house called the Dover Castle. At the western end of the street, set back from the road, stands an ancient, well-preserved Wealden hall house, on land called Claxfield Farm, Lynsted. Wealden hall houses, built by yeoman farmers, originated in the south-east of the Weald of Kent and remain prevalent in the Maidstone area. The half-timbered, late medieval house at Claxfield is a Grade II listed farmhouse, dating from the mid-fifteenth century. It is documented as the former abode of the ancient Greenstreet family. I was able to trace the family at Claxfield back to Reeve Johannes Greenstreet, 1494, from whom derived lines of descent via Ospringe, Eastling, Selling and Wingham. William Greenstreete was son-in-law to Lord Thomas Gillingham in 1250. John de Greenstreet was Prior of Rochester Cathedral in 1314. Sir Lawrence Greenstreete was recorded in 1451 and bore the family coat of arms.

So, I comprehensively traced a direct line of male descent via every one of my eight great-grandfathers and their families, through three centuries and more, up to the new millennium. This achievement was realised through various churches in north Kent, but mainly by researching deeply within the archives of Canterbury Cathedral. All the families were born and resided in Kent. Teynham, Wingham, Ospringe, Selling, Frinsted, Waldershare, the Isle of Sheppey, Walmer and Folkestone were the main places of residence in the line of my family tree. The Greenstreet men were mostly God-fearing, often connected with the Church as parish clerks or churchwardens. Further back they acted as King's reeves and stewards of Teynham Manor. The trades of the family were yeoman farmers, carpenters, joiners and boatbuilders. My eighth great-grandfather was a mystery, because of lost records during the civil wars.

When researched, most families are connected to fame, heroism or villainy, down the lines of descent. My own lineage was no exception. William Greenstreet, my third great-grandfather, was also first great-grandfather to the 1940s Hollywood actor, Sydney Greenstreet, born in Sandwich, Kent. Sydney starred in several films. He was an inveterate scene-stealer in Warner Brothers' *Casablanca*, *The Maltese Falcon* and *Background to Danger*. My grandfather Harry's brother, my great-uncle Thomas, was coxswain of the R100 airship, designed by Barnes Wallis, who was famous for the World War II bouncing bomb. Thomas Greenstreet flew the R100 from the Cardington mast to Montreal in Canada in 1930. In Canada, the crew were hailed as pioneers and heroes. Several banquets were held in their honour. Later that year, there followed the tragic crash of the R101, a sister airship which burst into flame whilst landing in France, killing most on board. Further airship programmes were then abandoned by the government, principally because of the Great Depression. The R100 was deflated and hung up in its shed, never to see service again. In my novel I included the true documented account of the Faversham witch trials. The trials related to Robert Greenstreet, Lord Mayor of Faversham, who did indeed preside over the hanging of three witches in 1645. Robert had an axe to grind. What misogynous villainy! During the turbulent times of civil wars, plague and witchcraft in the seventeenth century, some members of the Greenstreet family followed in the steps of the Pilgrim Fathers, by setting sail for a new life in North America. They settled in Newfoundland, Maine, Virginia and the Carolinas, where the name is prevalent and lives on.

From that late medieval house, situated at Claxfield, near Lynsted in the Teynham Manor, and once the home of the reeves of Teynham Manor, derived a dynasty which spread all over Kent. Thus, the pedigree of the ancient family name of Greenstreet was established. Still standing, this attractive jettied farmhouse, with its tall brick chimneys and framed vertical oak-timbered facade, was referred to in ancient Teynham Manor rolls as Claxfeldestane.

Paul Greenstreet – Author

Matador

For exclusive discounts on Matador titles,
sign up to our occasional newsletter at
troubador.co.uk/bookshop